Swallowed By Night

Copyright © 2026 by Jeremey Harrison

All rights reserved.

No part of this book may be reproduced in any form or by any electronic or mechanical means, including information storage and retrieval systems, without written permission from the author, except for the use of brief quotations in a book review.

This is a work of fiction. Any resemblance to actual persons, living or dead or actual events is purely coincidental. Although real-life locations or public figures may appear throughout the story, these situations, incidents, and dialogue concerning them are fictional and are not intended to depict actual events nor change the fictional nature of the work.

Published in the United States of America April 2026 by Jeremey Harrison.

Cataloging-in-Publication Data is on file with the Library of Congress.

ISBN: 979-8-9938684-2-4 (Paperback)

979-8-9938684-1-7 (ebook)

Author Website: www.jeremeyharrison.com

Editors: Ramona Mihai and Charlie Knight

Cover Art: Maria Arteta

Cover Design: Rae Valtera

It only makes sense to have my first adult romance be dedicated to

Michael

My Gabe, my Jude, and the only person I'd want to be with at the end of the world.

Content Warnings

Dear Reader,

Swallowed By Night may address some heavier themes that may be sensitive to some readers. Below is a list of potentially triggering content, and I encourage you to look over them before proceeding. I have done my best to ensure this list is complete, but if you feel I've missed one, please reach out to me through my website where I'll have a comprehensive list with updates.

- Sexual Content
- Foul Language
- Alcohol Use
- Abduction
- Use of Weapons (guns, knives, bombs)
- Descriptions of Blood, Injury, and Violence
- Manipulation and Gaslighting
- Death

Prologue

Not many people can say they witnessed the end of the world.

I did. And believe me, it's not something to brag about.

The piercing noise of a siren filled our house, startling me awake and causing a paralyzing fear to seep into my core. My father's frightened expression materialized before me, his brow creased with worry.

"Wha-what's going on?" My heart pounded in my chest, a rapid rhythm echoing in my ears as I sat up. Something was wrong.

"Mom's packing a bag. Get dressed—we have to get to the shelter in town." My dad's trembling voice cracked as he spoke, and he immediately erupted into a fit of coughs. "And put your mask on."

For over a year, we'd been living in a deadly pandemic. Masks became a constant accessory whenever we were in the presence of others, and leaving the house only happened when it was absolutely essential. Scientists called the sickness BRETH, an ironic name for a substance that invaded the lungs and airways, constricting the flow of air.

Conspiracy theorists circulated rumors, suggesting the sickness was manufactured, although there was little evidence to support their claims.

My father's worried face told me everything I needed to know and made my heart rate skyrocket—this was serious.

Sliding out of bed, the icy floor sent shockwaves through my warm toes. A shiver traveled up my body, and my shoulders tensed as I hastily made my way to the dresser. I quickly yanked a hoodie over my head, feeling its soft fabric brush against my cheeks, and pulled a pair of jeans over my underwear. Ravaging my dresser, I threw a few warm sweaters, pants, and a small pouch of emergency toiletries into an old backpack that was haphazardly tossed into the corner of my bedroom. "Are we under attack?"

Flickering shadows danced in our kitchen, where my father was frantically rushing around, grabbing papers from his desk and stuffing them into his briefcase. He paused for a moment and turned his bespectacled face in my direction. "It's happening. We need to get to a shelter."

Since the pandemic had started, a world war had been brewing, and the United States was on high alert for any signs of terrorist activity. Each day, mass panic spread throughout the world as bank accounts froze, websites went dark, and browsers crashed, leaving the internet inaccessible. It was declared a global cyberattack, spurring nations to ready their armies and nuclear arsenals for retaliation, despite no one knowing who was behind it.

With Wi-Fi and streaming as their only source, the televisions transformed into expensive rectangles, serving as wall decorations in every household. As a result, radio broadcasts and newspapers regained popularity. Tonight, the radio blared at full volume, and a monotone male voice crooned through the speakers, "This is a Wartime Broadcasting Service. A nuclear attack is imminent. Seek shelter immediately."

I instinctively reached into my back pocket to find my phone, its sleek screen casting a soft glow in the dim light surrounding me. I skimmed the defunct apps before clicking into my texts. Since the internet went out, my attempts to send texts had been futile, but I'd made sure to keep my phone charged to scroll through old photos.

It made me feel less alone.

I held hope that one day my texts would go through, especially in an emergency. My fingers glided over the screen like an Olympic figure skater before I pressed send on the text I'd been typing to my boyfriend, hoping he and his family were safe. I held my breath, willing it to go through, but my hopes were dashed when a red exclamation mark appeared next to my unsent message.

When the pandemic hit and technology still worked, Gabe and I were forced to spend a couple of weeks apart. We found solace in phone conversations that lasted hours every night, even when the world seemed to be in a constant state of chaos. The long-distance dating was fine until it reached a point where I couldn't resist the urge to lay my eyes on him. To touch him. I felt safe when I was with him, even when havoc was being wrought around me. We agreed to meet at a town park nearby, and from then on, I'd pop the screen from my bedroom window and sneak out to see him.

Even though my father had no issue with me being gay, if he knew I was sneaking out to blow my boyfriend, I'd never hear the end of it.

"C'mon, let's get going." My dad's gaze met my hands clutching the cell phone. "Why do you have that? You know it doesn't work."

"Gabe," I breathed. "I was hoping I could give him a heads-up about where we were going."

His face softened. "Vinny, I know you're concerned, but trust me, he'll be fine." He could sense my uncertainty from the mixed emotions displayed on my face. "Don't you think he'd want you to stay safe?"

One of the many amazing things about him was his ability to convince anyone to do anything, which is why he was so successful at work. He gave me a sympathetic sideways smile as if to acknowledge the internal battle I was facing, but our primary focus needed to be on *our* well-being.

And he was right.

Walking into the kitchen, I saw my mother checking to make sure the oven was off, even though we hadn't used it today. She was stunning, and we always joked that she resembled a delicate Victorian doll, but in reality, her beauty surpassed anything I'd ever seen.

"Ready?" Her brown doe eyes were large and frightened. "We don't have much time."

"Let's go." My dad wrapped his fingers around his jangling keys and sprinted outside.

With haste, I stomped out the front door, the sound of the frozen wooden steps groaning beneath me. My dad was already in the driver's seat, and the engine was humming. The moment I reached the last step, my foot unexpectedly slipped on the icy surface, forcing me to grab onto the railing with my arm to maintain my balance.

"Hurry up!" My dad's breath created a plume of smoke as he yelled out the window. "And be careful, it's slippery!"

As my mom gracefully slid around the hood of the car, I hurriedly shuffled my feet toward the nearest door. The cold metal of the handle touched my palm, and a loud crackling sound filled the air when the layer of ice shattered and fell away.

"We're all in. Go, go, go!" My mom's voice was shrill as she yelled to my father.

My body quivered, unable to distinguish between the freezing temperatures and the overwhelming fear of what was happening. We were in the midst of a possible nuclear attack. The government recommended drills to ensure we had a viable evacuation plan, but no simulation was never like this. It was evident my parents shared the same fears as I did, though they tried to hide it.

"Honey, can you drive faster?"

"The road's too slick." His eyes never left the road, never to so much as blink. "Both of you, put your seatbelts on."

The dark street was shrouded in a layer of white snow, giving the scene an eerie glow as we drove. Our car approached the stop sign at the end of our street, and its rear wheels suddenly jerked to the right, causing it to slide through the intersection. My hand instinctively grasped the seatbelt crossing my chest before the car came to a halt. From the front seats, both my parents let out a long breath of relief.

Thump, thump. My cheeks grew hot, and the beating of my heart was all I could hear. After what felt like an eternity, I finally exhaled the breath I'd been holding, desperate to steady my racing heart.

We continued to drive toward town, inching our way down the street as the endless expanse of the black road stretched ahead. Mounds of snow flanked the darkened street and twisted trees, their branches reaching out like long, bony fingers, ready to snatch us away. Everyone in the car was silent, except for the occasional deep cough from my father that pierced the stillness. I knew that once we reached town from our country home, we'd probably have to abandon the car, but it was eerie not to see a single headlight besides our own, and for the next mile or so, nothing else stirred in the darkness.

At least nothing else we knew of.

In normal weather conditions, it would take five minutes to reach town, but tonight, it seemed unlikely we would make much faster. Out of my peripheral vision, a red light flashed through the night. I squinted, straining my eyes to make out any shapes in the pitch-black darkness. "What's out there?"

My mother turned her head and gasped, causing my dad to quickly divert his attention from the road. The car lurched forward, indicating he'd put more pressure on the gas pedal. A sudden burst of red light illuminated the darkness, causing me to hold my breath in fear of being surrounded by whatever lurked in the shadows. A sense of foreboding slowly seeped into my very being as tears pricked my eyes.

We were passing a large, red barn that sat on top of a hill, surrounded by perfectly shaped pine trees. I knew we were getting closer to town once I saw the outline of the nostalgic Christmas tree farm we frequented every winter. The road, which had been flat and even for miles, finally started to descend. Red and blue lights blinked across the farm to our left, indicating a police vehicle coming down the road that merged with ours. A cluster of red lights illuminated an open field to our right, and as our headlights reached the top of the hill, it felt like all eyes were on us.

We zoomed down the icy hill, feeling the useless pump of the brakes as we tried to control the vehicle. The red lights from the field menacingly advanced toward the road, causing my father's breathing to grow heavier. Fidgeting with his glasses, he muttered something indiscernible under his breath.

"What's wrong, Sal?" My mother's voice trembled, and her eyes never left the lights outside. "What are you saying about Dante?"

My dad opened his mouth to answer, but instead, a piercing scream escaped his lips. Out of nowhere, a colossal gray creature leaped in front of our car, its glaring red eyes staring us down. The air was filled with the sound of screeching tires against ice as my father twisted the steering wheel, causing our car to veer off course.

The last thing I knew was the fear in my mom's face and the sound of metal crunching. She'd turned around to look at me, making sure I was okay. Then the impact jerked my body, hitting my head against the window before everything went black.

I knew I'd been unconscious for a while, yet it felt like only seconds had passed. The sounds of hurried footsteps echoed around me before a man shouted to someone nearby. "He's conscious!"

As more people ran to me, their footsteps and chattering grew louder. I wanted to ask what happened and where I was, but my brain wouldn't allow my mouth to work. I assumed I was in a medical facility, judging by the beeping and sterile smell around me, but each attempt to focus my eyes sent nausea surging through me, blurring my vision in a dizzying swirl. A sudden chill made me shake involuntarily, sending a jolting shiver through my body.

"He's in shock—bring more heated blankets!" An authoritative woman's voice rang through the area. "How are the other two? Status, please!"

"This one has BRETH," a man yelled to her. "His license says his name is Salvatore Asposito. We're pulling his medical records, but he's losing blood rapidly. I don't think he has much time."

Feet shuffled toward the woman next to me. "She didn't make it."

What are they talking about? Who was *she*?

A wave of nausea washed over me as I realized they were talking about my mother, my breath coming in short, shallow breaths. Could it be true she was dead? I strained my ears, trying to pick up any word, any whisper, any sound that might offer a glimmer of hope about my father or confirmation of my mother's death. The looming reality of losing both parents pressed down on me, a suffocating weight of grief and fear.

She sighed in frustration. "These two, the father and son, have the same blood type. Let's begin a transfusion. Hopefully we can save him."

There was a slight tug on my arm as it was lifted, and I felt a slight pinch before my vision went dark once again.

"This is working," the woman announced. "His body is taking well to the blood." I strained to catch every word of the frantic whispers around me. I finally heard her confused voice command those around her: "Test again for BRETH."

The room went silent, and my heart dropped. Was my father dead? What were they testing for?

As I drifted into unconsciousness, the voice of the woman doctor was a mixture of confusion and relief. "He…doesn't have a trace of BRETH left in his body. Is *he* the cure?"

And from that moment, I knew this was going to be an issue.

Chapter One

"Order for Vincent!"

The booming voice echoed through the bustling café, and I scrambled from the small table, clutching a book under my arm. The man extended his thick arm to me, his sausage-like fingers clutching a brown paper bag. "Thanks, Louie." I smiled and took it from him.

"Almost yer birthday, isn't it?"

I nodded. "Tomorrow, although I don't know why we keep track anymore."

We both laughed. I've been coming to this same coffee shop for years, and Louie was always behind the counter. He might appear mean with his bushy eyebrows and droopy mustache, but anyone who knows him well is aware that he's a big softie.

Two men in black tuxedos, each with guns strapped to their backs, approached the counter. With their black hair parted in the middle, high cheekbones, and pointed chins, it was hard to deny the striking resemblance between them. It was as if they were cast from the same mold, hinting at a close familial bond. Their seemingly serious dark eyes held a playful glint, hinting at mischief lurking beneath the surface.

"Hol' on one sec." Louie put one finger in the air and sidled over to the men to take their order.

I smiled and nodded, watching the men order their food with a casual familiarity, even though I'd never seen them here before. I couldn't tell if I was drawn to their physical features or simply captivated by the mystery of someone unfamiliar. We don't get many newcomers to this café, but I always take notice when we do. After they finished ordering, they smiled at Louie, their pink lips parting to show a row of white teeth before thanking him.

"So Vinny, any plans for yer birthday?"

The two men trailed behind me, their footsteps echoing softly on the tile floor. They settled to my left, with one leaning against the pastry case, patiently awaiting their order. My ears perked up, eager to catch every word of their hushed conversation.

"Are you thinking of going to The Carlton tomorrow night?"

"Thought about it," the other responded. "It's only open once a month, so why not?"

"I heard one agent is bringing some people from out of town."

I stole a look at the two of them, and after hearing the news, the one man's eyebrows shot up so high they nearly touched his hairline.

"Really?" he asked. "It would be fun to meet someone not from…here."

The laughter that tumbled from their lips was a joyous blend of anticipatory glee and playful mischief, like two boys on a playground.

Louie waved his hand in front of my face. "Hello? Vinny, you in there?"

Their conversation captivated me so completely that I drifted off, my gaze fixed on nothing in particular. I shook my head to gather my thoughts. "Sorry, yeah." I laughed. "No plans for my birthday that I know of."

He put his hands at his waist. "If I know Gabe like I think I do, he'll be plannin' somethin' fun for the two of yeh."

"Maybe." I feigned a smile. Gabe's not the most imaginative guy, and romance isn't exactly his forte, but watching Louie's reaction to us, you'd think we were the most perfect couple on earth. "Thanks for the sandwich, I'm going to head to the grocers before they close."

"See yeh tomorrow?"

"Only if you have my coffee and muffin waiting." With a wave, I said goodbye and paused before leaving the shop. I took a quick look back to see the two men grabbing their food from Louie, with one question running through my mind: what was The Carlton?

This morning, I woke with a chill and knew a hearty, comforting meal was just what I needed. A small grocery store, just a couple of doors from my apartment, was my go-to spot for ingredients when I wanted to cook. Tonight, I was determined to recreate the creamy pasta dish my mother would only make on special occasions, the aroma I still remembered from childhood.

As I meandered through the aisles of the store, I couldn't stop thinking about the two men. What was The Carlton? Why were they excited for out-of-towners to be there? Typically, only appointed officials are allowed to leave and enter our living area, so my interest was piqued. I wonder if Gabe knew.

"Hey, Vinny!" A man in a black tuxedo waved to me. "Happy early birthday!"

"Thanks, Jack." After waving back to him, I grabbed a

red pepper and placed it inside a plastic bag. I knew everyone here, and they all knew me. We see each other every day, and you learn a lot about them during idle conversation.

After gathering the last of the ingredients, I clutched the heavy bag of groceries to my chest as I waved to the store owner, Antonia, and headed back to my apartment. Walking down the road, I strolled past the clothing store and waved to Claudine, the head seamstress, who was busy crafting beautiful dresses by hand. Across the street, Kenny sat in his ice cream shop, watching the world go by with a bored expression. Each of the businesses was overflowing with patrons, all clad in black tuxedos and carrying assault rifles strapped to their backs.

My apartment was just a few steps away, but I stopped quickly to press the closest elevator button. The doors remained stubbornly shut, and no lights flickered on the panel.

It was worth a try.

I looked back at the long hallway of shops and businesses on the floor to my apartment. The soft glow of neon signs above each entrance cast a colorful light against the polished floor. The businesses were designed to give the illusion of freedom, but behind the facade of open doors, their owners cater exclusively to the powerful—appointed officials, law enforcement, and me. This carefully constructed illusion offered only a deceptive taste of freedom. My world barely extended beyond this floor, and at night, I was trapped within the confines of my penthouse suite.

It was the perfect gilded cage. And I was its only prisoner.

After putting the groceries away, I grabbed a long-stemmed wine glass, pulled on a plush white robe, and uncorked a fresh bottle of rich, deep cabernet. I took a sip of the wine, savoring the intricate notes of fruit and spice as I gazed out the floor-to-ceiling windows of my penthouse. The sun sat low in the sky as if it were too lazy to reach higher, but nevertheless, its rays lit the barren wasteland below. The sight before me was a stark reminder of winter's harsh embrace: frost-kissed fields, skeletal trees, and a desolate village seemed to echo with the silence of forgotten lives.

That's the thing. After an apocalypse, nature will always carry on.

Despite the discovery of a cure for the devastating sickness sixty-five years ago, the world still descended into the chaos of The Great World War. Those who survived the pandemic were not spared from the devastation of the nuclear attacks. There was a winner who emerged from the war—my father. He used the war-torn world as a platform for his capitalist ambitions, creating massive Elysium structures to attract the wealthy and powerful. Each of the large buildings was encased in a special film designed to absorb nuclear fallout, offering a safe haven for its inhabitants who were equipped with all the necessities for life. These sprawling buildings provide safe and comfortable living quarters for every cured person with the financial means to reside there.

America, am I right?

Though I live in the world's grandest and most protected Elysium, my view is mainly limited to the confines of my opulent penthouse, rarely venturing beyond its walls. My father makes sure of that. His overprotective nature keeps me confined to my floor, never allowing me a moment of freedom.

A muffled knock, followed by the electronic beep of a key card, breaks the quiet of my apartment. Sipping my wine, I continue to gaze out the window beyond the large stone wall that protects us, knowing the small number of people with access to my penthouse couldn't possibly pose a threat.

An annoying squeak from the door made my jaw clench, a sound I'd grown weary of despite my numerous requests to the maintenance team for repair. Within moments, strong arms wrapped around my waist, their grip firm and reassuring, and a hard chest pressed against my back. An intoxicating scent of vanilla and sandalwood filled the air as a head of slick brown hair brushed my shoulder. Two soft lips met the curve of my neck, and a warm caress melted me into the moment.

"Happy birthday," Gabe cooed in my ear. Goosebumps sprang up on my arms as the frigid air from his breath brushed against my skin.

"Not quite," I corrected, my body leaning into his. "The first frost always comes on my birthday, half a week before winter."

Gabe nods, his chin resting on my shoulder, following my gaze. "I felt it coming in the air, the chill always bites before it comes."

When my father and I were released from the hospital, Gabe was already ill, and tragically, his parents both succumbed to the same sickness. We wept together, hearts heavy with the loss of our parents, but I was determined to use the newfound cure to save him.

And I did.

When I moved into Elysium, Gabe asked my father if he could be my personal bodyguard; no one else would do a better job at protecting me than him. My dad wholeheartedly agreed, and I couldn't imagine anyone else living in this fucked up world with me. Over the years, our relationship only deepened, growing ever more entwined as we spent so much time together.

The sex is an added perk.

I spun around, turning to face Gabe. His glittering brown eyes and playful smirk made my knees weak. His skin was a mixture of rich brown hues that gleamed in the sunlight, and his physique was practically divine. I was pulled into his embrace, the strength of his arms surrounding me with one hand resting on my back, while the other gently lifted my chin. His touch sent shivers down my spine. Our lips met, delicate and sweet, but then quickly blossomed into a ferocious intensity as his tongue danced with mine.

His hand tightened on my back, pulling me closer, while his other hand gently brushed a stray strand of black hair from my face. Our tongues wrestled and intertwined, a passionate battle fought within the confines of our joined lips.

I loved kissing him. I couldn't get enough of it.

A mischievous glint crossed his eye. "Do we have time?"

I nodded, and a wide smile formed on his lips as he pushed me against the dining room table, his groin poked against the inside of my thigh. My body trembled thinking about him, yearning for him. Our lips remained locked as I frantically tugged at his shirt, pulling it over his head. The afternoon sun painted his skin, highlighting every contour of his body. I put my lips to his chest, his nipples hardening with the cool of my breath.

I tugged at the sash of my robe, the fabric bunching in my hands. With a final, frustrated jerk, it gave way, tumbling to the floor and revealing my naked form to his gaze. A look of lust crossed his face, and his eyes gleamed with desire as he scanned me. Leaning against the table, I slipped my fingers into the waistband of his pants and drew him closer between my legs. I knew in this moment that I was his god.

And he worshiped me.

With a deliberate tilt of my head, I let him know exactly what I was searching for. Desire coursed through me, leaving a tingling trail of electricity along every nerve. The soft touch from his lips brushed my neck, followed by a sharp sensation as he sucked until my skin turned purple. I needed this. A strangled moan escaped my lips, and I knew he heard it because immediately after, his teeth sank into my flesh, piercing my fragile skin with agonizing sharpness.

Did I mention we were vampires?

"Suck me," I whisper, letting it come out as almost a breath, or else I'd let out an almighty moan from the back of my throat.

Gabe didn't need further prompting. His fangs sank deeper into my neck, drawing a crimson trail that painted his mouth. Every cell in my body thrummed with a primal fear, drawn towards the sharp, metallic bite of the fangs that were draining me. It was as though a thousand tiny insects were crawling under my skin, each one a whisper of pure delight, their movement an intoxicating wave of ecstasy.

Gabe wrapped one strong hand around my cock and began stroking. The rhythmic friction paired with his fangs in my neck caused my breath to deepen, and I closed my eyes, sensing all the blood flowing to Gabe's member. His manhood gradually swelled until it was fully erect, sending shivers of anticipation through my body.

A smirk played on his red-stained lips as the weight of his thick cock pressed against me. Lifting me, his fingernails dug into my lower back. The sharp sting of pain was a welcome distraction from the intoxicating thrill I just savored.

"Do you want this dick?" Gabe's voice growled in my ear between his heavy breaths.

After an affirmative moan escaped my lips, he flipped me onto my stomach, my hips resting precariously on the edge of the dining room table, the cold wood pressing into my skin. Hearing the familiar click from a bottle of lube, he grabbed the base of his cock and entered me. Stifling a moan, I bit my lip as he eased his way into my core.

"What a good boy you are," he cooed.

Whenever we were intimate, Gabe's approach was direct and focused, without any unnecessary delays. Vampires often feed while engaging in sexual activity because their arousal diminishes once all the blood collected from their host is consumed or redirected. The quick and intense lovemaking was aimed at reaching climax before losing arousal.

Once he was fully inside me, Gabe's eyes rolled in his head, taking a few intentional strokes. Immediately after, he pushed against me forcefully, extinguishing any sense of romance or desire. I knew every move he was going to make by the sound of his breathing and body language.

I stole a glance back and saw his mouth wide open, occasionally biting his lip as he continued to pound me. I wished the intense passion we had before making love lasted throughout the entire experience. I'm not sure what making love actually feels like—this is all I know.

This is what I accept.

I carry on, I carry on.

Chapter Two

Gabe's rough stubble grazed my cheek as he kissed me awake, a familiar warmth spreading through me alongside the gentle pressure of his lips. I peered at his elated smile while his honey-golden eyes radiated enthusiasm in the gentle morning light. Leaning on his elbow, his slick hair still perfectly in place, the blanket revealed half of his toned abs. His usual demeanor was strong and silent, a quiet strength, but I was the only one who could coax out his playful side.

"Happy birthday, handsome." He smiled at me, and the crinkles in the corner of his eyes deepened. "Officially."

I pulled his face toward mine, engulfing my lips with his. Here we were, another birthday. I appreciated how he still got excited about these things because I found myself feeling disconnected year after year. Sometimes, I even forgot when his birthday was; he didn't care, though.

"How old are you now?" He winked at me as a spirited glance danced in his eye.

I raised one eyebrow. "I'm officially *twenty-one*."

"Hmm." He pursed his lips and silently counted his fingers in faux wonderment. "So that makes you…eighty-six years old, right?"

"Asshole." My fingers tightened around the soft cotton pillow behind my head as I swung my arm, making direct contact with the side of his face. I wasn't expecting his sass so early in the morning.

"Hey, hey, be careful, old man!"

We both laughed at his stupidity, but he was somewhat right. Following the distribution of my blood, we observed a noticeable slowing of the aging process in those who received the cure compared to those who hadn't. So technically, I'm twenty-one in vampire years but eighty-six in human.

A serious expression took over my face as I hooked my knees around his waist, mounting him. With my arm outstretched, I clamped down on his neck, pressure building with each tightening squeeze. "Stop with the old man shit."

"Are you trying to make me horny? Because it's working." He licked his lips, and his fangs retracted. "But we don't have time for shenanigans. You have an appointment with your dad today."

Oh yes, my yearly scheduled meeting with my father—great. I yearn for the comfort of our past, the days of togetherness and happiness, filled with sweet shared memories. Now he's strictly business. Even in our shared moments, a chilling sense of distance replaces the easy camaraderie we once shared. He saved the world; he's a worldwide treasure. But even though he's different, the dad I grew up with remains in my memory. I long for those days, for that normalcy.

Gabe's lips found mine one last time, a long, passionate kiss that left me breathless. "Hey," I said after he pulled back. "I have a question for you."

"Anything."

"What's The Carlton?"

A sudden rigidity seized him. He stood frozen, and the air was thick with tension. "How do you know about that?"

I shrugged and slipped out of bed. "I heard two guards talking about it at Louie's yesterday. They said there's a rumor people from other Elysiums would be there."

"Who were they?" Gabe's voice was a low growl, and his eyebrows furrowed in a deep frown.

"I…I don't know. I've never seen them before." It had been years since I saw him so taken aback and angry. I knew this must be something I shouldn't know about. "What's happening there?"

His eyes searched mine, a silent question hanging in the air as he struggled to find the right words. "It's a party," he admitted. "Anything goes at The Carlton. That's why people like it so much."

"What kind of stuff?"

"It starts as a club, so the normal debauchery: drinking, drugs, you name it. But then there's the back rooms…" He paused, his brow furrowing as he considered whether to go on. "It's all sex stuff, different rooms for different things."

Saying The Carlton sparked my curiosity would be an understatement. The idea of going to a club or a sex party sounded intriguing, even though it was something entirely new to me. Cooped up on this floor, my life became monotonous, so any new experience, no matter how small, was appetizing. I wouldn't partake in any activities because I am committed to Gabe, but it would be fun to see it all. "Have *you* been to The Carlton before?"

"I need to know who those officers are. They aren't supposed to discuss outside activities while on the job." His face grew red, and his shoulders tensed. "Don't ask about it again."

I jumped in the shower, allowing the hot water and steam to cleanse my body, but my thoughts remained wild. Gabe's reaction to The Carlton had me even more intrigued. I needed to find a way to sneak out—the idea of feeling alive again was too tempting to ignore.

"Hurry up in there." Gabe banged on the door. "We can't keep your dad waiting; he's a busy guy."

I rolled my eyes. Yeah, he was busy. Busy enough that I had to schedule time with him, his own son. Whenever I see him, the rules are simple: stand up straight, say what he wants to hear, and try to entertain him. Like I'm a fucking clown. As a reward, he'll lock me away for another year.

I stepped out of the shower, the heat of the water still on my skin, and roughly dried my black hair before sweeping it to the side. Wiping away the misty film on the mirror, I patted a tinted moisturizer over my cheekbones and forehead, and the cool metal of a cologne roller glided under my sharp jaw. Adding a light pink balm to my thin lips, I smiled at my reflection, but my eyes immediately went to my fangless mouth. Not having them set me apart from the other vampires. It was like a sick joke.

I slipped into a cream-colored turtleneck, tucking it into gray plaid pants. Fixing the sweater around my neck, my gray eyes flickered as I grazed my sharp chin. "I'm ready."

We exited my penthouse, and the sleek chrome of the elevator doors remained closed before Gabe swiped his key card. I wish I could have one—to be able to go anywhere in Elysium by myself. Stepping into the cold, metallic box, his finger brushed a glowing button, and the elevator shuddered to life, carrying us to our destination.

You'd think annoying elevator music wouldn't be a thing after an apocalypse, right?

My thoughts are permeated by the lilting music coming through the speakers built into the corner of the box. I hated going to my father's office—The Room of Empty Promises, I called it. Despite my love for my father, I knew his pronouncements were often designed to please me, regardless of their truth.

Typical parent, right?

Once pressed, the elevator buttons glowed an eerie white, casting a dim light in the otherwise dark space. The mirrored walls reflected my face as I shaped my lips into a smile, a bitter, rehearsed expression for the vows my father would soon break. Despite the legends, a funny thing about vampires is that our reflections are perfectly clear. The whole farce was nothing more than fiction.

Gabe's gaze lingered on the noticeable bulge from my pants before quickly looking away when he realized I caught him. A smirk crossed my lips. "I was going for a hot teacher vibe with my outfit."

"Then call me your student." He shook his head, trying to recalibrate his thoughts. "I have to stay focused." He straightened his stance and placed both hands behind his back. The elevator made the familiar *bing*, indicating we reached our destination.

The elevator opened, revealing a small, dimly lit lobby. A lone man in a tuxedo and black bow tie stood at the far end, his arms crossed, silhouetted against the dark wood of the two doors beyond. As we strolled toward him, I shook my head at the overly formal uniform he makes his staff wear.

My heart leaped as a massive painting came into view.

The canvas was alive with a ship tossed and turned by a raging sea, its colors vibrant and full of movement. I'd loved this painting since I was a child; each viewing revealed new details. Most recently, I noticed a tiny green bird perched subtly atop the crow's nest, its green feathers almost blending into the background.

"We're here to see Mr. Asposito." Gabe reached into his back pocket and pulled out a crisp white card, flashing it at the guard.

It seemed as if the guard's eyes hadn't moved from their spot, but a flash of light glinted in his pupils before he turned. The hinges of the large doors groaned as he opened them. A shaft of brilliant white sunlight cut through the foyer's cool fluorescent light, revealing the dark, opulent grandeur of my father's office.

We trudged through the doorway, the ceiling lifting higher than the room we'd just left, revealing a breathtaking expanse of painted frescoes and intricate carvings. My father's office, designed as a pre-apocalypse grand study, boasted wooden walls lined with overflowing bookshelves, the scent of aged paper and leather filling the air. A small, plush velvet settee and armchairs sat beside a bar overflowing with every imaginable liquor, the crystal cocktail glasses gleaming regally in their display case. Sunlight streamed through the large, outward-slanting windows on the far wall, illuminating a massive mahogany desk. Its exterior was intricately carved and dominated the center of the room.

My father sat behind the desk, never once looking up from a pile of papers he was reviewing.

We walked toward him, and as we reached the marker used to indicate guests to stop, Gabe cleared his throat. "Sir, I've brought Vincent to see you."

When he heard my name, my father froze, his head

snapping upwards, a look of surprise and excitement washing over his face. He had a timeless look about him—a thin man in his mid-fifties with high cheekbones and dark-rimmed circular glasses resting on the bridge of his nose, just below his arched eyebrows. The first thing anyone noticed about my dad was his impeccable style—a perfectly tailored suit, always complemented by a brightly colored bow tie and socks to match, creating a vibrant, eye-catching ensemble. Today, he wore a mustard-colored jacket with a brown Burberry vest and a blue collared shirt underneath. The deep navy of his pants echoed in a subtle border on the pristine white pocket square peeking from his coat.

My dad rose from his desk, the chair legs scraping against the wooden floor, and outstretched his arms. "Vinny! My boy! Happy birthday!"

He walked over and embraced me in a warm, affectionate hug. The familiar scent of musky cologne, mixed with the faint sweetness of bourbon, enveloped me. "Hi, Dad."

His thin lips disguised the bottom row of his crooked teeth, and his green eyes twinkled in the light within the room. Crows' feet line his temples, each ridge telling a tale of a time that has long since passed. "How are you, my boy?"

His words are soft and meaningful. He loves me. A noticeable pressure builds behind my forehead, and I brush away the wetness gathering in the corner of my eyes. Though time apart sometimes hazes my memories, his presence when I see him again is like a magnet pulling me in. The sound of his voice was nostalgic, bringing me back to simpler times. "I can't believe I'm finally twenty-one; it feels like it took forever to get here." I laugh at my comment because it truly did take too long to reach this age.

"Well, you look amazing," he cooed with a proud smile. "Since you're *finally* of legal age, would you like a cocktail?"

We both smirk, sharing an unspoken memory of the old days when the legal age for the consumption of alcohol was twenty-one and how long ago that actually was.

"It is truly a blessing how fortunate we are to have each other in our lives for so long."

I nodded, knowing what was coming next.

"Do you remember how all of this started?" His eyes became glassy. "Time has an interesting way of fading memories. Do you remember her?"

Of course I do. My mother was the light of his life and my best friend. She introduced me to the best songs of the '90s and showed me how to bake the perfect batch of chocolate chip cookies. Even now, the mere scent of their sugary sweetness brings an involuntary smile to my face. Her laughter was as bright as the sun, and her smile could light up a room.

The haunted look on my mom's face as she frantically scanned the backseat, searching for me right before she died, is an image seared into my memory, still haunting my dreams. It was the last time I ever saw my mother, and a piece of me and my dad died with her that night.

Since then, my father spent countless hours hunched over his workbench in the lab, the only light the eerie glow of his equipment as he examined my blood, a crazed look in his eyes while he studied how it healed him. Over the next few years, he healed those affected by the pandemic, primarily politicians, world leaders, and influential celebrities.

This was the beginning of his monopoly, the start of

his power. Little did he know, all the people he healed with my blood were turned into vessels that craved my blood to live.

I've always been proud of creating a race more advanced than humans, but as the years went by, my heart ached with guilt.

I helped to create the end of humanity.

Chapter Three

My father handed me a crystal glass, its surface gleaming, filled with a rich, amber liquor. A large cube sat in the middle, like an island in the vast ocean. I felt a sudden surge of anticipation for the celebration as he smiled and lifted his glass in a toast, inviting Gabe and me to follow suit.

With our arms raised like a pyramid, my father proclaimed, "To Vincent!"

We clinked our glasses together, and a bright, cheerful sound echoed through the room as the cool, smooth glass touched my lips. A fiery sting shot across my dry lips as I tasted the alcohol, followed by a rich, smoky caramel sweetness that filled my mouth. It felt as if a scorpion injected poison into my throat, and the sharp, burning pain made me cough uncontrollably while my face contorted in agony.

I hated his alcohol; I much preferred wine.

"A delicious vintage I've been saving for a special occasion." My father quickly finished his glass, a satisfied look of wistfulness on his face as he set the glass on the bar. He smacked his hand against his forehead. "Silly me, I forgot something." He approached the mahogany desk, and I heard a drawer open. He beamed with a child-like smile as he clutched a small square box with a red button to his chest. "Go ahead."

My father's flair for the dramatic made me stifle a laugh. He watched, eyes alight with anticipation, as my finger pushed the button. A light glowed from the center, and within a second, the air filled with confetti, and balloons rained down from the ceiling.

His lips curved into a gentle smile as the vibrant, confetti-like pieces of paper fluttered down, blanketing his suit. "Isn't that fun?" Warmth and happiness radiated out of him, emotions he doesn't feel very often. He placed a hand on my shoulder. "What are your birthday plans?"

I shrugged, shaking the confetti from my hair. "I'm hoping now that I am officially twenty-one, even after sixty-five years of birthdays, I can do more outside my room?"

My father's smile faded, his eyebrows furrowed as his face fell, worry etched deep into his skin. Clearing his throat, a nervous cough echoed the tension in his shoulders. "Is your room no longer comfortable to you? I can fix whatever you don't like."

"The room is amazing, Dad. I appreciate you creating everything to make me comfortable," I began, "but I really want to create relationships with the other people in this Elysium, maybe even get a job."

His eyes grew wide. "A JOB? Absolutely not, I vowed to take care of you for the rest of your life. I am sorry, but that's simply out of the question."

I watched Gabe's fingers fidget in his hair, a clear sign of his unease, but I didn't care. "This may come as a surprise, but I'm not your *prisoner*. Let me actually *do* something."

"Sir," Gabe's deep masculine voice interjected. "My apologies—"

"Don't apologize for my son's outburst." His calm voice, devoid of any emotion, sent shivers down my spine more than any raised voice ever could. He lifted his face to the sky and squinted before another sip of his drink. "You're right, my boy, you are responsible, and I should recognize that to show you my trust. So how does this sound to you?" He turned to me, both his hands gingerly on my shoulders. "I'll allow you to leave your floor, but only if Gabe accompanies you." He paused, a smirk playing on his lips. "Do we have a deal?"

I knew he was lying to me. This was his way, always saying exactly what I wanted to hear. I forced a smile before answering. "Deal."

His lips curled into a smirk, and he winked at me, a triumphant glint in his eyes. "That's my boy, you never give up." He turned to Gabe. "I'll give orders first thing in the morning to halt all other responsibilities he has to focus on you and your protection." He turned to the muscled man. "Please ensure you report to me tomorrow to discuss your new role."

He nodded to my father, his hands fidgeting behind his back. "I was going to ask your permission in private, but with this new development, I think it's appropriate." Clasping his hands behind his back, he puffed out his chest. "May I ask for your permission to take Vincent to Smoke for his birthday tonight? Rest assured, I'll request an exclusive table in the VIP area so we'll not be bothered."

I knew Gabe was essentially calling my dad's bluff and could practically feel the tension in the air. If he doesn't let me leave this floor, his lie will be obvious; however, if he does, I know this is a single exception. The thought of having a meal at Smoke, the chicest place in Elysium, sent my heart soaring. Getting a reservation at this restaurant is nearly impossible. It's one of the most exclusive in the world, with a menu curated by top chefs, each dish a masterpiece.

Regardless of my father's response, a rebellious determination to break free from his watchful eye was coursing through me. Even if he allowed Gabe to take me out, I knew it would be a temporary freedom, and I'd soon return to the suffocating confinement of my floor. I'd be stuck in the same endless cycle that had trapped me for another sixty-five years.

A stern look crossed my father's face as he raised his chin, a sharp tutting sound escaping his lips. His eyes lingered on my boyfriend's face, a silent question in their depths, before lightly patting him on the shoulder. "Of course you have my permission. This will be a birthday to remember." He stuck out his forefinger sternly. "Be careful with him tonight, our enemies have been quiet, and the Dogs still roam outside Elysium."

Gabe put his hand over his heart. "You have my word."

"Ah, to be young again." My dad got a faraway look in his eyes, like he was recalling a long-forgotten memory.

He always says we're young, but maybe he's too old to remember. Like everyone in Elysium.

The Dogs were always a concern. During the war, the government told its citizens they were created to keep an eye on their enemies, although they also monitored their underlings. The Dogs were cold, metallic figures made of hydraulics and steel with brains programmed to record and relay all interactions back to their controllers. Once the government began to fall, the Dogs turned against their own creators, turning feral and deadly. Once they went rogue, they formed vicious packs and were determined to kill anyone who stepped in their path.

We have one rule known to all: stay inside, and they'll leave us alone.

"We know our enemies control the Dogs, so their silence concerns me. Please be alert, you know how I feel about them," my dad almost spat his words. Though he remains silent, the rumor persists that his closest companion, Dante, allied with the humans in their war against us. In the early days, my dad used to say it was the biggest betrayal against him, and we dared not speak his name around my father. A century is a short time for vampires, yet long enough for Dante to surely be dead. We haven't had an attack from the humans in years, but that didn't stop my dad from being constantly paranoid.

There was a brief moment of silence before my father turned and embraced me one more time. "Don't stay out too late tonight, you have Extraction first thing in the morning."

Even though I've helped to give him his empire, he knew how to deliver my fear.

There was nothing I hated more than Extraction, and sometimes I wished my blood wasn't the cure. I didn't ask to be the savior, but our scientists say I'm an anomaly, healing the sickness and turning everyone into blood-drinking beings was something that just…happened. Unexplainable. There might be others like me in the world, but so far, none have been found, and even if they were, they'd probably face the same fate as I: locked up and drained once a year.

The day after my birthday, when my blood is at its most potent, I'm taken to a sterile lab. During the Extraction, they meticulously drain my blood, leaving only the barest minimum. For days afterward, I'd feel like a snail covered in salt: withered and used from the outside in. From there, the doctors replicate my blood in mass amounts and send it to all of the Elysiums across the world to continue the vampire line.

Only *my* blood can satisfy the hunger that dwells within each of their souls.

"Do I have to?" I asked, exasperated.

My dad's nose wrinkled. "You know that all the blood we make has an expiration date."

After a year, the replicated blood begins to degrade, losing its life-extending properties and making wrinkles more noticeable, a tangible reminder of its potency. Despite our fangs and thirst for blood, we share a common trait with the humans: vanity.

Plus, expired blood tastes terrible. Needless to say, if they don't have to drink it, they won't.

"You're *special*, Vincent." His voice softened, like he was complimenting me. "Only you were able to save humanity."

"Special?" I asked, lifting my lip. "I don't even have fangs! It's like I was half-baked compared to everyone else."

He smiled, a twinkling in his eye. "But how good does your blood taste?"

He has a point. I was able to drink the blood he made in his lab after the Extraction, and it's delicious—an indescribable taste, but one that's completely intoxicating. With one touch to your lips, you needed more.

My father's receptionist entered, advising he was being summoned to another meeting, and we were quickly ushered out of The Room of Empty Promises. Before dismissing me to my penthouse prison, my dad beamed one last smile. "Happy birthday, my boy, I hope it's one to remember."

Me too, Dad, me too.

The elevator doors slid shut, and as we ascended, the smooth, metallic walls reflected the artificial lights while my amazement at my own naiveté grew. It was miraculous how much I still loved my dad, even though he gave me every reason not to. How can he go anywhere he wants, but I'm stuck on my floor of the building? In my heart, I knew his actions, though sometimes confusing, stemmed from a profound and protective love. We only had each other.

Opening the door to my penthouse, Gabe pulled me close and planted a kiss on my lips. "I have to get back to work, but I'll see you later." He smiled and bit his bottom lip. "Happy birthday, handsome."

The sun was beaming on the frozen landscape outside, and I knew exactly how I wanted to spend my afternoon. Years ago, I told my father I wanted to learn how to swim, so he ordered our engineers to design a solarium outside my penthouse, complete with a pool and hot tub. It may be in single digits outside, but in my solarium, it was warm.

I slipped into my bright red Speedo and tossed a fluffy towel over my shoulder. The humid, warm air from the solarium rushed into my penthouse, and a wave of heat pushed against my face. With a contented sigh, I plopped into a beach chair, tilting my face toward the sun's warmth shining through the clear glass.

I've never really been sure why I have always been able to go into the sun, but nobody else in Elysium can. One time, a vampire stepped outside during the summer, and within minutes, their skin started melting off, probably due to our extended age and how pale we all were. But no matter how long I basked in the rays, I never tanned; my skin absorbed the heat, untouched by any color.

I suppose being pale was preferable to being dead.

I loved the feeling of the sun on my skin; my cold body craved its penetrating warmth. Once my skin vibrated with heat, I stood from my chair and lowered myself into the inviting pool. The cool water enveloped my body, each ripple parting as I moved, a gentle caress against my skin. Swimming to the far end of the pool, I rested my arms on the cool, smooth brim, allowing my body to gently float behind.

The barren world outside Elysium was both beautiful and sad at the same time. The war demolished everything in sight, and there weren't enough humans who found it worth rebuilding. Although if they tried, the vampire army would likely take them out.

In the distance, I caught sight of movement. I removed the designer sunglasses from my face to get a better look and see a pack of Dogs running together around a cluster of rusted automobiles that had been taken over by the elements.

As much as I despised the Dogs for what they did to my mother, I have a deeper hatred for the humans. They're still out there, plotting to take my father down. Blaming him for their misfortune. Despite their small size, their repeated attempts to attack Elysiums across the globe have all failed, highlighting the strength of the vampire army. The continued activity of the Dogs suggests that some humans still survive, though it has been a long time since anyone has reported seeing them. It's disgusting they use the Dogs as a fear tactic to keep us locked inside, although what better place to be than a self-sustaining paradise?

Sixty-five years ago, amidst the ashes of a broken world, the desperate humans forged a rebel group and called themselves Unicorns. Initially, this devout group, believing themselves untouched by evil, fought vampires in God's name, coining their name to reflect this perceived purity. A battle of the strongest ensued, but my father's army was greater than theirs. Their only upper hand is their control over the Dogs. Once the vampires forced the humans into hiding and their religious beliefs crumbled, they left their mechanical mutts to keep surveillance.

Even though I hated them, I sometimes identified more with humans than with vampires, which is why I felt the need to do something rebellious. The excitement of sneaking out from my floor was too enticing, and I couldn't stop thinking about it. I craved going to the party at The Carlton, simply to dance and feel free.

I got lost in thought, formulating my plan, completely entranced by the pack of Dogs running together in the distance. Not much could be seen from my vantage point, but their powerful hind legs propelled them forward with each powerful leap over the snow-covered wasteland below. At night, you're sometimes able to see the Dogs' glowing red eyes, and whenever I see them pierce through the darkness, I'm reminded of that fateful night. Like my father, they're biding their time, waiting for me.

Well come get me, mother fuckers.

Chapter Four

As the afternoon unfolded, I found myself unwinding around the solarium, lazily going from pool to beach chair. In between reading my book, my thoughts kept circling back to The Carlton. The idea of it set my body abuzz, igniting a relentless itch that needed to be scratched. How would I manage to get there? Should I sneak away tonight?

As the sun dipped below the horizon, casting long shadows across the landscape, I knew Gabe would be arriving soon to take me to dinner. I wrapped a soft, blue and white striped towel around my waist, the cotton cool against my skin, and flicked a pair of sunglasses from my head to my face before returning to my luxurious penthouse. I slid the door open, taking a glance at the mountain of birthday gifts sent to me by the leaders of all the Elysiums across the world. I used to get more, but the pile slowly diminished year after year. I guess if you're not visible, you're forgotten.

Not to sound conceited, but it's the *least* they can do for me after preserving their lives year after year.

I scanned the boxes, disregarding ones with logos depicting fruit or an arrow because I knew there was nothing in either that I wanted. Few corporations survived the apocalypse, but these two did. Go figure.

A few designers sent me exquisitely crafted gifts of men's couture from their upcoming collection, each piece a testament to their precision and care. I love being ahead of the trends and getting these exclusive gifts, although almost nobody saw me in them.

But now they will, my father promised. We'll see.

A sharp rap echoed from my door, followed by the satisfying click of the electronic lock retracting. Gabe walked through the door, a smile playing on his lips, looking more handsome than I'd ever seen. Usually, I see him in his crisp, starched military uniform, but tonight, he was strikingly different in a smooth, cream-colored suit. The jacket was open, revealing a stark, white dress shirt underneath, and his cropped pants fit him in all the right places. A beautifully patterned red-and-white pocket square was tucked over his chest, giving the ensemble a pop of color and added elegance. His hair was pushed back, with one strand popping out of place across his forehead.

He smiled when he saw me ogling him—I swear my tongue must've been hanging out of my mouth.

He held up a crisp pair of black pants and a tuxedo suit, a grin splitting his face. "What do you think about my new uniform?"

"Oh, right, for your 'promotion.'" I raised my fingers, mimicking air quotes, a silent acknowledgment that little would likely change. If anything, the only difference would be in his uniform.

With a dramatic flourish, Gabe flung the tuxedo onto the couch, then presented a stark white box tied with a black velvet ribbon, its smooth surface gleaming under the light. The signature packaging was a dead giveaway it was from one of my favorite clothing designers. With an emphasis on quality over quantity, he limits his yearly output to five shirts, each made from the world's finest textiles, the richness is evident in every detail. I only have two of his pieces in my closet…and I cured the damn pandemic. My breath caught in my throat, but I managed to croak, "For me?"

I tugged gently at the beautiful bow, enjoying the soft, downy feel of the fuzz against my fingertips. Lifting the top of the box, tears welled in my eyes. I was speechless at the garment's beauty. A silk-collared shirt sat inside, light as a feather and folded to perfection. The soft sheen of its dark fabric caught the light. I traced the hand-stitched lace, its threads cool and delicate against my skin, and each of the almost-invisible marble buttons was tiny a masterpiece on the richly textured shirt.

It was a captivating blend of masculine and feminine aesthetics, punctuated by a subtle hint of edge. Perfect.

Nestled atop the shirt was a small box, containing a stunning silver chain bracelet. "Gabe, you didn't have to…"

"I wanted to," he interrupted. "You deserve to look absolutely perfect for your first night out in Elysium, so I contacted your favorite designer to custom-make the shirt to your exact measurements."

"Thank you," I breathed as I slid closer to him. Putting one finger on his chest, I seductively flitted my eyelashes, my gaze lingering on his mouth. I bit my lip, a smirk playing on my face as I threaded my fingers beneath the lapel of his jacket. "You look very handsome tonight, too."

A slow smirk stretched across his lips as his large hands cradled my face, and he pulled me into a tender kiss. As he finished, he gently nibbled on my bottom lip, leaving it flushed and tingling. "We'll save this for later."

"We have plans after dinner?" I asked coyly.

His pink tongue grazed his fangs before licking his lips. "We're not having dessert tonight. There's no slice of cake that's sweeter than watching your toes curl in ecstasy and hearing your throat whimper for more."

His comment brought my mind back to what happened at The Carlton. What happened inside? Would I be safe? I needed more information, especially if I was planning to sneak away. Tonight may be my only chance.

I pulled away, my fingers finding the edge of the damp towel before it slipped from my grasp and fell to the floor. Without averting my gaze, I watched his expression change from amusement to lust when he noticed my skimpy swimwear. I slid my thumbs inside the Speedo and smoothly shimmied out of them, leaving me fully exposed to his gaze. With a gentle touch, I traced my fingers down my body and covered most of my dick, leaving just the base of my shaft visible. The easiest way to get what you want from a man is to toy with him.

Call me Mattel.

"D-don't," Gabe stammered, letting out a long breath. "You're making me want to suck you."

As I stepped into the black pants, a coy smile tugged at the corners of my lips as I allowed him to savor the slow, seductive inching over my hips. "Can you help me button them?" I angled my body in just the right way, thrusting my pelvis forward.

Gabe knelt and licked his lips before deftly zipping my pants and securing the button around my waist. "You're a bad, bad boy, Vinny."

I shrugged my shoulders as I dropped the bracelet into his palm. "I always thought I was your good boy?" A smirk played on his lips at the name he called me in the bedroom. He clicked the bracelet's clasp into place, and I knew I had him where I wanted to get more information. "Tell me more about what's happening at The Carlton tonight."

He held the bracelet around my wrist, but at my question, his grip tightened around my arm. "The Carlton is dangerous, don't even think of it because you shouldn't know. It's not a place for someone like you."

"Someone like me?" I snidely said. "What does that mean?" In all honesty, I knew what he meant—The Carlton was a club which doubled as a sex party, attracting anyone who needed to escape their mundane existence. Someone like me. "I think the sleaziness and danger make it all the more exciting."

Gabe's voice got stern. "It's outside of Elysium. You're not going there, and that's final!" His hands threw my wrist away, and a glint of anger flashed in his eyes. "The Carlton cannot compare to what I have planned for you after dinner."

I reached one arm to the back of his head, his dark hair entwining around my fingers like vines as I kissed his neck. His nose extracted a quiet moan, and his hand never left mine.

He pushed back abruptly. "Stop distracting me, we have to go. Our reservations are coming soon."

"Lemme put on the shirt, I promise I'll be quick." Ripping the shirt from his grasp, I dashed away, my heartbeat pounding in my ears as I scrambled into my room and slammed the door. Standing in front of a full-length mirror, I slung the shirt over my messy black hair and around my shoulders. The fabric was heaven on my skin; it felt luxurious. I fastened each button slowly, taking in the details of the garment, then stepped back to admire the meticulous craftsmanship, the way it draped perfectly, and the rich texture of the fabric against my body. Hints of white skin peeked through the delicate lace, creating alluring layers of depth and texture.

Flicking some light mascara on my eyelashes, I gave myself a small fangless smile. I looked like a badass. I felt like a badass.

Butterflies were frantically flying through my body. I couldn't believe I was actually leaving my floor for the first time in sixty-five years. It almost seemed like I was in a dream, and at any second, I'd wake up.

Taking one last look in the mirror at my impeccable look, I met Gabe in the hallway of closed shops and cafés that were made for me. He swiped his keycard and pressed a button, a small white ring illuminating the downward-pointing arrow. As the doors opened, I watched as Gabe tucked the card into the front pocket of his suit.

Once the doors reopened, a wave of anxiety reached me. This was the first time in sixty-five years I was leaving my floor. What if it wasn't as magical as I hyped it up to be in my mind? Stepping out of the elevator, my head swiveled constantly, and the pit in my stomach disappeared. Vibrant colors and sounds within Elysium surrounded me as we walked toward the restaurant, a symphony of sights and sounds assaulting my senses. Passing London-style pubs, we noticed the aroma of freshly brewed coffee from French cafés and bookstores with shelves overflowing with books, just like in a movie. I almost forgot there was so much more than what was on my floor. Toys, games, and even non-designer clothing had their own storefronts.

I guess fast fashion hadn't died with everything else. Gross.

People bustled along the walkways, the rhythmic shuffle

of their feet a steady drumbeat against the floor. Confined to my floor for years, seeing the same faces daily, I was amazed by the surprising diversity of those around me—their laughter, the way they moved, all subtle differences that set each one apart. They had their own identities. As we walked by, so many people caught me staring, their faces scrunching up in confusion and suspicion as they likely wondered what was wrong with me. Every time I saw someone's confused face, I realized I'd been looking for too long.

If I were being honest, I kind of expected all eyes to be on me. Maybe if I'd gotten out sooner, I'd be seeing the reactions I expected, but after being hidden away for sixty-five years, maybe they all forgot about me? They must not know who maintains their survival. Could they all be living in ignorance?

"You're quiet," Gabe said, his eyes darting back and forth. "Could it be that you're...*shy*?"

Hearing the unusually light and teasing tone in his voice calmed me, a welcome change from his usual demeanor. Although he's not working right now, I knew he was on high alert. "Never," I answered. "There's just so much to see down here!"

A laugh escaped from his throat. "Believe me, it's much better upstairs. You'll find out soon enough once you're able to be down here more."

I didn't exactly know what he meant, but Gabe slipped his hand into my palm, our fingers interlocking as he expertly navigated through the labyrinthine Elysium. A large open area overlooked different levels of the safehold spread before us. Lush vines and emerald leaves cascaded from the high ceilings, forming a vibrant, living curtain that filled the space.

I'd always wanted a garden but never thought it would survive.

A thin waterfall, sounding like a gentle shower, rained through the leaves, cascading into a moss-covered basin below. The scent of damp earth rested in the air, a lush, wild feeling that gave the perception of truly being outside. I half expected to see the flash of vibrant plumage or hear the whoops of monkeys as they swung down from the thick, tangled foliage.

"Go to the right."

Turning my head to where Gabe pointed, I saw a long hallway filled with shops, their colorful signs, and the murmur of shoppers filling the air with a lively buzz. At the end, a large neon sign pulsed with a bright, white light, its lettering a stark contrast against the darkness, like a beacon in the night. The letters looped into one another, like a messy scrawl to spell one singular word: SMOKE.

Chapter Five

A thick, grey mist, cold and damp, clung to us the moment we stepped through the arched doors, obscuring the restaurant in an alluring veil of mystery. The thin, acrid smoke snaked around us, its tendrils tugging at our clothes, lightly brushing against the crisp edges of Gabe's perfectly ironed shirt.

"Rodriguez, for two?" Gabe's unruly eyebrows shot up as he acknowledged the staff, his smooth voice a low murmur in the otherwise silent room.

With a sly smile playing on the host's lips and one eyebrow arched high, the short blond man regarded my boyfriend with curious interest. Situating himself behind Gabe, the blond host assisted in removing the cream colored suit from my date's muscular body and folded it over his arm. Tucking a piece of his long blond hair behind his ear, the host fluttered his long eyelashes, and sweetly gestured ahead. "Right this way."

The man's desperate eyes, filled with pleading that bordered on pathetic, made my stomach churn, and my face contort in disgust. A sickeningly sweet, almost chemical smell of cheap cologne hit me as the host led us through the dimly lit restaurant to our table, hidden behind heavy, velvet drapes. The circular table, draped with a crisp white tablecloth, was dimly lit by a single candle, its flickering light casting dancing shadows on the polished wood.

Gabe scrambled to pull the chair out for me, and the chair legs scraped against the hardwood floor before I sank into the plush, velvet cushion. My eyes sparkled as the candlelight flickered, reflecting warmly on the polished silverware, which highlighted its gleam against the grey stone chargers. A starched black napkin, folded with precise angles, rested on the plate. I unfolded it, the crispness whispering against my fingers, before laying it across my lap.

With a flourish, the blond host revealed two crisp menus clutched to his chest, a slight smile playing on his lips, before Gabe held up his hands. "No need for menus tonight, I'll order for my handsome date."

A wide grin spread across my face as I watched the host purse his lips, a clear sign of disapproval, before hastily retreating from our table. The beauty of the restaurant was truly stunning. The black walls, carved with intricate, swirling embellishments, seemed to writhe under the weight of a thick, smoky plume hung from the ceiling like a heavy trellis. The lone candle flickered, its muted light a fragile beacon in the overwhelming darkness, like a will o' wisp, beckoning yet elusive.

"Gorgeous place, isn't it?"

I nodded, and a man materialized from the shadows, his movements fluid and quiet as he poured a rich, crimson liquid into our wine glasses. A stray bead of purple dye snaked its way down the bottle's neck, absorbed instantly by the white tablecloth, leaving only a faint purple stain.

With a flourish, the man displayed a crystal decanter, its facets catching the candlelight and sparkling like a thousand tiny stars as he delicately tilted it toward a small rocks glass. A rich, red liquid, like thick honey, poured from the decanter, coating the glass with its syrupy texture and deep color.

"Fresh blood and vintage wine, a perfect combination." Gabe lifted his wine glass, the candlelight dancing in his brown eyes, reflecting the warmth of the moment as he looked across the table.

I shuddered while looking at the blood as the Extraction scheduled for tomorrow morning ran through my mind. I raised my glass to meet his, and the delicate tinkle of crystal against crystal echoed softly in the quiet room as our glasses met. Raising the thin goblet to my lips, the intoxicating aroma of the blend filled my senses before I took a sip, a symphony of flavors exploding on my tongue. The wine was layered with initial flavors of cranberry and blackberry, followed by a cascade of black cherry and a subtle warmth of spice. The wine's flavors were soft and enveloping, with a bright, balanced acidity that danced on my tongue, making it one of the most pleasant glasses I've ever tasted.

"This is a beautiful red," Gabe acknowledged as he took a sip. "This particular wine was shipped from our partners in Italy and produced only in small batches for optimal flavor. Wonderful, isn't it?"

"With the blood infused into the wine, it tastes like… me." I smiled, knowing it was an inside joke between the two of us whenever blood was involved. "But in all seriousness, I've drank a lot of wine, but this is special."

A wide grin stretched across his face, his white teeth flashing in the dim light. "Anything for you, Vin." He leaned across the table and touched his lips with mine. The kiss was passionate and meaningful, a silent language of longing and desire spoken only through the gentle pressure and warmth of our lips. "I love you."

His touch, though tender, sent a jolt through me, causing my body to stiffen in response. Gabe didn't kiss me outside of when we were nearing intercourse. Over sixty-five years of knowing each other, the non-sexual kisses we shared were so few, they could be counted on both hands. "I-I love you too?" I didn't mean the words to come out as a question. Looking into his handsome, yet hopeful face, I knew why. I did love him. He'd been my rock, a steady presence through the storms of my volatile emotions, frustrations threatened to consume me, and grief that threatened to break me. I knew I could rely on him.

But is that enough for me?

The server, a shadowy figure barely visible through the misty darkness, returned bearing two small plates overflowing with frizzy green leaves. He carefully placed the pristine white dish on the charger before us, then vanished as quickly as he'd appeared.

"After dinner, I have a surprise for you." Gabe reached out and lightly held my fingers in his hand. "I booked the observatory for your birthday. The stars will be bright tonight."

I feigned a smile, knowing full well his intention was to fuck under the stars, before using my salad fork to stab a piece of lettuce. My mouth was instantly enveloped with a sharp taste, as if a bee had stung my tongue. I looked toward Gabe, who was chewing with no indication anything was wrong. Was it just mine? Taking a long sip of the refreshing water, I cleared my throat, feeling my vocal cords loosen.

He swallowed. "I figured it would be like when we used to meet in the park."

"I wish we could go back," I admitted. "Everything was just so…different. Easier." I took another bite of salad and winced once again. I thought maybe I was being overdramatic, but it was just as bad as I remembered. "Is this salad—"

"Terrible? Yes," Gabe finished.

Our loud and unrestrained laughter shattered the night's stiff formality, breaking through Smoke's suffocating atmosphere. I stole a glance toward the other tables illuminated by candles and wondered if the other patrons were wondering why we were snickering to one another.

I loved it when he loosened up; it reminded me of how we used to be. As hot as he looked when serious—his jaw tight, eyes narrowed—seeing him genuinely laugh felt like winning the lottery. My heart ached every time his eyes crinkled from his wide smile.

The waiter appeared once again. "Are you enjoying the salads?"

Gabe and I stole a glance, a silent communication passing between us as I bit my lip to stifle a snicker.

"It's great," Gabe answered and held the plate out. "I think we're saving room for dinner." With the vile appetizer cleared from the table, his intense gaze seemed to see past my very soul. "I know I ask this every year, but what are you looking forward to?"

Seeing The Carlton tonight.

Since leaving my floor, I was aching to see more of Elysium. The world seemed to open up to me within a matter of hours. "Not sure." I shrugged. "I think getting my father to let me out of my room is a huge step, so I'm excited to build more relationships with other people. There's still so much I don't know."

"Like what?"

I had to change the subject so I didn't give an indication that I was itching to sneak away. I needed to deflect the conversation back to him. I arched my eyebrows, and my voice took on a playful, teasing tone. "For example, I don't even know your middle name."

Gabe tilted his head back, a hearty laugh booming from his chest before he took a slow sip of the smooth, red wine. "My middle name? Is that really what's been keeping you up at night?"

"I've never thought about asking." Lifting the wine to my mouth, I took a swig, mirroring him. "Tonight was my first time in Elysium. I don't know what I don't know until it dawns on me."

He nodded and closed his eyes, a smile on his lips. "Edward," he breathed. "As embarrassing as it is to say it, my middle name is Edward."

I squinted at him, furrowing my forehead. "Why's that a name to be embarrassed by?"

Gabe rolled his eyes. "Do you really want to know?"

I nodded expectantly, my fingers laced together, with my chin resting on my hand.

He let out a dramatic breath of air. "I'm not sure if you remember the book series, Twilight, but my mother was obsessed with it. Originally, she wanted it to be my first name, but my father wanted to name me after my deceased uncle, so they agreed on Edward as my middle name."

"Twilight? The book about vampires?" An unbelievable laugh, full of unrestrained joy and surprise, escaped my mouth.

"Ironic, right?" A laugh escaped his lips.

"Gabriel Edward Lopez," I whispered. "I love it." Knowing this piece of information only opened my heart more for him. You'd think we'd know every detail about each other after sixty-five years, but these small, easily overlooked things slipped through the cracks. I suppose we thought we had all the time in the world to get to know each other since aging was so slow.

"I need to ask." Gabe reached over, holding my fingers in his palm. "For someone who has it all, why are you so keen to uproot it all? Every person in the world would love to switch places with you."

My heart fluttered as his thick thumb caressed the back of my hand. Draining the last drop of wine, I shrugged. "I don't know... I just want to be *excited* about life again, you know? Being alone so often, I've had a lot of time to contemplate my life. I don't know who I am, what I'm doing, or where I'm going—that's why I told my father I want a job. To find some sort of...fulfillment. I can't remember the last time I was truly happy or excited." Gabe's brow furrowed as he looked at me with confusion, making my cheeks burn with embarrassment. "I'm sorry, I'm rambling."

"You don't feel happy or excited with me?" Each word contained an underlying tinge of disappointment.

"That's not what I meant." My heart felt like someone stabbed a wooden stake through it as I shook my head. I didn't mean to hurt him, and his quick temper prevented any meaningful discussion, so we never get to have these types of conversations. "It's hard to explain, I just feel unfulfilled with...life. You're the only thing I have to look forward to every day. How sad is that? It's like I don't know how to be happy anymore."

Cupping one hand to the side of my face, Gabe's breath hitched as he gazed into my pupils, searching for the flicker of love reflected in their depths. "Vinny, I want to be the light in your darkness because that's what you are to me. I'd do anything for you. You brought me back to life when my entire world seemed to end. You're my family." Wetness coated his eyes, and he turned away.

I knew I was all he had. After his family passed from BRETH, he was all alone, and this was the time we helped each other the most. Tension coated the air around us, like it was being pumped through the ventilation. I pushed away from the table and embraced him, the solid weight of his broad shoulders a comforting presence against my arm. "I love you, Gabe. You're my family too." He sharply inhaled a long breath of air, which was my indication he needed a moment to himself, but knew acknowledging it would only upset him more.

Damn toxic masculinity. The wine also didn't help.

"I'm going to use the restroom." He turned his head, and I offered a reassuring smile, hoping to calm his worry. "Don't worry, I'll be back for dinner, it should be here soon."

He nodded, and without another second, I strutted toward a light-up sign that gestured patrons to the lavatories. Before taking the turn, my feet halted as I stood at a crossroad. Should I continue my way to the restroom or turn toward the exit? The angel on my shoulder reminded me that I promised Gabe I'd be back shortly, but the devil was pulling me toward the key card tucked into his coat pocket behind the host stand. Do I choose to continue my birthday with Gabe, eating disgusting food, and ending with quick, emotionless sex? Or do I choose adventure and risk my boyfriend and father being mad at me?

Weighing the pros and cons of each, I found my head bobbing back and forth as I contemplated my options. Tonight has been absolutely perfect. I loved getting off my floor and seeing more of Elysium, and I truly felt loved by Gabe. But...even if I chose to have fun, how long can he and my father *really* be mad at me for? They need me to survive.

Anticipation bubbled in my stomach, and the overwhelming heat inside the restaurant made me feel faint before my feet moved, taking me to my destination. I've got nothing to lose and everything to gain.

"Excuse me," I smiled at the blond host. "My date asked me to grab something from his coat, can you grab it for me?"

I chose excitement. I chose myself.

Chapter Six

Elysium was situated at the heart of what was once a sizable city and now sits within a massive stone wall, its only defense against the dangers beyond. The original name of the city, lost to time, is now known as The Wastes, a desolate landscape of crumbling structures and whispering winds. The once-thriving city was now a skeletal frame of crumbling buildings and silent streets, and those who were wealthy enough, escaped to Elysium. Over time, the city decayed into a slum, the forgotten buildings casting long shadows over streets choked with poverty and refuse.

The Wastes are home to Exiles—criminal vampires or those who have been shunned because they couldn't pay their taxes. When you are deemed an Exile, you're thrown to The Wastes, where you soon become starved for blood. Your body slowly uses all the food reserves it stores, and as it does, you feel weaker, and your skin will become dry. Eventually, brain function begins to shut down and your body starts withering from the inside out. Before death, Exiles are alive, but only just. It's a terrible price to pay, although they can return to Elysium if they pay their dues to society. Driven by the desperate hope of reaching the paradise above, most will risk anything in The Wastes, making them incredibly dangerous.

I walked down the dusty and desolate streets that snaked through the city, crossing my arms across my chest from the frigid cold outside. The cracked, decaying walls of the buildings loomed over me, their silent stories whispering of a grandeur lost to the war and were stained with centuries of grime. A thin layer of snow crunched underfoot, and the dim, flickering lights in windows cast long shadows on the snow-covered street.

I assumed, by the gossip, that it would be a busy night at The Carlton, but my eyes didn't catch any sign of movement. Turning my head toward the snowy ground, I saw the imprints of several pairs of feet heading toward the town square, their patterns slightly veiled by a light dusting of fresh snow. I followed the trail, the moonlight illuminating my path, until I saw a large fountain shimmering in the pale light. Walking around the empty basin, I ran my fingers along the surprisingly thin layer of ice atop the undisturbed snow, feeling its brittle texture.

Rough, uneven piles of snow were heaped around the square, some near the fountain and others pressed against the cold stone of the surrounding buildings. Passing one of the mounds, I stifled a gasp as a thin, cold hand clamped around my ankle. My wide eyes, filled with shock, looked down as my mouth dropped open at the sight of an Exile on the brink of death. Its withered, yellow-gray body looked brittle, and its bony fingers, thin as twigs, seemed as if they might snap if they grasped too hard. Its face was terrifyingly gaunt, and thin wisps of hair stuck out from its skull, reminiscent of a decaying zombie from a vintage horror movie.

"Blood…please." A raspy, broken voice, barely a whisper, escaped their cracked lips. "I can...smell the blood. Please help...me."

With a sharp yank, I pulled my foot from the Exile's grasp, eliciting a high-pitched shriek piercing the air. I wasn't sure if it was in pain or upset that I got away.

Secretly, I hoped it was in pain for startling me.

I eyed the towering mounds of snow, their surfaces trembling slightly, and noticed they were shaking. These beings, on the brink of death and their bodies wracked with chills, were too weak to lift a finger.

Following the icy trail leading away from the town square, I rounded a bend and found myself atop a tall stone staircase, completely glazed with ice. Latching my hand firmly around a rusted metal railing, I slowly made my way to the bottom, taking care not to cause injury to myself. The bottom of the stairs led to the remains of a charming park, and I could almost smell the freshly cut grass and hear the laughter of children on a bright sunny day. Years of neglect dulled the playground's charm. The central pavilion was weathered, a broken seesaw lay beside it, and a rusted death-trap of a jungle gym stood nearby.

I couldn't help but empathize with the park, a place that was once filled with happiness, but was now a shell of its former self.

The din of the night was creeping over the town, and my stilted breathing blew white clouds into the air. Following the footsteps, I rounded a corner into a narrow alleyway, where an ominous red glow was emanating at its end. A five-story brick building, weathered and worn, met my gaze as I peeked around the corner. A large, buzzing neon sign in swooping red letters cast a lurid glow on the alleyway that read, The Carlton.

I raised a skeptical eyebrow, noticing the unsettling absence of people outside the building or behind me, not a single sound or movement. Was there another way to get here that I wasn't aware of? Anxiety told me not to continue further, but I pushed it aside and, without another thought, stole down the alleyway. The faded grandeur of The Carlton, dwarfed by the towering buildings around it, whispered tales of a bygone era as a charming boutique hotel. The beautiful glass turnstile and vibrant awnings were now just memories, replaced by decaying wood and boarded-up windows. A small metal door, painted a dull grey and bolted shut, served as the hotel entrance, its sheer weight and imposing presence hinted at a deliberate effort to keep people out.

Or in.

Wrapping my fingers around the cold, metal handle, I pulled with all my might, but the heavy door remained stubbornly shut. Hesitantly, I knocked, but nothing happened. I heaved on the door one last time, the cold metal biting into my palms before letting out a frustrated groan and throwing my arms up. How could I come this far to let a door get in the way? I wasn't about to give up now.

"How many?" a voice came from behind the door.

A metallic partition slid open with a grating sound, revealing a face pale as bone, and dark eyes that seemed to absorb the light. I don't think I should be here... Have I made a mistake? Gabe told me The Wastes were dangerous. Why didn't I listen? "J-just me."

The large metal door opened with a low groan, revealing a small, dimly lit foyer, plush chairs, and mirrored tables gleaming faintly under the sparse lighting. A single, lopsided chandelier cast long, distorted shadows across the dilapidated lobby. The smooth white and black tiles shifted beneath my feet from ages of decay as I approached the wooden desk, where a wizened vampire sat hunched over, his long, hooked nose nearly touching the ancient, leather-bound book before him. Bits of white hair peeked from his ears, contrasting with the sharp gleam of his black eyes, which sparkled merrily behind his small, round glasses.

As I approached the desk, the old man moved away from his worn novel and fixated upon me. "Welcome to The Carlton, will you be joining us tonight?" His raspy and dry voice had a curious lilt at the end of each phrase, as if every sentence were an unspoken question.

I nodded, wondering if I should turn and run out the door. Was this a mistake? What was I getting myself into?

"Ah, a first timer." His smile was sharp, and a flash of white teeth glinted in the dim light, catching my eye. The man rummaged under the dusty desk, his knuckles cracking as he held a dented metal bottle to me. "The party is in the ballroom on the first floor; you should have no problems finding it. That damn music is so loud." He shook his head, and his lip curled. "With entry, you have access to all five floors of the hotel. Each level has at least one bar where you're welcome to fill your bottle with blood, free of charge."

A gust of frigid air rushed in as the door behind me swung open, making me shiver violently as the cold seeped into my bones. A strangled gasp escaped my lips as my head slowly turned, expecting Gabe's furious glare behind me. Instead, I saw a tall, slightly overweight, bald man in a rumpled suit, his upturned nose wrinkled as if he'd smelled something rotten.

I swung my head around to be out of eye sight, knowing full well his outfit meant he was a politician of some sort. If he recognized me, my father would instantly be alerted to my defiance, and I'd find myself back in my penthouse within seconds. Turning to the old vampire behind the desk, I nodded. "Understood, thank you."

"One moment, young man." He held up a finger, its skin so wrinkled and prune-like that it looked as though it was soaking in water for years. "If you choose to go to any other floors, you'll need to purchase a locker. You cannot wear outside clothes on those floors; there are robes in each locker."

Fuck. I didn't even think to take some coins from my stash before I left my penthouse. I've never had access to actual money, just the few stray coins or crumpled dollar bills I managed to find here and there. Everything I've always wanted has always just been…paid for. For sixty-five years, money was never a thought or concern for me. "I-I'll just go to the party," I mumbled.

The man behind me dropped a few coins on the desk, each leaving a dull thud on the wooden desk. "I'll pay for him tonight." He gave a sly wink as his lips curved into a slight smile. "I hope to see you inside."

A hand brushed my butt, the unexpected touch causing me to stiffen, and I instantly slapped his hand away. My skin tingled with a mixture of anger and revulsion. "Thank you," I muttered before grabbing the gold keychain the old vampire man was holding.

"Enjoy yourself, wherever the night may take you." His words, accompanied by a sly smirk, caused a buzzing sound to fill the lobby as the lights on the large metal door switched from red to green, a low hum vibrating through the floor.

Chapter Seven

The music vibrated through my veins like tiny bombs, each beat a little explosion of sound and feeling. It felt as if my pulse melded with the powerful bass line emanating from the speakers next to the DJ. I didn't know the music, but it didn't matter. I danced with my arms flung high and a smile playing on my lips as the vibrant music filled the air with a joyful, swirling energy of notes and rhythms. This was what it felt like to be alive.

And I was obsessed.

Multicolored lights strobed alongside the heavy beat drops, painting the swaying crowd in a hypnotic rhythm. The bass thrummed through the floor and crawled up my body. Flashing light sticks and neon props created a dizzying spectacle, their movement a blur of color against the darkness, while a tangible energy vibrated through the crowd. It was like I was in a movie, and everything was happening in slow motion. Swaying my hips and moving my feet to the rhythm, I let my body take control, feeling the music course through my veins.

Though the room was full of vampires, the air was

warm with the combined heat of our bodies. The cold metal of the bottle, hooked onto my belt, clinked rhythmically against my leg with each step, a constant reminder to stay hydrated.

Snapping out of my euphoric state, I opened my eyes to a world of vibrant colors and unfamiliar sounds, feeling like a newborn taking in the world for the first time. The flashing lights blurred my vision, and each face became a jumbled mess of features, making it impossible to recognize anyone. I was dancing by myself, but it was clear I was in the minority. A couple engaged in an intimate kiss caught my eye to the left, while a group of girls danced energetically together ahead.

Time became meaningless, but the gnawing thirst was real, and I knew I needed to fill my empty canteen as quickly as possible. Pushing through the throngs of people, I made my way to the bar. With a sigh, I leaned on my elbows, the bar's dim lights reflecting on my wet hair as I ran my fingers through it, waiting for the bartender to notice me. I noticed two men, one of whom gave me a brief, almost imperceptible nod.

"Hey, don't we know you?" one of the men yelled over the blaring music.

I shook my head and turned away from them, scurrying away to not be seen. I knew what would happen if anyone recognized me, and I was having too much fun to go home. Plus, even though the rest of The Carlton was a bit sleazier, I wanted to see more.

With a burst of adrenaline, I raced for the exit, my fingers hitting the elevator button for the hotel's second floor. The old metal doors groaned open, and I leaped inside, slamming the button to close them with a frantic push. With my back to the metal interior, I sighed in relief as they sealed shut, keeping out all others.

Barely a moment passed before the doors re-opened with a slight creak, revealing a small, empty foyer and two plain doors directly across from one another. Walking through the door marked with a man icon, I was thrust into a room that reeked of sweat—a locker room whose smell instantly turned my stomach.

Before the apocalypse, the locker room at my school always felt like a battleground. Was I going to get caught in an explosion of name-calling, or was a bomb of toxic masculinity going to go off? Would I get shot by snide remarks from metaphorical guns or be left alone to fight another day? As an openly gay guy in school, being around straight men was always anxiety-inducing—what would they do and what would they say if I accidentally glanced anywhere but directly in front of me?

With my arms crossed and shoulders tense, I walked through the locker room, taking care not to look anywhere there was movement. Reaching the back of the room, I found an empty locker in the corner amongst the faded red metal lockers. A rusty groan echoed from the door as it swung inward, revealing a lone white robe hanging limply from a hook.

Here we go.

I untied the silky shirt around my waist and carefully hung it from a hook inside. I grabbed the soft cotton undershirt, pulled it over my head, and shimmied out of my sweaty pants. As my belt hit the tiled floor, a metal clank sounded through the area. Together, I rolled them into a ball and threw them inside. I looked down at my exposed body and looked past the small tuft of hair in the center of my chest. Do I wear my underwear?

I returned to the battlefield and glanced at those around me. While one man, with a sagging belly, paraded around in his birthday suit, another man swiftly discarded his clothes to slip into a robe. I diverted my eyes before each of them could notice and let out a sigh of relief—no need for open fire today. I lifted my head, the fluorescent lights reflecting harshly, and squinted to make out a faded sign hanging from rusty chains above the lockers that read, 'No outside clothes beyond this point.'

Well, there's my answer.

As I wrapped the scratchy robe around my shoulders, it served as a barrier from the prying eyes of others while I discreetly removed my underwear and placed them with my other possessions.

I did it.

I didn't think I'd be comfortable being naked in public, but I suppose when everyone else was, what's there to be embarrassed about? A tremor ran through my body, a mixture of jittery nerves and excited anticipation. I pushed the sense of guilt nagging at me to the side. I wasn't going to cheat on Gabe; I was simply there to observe and soak in the atmosphere. With a deep, steadying breath and a long, releasing exhale, the quiet confidence settled over me, and I was ready to explore the upper floors of The Carlton.

Hotel room doors lined the dimly lit hallway on each side of me, with a strange energy emanating from each of them. Many rooms were closed, their doors silent and still, but I couldn't help but peer into the ones that stood slightly ajar. As I walked by, I saw a solitary woman sitting on a bed, naked, gently playing with her nipples under the flickering light of the television. I grimaced as I turned my head across the hall, where a young woman had an older man blindfolded and handcuffed to the bedpost.

The Carlton's reputation for catering to every imaginable vice preceded it, but the reality of stepping inside was an experience I didn't expect. Ever since I first heard the two at Louie's talking about this place, it was like a magnet drawing me closer. It wasn't the lure of music, sex, or drugs but more as an act of defiance—an escape to the wildest place imaginable, far from the confines of my own floor.

The hallway opened into a cozy scene: a small bamboo bar, the pale wood gleaming softly, surrounded by comfortable rattan chairs. Multicolored plastic cups, shaped like coconuts and slightly sticky from condensation, held refreshing drinks and cocktails.

A joyous scream, sharp and high-pitched, echoed off the walls from beyond the bar. Craning my neck, I saw a crowded, steaming hot tub attached to a swimming pool, overflowing with naked, glistening bodies. The yelp came from a blond woman who had one leg in the air and a man's arm hooked around her neck from behind, her breasts bobbing against the bubbling water.

I knew the additional floors outside the party would be scandalous, but I didn't expect everything to be so…open. A tingle stirred underneath my robe as a couple of well-endowed men passed by and posted up at the tiki bar.

One of them noticed me staring and slowly spread his muscular legs, making his presence more pronounced. "You lookin' for a drink?"

I gulped. Boy was I.

"Uh…I'm all set!" A nervous giggle escaped my lips as I tapped the cold, metallic bottle at my hip, brushing my semi-erect member out of the way. "Thanks for the offer." Mortified by my own lame words, I cringed and fled, my steps echoing as I bounded up the carpeted stairs to the second floor. At the top of the stairs, a long, dimly lit hallway stretched before me, splitting into three mysterious directions with three signs hanging above each. "Sauna, steam room, or…playroom?"

I knew two of the three, but the lingering chill from the

outside air still sent shivers down my spine. Turning left, I grasped the hot, smooth wood of the sauna door and pulled it open. The hallway was filled with the comforting warmth and the distinct, pungent smell of cracked wood. Walking into the warm room filled with wooden benches, I paused. Two women with blood dripping from their necks were bent over the bench, while two men grasped their hips, thrusting behind them. "S-sorry," I stammered.

"You're welcome to join!"

I closed the door behind me and returned to the hallway, my eyes lingering on the steam room door. Startled, I quickly jumped back as a dark figure slammed against the glass, and a throbbing cock was the only feature unobscured by the billowing white smoke. My mouth dropped, hoping no one was hurt, but the moans of pleasure seeping through the door reassured me everything was fine.

To avoid disrupting the activity in both areas, I quietly walked down the hallway toward the playroom. I'd seen more tonight than I ever have in my eighty-six years of living.

And I felt on top of the world.

I suppose I should feel scared because there truly were no rules here, but my intrigue dispelled any fear in my body. I've never seen another man's body besides my own and have never seen another man's dick besides Gabe's. As naive as it may sound, I never considered the fact that penises could be so vastly different—I knew they could vary by length and girth, but each was unique to its user.

"Speaking of cock," I said under my breath as I arrived in the playroom. A multi-level area opened before me, each level showcasing unique furniture styles, but at its heart was a mess of intertwined bodies. This room was an orgy of epic proportions, and the diverse moans of pleasure echoed throughout the room. Around its perimeter were a few leather slings, each occupied and rocking back and forth.

I was approached by a woman with red hair twisted into a bun and wearing black eyeshadow, her naked form exuding confidence as she brushed against my elbow with her large breasts. "You joining, handsome?"

"Oh... I don't think so." She seemingly came from nowhere, catching me off guard. "It's my first time, I just came to watch."

"You like to watch, got it." The woman lifted her eyebrows, a nostalgic smirk pulling at her lip. "I remember my first time here, said I was just going to watch, too, but as soon as I saw Israel's dick, I knew I had to try it out." She nodded to a dark man who was feeding on a woman while thrusting into her. "Don't be afraid."

"I-I have a boyfriend." A pang of guilt pierced my heart as I thought of Gabe.

"We all do, honey." She smiled. "If you don't want to be with a woman, most of the guys here are okay with getting fucked, too." A leather harness encircled her waist, with a ribbed silicone replica of a man's erection at its center.

"No, it's fine, thanks." A laugh, tight and uncomfortable, escaped my mouth, not knowing exactly how to communicate. Despite my discomfort, I couldn't deny I was slightly turned on. The raw, untamed sexuality on display without any inhibitions almost tempted me to join.

Almost.

The woman lifted a metal bottle to her lips, and blood poured down her chin onto her breasts before she shrugged. "The dominance turns me on, I guess." She grasped the faux cock with her fingers. "Plus, with one of these, you get deeper into them than they ever could with you...and it lasts longer." She held it out to me with expectant eyes. "I promise to take it slow, wanna give it a try?"

Summoning a polite smile, I shook my head, the muscles in my face feeling stiff from the effort. "You go ahead, have fun with Israel…and everyone else."

"I'll be here if you change your mind, handsome." She left my side and rejoined the throng of bodies, the murmur of voices, and the press of people closing in around her as she put one hand on the dark man's shoulder. Within a moment, his eyes widened, rolled back in his head, and his body shuddered with overwhelming ecstasy.

Chapter Eight

Leaving the playroom, I made my way up the staircase, the echoes of moans fading with each step. What other scenarios would I find myself in? With each step towards the fourth floor, I found myself contemplating whether Gabe ever set foot in this place and experienced the offerings of The Carlton. Surely his knowledge of this place couldn't have *just* been from his friends at work, right?

Upon reaching the top, I was surrounded by more neon signs, casting a vibrant glow. Whispering to myself, I read each of them. "Shower Room, Dark Room, Executive Lounge, or Diamond Bar?" I had an assumption about what was happening in the shower and dark rooms, but my curiosity piqued in the lounge and bar. Even better, both of them were in the same direction.

A bald man stepped out of one of the rooms as I walked down the hallway, casting a curious glance in my direction. With a smile, he took a few steps forward and gently grasped the doorknob of the adjacent room. With a final glance back, he reached for the sash around his waist, letting the robe fall to the ground with a soft thud. "Like what you see? Wanna come in?"

If I were being completely honest, I didn't like anything he was showing me. I may have been living under a rock for sixty-five years, but that didn't make me desperate. Despite his thin frame, he had a noticeable protruding stomach, and his small, shriveled penis hung limply between his legs. I shook my head and pointed straight ahead. "Nah, I'm heading to the Executive Lounge."

"Ah, the Executive Lounge, you don't look like a dirty boy." He opened the door with a horny smirk and raised an eyebrow. "If you change your mind, you know where to find me."

Fat chance, buddy.

I moved along the hallway, consciously resisting the temptation to glance into the rooms. What I originally found exciting was starting to become irritating as more and more people kept asking me to join them. I kept my eyes fixed straight ahead, where a looming black metal door marked the end of the hallway. The chaotic energy emanating from it was strangely alluring, pulling me closer. My hand grasped the handle, but it didn't move—the door was locked.

Suddenly, a beep came from inside, and a man emerged, freezing in his tracks once he saw me. "You coming in? Maybe I'll stay."

I swayed on my feet to catch a glimpse inside, where people in tuxedos were surrounded by naked men and women. Situated around the stage, plush lounge sets provided a comfortable view of the woman spinning around the pole. The room was filled with crystal decanters, their contents a mix of blood and liquor that they were drinking straight from the source. My breath caught in my throat as I realized all of these men were employed by my father. I put on my most innocent smile and casually ran my fingers through my hair, feeling the strands slip between my fingertips. "I think I got turned around. Do you know where the Diamond Bar is?"

Raising an eyebrow, he pointed down the hallway. "It's straight ahead, you won't be able to miss it." With a mischievous grin, he bit his bottom lip and winked. "But would you rather join me downstairs in the playroom?"

I fanned myself before responding. "I just left and needed to refresh myself." Playing coy seemed to be working well, judging by how the man's eyes lit up with interest. I was in control of this situation.

"Come find me when you're finished." Before departing, he winked at me one last time.

As I turned down the hallway, a surge of newfound confidence rushed through me with each step. The allure of The Carlton finally made sense to me: in here, you can be whoever you want.

It was also an ego boost knowing he was staring at my ass as I walked away.

Turning the corner, I felt like I stepped directly into the glistening jewels of a chandelier as I neared the Diamond Bar. Looking up, I was surrounded by twinkling lights and intricate jeweled decorations cascading from the ceiling to the floor. The bar in the middle, where all the stringed tassels gathered, created a dazzling display of rainbows on the floor as light refracted through them. On the mirrored shelves behind it, various liquor bottles were arranged, each shimmering with its own distinct glow.

I found a spot at the bar, crossing one leg over the other as I settled into the seat. The bartenders were busy, creating intricate cocktails with freshly muddled fruit. The sound of ice being thrashed around in a cocktail shaker was music to my ears.

Using his arms as a brace, an elderly man with a bow tie and a mustache leaned over the bar. "What would you like tonight?"

Ruffling my hair, I aimed for a carefree, relaxed look, which drove men wild. "Dirty martini, rocks on the side."

Out of the corner of my eye, I saw a man take a seat beside me, his broad stance almost brushing against my leg. With a quick glance, I noticed his average physique, overshadowed by a dense layer of chest hair peeking out from the white robe. His small eyes squinted as his full lips curved into a smile. He wasn't unattractive, but not someone I'd typically go for.

But who cares? I can be anyone I want.

The bartender returned, tipping the contents of the shaker into a martini glass in front of me. The red pits within the sage colored olives stood out like beacons as the liquid poured over them, creating a stunning visual contrast.

"Martini, nice," the man beside me acknowledged and dropped a few coins atop the bar. "I'll take a Manhattan." The bartender nodded in acknowledgement before disappearing to mix the alcohol. "My name's Trent, how 'bout yours, handsome?"

Taking a sip of my martini, I racked my brain, trying to come up with a suitable name to give him. His voice sounded familiar, making it difficult for me to concentrate. "Jacob." As the name forced itself out of my mouth, it took everything in my power not to chuckle, as it was similar to Gabe's middle name.

"Jacob," Trent repeated, letting it sit in his mouth as he raised his glass to take a sip. "Is it your first time here?"

I shook my head and shrugged. "I've been here a few times, although not as often as everyone else, it seems."

He licked the liquor off his lips, a knowing smile

playing on his face. "It breaks up the monotony of our day-to-day. Reminds us what it's like to be human, you know?" He took another sip before turning back to me with a smile, his fangs glistening in the light. "I saw you coming out of the Executive Lounge. Do they pay you to be here?"

They wish.

My cheeks flushed. "I wasn't coming out of the lounge. I was curious about what was inside."

"You know, I've heard that The Carlton is the headquarters to all security within Elysium. They monitor the cameras and can even open the wall outside from somewhere within this hotel."

"Interesting," I responded, not remotely attentive to the conversation. "You can't believe every rumor you hear. I mean, *you* thought *I* was working in the Executive Lounge."

"Forgive me for that." His slight lean towards me allowed his large hand to softly stroke my leg. My conscience continued vollying my morals. Playing along with this man wasn't cheating, right? "The reason I made that mistake is because you're so handsome. Can you blame me?"

With a slight movement to readjust his palm, I felt my body tense as his thumb brushed against my thigh. "Um... thank you," I answered, shifting uncomfortably in my seat. "You-you're a good-looking man yourself." My facade was beginning to crumble, and the unexpected sensation of a physical touch caught me off guard.

"You think so?" He put his free hand on my other leg. "Would you like to pay me back for getting you in here tonight?"

His voice triggered a sense of familiarity, but it wasn't until now that I connected it to the man who paid for my entry downstairs. He looked different without clothes, although I hadn't studied him before. With a shake of my head, I pushed his hands off my legs.

Trent leaned forward, putting his head near my neck. "I can smell your blood through your skin, and its scent is divine." He tightly grabbed my leg with one hand while placing the other on the side of my neck, his fangs fully extended. "Would you mind if I had a taste?"

"Don't." Even as I attempted to twist around in my chair to avoid him, he kept me securely ensnared between his legs. I'd heard rumors of vampires not knowing their true strength and killing others. I didn't want to test the theory tonight.

"I…I need to," he whispered in a seductive undertone. He savored the scent with closed eyes and took a deep breath through his nostrils, releasing a faint moan. "I need to have a taste." He wrapped his fingers around my neck, the rough skin of his thumb caressing my jaw as he tilted my head.

"S-stop," I spat, trying to wriggle away. The thought of causing a commotion or yelling crossed my mind, but I quickly dismissed it, knowing it would only lead to people arriving and ultimately alert my father to my sneaking away. I prayed the bartender would pick up on the distress in my facial movements and step in to help.

Within a flash, my body was free. Feeling his grip loosen, I immediately stood and checked my neck for any holes or protrusions, relieved to find none. "Fuck you." I spun around, and my heart raced at the sight of Trent being held against the bar, a knife dangerously pressed against his throat.

Gabe was an inch away from the man's face and growled, "Get the fuck away from him."

My boyfriend's anger filled the room, causing me to momentarily forget the familiar face of the man before me. As he moved swiftly, the sash around his waist came loose, revealing his muscular physique. With his wide, feral pupils and taut, bulging muscles, he looked like a coiled spring ready to unleash. While his appearance may have been off-putting to others, I found myself captivated by his wild look, feeling a mix of fear and desire as I nervously bit my lip.

"Get the fuck off me!" Pushing Gabe backward, Trent wasted no time in making a swift escape, scurrying away as fast as he could.

Gabe kept a steady gaze on the man until he vanished down the hallway. Turning his head in my direction, he glared at me, feeling like piercing daggers. "What the hell were you thinking coming here? How can you be so—so stupid?"

The way he stared at me, I knew I was in trouble. I hurt him. "I-I just wanted to see what it was like."

"Do you know what a stupid idea that was, Vin?" Flakes of spit flew through the space between us as he reprimanded me. "When I realized you weren't coming back from the bathroom at Smoke, I looked everywhere for you. I thought I was so dumb for thinking you'd come here, but in my gut, I knew. I checked every room in this place, hoping some creep like that guy didn't force themselves on you. If anything were to happen to you, I...I wouldn't be able to forgive myself."

"You don't have to worry about me." I crossed my arms. "I'm a grown man and can handle myself. I'm not as fragile as you and my father think."

His eyes held a lost expression, as if trying to comprehend something unfamiliar, while he nervously bit the inside of his cheek. "I know you're strong, but The Wastes themselves are dangerous. You never know who could be in The Carlton."

"It *is* dangerous," I admitted. "But I've never felt more free, you know how badly I want to be off my floor."

"I can show you new experiences. We can do them together now that your father has given the order to allow you to experience Elysium. You don't need to put yourself in life-or-death situations to feel something."

He was pleading with me. His facial expressions shifted from anger to a sorrowful gaze, as if he finally let go of his fear, and his emotions were rising to the surface. I nodded. "Let's go home."

"Hold on." The furrow in Gabe's forehead went smooth, and a light glinted in his eye. "Since we're here, let's have some fun."

Without a chance to react, he swiftly pushed me against the wall and knelt before me. Using two fingers, he peeled back my robe and engulfed my member in his warm mouth. He seldom exhibited this behavior, and I didn't have to drain his blood to be fully alert. My body was trembling with the rhythmic thrusts of his head and the soft tissue at the back of his throat.

The onlookers at the bar, still buzzing from the earlier commotion, couldn't tear their eyes away as Gabe skillfully sucked me off. If I were being honest, the people watching us made the experience all the more pleasurable. Gabe ran his tongue along the bottom of my shaft and began rolling his wrist along the base of my cock. Release was building inside of me, but I held back.

"Is this what you wanted?" he asked me again, pausing momentarily, his lips shining with precum.

"You need to finish me." I gasped. "Please."

Right before he could carry on with the act, darkness engulfed the entire area, and all the lights went out. Gabe quickly stood up, wiping his mouth, as the onlookers in the bar let out subdued yelps. What was happening?

We were surrounded by flashing red lights, flickering rhythmically in the darkness. A blaring siren surrounded us, and Gabe's brows rose in response. He was scared. Screams filled the bar, bouncing off the walls as people frantically fled down the hallways.

Gabe's firm grip on my shoulders was his way of ensuring I was paying attention. "Something's happening. We need to get back to the locker room so I can protect you." His voice got stern, and he spat, "You cannot leave my side, so don't get any ideas to disappear on me again."

Despite my confusion about the situation, the flashing lights, alarm, and Gabe's swift transition to bodyguard mode left no doubt things were serious. Running through the chaotic hotel, we held on to each other tightly, navigating the crowd and avoiding slippery surfaces. The loud bangs and gunshots could be heard from outside the building. The terror within me steadily built before a deafening explosion shook the hotel to its foundation.

Were we under attack?

Chapter Nine

Sitting fully clothed on a bench within the locker room, I waited for Gabe to come collect me. He threw on his clothes, a frantic energy in his movements, and urged me to stay put as he rushed outside to investigate. A handful of people remained in the area, as the majority of the hotel guests had fled toward the exit, some clothed, while others were completely naked.

So here I sat.

The sharp crack of gunshots echoed outside, each one sending a shiver down my spine. What was happening? Were we truly under attack? I'd been sitting here for what seemed like hours. "Gabe?" My voice came out in no more than a whisper, although I didn't exactly know why. Fear had a tight grip on me, making every sound, every moment, feel like an eternity.

I waited, listening for any sound, but his voice remained absent. I tentatively stood and walked through the silent, empty locker room, hoping to see my boyfriend. But there was no sign of him. Where could he have gone? Do I continue waiting for him? A loud explosion, as if answering my question, rocked the building, the shockwave seeming to hit me directly. They were getting closer.

I couldn't sit here and wait for him; I knew I had to get out for my own safety. Fear gripped my throat—did something happen to Gabe? I ran out of the locker room, taking the stairs to the ground level, which opened into an empty ballroom. I sidestepped piles of brightly colored confetti on the floor, the silence amplifying the emptiness of the now-unmanned front desk. I pushed the metal door open with all my might and scurried down the alleyway, seeing the once-empty park now full of people. The night was alive with the roar of the fire, its orange flames licking at the snow, leaving behind a grim trail of black soot in the snow underfoot.

I peered out from the alley's shadows and got my first glimpse of the chaos outside the infamous hotel. A wave of men in matte black armor surged through the streets, and the cold, hard gleam of their weapons reflected in the dim light. I could tell they were drunk on blood for the occasion because they each had a crazed look in their eyes, and their fangs were completely bared in maniacal smiles. It was the vampire military.

A wave of people surged past me, their bodies brushing against mine as I strained to find Gabe. Flattening myself against the stone building, I shimmied out of the alleyway, the snowy ground crunching softly under my shoe. Every time the deafening sound of gunshots pierced the air, I froze, the yells of the crowd a terrifying symphony around me.

Charred wood and debris littered the ground, the acrid smell of burning wood stinging my nostrils as tendrils of smoke swirled around me from the fires consuming the skeletal trees. The commotion in the park died down as a crowd of vampires stared at their enemies—figures in powerful white coats, their faces hidden behind menacing metal masks. Sleek guns were clasped in all the vampires' hands, yet these newcomers brandished weapons like axes, outdated firearms, and arrows readied in their bows.

How barbaric.

A gunshot shattered the morning calm, and one of the white-clad intruders crumpled to the earth, crimson staining his companion's clothes like an art canvas. In that moment, all hell broke loose. The composed groups on both sides, their faces grim, dispersed, and the sharp crack of gunshots echoed through the air. More soldiers from both sides poured into the area, their boots crunching on the gravel, completely covering the park. I watched in horror as a missile, screaming through the air, slammed into the top of the building next to me, shaking the ground.

Before I was hit with debris or crushed under a falling building, I made a mad dash to the staircase, the gritty dust stinging my eyes, and turned right, seeing the broken peak of the fountain in the town square, its once-graceful curves now shattered and distorted. Hurrying up the road, I couldn't help but feel a pang in my heart as I ran past the mounds of snow in the area, knowing the starved vampires couldn't save themselves from the invasion.

Fear gripped me, pulling at my mind and reminding me that my father and Gabe were right: The Wastes were dangerous. A deafening roar filled my ears as I was lifted off my feet and thrown violently across the walkway. The screams abruptly ceased, replaced by an unsettling quiet that felt heavier than any sound. Through my blurred vision, a plume of smoke rose into the air from a recently detonated explosion.

The icy snow clung to my face as I lifted my head, and a jolt of adrenaline surged through me, feeling like a swarm of bees buzzing beneath my skin. I was scared to move, nervous in fear that if I did, I'd be the next one shot. The people clad in white who I assumed were the Unicorns infiltrated the area. A bloody battle raged around me—vampires, with their fangs and talon-like fingernails, clawed at the human bodies, the air thick with the coppery tang of blood and the screams of the dying. Crimson blood, like a macabre stain on a pristine canvas of snow, mirrored the robes of our enemies.

We were winning.

A vampire guard was backing his way toward me, and I reached out my hand to grab his ankle, hoping he didn't mistake me for an Exile. He swung his gun downward, the cold steel glinting menacingly as I stared down its barrel. I couldn't do more than whisper, "H-help me get back inside?"

The man paused, carefully weighing my question before giving me a slow nod and placing a firm hand on my arm, pulling me upright. Crouching low, I hid behind the guard, his finger tightening on his gun's trigger. Fear pulsed through me, making my body shake uncontrollably as we inched backward toward the old fountain. Every step I took was stunted, hoping I didn't get caught in the crosshair of a stray bullet by slipping on a sheet of ice or stumbling over a stray Exile lying in the street.

As we reached the stone fountain, a white-clad figure darted from a shadowed alcove high above, startling us. The guard in front of me swiveled his body and shot the intruder; their lifeless body fell to the ground in a puff of snow.

A shared glance passed between us, our exhaled breaths hanging like small, white puffs in the frosty air. The shocking realization of our near-miss was shattered as two more people launched themselves from a surrounding high-rise. A series of deafening gunshots ripped through the air, and I instinctively threw my arms in front of my face. One of the intruders, his white clothes stark against the night, stumbled backward as his accomplice lunged, the pale glint of moonlight on his knife.

The man's firm hand clamped down on my arm, yanking me down as he crouched beside me with his arm in the air. The assailant halted midair before collapsing to the ground with a sickening, hollow thump.

"Are you okay?" the guard quickly asked.

"I'm fine." I was immensely thankful for this guard risking his life for me. Hearing the gunshots, more and more people entered the area as vampires and intruders mixed in a swirl of white and black. It was impossible now to see who was winning the fight.

The guard turned to me, his helmet covering all but his mouth. A wispy, light-colored mustache sat on his upper lip, his fangs glistening. "Take a right behind the fountain and run straight ahead, I'll hold them o—"

With a terrifying whoosh, a sharp arrow plummeted from above, impaling the guard next to me. A cold dread washed over me as the arrow's tip rested mere centimeters from my body. He collapsed onto the cold, hard ground, blood blooming crimson on the grey stone walkway. My eyes briefly left the still form of the dead man, and I saw someone in stark white robes raise their bow, the next arrow aimed straight at my chest. A wave of paralysis washed over me, but impulsively, I threw myself into the basin of the fountain. Like the whisper of the wind, a whoosh sliced through the air above me, the sound of an arrow missing its mark. "It's now or never."

With a mighty push, I jumped from the empty fountain and ran faster than I'd ever imagined toward Elysium's entrance. Following the soldier's directions, I found myself in a narrow, dark alley, with the sliding doors waiting for me ahead. My mind replayed the scene—the kind guard, his lifeblood seeping into the earth, his eyes wide and staring—and a wave of nausea washed over me. I couldn't help but keep thinking that coming to The Wastes was a bad idea.

My heart hammered a frantic rhythm against my ribs, a deafening drumbeat obliterating all other sounds as I remained glued to the doors ahead. Between the rapid, frantic thumps of my heart, a faint, melodic tinkling like tiny bells drifted down from above. I saw arrows clink and ping off the glass, their metallic sound echoing, while small bullets peppered the ground around me like a sudden hailstorm.

Seeing the protective glass outside Elysium was as strong as they advertised, allowing me to breathe a sigh of relief. Once I get inside, I'll be safe. I reached for the glass doors when a deafening explosion rocked the building, the force lifting me off the ground and hurling me through the doors.

My body hit the hard floor, and I lay there for a moment in an attempt to catch my breath before a realization hit me. I wasn't safe yet. "I need to get back to my room."

I walked down a long, dimly lit hallway, the only sound my own footsteps echoing, until I reached a row of elevators standing in perfect formation. The emergency lights in the hallway flickered, casting an eerie, strobe-like glow. The shadows that moved along the walls seemed to writhe and shift, as if something were lurking within, ready to pounce. It was strange that it was just me. I assumed everyone got inside before the intruders fully invaded.

Pressing the elevator button, I rolled my eyes when no light emitted from the box, indicating it wasn't in working order. With the power out, the building was plunged into darkness as I climbed the seemingly endless stairs to the top floor. I rounded the corner to find a lone door at the top of the staircase. My hand grasped the cool, smooth handle and pulled—locked, a small, disappointing thud punctuating the quiet. "Ugh, of course," I whispered to myself. Reaching into my pocket, I retrieved the cool metal key card and slapped it against the unresponsive pad. Nothing. Probably a security measure for instances like this.

"Need some help?"

Gabe's voice startled me, and I whirled around to see him standing behind me. His clothes were torn and ragged, revealing patches of skin beneath, a gash marred his cheek, and he clutched his bleeding right arm. Beads of sweat clung to his temples. He looked scared, even though his voice sounded calm. "Where the hell've you been? You scared the shit outta me! Are you okay?"

"Where have *I* been?" He looked taken aback. "Where have *you* been, Vinny? I looked everywhere in The Carlton, and you just ran off…again!"

I shook my head at his accusatory tone. "I waited in the locker room for you for so long, but once I heard all the explosions, I left because I thought maybe you went to help the army when you heard the siren."

With a firm grip on my shoulders, Gabe made sure our eyes locked, his expression serious and unwavering. "Do you know how scared I was for you?" He wrapped his arms around me and pulled me in for a hug filled with relief. "I saw that fucking Unicorn nearly kill you at the fountain, and I think my heart stopped. I can't lose you, Vin."

I held him close, savoring the feeling of his arms

around me and offering a silent prayer of gratitude for our survival.

"I need to get you to your room. It's the safest place for you, away from any potential danger." Gabe's words were barely out when he clicked his fingers against the keycard, the plastic face popping off to reveal tiny numbered dials. Completing the code, a faint click echoed from the door's mechanism, signaling the lock's release. "All keycards have a backup battery for instances like this." Gabe looked at me with a smug smile. "By the way, can I have my key back?"

I held out the crisp, white card, its edges sharp against my fingertips, and he snatched it away, tucking it into his back pocket with a swift motion. As we entered the stairwell, the echoing silence amplified the sound of our footsteps, and I looked up at the countless floors stretching before us. "I don't suppose the elevators have a backup battery, right?"

He laughed from inside the doorway. "Yes, they do, that's what I just activated. The keypad temporarily unlocks this stairwell and allows us to use the elevator inside."

I'm not religious, but thank God.

A lone metal door, dented and scratched from age, was bolted to the wall to our left. Pressing the metallic button, a small light illuminated the knob, and within seconds, the rusty doors groaned open.

After pressing the top button, the elevator rumbled to life with a low, vibrating hum. "So what's going on out there?"

"The Unicorns launched an invasion," Gabe calmly explained. "We've speculated an attack was coming; we just didn't know it was going to be tonight."

I nodded, remembering a prior conversation. "My dad

did say our enemies have been quiet, but what are they looking for in The Wastes?"

"They can't get inside without going through The Wastes first." His eyes shifted away. "I've been told they're looking for a way to kill all vampires, and they think the key is hidden somewhere in Elysium."

"Is it?"

He shrugged. "No idea. I've never been told of a trigger that would kill all the vampires in the world, and I don't know why one would be made."

The elevator doors slid open, revealing a dimly lit hallway, the silence broken only by the faint hum of machinery. Only the dim glow of the keypad to my apartment broke the darkness of the hallway. With a slight wave, Gabe's card unlocked the door.

Placing one hand on the handle, I opened it ajar. "You'll protect me tonight?"

"Absolutely." He smiled. "I first have to report to your father that you're back safely and get my arm bandaged, then I'll be right back."

"Deal." I smiled at him, at my boyfriend. "Thanks for looking out for me." Stepping inside the penthouse, I lingered on the man in the hallway who constantly put me on a pedestal. The door clicked shut, and I eased myself into the kitchen, pouring a glass of rich red wine. Its taste did little to calm my nerves.

I was safe.

"What a crazy birthday," I murmured to myself, taking a sip of the spiced red wine. The adrenaline wore off, and a wave of heavy-lidded fatigue washed over me, my senses dulled like a foggy hangover.

"Hello, Mr. Asposito."

My grip on the wine glass tightened as a man in pristine white robes, his light hair entered my view, the air around him thick with unspoken power. The mask obscuring his face was crafted from metal and shaped like a horse's head with a tiny horn jutting from its brow.

A Unicorn.

The man's sudden appearance startled me, a gasp escaping my lips as my grip on the wine glass loosened, sending it tumbling to the ground with a sharp shattering sound. Purple liquid pooled at my feet as bits of glass tinkled on the floor. "W-who are you and what do y-you want from m-me?"

The man clasped his hands, his knuckles white, and spoke in a calm voice that resonated with authority. "No harm will come to you as long as you do as I say."

So much for being safe.

I nodded, and the cold steel of the handcuffs clicked shut around my wrists as the man secured them behind my back. From behind, he wrapped a coarse white fabric around my mouth, the rough texture scratching my lips as he bound it tightly to the back of my head, silencing me.

Usually, handcuffs and a gag would have a different effect on me.

"Please follow me."

His hand was placed in the middle of my back, urging me forward. We walked along the plush carpet, which reached from the penthouse to the elevator, and pressed the button. I stared at the button, a silent prayer on my lips, willing the power to be off, but the doors slid open with a hiss of compressed air, a chilling sound in the sudden silence. The man reached into his front pocket and swiped a white card. The doors closed, and the vestibule descended through Elysium. As the screen inside counted down the numbers, it halted at floor thirteen.

The doors slid open, and two blood-soaked figures in white robes collapsed onto the floor, a hollow sound accompanying their fall. The man's hand on my back urged me forward as I stepped over the corpses, their cold, vacant eyes staring up at me from the blood-soaked ground.

I'd never been to this floor, although that isn't surprising. We were in a sparsely furnished lobby with dead vampire guards in tuxedos strewn over the floor. A throng of Unicorns stood before us, encircling the final two vampires.

My heart leaped into my throat at the sight of Gabe and my father, fangs bared, standing back-to-back. I gasped and tried to yell, but only choked, muffled sounds came out.

"At ease," the man instructed the other white robed individuals. A sudden shove sent me to my knees, and he gestured toward my boyfriend and father. "Salvatore Asposito, I'm pleased to make your acquaintance."

"What have you done to my son?" My father's eyes narrowed to slits, his face pale and tense, and he spat his words like venom, a cold fury radiating from him.

"Vinny, did they harm you?"

I quickly shook my head, my scared heart pounding in my chest. The man promised I wouldn't be harmed, but what about Gabe or my dad? Never before had I seen them both so sharply peaked and furious, their voices sharp and their bodies tense. A fierce, infernal light blazed in their eyes as they focused intensely on the man.

"I can assure you that not one hair on your precious son's head has been harmed and will remain that way as long as you do what I ask."

"I'll kill you before you lay another finger on him." With a fierce cry, Gabe launched himself at the man, only to be stopped short by the sharp crack of a Unicorn's gunshot, the bullet ripping into his shoulder. With a yell, he plummeted from the air, clutching his smoking, sizzling arm wound.

"Our bullets are infused with silver, and before you say anything—we know they won't kill you because you're vampires, but they do more damage than a normal bullet."

My dad raised his hands, his knuckles white, and a vein throbbed in his forehead as his anger swelled. "Let my son go, I'll do whatever you want. Take me if you'd like!"

"We don't want you." The man laughed, a sound that resembled water bubbling in a drain. "I'll release your son and signal my troops to retreat if you do one thing for me."

"Anything." My dad sounded defeated as his eyes darted between me and the man.

"Open the vault."

"Do it," Gabe moaned from the ground, his blood pooling on the floor.

"I-I can't," he whispered. "W-what if we supplied you with advanced weapons to fight against the Dogs? Or-or I could build an Elysium for humans only, to protect you and your family?"

I turned from my father's pleading gaze to the imposing figure beside me. I'd give anything to see the face behind the mask at this very moment. Was he contemplating my dad's offer?

He shook his head. "Open the vault, or I take your son. This is your choice, Mr. Asposito."

My father went quiet, his face a mask of silent contemplation, and I silently pleaded for him to choose me. He *would* choose me, right? He always told me I was the most important person in his world. Why was he taking so long to make this decision?

My father looked away, his jaw tight, avoiding my gaze. "Take him."

"WHAT?!" Gabe yelled as he stumbled to his knees.

"Dad?" My voice came out in a whisper as the shock of what I heard manifested at my core. "Are you serious?" Did that really just happen?

My mind went hazy as I tried convincing myself I didn't hear him correctly. My legs felt light, as if I were going to collapse. What was going to happen to me? Surely Gabe wouldn't let this happen.

A deafening explosion ripped a gaping hole in the wall, revealing the chaotic world beyond, the air thick with the smell of smoke and dust. A cool breeze blew into the lobby as wisps of snowflakes danced inside. With a roar of its engine, a large helicopter settled over the hole, and a massive door extended, forming a walkway inside.

"You made your choice," the man spat at my father, and he roughly pushed me toward the helicopter, shoving me inside.

"Dad!" I screamed. "Just give them what they want!" My voice came out as a shrill wail, as if this were my last moment of life.

Maybe it was.

Above the insistent thrum of the helicopter, I heard Gabe's desperate, increasingly frantic shouts directed at my father. His words were a jumbled mess, barely audible over the deafening sound of the helicopter blades.

Before the door closed, I took one last glance at my father, tears blurring my vision, and he remained stubbornly avoidant to my gaze. He stood there, head bowed, shoulders slumped, a picture of utter defeat. Only one thing was running through my mind: what's going to happen to me?

I carry on, I carry on.

Chapter Ten

I was frozen in fear, the deafening noise of the helicopter thrumming through my body. The men around me, still wearing their metal horse masks, sat silently along the perimeter of the vehicle. Shimmering faintly in the dim light, their white robes brushed the cool metal floor as we flew through the sky.

Did I really just get kidnapped by *humans*?

My lip snarled behind the contraption affixed to my face. The cool metal of the helicopter rested on my fingertips as my arms were still handcuffed behind me. I was trembling, both from fear and the cold temperature, but I refused to let them see. My mind was reeling, a jumble of terror at the possibility of death and a torrent of unanswered questions. Surely my father had a valid reason to offer me to the rebels, right?

The light-haired man who surprised me in my penthouse stared at me through his mask, his eyes glinting from the controls at the head of the helicopter. He was slightly shorter than the other men, his blond hair pulled back tightly.

"Sir, we're descending," one of the men piloting the helicopter gruffly said in the front seat.

He nodded and crawled over to me with a metal contraption clenched around his fingers. "I'll remind you," his voice was stern, "cooperate and you will not be hurt." With a sharp snap of his fingers, two men, one on each side, grabbed me and pinned me down. "Open your mouth."

The rough fabric was pulled from my head, and I stubbornly refused to open my mouth. I wasn't following their direction. Two strong hands, rough and calloused, wrapped around my jaw, forcing my lips apart. The man's hands moved quickly, attaching the complex metal device to my mouth. The arms of the contraption extended and latched onto the hook toward the back of my neck.

They must not know I don't have fangs. Idiots.

"This is for our protection," he explained. "Is it too tight?"

Ignoring the question, I craned my neck, peering through a tiny, square window at the world outside. The ground was covered in a thick layer of untouched snow, snowflakes whipping past, obscuring my vision. A hole in the ground below opened inward. The black rectangle looked ominous as we headed straight for it. The helicopter shuddered to a halt, its descent slow and measured, reminding me intensely of the smooth, silent elevators in Elysium.

As we disappeared into the dark hole, bands of white lights sprang to life within the helicopter cabin, illuminating the metallic surfaces and our anxious faces. The man's hand, resting on the cold, metallic handcuffs, signaled me to stand, and I flinched at the harsh, blinding brightness. I stirred, my knees cracking like twigs as I extended both legs with a grunt.

"Did he just growl at you?" A man in front of her laughed behind his mask. "Make sure the thing around its mouth is tight." Lifting his black boot, the man exited the helicopter and twisted a silver-handled flashlight.

"Idiot," a man behind me muttered as he pushed me forward.

Stepping from the helicopter, I was met with a dozen blinding circular orbs of light, each flashlight held by a robed figure, their beams intense. I squinted, unable to shield my eyes from the harsh glare despite struggling against my bonds. The lights swung wildly, and he gestured me toward a large metal cart, its wheels rusted and set on two ancient, groaning tracks.

"Get in."

I nodded, taking a moment to try to see through the mask placed over the man's face. A glint of unexpected kindness shone through the mask's eyeholes, piercing me with their warmth. I inhaled deeply, the musty scent of damp earth filling my lungs before settling onto the frigid metal seat. The robed men joined me, and the cart rumbled to life. Two orange lights blinked on at the head of the vehicle, casting an eerie glow on the damp tunnel walls ahead. A loud, ear-splitting screech echoed from beneath the cart, making the wooden structure shudder violently before it lurched forward.

The only sound in the dark tunnel was the rhythmic click of the cart's wheels on the tracks, the orange light ahead cutting through the inky blackness. Where were we? The jarring turns and bumps made the ride feel precarious. It felt unreal, like a movie set, but the bumpy road made me fear I'd be thrown from the vehicle at any moment. Peering through the inky black surrounding us, the beam of light cutting through the oppressive darkness,

I almost expected something to jump in front of us, scaring me nearly to death.

But nothing did.

The cart came to a stop, a gentle bump that jolted me back to reality, and I realized I'd lost all sense of time. It felt like I'd been in the cart for hours, although my sense of time was skewed from the helicopter to where we were now. It could've been minutes, but it could've also been much longer. A dim, white bulb sputtered to life, its weak light barely illuminating a cold, metallic ladder ascending into the darkness above.

The blond-haired man behind me pointed toward the heavens. "You three climb up and let us know if the coast is clear. I'll need to free his hands to climb, but as soon as he gets to the top, I want him in handcuffs again."

The white-robed men nodded, then scurried up the rusted metal ladder one by one, leaving me alone at the bottom. I shook my head, the murmur of their voices washing over me like a wave, as they spoke of me as if I weren't there. A lesser human. A monster.

The man beside me seized my hands, his whispered breath hot against my ear. "I trust you not to try anything sneaky. We have men armed, and we'll not hesitate to shoot you."

I nodded, and with a click, the pressure of the handcuffs eased on my wrists. I tried to talk and ask where I was being taken, but the metal constraints made my words sound nothing more than a jumbled mess.

A slow shake of his head, followed by a finger to his masked lips, conveyed a clear message of silence. "You won't be harmed as long as you cooperate."

Hesitantly, I nodded. He sounded genuine, like I could trust him. But to what extent? He'd been true to his word thus far; I just needed to know where I was going before I made a move. With a deep breath, I placed my foot on the cool, metal bottom rung of the ladder and carefully climbed upward, following orders.

Reaching the summit, I was suddenly surrounded by a snowy tundra, the biting wind whipping around me. Pulling myself from the cold, damp darkness of the hole, my eyes burned from the sudden brightness of the blinding white landscape. Even though I may not be human, I do still get cold. It's just not as much of a shock as it is to humans. Two hands fastened themselves under my arms, and the sudden pressure was alarming as they secured fresh metal restraints around my wrists.

A cold wind swept across the open ground as the remaining abductors crawled from the hole, quickly pulling their hoods low to protect themselves from the elements. "Let's go," one of them said, gesturing to me. "This quell will slow us down. Do you need a jacket?"

I shook my head. The cold pierced me to my core, but my body would soon acclimate. If we didn't keep moving, my body would begin to use as much blood as needed to feed me until I ran out and started becoming an Exile. Plus, I didn't want to ask them for any favors. I was strong, and I wanted them to know it.

The wind felt like a wall in my face as we traveled through the waist-high snow. Due to the quell, we were unable to see too far in front of us. The inky darkness reminded me of being in the cart, but wisps of white danced around us and continued to coat my eyelashes. The swirling snow obscured my surroundings, a biting wind whipping around me as the white-robed figures huddled closer, rubbing their arms for warmth. I thought I saw a flash of red catch my eye, but when I turned, it vanished. Paranoia was seeping into my body.

A high-pitched yell cut through the quiet as a man

behind me screamed. With a twist of my body, I saw a horrifying splatter of blood, stark and shocking against the untouched white of the snow. I followed the glistening trail of blood, each droplet falling from an angular metallic mouth.

It was a Dog, up close and personal.

The Dog ripped off one of the robed men's arms, the severed limb dangling grotesquely from its jaws, blood dripping down its snout. Its black eyes narrowed, the red irises gleaming like embers through the swirling snow. Its sharp teeth were bared in a snarl, its ears perked straight up, and a growl rumbled in its chest.

"Fuck," one of the men yelled. "A pack of Dogs is heading our way."

My heart stopped, and my body froze. I hadn't seen a Dog or been in danger since the night my mom died. Am I next?

A rapid series of gunshots shattered the silence, immediately followed by a Dog's entertained yelps. One bullet reached its mark, the impact sending a spray of dark liquid spurting across the cold, white snow. With worried whimpers, the pack of Dogs formed a protective circle around their injured brother, allowing it to retreat.

A tremor ran through me. I'd never been so close to death in years, and the fear was paralyzing. A thought struck me—don't the humans control the Dogs? Reaching to my face with my bound hands, I pulled at one of the contraption's arms, breaking it off into my hand. "Can't you turn them off?"

"What are you talking ab—" The man's words were cut short as a Dog, barking fiercely, leaped and knocked him to the ground.

Three more Dogs emerged from the swirling snow, their sharp teeth bared in a guttural growl that vibrated in the frigid air. Perfectly triangular teeth lined their mouths, glinting ominously. With each step, a rusty, mechanical creak echoed through the air, like an old clockwork toy. White tendrils of smoke curled into the crisp morning air as the Dogs' breaths hitched, heavy and ragged, their oil-slicked tongues lolling from their mouths.

"Someone help me!" The man punched the Dog that was pinning him into the snow.

As the blow landed, the Dog's metal eyelids flickered shut, reducing its red pupils to two tiny points. A gasp of horror escaped my lips, and my body froze as I watched the Dog's jaws clamp down on the man's face with a sickening force. Fresh blood pooled over the white snow, dripping from the mechanical creature's chin.

Their tails curled along their spines, and the Dogs crouched down with their hindquarters in the air. The next few moments were a chaotic blur of snarling Dogs, lunging bodies, and the deafening blasts of gunfire echoed through the air. A spray of black oil splattered the ground as the men's terrified screams echoed around me.

I watched as one man was thrown to the ground, the impact muffled by the thick snow, while another stumbled, his useless gun clutched in the Dog's jaws. A large man in front of me expertly shot at each of the Dogs pouncing at us, keeping them at bay as more emerged from the snow. It was like they were hiding in the swirls of snow in the wind, biding their time in the middle of the storm until they're needed.

I needed to get out of here.

While the Dogs were focusing on my robed captors, I ran. My heart hammered against my ribs, a frantic drumbeat against the roar of the Dogs and the shouts of my kidnappers as I focused on escape. The cold wind rushed into my face, like a frostbitten punch. The snow was so deep and powdery that with every step, my knees rose higher and higher as I ran. I knew I had to keep pumping my legs to get away.

A sharp yank on my loose pants pulled me to the ground. With a wad of tattered cloth clutched firmly in its teeth, a Dog stopped me from fleeing. Without a second thought, I yanked on the pant leg, the fabric tearing with a satisfying rip.

Though still cold, the snow felt almost warm against my frozen skin. A powerful force slammed into my back, sending me sprawling into the powdery snow. A bloodthirsty Dog, its eyes burning red with hunger, glared at me, its low growl vibrating in the air.

It sprang at me again, its weight pressing me into the soft, cold snow. The impact knocked the air from my lungs. Its metallic breath reeked of gasoline on my cheek. My ears caught a faint whirring behind the Dog's head before they turned to black. The creature paused, a strange familiarity in its stance, and I screamed, a futile sound in the carnage around me. Knowing my fate was sealed, I squeezed my eyes shut, waiting for my life to end.

Would my father be sad I was gone? Maybe it's wishful thinking.

A gunshot rang through the air, hitting the Dog with a metallic *clank*. With a sharp jerk of its head, it shifted its gaze from me to its new prey. The creature's body slid off my shoulders, its legs spreading wide as if to shield me from the gunshot.

The light-haired man in a unicorn mask dashed over, his fingers trembling. "Are you alright?"

My breath was heavy, but I managed to nod. I stretched my bound hands towards the man's, and felt him pull me upright. "Come with me, I need to make sure you're safe." His voice was light, yet concerned.

A snarl ripped from the Dog's throat as it sprang between us, its jaws snapping shut inches from the masked man's face. It looked back at me with its coal-black eyes before throwing its heavy, muscular body into me, sending me sprawling to the ground once more.

"Don't touch him!" The masked man jumped into the air, a knife glinting in the moonlight.

With a snarl, the Dog's head whipped around and lunged at the man, who was arcing through the air. With his arm outstretched, the blade sliced through the beast's underbelly, a wet, tearing sound accompanying the swift motion. A single, piercing yelp escaped its lips before it disappeared into a billowing cloud of powdery snow. It was dead.

He saved me.

The man ran back to me and asked again, "Are you okay?"

The world was melding together. I wasn't sure if it was a trick of the snow or if something was wrong with me. My head spun, but I managed to whisper, "I-I'm fine." He lifted me from the frigid, snowy ground, and a wave of dizziness washed over me as the world swam in and out of focus before darkness closed in, and I collapsed.

Chapter Eleven

Am I dead?

The words swirled in my head like a storm, each a crashing wave as I lay with my eyes closed. A comforting darkness shielded me from the unknown, and I hoped when I opened them, I'd be back in my penthouse apartment, the gentle snores of Gabe a familiar solace beside me.

In my soul, I knew that was only a hope.

The cold, hard metal slab pressed into my skin as the smell of mildew and damp earth filled my nostrils. I slowly lifted my eyelids with a deep breath, the world blurring into focus after so long in darkness. I was lying on a small, cold metal cot with a thin, scratchy sheet stretched taut over it and bolted to the wall. Enclosing me were three walls of thick, gray stone, each radiating a chill that permeated the air, and a row of unforgiving metal bars confining me.

I was in jail. I almost forgot these existed outside of movies.

Memories from the night prior flooded my mind, and

my father's betrayal left a bitter taste in my mouth. Lifting my body from the bed, the cold metal of the handcuffs bit into my wrists as I sat up and felt the unforgiving metal contraption still clamped over my mouth. I managed shallow breaths, but my jaw was locked, barely able to open more than an inch. Luckily, the arms were still missing, so my speech wasn't completely distorted. I wore loose canvas pants, a shirt with a gaping neck hole, and heavy, clunky shoes that felt like lead weights.

Where the hell was my couture?

"You're awake," a voice observed from outside the cell.

In front of me, a person in a pristine white robe sat silently on a roughly hewn wooden chair. Even with the horse mask obscuring his face, his voice and the mischievous sparkle in his eyes were unmistakable. "You-you're who saved me from the Dog. But why?"

He also kidnapped me, but I wanted to keep the conversation positive. I know I'd be able to get more out of him being nice than the latter.

"I've been waiting for you to wake since we brought you here."

His evasion of my question, a blatant non-answer, sent a firestorm of anger through me. These people kidnapped me from my home, put me in a deadly situation, and worst of all, completely ruined my couture. I needed to know who was at fault and who gave the orders to tear me away from my father. "Why'd you take me?"

"Sorry, buddy." The person on the other side of the metal bars shook his head, and a mess of blond hair waved to and fro. "That's not my place to tell you."

Buddy? The comment caused all the blood to rush to my face and made it burn with anger. My hands clenched into fists as I yearned to rip off his mask. "TELL ME!" Who was he to deny me a response? I'd been locked up for most of my life, living blissfully without answers. I refused to continue that pattern, whether inside or outside Elysium.

"Whoa whoa, vampire boy, calm down." A heavy metal door slammed shut in the distance, the sound echoing through the corridor as the person opposite me bolted toward the cell. "You'll get your answers, I promise. Just cooperate."

This is becoming a trend. Keep being a good boy and follow directions. Just like at home. Well, guess what? You chose the wrong guy to fuck with.

Four figures in white, their faces obscured by masks, entered the jail and approached my cell, their footsteps echoing eerily in the silence. A man with a low voice boomed through the stone prison. "He's being summoned. They've waited too long."

The man waiting outside my cell nodded, his shadow falling over the four others as he towered above them. Five heads turned toward me, their eyes curious and their faces etched with anticipation, as one reached into their robe pocket to fetch a key.

A stern woman asked, "Does he need to be sedated?"

Be calm. Be calm. I was trying to remind myself that I needed to keep a level head if I wanted answers. My guard was up in case a needle or a weapon emerged from those white robes. I couldn't be held accountable for how I may react. I wasn't much of a fighter, but what more did I have to lose?

The tall man sitting in the wooden chair shook his head. "He's likely still unstable; he just woke up."

The four figures, arranged in a diamond formation, turned their masked faces, a silent nod confirming their acceptance of his word. One placed the key into the lock, and the door opened with a rusty screech, the sound echoing in the still air. Every fiber of my being screamed at me to attack, but I forced myself to breathe deeply, fighting to stay calm amidst my rising panic.

With tense bodies and hesitant steps, the four people entered the dimly lit cell. Each spread out in a semicircle, their footsteps crunching on the gravel as they advanced. I caught sight of pistols clutched in each of their hands.

They were closing in on me. Breathe. Breathe. I knew if they touched me with any bit of force, I was going to fight back. All I could do was hope the man's promise was true—if I cooperated, they'd tell me the answers I was looking for and, hopefully, I'd be able to get back home.

A tangle of arms seized me, rough hands gripping my clothes, while a cold gun barrel pressed hard against my spine. "Don't get any funny ideas," the woman in the mask sternly warned.

I nodded, and the two men clasped one long string around my neck, like a leash. Together, with their hands on my arms, I was pulled upright, their bodies leading the way as they forced me to follow, the rope yanking painfully whenever I lagged. The weight of the gun pressed against my back, the woman behind me never letting it stray.

As the guards led me from the jail, hurried footsteps from the other cells scurried through the corridor. Like chips of obsidian, their eyes glinted in the dim light as they tracked my every movement like curious cats. Some hissed at the white robed people while others screamed indiscernible vulgarities. Once the heavy metal door slammed shut with a definitive clang, all sounds from the jail were silenced.

We wound through hallways upon hallways, the flickering fluorescent lights casting long, dancing shadows on the walls. The cold stone of the labyrinthine passageways twisted and turned, and I felt like a mouse in an experiment. Eventually, they brought me into a large, high-ceilinged room with a circular desk in its center. String lights were wound around the ceiling, and each of the yellow bulbs pulsed like veins in a body. Four people in white robes and metal horse masks sat around the table.

The man with a deep voice beside me boomed, "We brought the vampire."

"You may go." The robed figure at the head of the table rose, causing the four surrounding me to bow their heads before departing the room. His voice, smooth and low, carried an unshakeable confidence.

The man reached to his face and clasped his fingers around the snout of the metal horse mask, exposing his silver hair, sleek and pulled back tightly. A spider web of deep wrinkles covered his face, furrowing his brow and crinkling the skin around his faded light blue eyes. His demeanor exuded intelligence and exhaustion, like he stayed up too late at night studying. His thin lips curved into a slight smile, a dusting of light white stubble accentuating his sharp cheekbones and chin. Even though this was the first time I'd met him, his presence resonated with a deep familiarity—a warmth that felt comforting and unsettling, like a half-remembered dream.

Despite the rage boiling in my being, this man seemed to put me at ease. Well, as much at ease as my body would allow. I couldn't imagine yelling at this man, he looked so kind, and I found I had to keep reminding myself he was the enemy. He kidnapped me.

A heavy silence hung around us as if everyone was afraid to break the quiet. But not me. "Why am I here? What do you want from me?" The stiff metal of the muzzle pressed against my skin, muffling my words, but my voice remained steady, filling me with quiet pride.

"Knowledge," the man answered in a calm and cool voice. "We need to know how to deactivate the Dogs."

My eyebrows shot up in astonishment at the unexpected answer. Was he toying with me? Was this a trap? My eyes darted around the dimly lit room, the shadows playing tricks on my already muddled thoughts. "Everyone knows the humans control the Dogs, so what do you *really* want?"

The man's eyes flickered, a mixture of confusion and suspicion clouding their depths, as his forehead creased in a deep furrow. In a low and solemn voice, he answered, "We, the humans, do not control the Dogs."

My stomach lurched and felt hollow. How could this be true? Is he lying to me? I do have to admit, this information made perfect sense, given both sides were sworn enemies and locked in a bitter feud with no communication. If the vampires don't control the Dogs and neither do the humans…was there another threat unknown to us?

The air in the circular room grew heavy, and the only sound was the low hum of aging light bulbs. The man and I silently stared at one another, a tense silence in the air, both afraid to break it and reveal the cards in our hands.

As if I had cards to show.

The man took a sip from a metal bottle, and rust-colored liquid dribbled down his chin, staining his white uniform. His piercing blue eyes dropped with a look of disgust as he hastily wiped away the droplets. "Ugh, I wish we could find a way to get adequate drinking water from these old pipes." With a frustrated grunt, he furrowed his eyebrows as he twisted the cap back onto the water receptacle.

"Who are you?" I asked. This man wanted information from me, yet I had no clue who he was or where I'd been brought.

I watched him exhale a long, slow breath, and in that moment, I wondered if the change of subject brought him relief. "My name is Arthur. I'm the leader of the remaining humans on this planet."

"That you know of," I blurted. "But anyways, my name is—"

"Vincent, the son of Salvatore Asposito. I know who you are."

A sour taste filled my mouth, and my lip curled into a snarl. "What do you want from me?"

Arthur clasped his fingers together. "Initially, we hoped your father would willingly share the knowledge we were looking for, but his resistance left us with no choice but to extract it from him by any means necessary."

"Me," I whispered as the realization struck. "You know my father will do anything to get me back."

"Will he?" Arthur's eyebrows raised before an amused smile danced at his lips.

If I were being honest, I wasn't sure. Even though it appeared to be a difficult decision, he made the choice to let them take me. In my heart, I know he truly cares for me, but my brain questions if his love is influenced by the wealth and power I've helped him attain. If I were replaceable without impact on him, would getting me back be any of his concern?

"Tell me what *you* know about the Dogs."

What wasn't he understanding? I told him I knew nothing that could help him. He must be toying with me. I searched his light blue eyes, cold and unyielding like polished steel, for any hint of a trap, but found only an unsettling calm. "I have always been told humans controlled the Dogs. That's why we fear leaving the Elysiums."

"And *we* were under the impression the vampires gave

the Dogs their orders." A squint creased his forehead, a silent challenge as he searched my expression for any trace of falsehood, but I met his gaze with unwavering truth. "It seems our separation may have created miscommunication, and the Dogs have their own owner. Someone... different than who we initially thought."

"Dante?" The only person I thought of was my father's old business partner, a man whose betrayal left a lasting scar. I searched his face intently, hoping to find a flicker of familiarity, but his expression remained blank.

"Who's that?"

I shrugged. "I'm not sure. I thought he had more involvement with the humans."

"His name does sound familiar." Arthur squinted as he thought. "But I'd have to look into our records for more information. Do you think he controls the Dogs?"

I shook my head. "He'd likely be long since dead by now." This news was what I feared. For years, we've been at war with the humans, each side trying to eliminate the other for dominance over them and their pets, but the reality was so much worse.

Arthur lifted his heels, his gaze lingering on the door behind me. "Bring in the Dog!" He snapped the metal mask back onto his face before turning to me. "You'll get to meet your friend from last night again."

More people entered the room behind me, their footsteps short and intentional, as if they were pulling something behind them. Turning, I saw two burly men in white robes, their faces grim, carrying a Dog on a rough-hewn wagon. The Dog had its legs tied together, a metal muzzle around its mouth, much like mine, and a blindfold over its metallic screened eyes. The beast's terrifying presence caused my body to tense; this was the Dog who tried killing me last night. Its sharp claws and teeth sent a jolt of primal fear through me. "W-what's that doing here?"

"For years, the threat of the Dogs has halted our advances to eradicate the vampires. Our hope is without those…" Arthur paused and hesitantly gazed in my direction. "Abominations, we'll be able to live freely and create a new era of humanity."

"But now we know neither side controls the Dogs, we can try to find out who does and work together, right?" I truly believed this was a possibility. "Which could start a new generation of humans and vampires living in harmony."

Arthur shook his head. "The vampires won't allow that. They believe themselves to be superior to us, and that is why we have been hunted for years and forced to live in fear. There is no world where humans and vampires are harmonious."

"That may be true right now, but things can change."

"I'd like to believe that." He let out a breath in disbelief. "But based on history, it's unlikely."

I watched as Arthur walked toward the restrained Dog and placed one hand on the blindfold. His fingers untied the fabric, releasing a burst of red light that filled the room. A menacing crimson glow emanated from its eyes as it locked onto each person, and a cold dread seeped into my soul.

"We've tried to apprehend a Dog for years, but once they're injured, more to come assist, and the maimed retreat very quickly to an unknown location for repairs." Arthur's voice lifted higher as he spoke. "Their nest, as we call it."

I was transfixed on the Dog, and my gut told me it was biding its time to strike. Fortunately, the snarling beast remained tied up and continued scanning everyone in the room. Its black pupils dilated when its head landed on me, and a soft, almost mournful whine escaped its mouth. The sound from the beast was somber, as if it were singing a sad song. It knew it had been caught and its life would soon come to an end.

"Our military and intelligence will dissect this Dog to understand where it retreats when injured. Any information you may have on deactivating them would be helpful."

Sadness radiated from within the creature, like we were connected. Its rage quelled, and emptiness overtook its being. Where did this come from? I hated them for all the death they've wrought. A fire of rage ignited in my gut, and a burning spread through me like wildfire. "Why do you have to kill it? Can't you hear it's scared?"

"Humanity from a vampire? That's new." Arthur laughed, his tone bouncing off the walls. "Did the Dogs show us mercy as they killed countless humans, tearing them limb from limb? What about the vampires? Did the Dogs show them mercy when they encountered them patrolling outside your resorts?"

His words, dripping with contempt, were making me furious. He was degrading me and the other vampires. I understood there was hatred between the two races, but our core values are the same. We're all monsters disguised as heroes in life. Everyone may have different perceptions of your identity; however, actions will reveal your truth. "I…I'm not like everyone else in Elysium."

Arthur's eyebrows arched, and his pupils scanned me. "And why is that?"

Do I want to tell him? If I do, it could develop some trust between the two of us. "Take this thing off my mouth, and I'll show you."

He paused, his brow furrowed, clearly considering whether I was trying to deceive him. He could clearly see my bound hands, assessing my low threat level before casually circling behind me. The cold metal brace shifted against my teeth as he fiddled with it, before it clattered to the ground.

"Thank you," I sincerely acknowledged. With a wince, I rubbed my aching chin, then slowly opened and closed my mouth, the movement sending a dull throb through the jaw.

"Now, pray tell, how are you different, Mister Asposito?"

It took everything in me not to roll my eyes, but he was staring at me expectantly. With a nervous tug, I hooked a finger inside my mouth, pulling my lip high enough to show a flash of teeth. I watched the confusion on his face melt into amazement as he realized the absence of fangs.

"My, my, you *are* different. What are you?"

"I've never had them," I shrugged. "And if you were wondering, I can go out in the sun without burning, too. I don't know what it means, but my entire life, I've wished I were more like my friends and family instead of…"

"More like a human?" Arthur quietly finished my sentence, and I acknowledged by nodding. "You certainly are an interesting person, Vincent."

"Can you also unbind my wrists?"

He nodded and brought a small rectangular box onto the table. Carefully opening its top, he revealed two brass rings. Turning toward me, Arthur clasped each of them around my wrists before unlocking the handcuffs. "These bands will allow you to walk our compound freely, but the doors to the exit will not open for you. A guard will accompany you at all times, so be aware that if you make one wrong move, your life will be over. I am trusting you around my people."

Just like at home.

I nodded in understanding. "May I ask for different accommodations than the prison?"

A smug smirk crossed Arthur's face. "Missing your penthouse?" We stared into each other's eyes, a silent moment stretching into an eternity, before his laughter broke the spell. "We have a spare room where you can sleep."

"I'm thankful," I whispered. So far, I haven't felt threatened by the humans, besides the obvious kidnapping, and they have allowed me to have more freedom than I did in the Elysium. Arthur felt safe, almost like he was looking out for me.

"Jude, please enter."

The door behind us swung inward with a loud bang, making me jump and my heart race as I saw who entered. It was the guy from the prison, the one who saved me from the Dogs, the one who kidnapped me.

The man walked past me and took his place next to Arthur, who put one arm on the man's shoulder. "Vincent, meet my son Jude. He'll be your guard for the rest of your time here. He's been instructed to keep the residents of our village safe." He paused and shot a quick sideways glance at the man next to me. "This means he'll protect you, but consider this a warning: he also has clearance to restrain you. If harm comes to any human by your hand, all personnel have been advised to kill."

Jude ran his fingers through his perfectly coiffed blond hair, the soft strands falling over his forehead. From there, he detached the unicorn mask to reveal his face.

Despite being threatened, I'd be lying if I said he didn't take my breath away.

His bright blue eyes pierced me, making me feel completely exposed, while a smirk curved his plump lips. With a jawline as sharp as a freshly honed blade and eyebrows pulled down in a determined frown, his face was a mask of resolute intensity.

"Hello, Vincent." The smooth tones of his voice, reminiscent of his father's, were punctuated by a relaxed, almost careless, delivery. "May I show you to your quarters?"

Hesitantly, I nodded, but my heart would not stop fluttering as he put his hand on my back to lead me out of the chamber.

Chapter Twelve

Keeping my head down in the dimly lit hallway, I noticed the worn carpet, its faded stars and planets barely visible against the dusty purple background. It was familiar in a way, something that was hiding in my memories I couldn't pinpoint. Silently, Jude led me down a series of dark hallways. The small lights in the walls flickered, casting dancing shadows down each corridor.

We passed numbered doors until we reached the last labeled with a large number one. A grimy, empty glass counter stretched to my left, its only feature a strange contraption about an arm's length long, bearing the ghosts of faded, peeling labels. A second glass box stood adjacent to the first, its metal bucket hanging motionless, reflecting the sterile gleam of the surroundings. We found ourselves amidst a silent graveyard of machines, their decaying metal hinting at where we were.

Outside the prison, I turned and saw a faded sign above the entrance, with lines of dead lightbulbs circling it. A marquee of faded, almost illegible letters from the last film hung below. "A movie theatre?"

"I guess that's what they were called back in the day." Jude shrugged and followed my gaze.

"Wh-where are we?" I spun in a circle, taking in my surroundings. Straight ahead, a long hallway lay directly ahead with two men standing guard before a heavily bolted door, while the opposite end opened into a spacious area.

"It's where we live and are safe from the vampires and Dogs. We call this place Silvertown after the village that was here before your kind took over."

My kind? This guy really knew how to get under my skin.

I nodded slowly, a nervous sweat on my brow. I remembered Silvertown from before The Great World War; my father and I used to drive through it, but I didn't necessarily want Jude to know that. His scrutinizing side-eye made me uneasy. I didn't know if I could trust him.

"Years ago, the original Unicorns converted this large abandoned building into our home." He looked toward the upper levels and shrugged. "It may not be pretty, but it's all we have."

We walked in silence, a noticeable gap between us, yet close enough where he could easily catch me if I wanted to run away. On either side, doorways lined the hallway, each secured by heavy metal bars which looked cold and forbidding in the dim light. With no one around, I scanned the shadowed area beyond the gates, straining my eyes, but saw no one. One doorway, draped with a darkened rainbow of fabrics, hung in a grimy window, hinting at the treasures within.

Where am I? What is this place?

I followed Jude, who had his chin high and arms swinging rhythmically, taking long strides, the ground firm beneath his feet. His confident stance made me acutely aware of my own posture—I was walking with my arms defensively crossed, as if anticipating an ambush or a sudden attack. I focused on my breathing, trying to slow my pulse, but the anxiety remained a heavy weight on my chest. Regardless, I was a kidnapped prisoner for an unknown enemy group.

Ahead, the hallway opened into a brightly lit space, a visible contrast to the dim, shadowy corridor we were leaving behind. Vivid colors exploded before me, jolting my senses awake. Sunlight streamed through the large skylight, illuminating the vibrant green leaves of the plants and trees reaching toward the light. It reminded me of the center of Elysium near Smoke.

Jude paused, his eyes flickering to the light above, then to me. "Can you—"

"—Go into the light?" I knew what he was going to ask. What an idiot.

He nodded, looking genuinely curious.

I raised an eyebrow. "What are some things you *humans* think about vampires? I'd *love* to know."

"Just what we've been told throughout the years and in stories." He shrugged. "Things like they suck blood, can live forever, cannot be in the light, have hypnotic powers, and sleep in coffins. I've even heard rumors they can sparkle, although I don't know how or when that would happen."

Hypnotism? Give me a break.

I stifled a giggle at the sparkle comment, thinking about Gabe. "It sounds like I have a lot to teach you about *my kind*." I rolled my eyes and let out a heavy breath. "Vampires are not like the terrible beings in myths, although we share some similarities. We age differently from humans and need blood to survive. The only truth to the rumors is that we cannot be in the light for long periods. But most misconceptions around vampires were completely made-up for entertainment purposes."

"What about fangs?" He pulled back his lip, baring his teeth. "You do have fangs, right?"

I shook my head and lifted my lips. "Not me, but everyone else does."

"So…you're different?"

I nodded and shrugged. "And to answer your initial question, I also can go into the light without being hurt."

He narrowed his gorgeous blue eyes, intensely fixing on my face as if to gauge my honesty.

We walked toward the bright light, its warmth beckoning, and my body ached for the sun's embrace. Jude's intense gaze on me, and a slight smirk played on my lips as I stepped into the warm sunlight.

In the center of the area, the morning light glinted off the dew-kissed vegetables and fruit as humans worked diligently, their movements precise and efficient as they harvested the bountiful crops. Looking around, I saw levels of floors above me, all converging here. "Is this a…mall?" I hadn't thought of a shopping mall in years. The few remaining ones were mainly deserted before the war, and the rise of online shopping during the pandemic rendered them almost obsolete.

Jude nodded. "Silvertown Mall is what it used to be called, but now it's our headquarters. It's two floors, and each wing has its own community. Judging by the light, everyone will be waking up soon." He pointed in three different directions. "The north end houses the people who grow and prepare food, the east side is home to all the healers, and the western area is home to our maintenance workers and technologists. We all have a part to play in our survival."

"What about the south end of the mall?"

"Oh, wouldn't *you* like to know?" Jude paused before laughing.

Was he flirting with me? What's going on here?

With an irritating smirk, he pointed down the hallway we had just come from. "That's the military wing, where all our weapons are stored. It has the jail, the exit, and the entrance to the lower levels. The south wing is completely forbidden to everyone unless summoned."

"So which wing of the mall am I going to be part of?" I prayed he didn't say I was returning to the movie theatre to live in a jail cell.

"You'll be in the south, so I can keep an eye on you. You'll be locked inside a small room right next to mine. Wherever you go, I go."

Well, it wasn't a jail cell, but I was a prisoner all the same.

Almost as if a switch was flipped, people—humans—crowded the center of the mall. They scurried from each corner of the building, their footsteps echoing on the cold tile floor as they crowded to the center. Ragged and faded, their brown, green, and white clothes looked like they'd been scavenged from a dumpster. It looked like safety pins held their clothes together, while others had drab and faded colors splashed amid the dim tones. The cold from outside painted their cheeks a rosy pink, and their hair, tousled by the wind, framed their faces.

In Elysium, the vampires always looked like they had stepped out of a Vogue magazine, radiating an aura of chic, modern style. Yet, looking at these creatures, there was a noticeable difference from what I was used to. The unpleasant smells from the humans filled my nostrils, causing me to scrunch up my nose and try to discreetly mask my revulsion.

"Are you hungry?" Jude lowered his eyebrows, his

mouth slightly open in a silent question, a furrow in his brow. "Err...do you eat food?"

A wave of fury washed over me. Were all humans *this* stupid? "Even vampires eat food, idiot. We don't just sit around and drink blood all day." I knew my tone was harsher than expected, but his ignorance annoyed me.

He held his hands at chest level, his body language signaling me to calm down. "Chill, vampire boy, I'll grab us some breakfast, stay here." Jude pushed through the crowd toward a row of carts full of people grabbing the food on display.

I could run and try to escape. He left my side. Was this a trap? A trial to see what I'd do?

A flock of children pushed past me, their laughter echoing as they danced, their energy infectious. Vampires weren't able to have children, but that didn't stop us from trying. Turning seemed to mark the end of our fertility, as if our sperm and eggs died along with us. The early years of Elysium were marked by tragic struggles: countless couples tried for children, only to face the devastating consequences of miscarriages or infertility. Eventually, we accepted the harsh truth and just gave up trying to procreate.

The children's laughter reached my ears; it sounded like magic bells floating through the air. Euphoria surged through me, a grin splitting my face as I watched them, their happy squeals and shrieks creating a symphony of delight. Their carefree innocence awakened something inside of me—probably the nostalgia of the children I once knew.

"Whoa, this is different." Jude laughed, a bright, joyous sound, as he returned, holding a small, paper-wrapped package. "I didn't realize you knew how to smile."

Snatching the food from his hands, I shot a look at the

man next to me, my heart pounding as I tried to regain my composure. I hadn't seen a child in a long time, so their presence shocked me, but I didn't want Jude to think I was going soft, so I tried to remember the gross things about children—the sticky, snot-filled noses and the smell of vomit on their clothes. My smile faltered, a frown tugging at my lips as I silently unwrapped the tasteless, grey-tinged food. "What is this?"

"It's what we have every morning, a veggie, egg, and cheese bagel."

A warm sandwich, about the size of my fist, lay nestled on the white paper. Its center displayed a muted layer of green, yellow, and orange. I scoffed. "No bacon?"

Well, this wasn't Louie's, that's for sure.

Jude's smile, a slow, crooked grin, turned towards me, one eyebrow playfully raised. "Bacon? Where do you think we have room for livestock? I'm sorry if this isn't up to par with the fancy vampire complex."

I liked someone who could volley with me, but I had to remind myself he was the enemy, no matter how attractive he was. These people kidnapped me. They took me from my home. From my dad. From Gabe. "But you have chickens for the eggs?"

"Nah." He shook his head. "Our eggs aren't real. The people in the north end of Silvertown found out how to make an egg substitute. It's not good, but it's the best we have."

I stared at the sandwich in front of me momentarily, debating whether I wanted to eat the fake food. I was used to real eggs and caviar in Elysium, not the faux food the humans offered. It was no wonder they all smell terrible. I had to admit, I didn't think I'd be able to muster any empathy for the people who kidnapped me, but seeing their harsh living conditions tugged at my heartstrings.

How could someone live in such squalor and think it was okay? I guessed if this was how it had always been, a kind of numbness settled in, and people adapted. They didn't know anything different.

In a way, they were a little like me.

Noticing my pensive silence, Jude chuckled once more. "Follow me, we have an appointment with a friend of mine."

He waved me left, toward the west side of the mall, pushing through the dense crowd. The sounds of chattering and the smell of egg wafted around me. The people surged toward the mall's center, a sea of bodies pushing and shoving until the path ahead narrowed to a mere sliver. Walking behind Jude, I spotted a dented metal trash can nearby and silently snuck my half-eaten, cold, and slimy breakfast inside.

Chapter Thirteen

The west side of the mall, home to the maintenance and tech staff, was immediately identifiable by the ubiquitous bags of cleaning supplies and batteries scattered across the floor. The sharp, clean scent of lemon and bleach danced in the air, a familiar comfort that reminded me of my penthouse after the maid's meticulous cleaning. My body cried out for the familiar embrace of my bed high atop Elysium, longing for its plush comfort and the sweet smell of fresh linens. A sense of hopelessness overcame me, knowing I may never feel relaxed in my own bed ever again.

As we walked through the west wing, the hallway was lined with repurposed shops, their former lives hinted at in faded signs and dusty displays. To the right, colorful mops and brooms leaned against sudsy buckets, their soapy scent filling the air, while the left side was a chaotic jumble of rusty metal parts and cracked computer monitors. The morning rush began, and the aroma of frying faux eggs reached my nostrils as people streamed into the shops with their daily breakfast sandwiches. I watched as men and women zipped into their bright orange maintenance jumpsuits and filled buckets with sudsy soap.

"Follow me, vampire boy." Jude waved me toward a shop to our left.

After rolling my eyes, I saw a blank space outside the storefront where the sign once hung, and I recognized the logo from years ago. I believe the shop once sold used CDs and DVDs. Years ago, I vividly remember begging my mom and dad to buy me a poster from this store. My mom said no, but my father secretly bought it and gave it to me on my birthday that year. He used to be so caring. The memories of those days filled me with bittersweet nostalgia.

Back when this mall was a vibrant shopping center, the store we stood inside was once a haven for vinyls, CDs, DVDs, figurines, and posters, but all that was now replaced with desks cluttered with tools, surrounded by piles of metallic junk.

Jude guided me to a desk piled high with defunct electronics. "I'm here to see Michael," he said to the tower of junk in a deep, authoritative voice.

A woman's head emerged from behind the haphazard stack of metallic objects with a bright headlamp illuminating her face. She brought a finger to the side of her frizzy hair and clicked the light off. "Uh...hi th-there, Jude." She squeaked, her voice high and trembling. "I-I'll let Michael know you're here." She scurried to the backroom and quickly returned. "You can go back there to speak with him."

"Stay here and don't do anything stupid," Jude instructed as he turned to the short woman before him. "This is Nessa. You two can...chat?"

As Jude retreated toward the back room with a sheepish grin spread across his face, I couldn't help but feel annoyed. Wasn't he supposed to watch me at all times? Or was this another test? This thought irritated me even further; it was like they were observing me, being given a test I'd never know if I passed. An experiment.

"Whatta man, huh?"

I looked at the rotund girl sitting in the chair, propping her face in her hands. She had wildly long brown hair that looked as if she'd been electrocuted a few times, sticking out at various angles. The metal frames of her glasses magnified her pupils, making them appear ten times larger, perched delicately on the bridge of her nose. Her light green eyes, sparkling with adoration, watched the man in the flowing white robe vanish through the nearby door.

"Who? Jude?" I asked, a slight uncertainty in my voice.

"Yeah, whenever he's around, I get all nervous and shaky." Swaying her head toward me, she sighed heavily. "There are a lot of men in Silvertown, but none are as fine as him."

"You need to get out more." I scoffed, a smile creeping at my lips. I liked Nessa; her presence was magnetic, and her innocence was refreshing compared to who I'd been around lately. Considering how annoying I found Jude to be, it was hard for me to agree with her.

"We don't have many men like Jude here." With a wistful sigh, she looked at me, her eyes wide and sparkling with mischief. "Although the rumor is he doesn't play for my team anyway."

I was surprised to hear this and unearthed memories from before the apocalypse. People were scared to be who they are for fear of ridicule. I guess that's one good thing about the end of the world—all the unnecessary hate ended. I supposed, even after all these years, humans will still be humans after all. In Elysium, sexuality wasn't discussed because everyone was fluid. There were no labels on the gender of whom you preferred because we desired everyone. Blood made us horny, and limiting ourselves would only lose precious time before it wore off. Just because I'd never been with a girl didn't mean I was opposed to it—I just found myself gravitating toward men.

A playful smile crossed her face, like a secret was about to be told. "Tell me *all* about the hot vampire men you have in the Elysium."

"Y-you know I'm a vampire? And that I'm gay?" Nessa's playfulness was infectious. My heart drew me closer to her. It was clear she didn't leave Silvertown often and found a strange reflection of myself within her.

"It's kind of obvious." She shrugged before looking expectantly at me. "Now spill."

I wasn't sure what was obvious, but I decided politeness was key—you catch more flies with honey than vinegar, as they say—so I grabbed a nearby metal chair and pulled it up to the desk. I leaned closer to Nessa, whose breath shallowed. The words were caught in my throat, a smile stretching wide across my face I couldn't suppress. "My boyfriend, Gabe, is *the* hottest. Tall, dark, and handsome—what more could you want? He's part of the military, so his body is muscle upon muscle. To boot, he has a heart of gold."

"Good in bed?"

My eyes rolled backward. "Amazing!" I had no one to compare it to, but I can assume he's better than most. "I wish you could see him, your mouth would drop as soon as he walked in the door."

She raised a finger, a serious expression settling on her face. "You have to promise me if there's ever a way to see him, you'll bring him to me first."

I laughed. "Promise." This was a breath of fresh air after the last twenty-four hours I've experienced. Even though she was a human, Nessa lightened the heavy cloud over my head. Between the bitter resentment in my body toward Jude and the other humans who kidnapped me, and the gnawing fear for my safety, her lightheartedness was a surprising and welcome relief.

"So if you're a gay vampire, does that mean…"

"I suck dick *and* blood? Yeah."

We both stifled a giggle as I gazed at the chaotic array of curly springs, wires, and tools scattered across Nessa's workstation. I gestured to a pile of cogs with a rusted wrench lying atop. "So what is it you do here?"

"I tinker." She shrugged. "We try to find ways to enhance the lives of humans using technology, but we have the same broken items we've used for years. Sometimes we get new things we've stolen from the vampires we find in dumpsters, but that's rare." She turned to me and covered her mouth. "Maybe I shouldn't have said that."

I shook my head. "There's so much waste in the Elysiums that whatever you're able to scavenge, no one would even know. I wish I knew where we threw everything away so you could salvage it."

She lowered her voice to a whisper. "Wanna see something I recently figured out how to fix and have hidden away, just for me?"

My eyes brightened, nodding. "I won't tell anyone."

Nessa pushed her chair backward, rolling across the floor before lifting her body upright. Her hips swayed rhythmically when she walked, her curly hair bouncing with each step. Reaching into the worn leather bag hanging on the wall, she gently cradled the object and held it close to her stomach.

"What is it?"

Nessa gingerly put a small, black circular item on the desk between us. The surface was marred by deep scratches, obscuring the words that had been scraped away entirely, leaving only faint ghosts of their former presence. Her eyes glowed. "It's a CD player. We haven't had a working one in years, and I stowed this away from our last shipment. All it needed was some light fixing and new batteries."

"Do you have any discs to play on it?" I was smiling, a thin veil over the laughter bubbling up inside me. "It does use discs, right?" The world's most prominent tech moguls were turned into vampires, giving all residents of Elysium access to countless digital music libraries, available anytime, anywhere.

"We got rid of most of the CDs years ago. I think someone told me they were used as kindling during the first winter after the war." Lining the outside, numerous silver buttons, each displaying a unique symbol, gleamed faintly. A press from Nessa's chubby finger on one of them caused a satisfying click as the lid opened. "But this had one in perfect condition."

"Can we listen?"

She nodded. "This is the last CD in the world, and even though it's so scratched and beaten up that it only plays one song, I love it." She plugged the white corded earbuds into the device and handed me one before putting the other in his ear.

A synth-pop tune with a driving bassline reached my ears, and a powerful beat drummed through my body. The soothing, wavy melody reminded me of being on a beach. Life seemed so much simpler before all this happened. The artist's high, breathy voice, a strained attempt at sultriness, filled our ears. A cringe reached my face as I listened to the music—I knew who was singing; she and her family were leaders of an Elysium on one of the coasts.

The final note faded, and Nessa's grin was radiant as

she looked at me. "This song gets stuck in my head for days. Even though it is something you can dance to, the lyrics are pretty deep."

I couldn't help but laugh out loud. "Pretty deep for her, sure."

"What's that mean?"

"I know the singer, her father was one of the first to purchase the BRETH cure. If I remember correctly, she produced only a few albums. This may be the last song of hers in the world." Her eyes narrowed, questioning my statement, so I had to clarify with more details. "Not because of the war or the vampire uprising, it was because she realized she couldn't sing without digitally correcting her voice."

"Digitally correcting her voice? How's that done?"

"A lot of singers used to do it before the war," I explained. "It was all a money-making scheme."

"I wonder how all their money is treating them now." She rolled her eyes and shook her head. "Do you want to listen again? You have to admit, it's catchy!"

She was right, as much as I didn't want to admit it, it was one of those songs that would worm its way into your head and never leave. I sighed and put the headphone back in my ear. "Replay it." Looking back over my sixty-five years, I couldn't remember a friend, besides Gabe, that I could do this with. I didn't know where my friends went before the war. They may even have found refuge in Elysium, but I'd never know unless they appeared inside my penthouse. I never realized how much I missed this camaraderie, how I craved it. Until now.

We listened to the song five times. The catchy beat and lively tempo had us dancing around the desk, swaying our bodies back and forth with our arms in the air, completely lost in the music. The music in my headphones created a bubble of carefree normalcy, blocking out the world's concerns. It was like we were at a sleepover, listening to music and gossiping about boys.

Until the music stopped.

The back door opened, and Jude emerged from behind. Nessa snatched the headphones from my ears, the music ending abruptly, and then slipped the CD player under a stained cloth. Beads of sweat gathered at her temples as she leaned her face into her fist, offering Jude a shy, awkward smile.

The man looked at me with an oddly amused expression. "Everything okay out here?"

I nodded and turned away from him. Why did he need to interrupt us? This was the first time I felt normal in years. "Nessa and I were getting to know each other." I flickered my eyes at Jude, who looked back at me with a cold stare. "I think we hit it off. It's nice to know *someone* likes me here."

"We're *definitely* friends," she agreed, her voice cracking. "Vincent is always welcome here. A-and so are you, J-Jude."

A sly smirk crossed Jude's face, and he bit his bottom lip.

Was he enjoying the attention Nessa was giving him? Were all humans this egotistical? Honestly, their need for attention was exhausting.

"Let's get going, vampire boy." He cocked his head toward the door. "I have to update my dad about what Michael had advised me."

"And what *did* you find out?" I asked through my teeth.

He squinted his eyes and held one condescending finger toward me. "Wouldn't you like to know?"

With a playful glint in my eye, I turned toward Nessa and winked at her. "I hope I'll see you soon. The stars may be blind, but hopefully they can convince Jude to bring me back to see you."

A wide smile lit up Nessa's face, her cheekbones pinching her eyes shut.

"What are you two talking about?" Jude's face twisted as he turned to us with a sneer. "Is this some code you two came up with?"

My cheeks burned as I fought back the grin threatening to split my face, our gaze never breaking contact. I incorporated the lyrics in my farewell, and she caught on. It was like we had a secret between just the two of us.

Before we could answer, a cacophony of screams sounded from outside the door. A sharp crack followed by a tinkling cascade of shattered glass cut through the terrified screams of the humans outside. Like a monstrous beast unleashed, a deafening roar ripped through the chaotic scene, draining the color from my face and leaving me weak with terror.

The Dog escaped.

Chapter Fourteen

Terrified humans swarmed around me, their faces etched with fear, each clutching children close as they desperately sought safety. The chaos that filled Silvertown reminded me of the night the humans invaded Elysium. The irony was not lost on me, and I secretly swallowed the laugh from escaping my throat. Now it was their turn to feel the fear I felt as I walked through The Wastes.

Serves them right.

My disdain held for a moment before I realized that, as much as I'd like the Dog to destroy this place and everyone inside, I needed to help to ensure my safety. The crowd was a sea of faces, but I desperately searched for Jude, hoping to see his blond hair above the milling people. I shoved through the packed crowd using my elbows to fight against the human current.

Amid the bobs of hair and blurred earthtone clothing, a stark white robe, pristine and smooth, appeared a few feet in front of me. Jude was pushing against the crowd, like a salmon attempting to get upstream through rushing waters. The sharp crack of gunfire echoed through the mall and was immediately followed by a low growl. Piercing screams cut through the air, sending a wave of panic through the crowd as they scattered, their footsteps a chaotic rhythm against the ground.

I swiftly followed Jude toward the chaos happening in the mall's middle. As I drew closer, the extent of the Dog's destruction became horrifyingly clear. Shattered remnants of wooden wagons, once laden with food, lay scattered across the floor, while the plants that once climbed the columns now hung loosely, resembling tattered ropes.

An army of men with guns outstretched was fanned out in a semicircle, their gaze never leaving the far end of the center. I saw the Dog to my left, its body low, front legs planted firmly on the ground, while its hind legs kicked in the air—a playful stance. Its tongue lolled out, a metallic pink, and its tail, a gleaming steel rod, shot straight up in gleeful anticipation. I knew if it were a real animal, its tail would be wagging.

It was enjoying this. It was playing.

A series of sharp, echoing gunshots ripped through the air in the mall, and the Dog ran straight toward the sound. Its body twisted and turned with impossible grace, each movement a blur as it dodged the hail of bullets. The creature sprang into the air, a chilling metallic shriek echoing as its maw opened, revealing wickedly sharp teeth that tore into the guard's head with brutal efficiency. Piercing screams filled the mall as more gunshots rang out, the sounds echoing through the corridors.

"Vincent, you shouldn't have followed me!" Jude yelled as he shoved my shoulder.

I was glued to the scene before me—the metal Dog's mouth clamped down on the man's head, its teeth grinding on the metal mask with a sickening crunch. His screams, raw and filled with terror, were the only sound until the creature twisted its head, and a heavy silence descended. A dark, glistening pool of blood spread around his feet before his body hit the ground with a definitive thud.

Crimson liquid, warm and viscous, dripped from the creature's chin as it spat out the dismembered head, its hungry eyes darting to another nearby man. The group stumbled backward, their guns outstretched, as the Dog's unpredictable next move sent shivers down their spines. Another series of gunshots cracked through the air, and the metallic animal again dodged each one with impossible grace.

It launched itself into the air, a blur of motion, and landed softly nearby. Fixed on Jude and me, the creature began to sprint, its approach a terrifying thud in my ears. Panting, two men ran toward the Dog, its head swiveling between them, a low growl rumbling in its throat. Its front paws lifted from the ground, landing on one chest, then sprang off to the other. The two men were hurled backward, their weapons spinning across the floor.

With soft precision, the Dog landed a mere couple of feet away. Many human guards stood at attention, weapons trained on the escapee, their faces grim, and fingers hovering over triggers, waiting for the order to fire. I watched as the Dog reared up on its hind legs, locked onto both of us.

My body was shaking. Is it going to go for me or Jude? What should I do?

A bark from the inside of the Dog escaped its mouth that sounded like a bear's roar. Dried blood, crusty and dark, clung to its lips as its neon red eyes darted to each person in the room, the chilling glint of them catching the dim light, and it inched closer to us. My body was frozen, every muscle rigid with fear, and once its sharp snout was less than a foot away, it lunged, a blur of teeth and metal.

In the blink of an eye, Jude launched himself, arms outstretched, sliding between the snarling Dog and me. It soared through the air, latching onto the white robe protecting the blond-haired man. I stood behind Jude, completely paralyzed in fear. The Dog's head snapped around so fast that time seemed to freeze; the air whooshed as Jude flew across the room and landed heavily with a muffled thud.

Terror seized me, making my body tremble violently as I stared into the Dog's unnervingly bright, electronic eyes. Like startled embers, the red irises flickered white before resuming their fiery red hue. These eyes are what haunted my dreams, what killed my mother.

My jaw dropped in shock as the creature turned, now fixated on the man it hurled across the room. With a powerful surge, the Dog reared, its hind legs propelling it into the air before landing squarely on either side of Jude, pinning him to the ground.

I turned to look at the guards surrounding the perimeter. They remained glued to the Dog with their fingers hovering inches above each of their guns' triggers. Are they not going to help? In disbelief at the spineless military, I ran to the nearest guard, wrenching the machine gun from their limp hands.

I may not care for the man, but I couldn't let Jude get his head ripped off, right? Although killing him could give me enough time to escape this godforsaken mall. With half a mind to make a run for it, I watched a trembling Jude struggle under the weight of the Dog and decided against my escape. We needed to work together to stop the Dogs.

I closed one eye, taking aim, but couldn't get a clear shot without the risk of hitting him, so I had to run directly into the line of fire to save him. Before my brain registered my actions, I slung the gun across my chest, and my feet pounded the dirty tiled floor.

The Dog's eyes narrowed, and Jude's face went pale as he braced for the attack. Was I going to make it? The Dog's grin stretched wider, its jaws falling open to reveal a terrifying row of needle-sharp teeth. This was my shot—without another thought, I launched myself into the air, muscles straining with the effort, a silent scream building in my chest.

I like to think of myself as a smart guy. This was not one of those times.

I collided with the Dog, the sudden weight of my body crashing down on my shoulder. After making impact, gravity took over, and my hip slammed against the hard floor; the sounds of screeching metal reached my ears. My heart pounded in my chest as I instantly leaped to my feet, my hands shaking so violently that I barely held the gun steady as I pointed it at the Dog. I knew the exact spot I needed to hit, but I had to get closer to line it up. I slowly shimmied to my left, hoping to get a closer shot of its head.

"Vincent, stop!" Jude yelled from behind me.

His words were muffled in my brain, like he spoke a foreign language. I was locked on the fallen Dog. For an animal that caused so much chaos moments before, it was strange that it was completely immobile. I crept closer, and as its head reared back, its eyes changed from red to a glowing white. Looking into its pixelated face, it was as if they held a deep sadness. As if it knew it was done for. As if it were giving in.

I remember feeling sadness for this creature at one time, like it burrowed its way into my heart. Any sympathy I had for it was replaced with pure rage after seeing the destruction it caused and the hurt it brought the humans.

"Goodbye, fucker." I pulled the gun's trigger, the sound echoing through the chamber.

Like a rusty hinge, a pathetic, tinny whine escaped the Dog's mouth before its body went limp, its head falling to the floor as if it were sleeping. Black oil leaked from its head, forming a dark pool beneath its body as its eyes blinked in finality.

Chapter Fifteen

"You saved me 'cause you liiiike me."

"Hardly," I huffed with my arms crossed.

Jude's incessant singing, which felt like hours, only lasted a few minutes, yet it still felt unbearable. We waited outside the cinema for Arthur to usher us inside, but Jude's constant talking annoyed me to no end. After I killed the Dog, its oil soaked into the ground as guards quickly took it away, and the maintenance wing swept in to clean up the scene. I looked at Jude, a sigh escaping my lips as I rolled my eyes. "Your kind would've found a way to have pinned this on me if I didn't save you. If anything, killing that Dog was avenging the Exiles from back home."

"Avenging them? Aren't they, like, shriveled up slugs?"

My mouth turned into a grimace. What an idiot. "They're still one of us. When they get too old and close to death, they're often thrown over the wall and fed to the Dogs. I hate that we do it, but it keeps the streets clean."

"Whoa," Jude breathed. "That's pretty savage."

I nodded. "I remember when Elysium first came into

existence, my dad needed to figure out how to punish criminals because the jail cells just weren't doing it."

"Right," Jude's voice was full of sarcasm, "just throw them to the Dogs, that'll teach 'em."

I shrugged. "Crime within the building decreased by at least eighty percent the first year, so yeah, I guess it did."

Jude's head drooped, his fingers nervously picking at a loose thread on his pants. "Speaking of your father, we thought that as soon as we took you, there'd be a horde of vampires on our doorstep."

Secretly, I'd been wondering this myself. Where *was* he? The vampires needed my blood to survive. Did they not care about me as much as I thought? Could it be possible they found a way to replicate my blood, and I wasn't needed anymore? My thoughts then turned to my boyfriend—why hasn't Gabe split the world in two to find me? The only explanation is that there's something wrong.

Something's holding them back.

I shrugged and shook my head. Giving a nonverbal answer was easiest for me; that way, there's no fear of word vomit showing my true intentions. My father always told me the remaining humans were master manipulators, so limiting our conversation was for the best. No way would these barbarians gaslight me into trusting them.

Thankfully, a booming voice from the movie theatre interrupted our conversation, startling us both. "Arthur will see you now."

Rising from the worn, plush chairs outside the cinema, we trailed the masked figure through the dimly lit lobby, its hallways twisting like gnarled roots. We stopped in front of a door with a large rusted seven on it. Without knowledge, this was a movie theatre; it easily could've been a jail.

Oh, and minus the cheesy star carpet.

We entered the room in a single file. The quiet hush of

the large, tiered seating area was broken only by our footsteps as we approached the four podiums at the head of the room. If I had to guess, this room was used for the leaders to provide updates to everyone in Silvertown—an amphitheater of sorts.

"Good afternoon, Vincent and Jude." The dim light of the walkway cast long shadows as we walked toward the front of the room, guided by Arthur's calm, reassuring voice.

"Hey, Dad," Jude saluted the man with two fingers.

I remained quiet. An eerie feeling overcame me as soon as I entered. The air felt tense, almost expectant. Arthur's usually warm and friendly face was now stern, his kind eyes cold and distant as he slid on the cold, metallic unicorn mask.

"The council will be joining us momentarily."

"The council? Dad, what's going on?" A slight gasp escaped from Jude's voice. He turned to me and whispered, "They only convene when something big has gone down, or a decision needs to be made."

I hid a smirk. Typical humans, easily enthralled by the smallest happenings, transforming ordinary events into overly dramatic affairs. There are always several hands in any decision, which is why the laws before the war were so outdated; it took forever to make real change. Their plans always seemed improvisational, changing constantly based on immediate needs and opportunities. I'd be lying if I wasn't interested in what they had to say, but I doubt it's anything life-shattering.

Three masked figures, cloaked in shadows, entered the room, their footsteps barely audible on the thick carpet as they took their places behind the podiums. Once everyone found their spot, a silent nod passed between them before the masks were removed, revealing their faces. To my left, a small man, barely half my height, stood beside a tall woman with wild, red curls. At the end was a person with long white hair, their gender indeterminable.

Arthur spoke in an authoritative tone, "The council has called you here to discuss the event that happened in the town square this afternoon. The Dog we procured escaped from confinement and attacked our people. We may have lost some lives, but we ultimately wanted to extend our thanks to you, Vincent." He held his hands out toward me and paused.

Were they expecting a reaction out of me? I didn't need their thanks. This was a ploy to give me false praise. I raised one eyebrow. "Is that all?"

"No," the red-haired woman answered. "We attempted to keep the Dog alive to study it and find its weakness or to see if we could find a switch to turn it off, but were unsuccessful. Our research caused it to enter its fight or flight and escape, which was an unfortunate mishap."

The short man on the far left yelled, "Bring in the Dog!" With his words lingering in the air, three large bodies carried the dead Dog and lowered it to the ground in front of us. The metal exterior showed a gaping hole, surrounded by a spreading pool of dark liquid smelling faintly of burnt metal.

I do have to say, seeing it dead gave me satisfaction.

With a sigh, the red-haired woman spoke again in her wistful, melancholic tone. "But good came from our folly. You were able to do what we couldn't—you killed the Dog. Typically, when a Dog is injured, its pack protects it long enough for it to retreat for repair. We were able to restrain it outside before it attempted to retreat."

What did they find? Where do the Dogs go for repairs?

The short man spoke again, "Our technologists were able to take it apart and found this in its head." He held out a transparent sphere the size of a baseball, and a light tinkling was heard throughout the room.

Squinting against the glare, I saw a tiny, red bean-like item inside the ball, almost too small to be real. The bean, desperate to escape, slammed repeatedly against the smooth, unyielding curve of the sphere.

"We believe this is a compass that aids the Dogs in finding their way back to their nest. Right now, the mechanism is prompting me to go west, and if I walk in that direction, the item sticks to the side of this sphere until it prompts me to turn."

The white-haired figure spoke, their voice a melodious blend, neither masculine nor feminine. "If we can find a way to disable the Dogs, we'd be able to send an army to the vampire compound."

Arthur's bright eyes gleamed in my direction. "Jude, as head of our strategic military force, I'm tasking you with organizing a small group to locate the Dog's nest. It'll be a dangerous journey, but a necessary one."

He nodded dutifully. "I'll begin the preparations tonight."

"And one more thing." Arthur's wrinkled face twitched with amusement. "Vincent will be joining you as well."

My face scrunched in disbelief. Did I hear him correctly? Silence descended, thick and heavy, as the adults froze, their expressions hardening. Jude and his father stared at each other, a silent conversation between the two as the weight of the moment was heavy in the air.

The white-haired council member's voice echoed through the room, dripping like poison. "Can he be fully trusted? He *is* a vampire after all."

"Yeah, you don't even know me." This was meant to be a thought, but my mind decided to have the words tumble from my mouth. Luckily, I didn't share my other thoughts

—was this his way of killing me? Away from everyone? Or was it my chance to escape back to Elysium? Everyone's gaze was on me, like daggers piercing my skin, their eyes burning holes into my soul.

"While I don't fully agree with my father's suggestion…"

"It's not a suggestion, but a requirement." Arthur's voice grew stern.

"Like I was saying," Jude's eyebrows furrowed before he turned back to the council, "I do have some reservations about a vampire joining my group, but I've watched him interact with care toward the residents and have gotten to know him a little since he's been here. He may be…" He paused, trying to find the words. "Difficult, but he saved me from the Dog. For that, I have to put *some* trust in him."

"And what if I don't want to go?" Decisions were made without my consent, just like my entire life in Elysium, and I wanted my voice heard. Especially by humans.

"Then I'll give my military personnel orders to eliminate you," Arthur spat. "As our…guest, you don't have a say in the matter."

I pushed down the laugh building in my throat and couldn't help but mutter, "Guest? More like a hostage."

Exasperatedly, Arthur turned toward the council. "If my status within Silvertown is on the line by having Vincent join this assignment, I'm willing to accept that risk. I believe in him."

I hated these people, but his words hit me like a punch to the gut, leaving me breathless and shaking my head. No one ever believed in me before. Surely this was him manipulating me, right? If not, his naivety would be his downfall if he thought that, because I saved him, he could trust me.

I couldn't deny his belief in me felt good, though. Like I mattered.

"You're endangering your son's life!" The red-haired councilwoman's voice rang. "How does he feel about that?"

"Let's ask him."

All eyes turned to Jude, who was fidgeting with his fingers as he weighed his options. Raising his head to the narrow-eyed adults in the room, he confidently nodded. "I'll take the risk."

"I trust you, my son." A smile tugged at Arthur's cracked lips before it disappeared and was replaced with a business-like demeanor. "A fully charged car will be available to you in the morning. You're free to leave, gather the group, and prepare for the journey ahead."

The four council members, their heads shaking in disbelief, replaced their metal masks before leaving their podiums and vanishing through the cinema door. With every departure, I felt the weight of their scrutinizing eyes, a silent judgment that chilled me to the bone.

Jude opened the door and led me to the movie theatre's entrance in silence, both of us contemplating the meeting we had, but for different reasons.

"Th-thanks," I muttered, breaking the silence.

I turned to him, and it was like I was looking at a different person. Jude's pupils flitted like trapped butterflies, reflecting the whirlwind of thoughts in his mind. No longer was his posture loose, but instead, it was stiff and rigid, and each word he spoke was clipped and precise. "I'll escort you back to your quarters for rest. I have a lot to do before we leave tomorrow afternoon."

I nodded; the man who was slowly opening up to me disappeared into his duties. In Elysium, I was used to Gabe taking time to distance himself from work, so it was a shock to see Jude like this. Maybe they weren't so different —one moment, he was the stern, disciplined military leader, and the next, a carefree goofball. The transition was so smooth it was almost unbelievable.

I much prefer the goofball.

He ushered me toward the south end of the mall, where he advised I'd have a room to sleep in. A left turn led us to a seemingly endless staircase spiraling downwards. With every step, I wondered if he was leading me into the pits of hell. Am I really going to sleep down here? Hey, at least it's not a jail cell.

"Vincent!" Leaning against the cold, steel door at the bottom of the creaking stairs was a girl about my height, her figure round and soft. A wide smile stretched across Nessa's face as we approached, her eyes sparkling with admiration. "Hey there, Jude." A tinge of pink reached the balls of her cheeks.

"Call me Vinny." I smiled. "What're you doing here?" I was thankful to see Nessa again. I needed someone to feel comfortable around because the Mr. Hyde that Jude turned into was *not* fun.

Heavy, metal doors lined the long, dimly lit hallway, each sealed tight, making me feel as if I were walking the passageway of a submarine. Thick bolts lined the outside of the doors, and the shining handle looked almost nautical.

Opening one of the doors, Jude held his arm out. "This is your room, *Vinny*."

My jaw was clenched, my muscles bunching and throbbing with barely contained fury. "*You* cannot call me that."

"Whatever." He rolled his eyes. "I have so much to do tonight, I can't be bothered with your games."

"Is it okay if Nessa hangs out with me for a while?"

"I'll need to lock you inside for the safety of Silvertown, so as long as she's okay with that, I don't see why not."

"Am I okay with it? Of course I am!" Nessa's excited sounds reverberated through the air. "We have so much to share, I need to know *everything* about where you're from!"

By that, I assume she meant boys.

A large bed sat in the center of the small room, flanked by nightstands holding lamps that cast a warm glow, and a bathroom was tucked away to the left. The small apartment was a far cry from my luxurious penthouse, but it could be worse.

Jude's head poked around the door. "Alright, have fun, you two. Make sure to get some rest, we'll be leaving in the morning."

Nessa gasped, her eyes wide with disbelief as the door clicked shut, the sound echoing in the sudden silence. "You two are going on a trip together? We have *a lot* to discuss."

I collapsed onto the surprisingly plush bed, sinking into its softness, as Nessa pulled out two bottles of wine and a CD player from the jacket slung over her shoulders. The promise of a night filled with the joyous sounds of laughter, the murmur of gossip, and lively music brought a smile to my face. I needed this. I couldn't tell you the last time I felt free. Felt fun. As much as I wanted to get home, how could I leave this freedom behind?

Chapter Sixteen

My head was pounding. Resting my cheek against the glass of the car, I sighed with relief because the cool felt nice against my skin. We'd been on the road for hours, the monotonous hum of the tires a constant drone, and although I longed to see the bleak, dystopian landscape, I couldn't bear to open my eyes.

My night went exactly as you'd expect—Nessa and I listened to the same song on repeat, its melody weaving through our laughter and gossip as we sipped wine. As much entertainment I got out of discussing Nessa's lust for Jude, as soon as the wine touched my lips, I couldn't stop. I'll admit, the wine tasted like vinegar, but I missed the carefree feeling of being silly and giggly with my friend, even if it was fueled by subpar alcohol.

Unfortunately, I was paying for last night's fun today.

"How're you doing back there?" Jude's head swiveled around the seat in front of me with a sheepish smile plastered across his face. "A little sleepy, are you?"

"Fuck off," I mumbled. He knew I didn't feel well, did

he *have* to be so damn annoying? Maybe I shouldn't have saved him from the Dog.

"Do you want some water?"

"I don't want your help." We don't get hangovers in Elysium because all our wine is infused with my blood. The chances of finding any to cure me in a van with six other people were scarce. Plus, I didn't want to start sucking on my wrist and give them a reason to be nervous.

"Alright." He shrugged smugly. "Then suffer."

"Been doing that since I met you," I mumbled, resting my skin against the cool glass again. When we first left Silvertown in the car, Jude turned the radio on and flipped through the channels. We sat in silence, listening to static for hours before he turned it off, leaving the air bathed in silence.

This was an absolute nightmare.

A large man, introduced as Three, sat beside me, sweating profusely on the car's cracked leather seat. Apparently, humans in the military used numbers as names. Jude tried explaining why, but I didn't care enough to listen. Both men were bald and had constant beads of sweat dripping down their neck rolls. Behind me, Eleven and Twelve, two blond women with knives strapped to their waists and hidden in their jacket pockets, glared at me with icy expressions from their seats. Driving the van was a man named Eight whose belly rested on the steering wheel.

Straight ahead, the sun's light blazed into the van in a fiery orange glow, indicating we had a few more hours before the sun dipped below the horizon. "Look at that building." Jude's fingertip extended, pressing against the window. "What's that place?"

I lifted my eyelids and saw a faded red building with a garden of broken cars in an old parking lot. The entrance was marked by enormous red balls and a heavy, circular sign, cracked and dirty, that leaned precariously against the jagged edges of the broken glass doors.

Eight, the large man driving spoke in a raspy, but gruff voice, "Sold guns, I'd assume."

"And knives," agreed Eleven from behind me.

"I dunno." Jude wrapped his fingers around his chin like he was thinking. "Maybe it was an indoor shooting range?"

I let out a breath of air—half laughing, half exasperated with the conversation from those in my company. "It used to be a store, and they sold everything from groceries to household items. I remember my mother used to bring me there, and we would travel up and down the aisles for hours."

With her shrill voice, Twelve asked, "Is that what you did for fun before the war?"

My lip curled before I answered, feeling her judgment. "No… Target always sold interesting items, things to make life easier you didn't know you needed."

"Like what?"

"I don't remember, that was over sixty-five years ago." I whipped my head around and shrugged my shoulders. "You know what? Let's play a game… The quiet game. Anyone who speaks loses."

A breath escaped her nose, and a silent chuckle passed between them. Their stifled laughter made me roll my eyes and throw myself back against the seat. My hands clenched, knuckles white, as I fought the overwhelming urge to turn and unleash my fury upon them.

"Whoa, whoa." Jude put his hands up. "Let's calm down and continue to get along. We have to work together to complete this mission." The gray sky outside shifted to a vibrant yellow twilight, and the red bean pointed straight ahead. "We're still on the right path. Let's find shelter before nightfall. The Dogs' night vision is much more precise than their eyesight during the day. How are we doing on power?"

Before the war, the world transitioned to electric vehicles, boasting batteries powerful enough for cross-country trips. With Silvertown's limited electricity, it took a week for a car to get a full charge, so I could imagine how long they were planning to ambush Elysium with the helicopter.

"We're doing good," Eight answered. "Only used about a quarter of our charge, so this should be enough to get us there and back home." He turned on the van's headlights and pointed ahead. "I'm gonna take this turn, and from here, it's a straight shot. We can find an abandoned house to sleep in for the night and get back on the road first thing in the morning."

"Let's do it."

With that, the van swerved left, its tires bumping over the uneven pavement, the jarring jolts punctuated by the occasional thud of a pothole. Was this the wrong choice? Is this bumpy road a metaphor for where we were heading? The buildings grew sparser as we drove, the last few stores replaced by a landscape of snowy white hills. The tracking bean remained straight as the twilight deepened, painting the sky with hues of orange and purple, and a chill wind whispered through the barren trees as the sun's last rays faded.

"I think we found our humble abode." Straight ahead and perched atop a hill was a small, two-story house, its paint weathered by sun and time. Eight smoothly turned the wheel, guiding the van into the driveway with a gentle sigh of the engine's quiet power, then switched the headlights off. "Let's bring our equipment inside for the night, making sure not to make too much noise."

I pulled the door's lever, the rusty mechanism

protesting with a screech, and stepped onto the frozen earth, hearing the satisfying crunch of frost beneath my boots. Eight ripped open the back doors of the van, tossing rifles, shotguns, and backpacks filled with supplies to each person as they piled out.

"You okay over there? I turned to see Jude struggling with four leather straps, each holding a heavy gun as he tried to secure them to his shoulders. I had to stop myself from laughing out loud. He looked like someone trying to carry too many grocery bags at one time. As soon as he gathered them, one loosened, fell off his shoulder, and went down his arm. I balanced the box on my knee and held out my arm. "Let me help."

With rosy cheeks from the cold, Jude paused, contemplating giving me a weapon before skeptically slinging one of the heavy guns around my shoulder. One by one, the rest of the crew walked toward the house, their footsteps crunching on the gravel path. We gathered on the creaky front porch and, without breaking eye contact, Three quietly twisted the doorknob and disappeared inside.

"What's going on?" I whispered.

"Surveillance," Jude whispered back. "He's making sure the house is empty. We not only have to worry about vampires and Dogs, but there may also be humans out here who have nothing to lose."

I had assumed the remaining humans were all in Silvertown. I never thought they would be living off the lam, being extremely careful the Dogs don't catch them, and scrounging for food. It didn't seem like a good way to live. A half-life.

Three reappeared in the doorway, his gun crossed against his chest. "All clear, come in."

The cold penetrated my core, and even though the house was empty, it felt warm. The air seemed thick with the weight of forgotten joys and sorrows, a reminder of the past lives that had once lived here. Old floorboards groaned under our weight, and flakes of snow littered the ground.

The house was small but had a warm, homey feel. We walked into a closet-sized room, with dirty shoes haphazardly thrown on the floor, and a tiny raincoat hanging on a hook. With a soft thud, I dropped the boxes onto the aged wooden table, disturbing a thick layer of dust that billowed into in a small brown cloud. The modest kitchen opened into a living room with worn couches and chairs arranged around a large, stone fireplace. A discolored rectangle where a television was once mounted sat above the hearth. To my right was a staircase that led to the second floor.

I walked through the house, pausing to study each faded photograph of a small family, their faces smiling up at me from the walls. They looked kind, their smiles warm and genuine, and they were dressed in clothes that screamed the nineties—plaid shirts and high-waisted jeans. The mother's curly hair, a wild halo of dark brown, contrasted with the two young boys' matching blond haircuts. The father's grin was wide and proud as he displayed an enormous fish to the camera.

I smiled at the pictures, remembering a simpler time. My heart yearned for those days back. When my dad was happy, and my mother was still alive. When I was a little boy, the only thing I was worried about was the best place not to get caught during a game of hide-and-seek. I turned to the fireplace and asked, "Do you think we could start a fire?"

Eleven jeered at me and threw a blanket into my arms. Her eyebrows rose in annoyance. "Yeah, start a fire if you want. The smoke will alert every Dog in the area."

"Yeah, great idea, idiot," Twelve condescendingly agreed, her eyes rolling as she let out a dramatic sigh.

Darkness fell, and the last sliver of light disappeared, leaving us in quiet darkness as we slowly unpacked our supplies for the night. My hand trembled slightly as I touched the aged, worn wood of the staircase railing, silently praying it wouldn't give way under my weight.

Thankfully, it didn't.

"Where're you going?" Jude's concerned face looked up at me. "We should stick together."

I shrugged. "Just going upstairs to find a bed to sleep in."

"Oh," Twelve elbowed Eleven. "The little prince wants to sleep in a bed tonight. I guess that means us peasants have to sleep on the floor."

Ignoring their taunts, I climbed the creaking staircase, my chin lifted in defiance. I didn't give the two immature women the satisfaction of throwing a comment back at them. Instead, I wanted them to revel in their words. After all, it looked like they were used to sleeping on the floor.

Which was the exact comeback I kept to myself.

Chapter Seventeen

With each step, the aged floorboards groaned beneath me, and as I reached the landing, I feared I might plummet through to the kitchen below. I took a left and found a room with a bunch of windows on one side. One was shattered, letting in the wind and rain, and the floorboards beneath it were warped and rotting from years of exposure to the elements. A large, antique chest sat in the center of the room, surrounded by an array of broken plastic toys and moldy stuffed animals. A colorful mat depicting a quaint town with winding roads and storybook houses was spread on the ground. I looked at one of the papers that had fallen off the wall, and it was a child's drawing of a rainbow with four poorly drawn people beneath it. In an almost illegible scrawl were the letters D-A-N-N-Y.

A slow breath escaped my lips as I pictured Danny and his family in the photos downstairs. What happened to them? Did they turn into vampires? Did they find their way to Silvertown? Or did they flee and possibly get caught by the Dogs? Whatever happened to them, I wish I could've helped somehow.

I pursed my lips together and moved to the next room, which was bathed in hues of an aged pink, almost white. A crumpled blanket lay discarded on the bed, a contrast to the otherwise perfectly ordered room. A purple stain spread across the white dresser, a small, overturned bottle of nail polish lying nearby, its sticky residue clinging to the wood. Opened drawers revealed a jumble of mismatched items: cheap plastic earrings, heavy gold bangles, and stiff makeup brushes.

A beautiful, jewel-toned box on the dresser made my eyes light up. Years dulled the paint on its outside to a dim hue, but the box was adorned with finely carved leaves circling its top, complemented by murky stones. As the mirrored lid clicked open, my reflection appeared, a perfect copy staring back from the polished surface. A faint, slightly off-key melody, barely audible, drifted from the depths of the antique music box, its notes softened and blurred by time.

"Shh!" a voice sounded from the doorway.

In a panicked jump, I slammed the lid shut. I turned to look and saw Eleven standing silently in the dimly lit hallway, her eyes fixed on me.

"What're you doing?"

"I dunno." I shrugged. "Getting a feel for who used to live here. Reminiscing of times before everything went to shit, I guess."

"I wish I knew what that was like," she admitted wistfully, her fingers tracing the worn wood of the doorway.

A sudden, sharp crash downstairs caused us to freeze, our muscles tensing. The shattering of glass sent a sharp, high-pitched ring through the air, followed by a monstrous bang—like the front door had been blown off its hinges by a cannon. Loud, angry voices started booming from the floor below.

"Who da fuck is in ma house? Ya'll fangers?"

A woman's voice, sharp and shrill, cut through the air with a shout. "Git outta here!"

I looked to Eleven, and she put a finger to her lips, her body tense as she flattened herself against the rough-textured wall.

"Fangers ain't welcome here!" With that, a gunshot pulsed through the silent house, the sound bouncing off the walls.

"We aren't vampires." I heard Jude attempt to explain to the intruders. "We're human."

The sounds of rapid gunfire echoed from below, a jarring cacophony that shook the ground beneath our feet. Eleven's grip was firm as she pulled me across the hall and into the primary bedroom. A huge bed took up most of the room, and next to it lay two nightstands, their drawers hanging open and contents spilled across the floor. The blankets lay in a haphazard heap, tossed aside in a rush.

"What the hell is happening?" I asked as she closed the door.

"Uncivilized humans, I guess." She shrugged, looked under the bed, and rifled through the closet as gunshots and screams rang downstairs. "I knew I should've brought a weapon with me, fuck."

The last gunshot echoed, then a heavy, unnatural silence fell over the house. Was everyone dead down there? I watched Eleven, her movements as silent as a shadow, tiptoeing toward the door, careful not to creak any floorboard.

I examined the wall and floor near the bed, noticing the fine spray of blood droplets scattered across the surfaces. Someone here must have had BRETH. Maybe that's why they left so abruptly.

From downstairs, Three's voice, a low murmur at first, then rising to a call, cut through the quiet of the house. "Roll call."

"Vincent and I are fine up here," Eleven yelled as she sidled down the staircase.

"I'm here," Twelve's voice shouted.

"Oh shit!" Eight shouted. "We're fucked! Grab your weapons!"

What about Jude? Why didn't he answer during the roll call? I heard the frantic patter of feet running back upstairs, which only added to the suspense I felt. I braced myself as the door burst open, revealing Eleven, her eyes wide with fear.

A thunderous bang shook the house, originating from downstairs, and then the horrifying screams of several men pierced the silence. There were gunshots, but even scarier, there were barks. The girl next to me was trembling, and her head stood at attention with every growl emitted from the Dog. "How many are there?"

With a shrug, she tightened her grip on two knives clutched in her fist. Her chest heaved, shallow gasps escaping her lips as her body shook uncontrollably.

"We need to help."

The girl next to me shakily grabbed my wrist. "W-we c-can't."

"What are we going to do? Stay in this room until the Dogs find us and die like the family that lived in this house? Not me. I'm going to help as best I can or die trying." I would've gone down when the humans ambushed us, but there wasn't enough time before guns started blazing. These were beasts I knew.

I eased the bedroom door open and peered outside—

the coast was clear. I took one step, and a floorboard creaked beneath me. With a shake of my head, I knew the creaks of the old house would give me away.

A screen door at the bottom of the staircase hung slightly ajar, revealing two glowing red eyes in the inky blackness beyond. They turned right in a slow, deliberate motion, then left, before finally locking onto me. The Dog, accompanied by some friends, let out a bone-chilling howl before bounding inside.

I had nothing to defend myself with. What was I thinking going into this blind? I watched as the Dog's eyes flashed from a furious, bright red to a cold, hard white as it bared its teeth in a menacing snarl. The next thing I heard was a whimper, a tiny, pathetic sound, as two blades whistled through the air behind me, sinking into the creature's eye sockets with a sickening thud.

I swung my body to look behind me. "Thank you."

Eleven shrugged. "I couldn't just let you die."

"No?"

Before she could answer, more yells rang through the house. "Get outta here, you filthy animals!" My heart inflated—that was Jude's voice. He was safe, and I needed to get to him. He needed my help.

The house shook with the renewed barrage of menacing barks and gunshots. With a whirring of hydraulics, a Dog turned its head towards me and its mechanical legs carried it swiftly up the stairs. Using both hands, Three clasped the metal tail and heaved backward with all his might, launching the Dog into the air. With a ferocious snarled response, the creature twisted its neck and sank its teeth into the large man's face, the sounds of tearing flesh and desperate cries echoing in the air.

Three's lifeless body slumped to the floor in defeat.

With blood dripping from its metal mouth, the robotic

Dog sprang into the air toward the staircase. As the beast soared through the air, I leaped beneath it, feeling the wind rush past me as I pounded down each step. Three's body broke my fall, and all I saw was Eleven's ghostly pale face. I didn't pause to think as I reached for the gun on Three's shoulder, firing five shots until it shared the same fate.

"Th-thanks," Eleven breathed.

"We're even. Let's go."

A deep scream from Eight sounded from the kitchen, and together, we ran to see where we could help. With a foot hanging out of its mouth, the Dog stood on the cracked tile floor, while the large man's face reddened as he clutched his leg. The beast twisted its head with a snarl, spitting the appendage out, and then thrust its paws against Eight's chest, pinning him against the wall. It surprised me that the metal animal could push back such a large man, but I suppose, without a leg, what more could he do? In a flash, the Dog's claws tore across Eight's body, tearing fabric and flesh before he fell limply to the floor.

Eleven had her jacket around her shoulders and reached into a pocket. The whoosh of a dagger as it flew from her palm missed my ear by mere inches. The blade tore through the Dog's pixelated eye, a distorted yelp echoing as it fled into the dark snow outside.

A weak moan came from the man at our feet. Kneeling, I supported Eight's massive head, feeling his breath's frantic, shallow rhythm against my hands. Gashes lined his body, deep claw marks oozing blood, soaking into his shirt; the crimson stain pulsed with each new bubble of blood.

Every exhale Eight breathed was filled with blood, and his internal injuries were rushing to the surface. His eyes, wide and glistening with unshed tears, turned to me in fear. Spitting out a mouthful of blood, he was able to croak, "Run."

My nose twisted, and my brows furrowed, scrunching my face. Was I about to cry? Rarely did vampires cry—maybe these humans were rubbing off on me. This was all too much. Where's Jude? I turned to Eleven, who stood frozen beside me, her eyes wide with a silent shock from the night's events. "We need to find your sister."

Racing outside, we saw a crimson trail in the pristine snow, leading directly to the van. Two silhouettes huddled in the front seats, barely visible in the car's weak interior light. Dogs circled the van, biding their time and looking for a way inside.

Eleven's breath hitched, a ragged plume of icy air escaping her lips. "Jude and my sister are in there."

I nodded. "We need to create a diversion to lure the Dogs away so we can get in and leave."

Pulling the last two knives from her belt, Eleven held them between her fingers. "I'll do it."

"You're coming with me; there has to be a way," I pleaded. "I refuse to let more people die tonight."

She shook her head. "With all this activity, the Dogs likely notified their pack, so more will be here momentarily. This is the only way. Tell my sister I love her."

My mouth opened to argue with her again, but I knew she was right. Cool wetness enveloped my eyes as I closed my mouth, nodding to her.

A nervous twitch played on her lips, her pale face a mask of fear. With an audible gulp, she fled around the side of the house, far from the parked van, her lungs releasing a high-pitched shriek which cut through the night. "Here I am, you mother fuckers! Come get me!"

Their ears pricked up, heads swiveling to pinpoint the source of the unfamiliar sound. With eyes blazing red, the Dogs bolted toward the girl, who vanished into the blanket of darkness and snow.

With a rush of adrenaline, I scurried to the van, my hands slick with sweat as I yanked on the heavy metal sliding door. Inside, Jude and Twelve's frightened, pale, and strained faces turned toward me.

"What—" The girl in the driver's seat began to stutter.

"Go!" I yelled, throwing myself in the van. "We need to go! Everyone's dead."

Without a second thought, Twelve slammed her foot on the gas, the engine roaring as the van lurched forward, accelerating to maximum speed in a blur. We haphazardly sped down the road with nothing but our heavy breaths to cut the silence. The snowfall was heavy, and the wind swirled each snowflake into a blurry white blanket across the windshield. The weak beams of the headlights barely cut through, offering little more than a hazy white expanse in the deepening darkness.

Gazing at the swirling snow through the windshield, a sense of déjà vu settled in, and I held my breath. Sixty-five years of memories resurfaced, and I was back in my dad's car, fleeing our house. A loud, jarring knock clanged from outside, rattling the van as it sped along. Peering out the window, three Dogs with glowing red eyes were chasing us.

"What do we do?" Jude's voice cracked. "They're running beside us, trying to hit us off the road."

The impact of the Dogs sent us sliding wildly across the slick, icy road, our bodies shifting from left to right. We all stared at each other in silence, unsure what to do, hoping the Dogs would get tired and leave us alone.

I knew that wasn't a possibility.

Our eyes were glued to the road in front of us when a flash of red caught our eye. A large Dog stood ahead, its teeth bared, attempting to block our path. Twelve yanked the steering wheel, and the van swerved sharply, tires screaming against the asphalt. A slick patch of ice, unseen beneath a dusting of snow, sent us skidding wildly out of control.

None of us had it in ourselves to scream as we slammed into the thick trunk of a tree, and a swirl of red lights surrounded us.

Chapter Eighteen

I was lying on the floor of the van when I came to, feeling nothing but the soft touch of snowflakes on my cheek. Glass crunched like a thousand tiny bones under my head, and its jagged shards were woven into my hair. I wondered if I opened my eyes, I'd be looking down at myself, like an out-of-body experience. The silence around me was deafening and scary.

Where's Jude? Is he okay?

Garnering courage after my first thoughts since waking, I slowly peeked through my eyelids. My brain pieced together the battered, vinyl seats of the van, and my body started shaking from the shock. I lay there momentarily, collecting myself and trying to stabilize my breathing, wondering if Dogs were around before making any moves. A high-pitched whistling wind was the only sound cutting through the otherwise still air around me.

Finally, I lifted my body, shaking bits of glass from my hair and clothes, the tiny, sharp shards bounced on the floor like deadly hail. I placed a hand on the smooth seat, then contorted my body to see the front of the van, completely overturned. In the driver's seat sat Twelve, her bloodied head bashed against the broken window. A thick brown tree branch extended from outside into the van, ending its descent through her temple. Twelve's face was ashen, her eyes vacant, the scarlet blood blooming on the snow visible through the shattered glass.

Hopelessness and fear washed over me. My throat tightened as my salivary glands surged, and I turned away, fighting the urge to be sick, silently praying Jude hadn't suffered the same fate. A massive tree branch ripped through the front seat, leaving behind a devastating scene of destruction, making it impossible to see Jude.

At least he wasn't impaled, right?

Lifting my body from the floor, I pulled myself over the cold bark. Straddling the tree, I leaned over and saw a man hanging outside the van by his seatbelt. "Jude? I scrambled over the branch, the rough bark scraping my skin, with Arthur's threat echoing in my head. My heart was in my throat, silently willing him to say something stupid. Anything. "Jude." I stared at his face, the involuntary warmth of tears blurring my vision as I searched for the slightest flicker of life.

A pained moan escaped his lips. "Va-Vin? What happened?"

Relief flooded through my body. He was alive. Kicking my foot over the side of the tree, I reached up and jumped to open the van door above me. Finding a place for my feet on the worn leather headrests, I climbed to the open door, the cool night air hitting my face as I exited onto the side of the vehicle. With the van completely overturned, I squeezed through the shattered glass to reach Jude's door. I noticed a jagged line of cracked glass snaking from the top of the window to the bottom, and without a second thought, I smashed my fist through it. The glass shattered into a thousand pieces, and I dove headfirst through the gaping window.

I knew I needed to get him out of the seatbelt—the only thing that likely saved his life—and my fingers trailed along his body, feeling the frantic pulse of his heart beneath his skin. I found the button, pressed it as hard as my fingers would allow, and unhooked the latch, grabbing his body before it fell over into the tree branch. A grunt escaped my lips under the strain of his weight; however, I summoned every ounce of strength to heave him through the window. Gravity was against me, but I needed to ensure Jude was alright.

I hoisted him out the window, his limp body a dead weight against my arms. My body slid against the freezing, metallic side of the van, and we tumbled together onto the cold, snowy ground. "Vincent?" Jude mumbled. "What happened? Where are we?"

He was stirring, and I let out a sigh of relief. "We're fine. We'll be fine." I was trying to sound reassuring, but I was anything but. We're in the middle of nowhere at night with the potential of a herd of Dogs to pounce on us at any moment. If someone described this scenario to me, I'd have said without a doubt, we were doomed.

And maybe we were.

He grunted beside me and sat up from the snowy ground, holding his head in his hands. "I'm ok, just roughed up from the…crash?" His eyes, glazed with shock, focused on the mangled wreckage of the vehicle as his mind frantically pieced together the prior events.

"Let's find shelter—it's a total whiteout, and it's getting colder by the minute." I squinted through the blustery night to try to see if there was a building nearby, but only white tendrils of wind and snow blew around us. Jude put his hands on the ground, trying to lift himself to his feet. "Be careful!"

He shakily rose to his feet, his body swaying with each gust of wind. "I'm fine. Let's start walking because we'll freeze if we don't move."

He was right—*he'd* likely freeze. As a vampire, I knew I'd last longer than him.

I nodded, my hand finding its way to his waist, offering support as he wobbled slightly on his feet. Together, we lumbered through the waist-high snow. The biting cold stole the feeling from my feet in mere minutes, leaving them numb and prickly. A fierce wind lashed our faces, each gust pushing us deeper into the inky darkness. The ground sloped upward beneath my feet, but my attention was on Jude, desperate to find a safe haven.

"What's that?" Jude asked, pointing straight ahead.

Outlined against the snowy darkness was a shadow of a small building. My body was shaking, so I knew he must have been absolutely frigid. With haste, we trudged on, in hope that the destination was somewhere we could stay for the night.

The building looked like a small barn, a simple wooden shack with a sagging roof and broken windows. Rotted wood and rusted nails barely held it together, but it was our salvation. The door opened inward, which was a relief; we didn't have to fight it against the snow.

A frigid draft howled through the dilapidated building, carrying a nauseatingly stale odor. I wasn't sure it was a trick of my mind from not being pelted by snow anymore, but I swear warmth began to spread through my body. Old hay lay strewn against the floor, some golden and others gray. Four small stables faced each other while various farm equipment leaned against the side of the barn to our left and right.

"It'll be a good place to protect us for the night." Jude was gazing upward at the cobwebbed eaves that held the shack together.

"As long as it doesn't collapse on us from the wind." I walked to the stables, rubbing my arms to generate warmth, and realized what the strong smell might have been. Carcasses of animals lay long forgotten in three of them, their bones brittle and crumbling. The fourth looked to be the cleanest—no bones or animal droppings were underneath the straw, although mice scurried from their home as we walked near.

"Let's sleep here," Jude suggested as he gazed at the stable. "Our bodies will generate heat, and we can create a nest with the hay as insulation while we sleep."

Where I'd be sleeping never crossed my mind when agreeing to come on this adventure. I didn't expect to be sleeping in a stable like an animal. Although judging by how the humans lived, I should've anticipated less, as this barn was nicer than what they're used to. My gaze drifted around the room until it landed on an empty burlap sack, its rough texture visible even from a distance, hanging limply from the wall. My numb fingers fumbled with the cloth before I ripped it apart, spreading the ragged pieces across the hay. Jude looked at me inquisitively, and I shrugged. "I guess we could use this as a blanket?"

He smiled. That damn smile. "Works for me."

I sat on the makeshift straw bed; it wasn't particularly comfortable, but I could feel the heat collect in the nest around me. My body ached and yearned for the comfort of my perfect bed. I lay my head against the cradle, and a wave of fatigue overcame me. I stifled a yawn, the chill seeping into my bones, and quickly pulled the scratchy wool bag over my body.

Jude's warm body settled next to mine, his back pressed

against me. I appreciated the respect he was giving me. I rubbed my legs together, thinking about Gabe and how I wished he were here to act upon my vampiric desires.

I kept my eyes shut, trying to fall asleep, but rest stayed just out of reach as my mind fixated on every subtle movement around me. The wind howled, and every gust caused the old shack to groan and shudder, threatening to tear it apart. From the other side of the ramshackle shack came the unsettling sound of metal chains, each link clanging against the next. In the back of my mind, I knew one of us should be keeping watch, but we were too tired to care. We put our faith in the shed to protect us from everything outside, yet every time I heard the rattle, I expected it to be a Dog that found its way inside. One of the most annoying things keeping me from sleep was Jude's incessant shivering.

My body was surprisingly warm, so I shimmied closer to Jude, lifting the sack to cover him. It only draped a sliver of his body, but the small amount of coverage seemed to quell his shaking.

He rolled over, and we came face to face. "Thanks for sharing with me."

His warm breath felt nice against my cold nose, and his light blue eyes were glowing in the darkness. Before I could stop myself, a sudden urge washed over me, and I leaned in to kiss him.

What was I doing?

His lips felt like plush pillows against mine, and I closed my eyes, picturing Gabe. Was this okay? Should I not be doing this with a human? I wondered if my hatred for Jude this whole time was lust, or if I was just desperate and delusional.

Desperate and delusional seemed better.

Jude's warm palm cradled my jaw, his thumb brushing

my cheek as our breaths mingled. His lips were warm against mine, and his thick eyelashes tickled my cheek. He drew himself closer, and my neck was lightly swathed between his lips. From deep within my throat, my vocal cords purred, and my back began to arch, yearning for a pair of fangs to sink into me. My writhing in ecstasy must have excited him as his erect member was grinding against my leg.

He pulled away from my neck, his touch lingering, before gently cradling my head in his hand. His fingers lightly massaged my scalp, each hair on my head tingling down my body. "Is this okay?"

Staying faithful to Gabe held me back, but I'll probably never see him again, right?

Fuck it.

I pulled him on top of me, lust blazing in both of our eyes. He deepened the kiss with his hand against the back of my neck, his other hand moving skillfully over my body. Our bodies were generating so much heat, the cold I felt earlier was a distant memory. All I could do was be here. In this moment. With Jude. I couldn't remember the last time I wanted to rip someone's clothes off them.

I grabbed his stiff cock through his pants, feeling its throbbing heat as I began to stroke him. My eyes widened as his girth swelled. I knew he was enjoying this as soon as he exhaled a large breath of air from his nose. He pulled back, muttering a low "fuck" before lifting his shirt over his shoulders.

We lay completely intertwined with each other, our lips never losing their wetness. His powerful physique was pressed against me, and I couldn't resist the urge to trace my fingers along his muscular chest. He moved his mouth to my neck, and his member throbbed against me as I moaned. His warm tongue glided down my neck, and each lick sent shivers down my spine and a gasp escaping my lips as his tongue reached my chest.

Why had Gabe and I never done more foreplay? Being intimate with Jude was sensual, whereas looking back, with Gabe, it almost felt…transactional. He'd sink his teeth into me, and we would get right to it before the blood left his cock, but with Jude, everything was different.

His tongue swirled my nipples, and it felt like every nerve in my body was standing on end. My breathing was heavy, and I wanted him to know how much pleasure he was drawing out of me. Confident in his actions, he traced his tongue slowly down my stomach, deftly undoing my pants with his hands.

"What're you doing?" I didn't know why I asked this.

He stopped abruptly, a sudden intensity in his gaze. "Do you trust me?"

With a heave, I rose from the straw cradle and bit my lower lip as I gazed at the gorgeous human before me. He was nothing like Gabe, who was shaved clean, impossibly lean, and a mass of rippling muscles. Instead, Jude was a bit wider, his broad shoulders hinting at strength, with a sparse trail of hair that descended his chest before vanishing below his waist. I shimmied out of my pants without a trace of doubt in my mind in this moment. "Yes."

Witnessing my enthusiasm, his pants slid down to his knees, and what I saw left me speechless. Emerging from his pants was the most beautiful cock I'd ever seen. The shaft curved slightly, with prominent veins running along its length, culminating in a glistening, plump tip coated with precum.

His grin widened as he took one last look at me, then planted his face between my thighs. As soon as his warm tongue wrapped around my cock, every nerve in my body stood at attention. The delicate way his throat closed around my manhood slowly helped me to let go of the nervous pressure building inside me. A thrilling anticipation built with each lap, his sudden movements electrifying me with a delightful rush. Jude's shoulders pressed against my legs, spreading them apart, while his hand firmly gripped my thigh.

My eyes rolled back, and the world swam into a blurry haze as my breath hitched in my throat. Heat built in my body as he gradually devoured more of me until his lips reached the base of my shaft. "Stop," I moaned, feeling Jude's fingers clutch my skin before his tongue kissed my stomach once again.

"Fuck," he whispered. "You taste amazing."

I couldn't speak. I saw spots invade my vision and disappear almost instantly. Jude looked up at me, his chin wet with a heartwarming smile.

I craved more.

I wiggled my pelvis closer to Jude's hips, giving him the knowledge it was okay to enter me. His blue eyes gazed downward, an appreciative smirk plastered across his face as he spat in his hand. There was a brief pause before there was a subtle pressure between my legs, his fingers skillfully moving before eventually reaching his mouth.

"Oh fuck." I whispered with a long, deep breath. I exhaled as he slowly eased into me, savoring the moment.

"Oh *fuck*," he breathed, almost as if in agreement.

Each inch of Jude was like an extra layer of pleasure as he buried himself deeper inside me. He lowered his body, his weight pressing heavily against my chest, and his breath softly grazed my neck. We gazed into each other's eyes as he began thrusting in and out of my hole. The perfectly timed movements, both fast and slow at the same time, were so much different than what I was used to. With

Gabe, our sex was quick and rough, but with Jude, it was sensual and passionate. I felt taken care of, like we were connected.

Like I mattered.

"You feel so good," he breathed and bit his lip, easing his way into me.

I arched my back, a low moan escaping my lips as waves of pleasure washed over me. Jude stiffened his body and began quicker thrusts once I let him know it was okay. I tried to stay quiet, but the feeling was like a wildfire, consuming me and making it impossible to hold back. I never understood when people compared sex to fireworks, but now I do.

It was like he was a match, and my name was dynamite.

As my leg pressed against his shoulder, he pulled me close and wrapped his arm around my neck to enthrall me in a passionate kiss. Our mouths pressed against each other with such ferocity that I thought we might merge.

"Do you like this?"

"I love feeling you inside me." With every kiss and thrust, his rapid breaths added to the throbbing pleasure in my dick. "But if you keep fucking me like this, I'm gonna come."

My warning was completely disregarded as his thrusts became deeper and stronger. "Then come for me," he growled.

Pressure built in my balls like I was ready to explode, and with one more thrust, I couldn't hold back any longer. An explosion of warm come radiated from deep inside my cock, spreading over my chest and neck.

A spark ignited in Jude's eyes as his hands clamped down on my hip, the pressure intense enough to leave crescent-shaped marks. His body tensed, muscles coiling like springs, focusing intently.

"Come for me, Jude," I cooed. "I need you deep inside me."

A series of perfectly timed breaths, each a silent puff of air from his mouth, preceded a face scrunching up as if he were about to sneeze. A series of moans escaped his mouth and I felt him pulsing inside me, warming my core before collapsing his body on top of mine. The air hung heavy and thick, clinging to our damp skin as he settled into the crook of my shoulder.

My body felt like it had released a lightning bolt, leaving me a shell of a man.

I couldn't remember the last time this happened.

My legs felt like jelly, but I've never felt so whole. Jude looked up at me once more, his eyes soft, offering one last tender kiss before we huddled under the rough burlap sack and fell asleep.

The two of us felt safer than we had in a long time.

Chapter Nineteen

The next morning, I stirred slowly, and my body ached like I had I completed a full workout. My stomach lurched violently, and a sour taste flooded my mouth as bile rose in my throat. I was entwined with Jude, my head resting on his chest, feeling the steady beat of his heart, my leg thrown over his. His arm, strong and warm, was wrapped securely around me, making me feel completely safe. I savored the morning light and the tranquility surrounding us. The scent of smoke and mint clung to Jude's skin, a fragrance I inhaled deeply, letting it fill me completely.

His eyelids fluttered open lazily, revealing a small smirk playing on his lips as he looked at me. "Good morning, handsome."

What did I do? Last night was surely a mistake. Even though any hope of seeing Gabe again was gone, I still felt like I had done something wrong. Was it guilt, or am I rejecting the thought of opening up to human connection?

I forced a smile, a strained grimace that didn't quite reach my eyes, before carefully pushing myself up from the hay cradle. I pulled on my shirt and pants and headed toward the dusty window of the barn. Wiping the grime from the dusty glass with my shirt, a ray of sunlight warmed my face. Outside was a winter wonderland—mounds of fluffy snow coated the rolling hills like clouds, and green pine trees held glistening flakes in their boughs. The world was bathed in the warm glow of the setting sun, looking like a perfectly crafted greeting card image. I had never seen beauty like this, being so high above the world in Elysium, but being fully immersed in the world at this moment, my breath was taken away.

While I marveled at the world's beauty, my mind kept wandering to what happened the night prior. The weight of my actions pressed upon my shoulders—Gabe's image burned in my mind, and the shame of sleeping with a human while abandoning the vampires left me questioning my selfish needs. I never felt so wanted and alive as I did last night with Jude. On the other hand, I don't even know if I will see Gabe again, let alone survive this adventure. I may as well have the best sex of my life, right?

Right.

Hands reached around my waist, startling me from my reverie, followed by the feather-light touch of lips against my neck. "You were amazing last night, Vincent."

"Yeah, it was…fine." His kiss sent shivers down my spine, and I wanted to jump on top of him once more before we left the protective barn, but I refrained. "You know, you can call me Vinny, right?"

"Oh, can I now?" He laughed. "I suppose last night made us a little closer than strangers." His pants hung low on his hips, creating a casual, relaxed look that slouched in the middle, exposing two defined muscles and a line of blond hair tracing up to his navel.

My eyes left his smooth chest as an irritating itch blossomed on my abdomen. A scratchy, crawling sensation covered my entire body, likely from fleas we picked up in our bed last night. "We have to be focused because it's just the two of us now. Without a car, we'll have to walk, and that leaves us open to attacks." As I spoke, I realized this task seemed more and more impossible. How were we going to get back to Silvertown? "Once we leave this barn, both of us need to commit to not letting any more lovey-dovey stuff get in the way of our mission."

"Yeah, absolutely." He nodded, a flicker of hurt in his eye. "I'll do anything to make sure you're safe out there."

With a dramatic shake of my head, I spun around, settling on the window once again. If anything, *I'll* be the one to protect *him*. I scanned the rolling mounds of snow in front of me, and my eye caught a pack of Dogs in the distance, running toward the middle of a valley. I squinted and saw the outline of a small village hidden in the snowy hollow, blending seamlessly into its surroundings.

"I'm shocked the Dogs didn't storm in here last night." Jude threw on his shirt. "Let's head to that village, Eight did say we were close."

I nodded and zipped a coat around my shoulders. I slung the heavy gun over my shoulder, checking the ammo count while Jude prepared to leave. We met at the barn entrance, where the cold wind whistled through gaps in the aged wood, making the metal chains jingle like wind chimes. "Ready?"

"One more thing before we go."

With a swift motion, he cradled my face in his palm and lightly kissed me. The moment our lips met, a jolt of electricity shot through me, so intense I expected lightning to explode from my fingertips. It was sweet, like a thick drop of honey that coated your tongue, yet left a craving for more.

He pulled away; it was all too sweet to last. "I needed one more before we left because once we leave, what did you call it? The 'lovey-dovey stuff' would be ending?"

I smiled. "Yes, we need to get back to Silvertown, and I'll be damned if anyone else dies. Especially you."

"We both agree—neither of us will let the other die, so we'll get through this together."

I pulled open the barn door, and despite the frigid temperature, the warmth from the sun felt nice against my face. Two pairs of leather boots were covered in dirt by the shack's entrance, and both of us slipped our feet inside before trudging through the snow. With each step, I had to lift my foot higher than my knee, my muscles screaming in protest, to avoid losing my balance. The snow was heavy, but just soft enough to fall through.

We walked in silence, making our way to the small town hidden in the valley. I was lost in my thoughts, and I'm sure Jude was as well, to the point where we forgot to talk to one another. There was too much spinning in our brains. What did last night mean to both of us? Is anything going to change? Were my feelings of love for Gabe even authentic? How did *I* feel?

The wind whipped snow into our faces as we walked, unsure of how long we'd trekked, until the small town gradually emerged from the swirling white. I was surprised by how close the village was, realizing I'd walked the entire way from the shack in a daze. It felt like driving home after a long day, the familiar route blurring past and the hum of the engine lulling your mind into a quiet fog.

"Vinny, look!" Jude pointed his finger straight ahead.

At the town's entrance stood a weathered, old gas station. Its rusted sign, barely legible from age and neglect, it loomed over rows of gas pumps, each surrounded by a cluster of abandoned cars and trucks. A small shop, with a faded white exterior and a blue tin roof, sat in the middle of the empty lot. The faded, cracked plastic numbers, once proudly displaying gas prices, now lay scattered below the sign, like fallen soldiers.

"Let's go inside and see if there's any food we may be able to eat."

I nodded and looked down the road, spotting a cluster of small houses lining the tree-covered street in the distance. The town had surrendered to the elements, nature reclaiming what was once its own. Cracks split the road beneath our feet, a thin layer of ice glazing its surface.

The air was thick with the smell of decay as I navigated the tangled mass of cars, their deflated tires choked by the remnants of vines that hadn't weathered the winter. Inside, assorted skeletons of dead animals lay scattered amongst old dolls and toys left behind by previous owners. The air felt still, like any sound would shatter the dystopian illusion in front of us.

"I'll go inside," Jude whispered. "Just in case there's rabid animals…or humans." He pointed to the pavement below my feet. "Stay here, don't move."

I nodded in understanding and heard the ringing of a bell as he entered the store. I pressed my face against its grimy window, trying to peer inside, but a thick film of brown sludge obscured my view. Using the sleeve of my shirt, I wiped the surface clean, making sure there was nothing nefarious waiting for Jude inside.

Peering in, memories flooded my brain. I remember going to gas stations like this as a child, begging my parents to buy me a candy bar. The gas station shelves were wiped clean, and old newspapers littered the floor, but my mind's eye pieced it all together from memory. I saw what this place used to be and the liveliness it once held.

I strained to see Jude through the grimy window, his bouncy blond hair the only feature visible before he vanished into the back of the building. Craning my neck, I tried to catch a glimpse of him, but he was nowhere in sight. I sidled along the outside of the building to clean the other windows, but just as I lifted my arm, something caught my attention in my peripheral vision.

A skeptical eyebrow raised, I turned the corner to find a row of electric vehicle charging stations, their cords snaking across the pavement like metallic serpents. At one time, these vehicles would've been expensive and highly sought after, but were quickly thrown away once the apocalypse happened.

Funny how useless money is when survival becomes more important.

"Vinny? Where are you?" Jude's voice had a tinge of fear in his throat.

Peeking from behind the corner, I waved to him, and his face went from frightened to relieved in a split second. As he jogged toward me, my eyes landed on his empty hands. "You didn't find any food?"

He shook his head. "Everything was completely bare, but I did find out something interesting." Jude walked to the charging station with a purposeful stride, opened the metal charging port, and stuck one of the hoses inside.

A small, whimpering beep sounded through the air. "...How?"

He shrugged, a smile pulling at his lip. "I don't know, but I heard a humming at the back of the store and realized it was electricity. There must be a power source somewhere in this town keeping the energy running. Let's charge this car, so we can get back to Silvertown to regroup."

I nodded, anticipation building in my chest as my mind raced with a million different scenarios. Obviously, Elysium had electricity, and the humans found ways to create it in their compounds, but how did this small, abandoned town have an energy supply? What other secrets are hiding in these streets?

Chapter Twenty

"While the car charges, let's try to find the town's energy source."

With a slow nod, the familiar tug of curiosity inched through my mind, a persistent hum beneath the surface of my thoughts. Why here? How is the entire town's electricity still running after sixty-five years? I wondered if we were walking into another nest of humans, but surely with the knowledge to create electricity, they wouldn't be feral, right?

The untouched pristine snow settled like a thick, white blanket. The skeletal branches of the trees clawed at the pale sky on either side of the street, and the brisk air painted my nose a rosy pink. Shivering slightly, I crossed my arms tightly across my chest as we walked down the chilly street, only to feel Jude's warm arm wrapped around my shoulders. It was like we were in one of the cheesy Christmas movies that played on loop in Elysium during the winter because people love living in nostalgia.

Honestly, it always made me sick. Watching movies

around the holidays was something my mom and I did—I haven't watched one in sixty-five years.

With each step, the snow crunched underfoot, a delightful sound as we neared a hill. The houses looked quaint and cozy, nestled side by side. Many looked run-down and old, but the grandeur of their design was still evident. They looked exactly as you'd picture small-town America: moderate porches with flagpoles that had tattered red, white, and blue colored cloth swaying in the wind. Each house possessed a fence encircling its perimeter; some were broken or had fallen over due to age.

"Pretty cool place, huh?" Jude asked once he saw my head swivel, gazing at the residences around me. "I'd love to have a house of my own one day instead of sharing a room with hundreds of other people."

"Yeah, I don't know how you barbarians do that." I bit my bottom lip. I didn't mean it to sound like it did. It just came out.

I swear.

"We wouldn't have to if the vampires didn't kill us if they found out where we were hiding, but maybe you forgot that."

My cheeks burned, and I wasn't sure if it was because of the temperature of the air or because I was embarrassed. I lifted my head, and his piercing blue eyes winked at me. "You're messing with me?"

A sheepish grin stretched across his face, and he shrugged his shoulders. "Yeah, but not really."

A nervous laugh broke the tension between us as we cautiously began to retrace our steps. "I do agree with you, though," I said, itching the underside of my arms. "I'd love to have my own space and have neighbors to make friends with. Back in Elysium, it's just me."

His eyebrows furrowed. "Just you?"

I nodded. "I wasn't allowed to leave my penthouse without authorization, which was rarely given."

"So what happened the night I met you?"

A laugh escapes my mouth, remembering the delicious thrill of defying my father. "It was my birthday, and I snuck out."

"Nice." Jude bit his bottom lip and put his hand on my shoulder. "I guess we each have our own completely separate gripes, but we can agree that our own freedom and space are important."

Before I agreed, a sharp tug on my arm shoved me downward onto the cold snow. I recoiled quickly, my heart pounding in my chest, to see what happened. Jude was next to me, kneeling with his head low.

A town square sat at the end of the road, an expansive area I assumed was once a small park with a church situated at its head. Scattered around the area were small shops perfectly spaced between each other, but the most surprising was what was occupying the space in front of us: Dogs. Lots of them.

The Dogs lazily ambled across the open space, their paws crunching softly on the snow, surveying their surroundings as others basked in the warm sunlight. If I didn't know better, these looked like real animals, like deer, grazing in a meadow. Two Dogs stood rigidly at attention, their watchful eyes scanning the area as if guarding something precious inside.

"Fuck! What do we do?" I mouthed to Jude. I knew any sound we made could alert them to our presence, and I'd rather not fight more than a dozen Dogs.

Clenching his fingers into a fist and extending his thumb, Jude mouthed words back to me. "Head back to the gas station?"

My head turned to the Dogs in front of the church.

What could they be guarding? What is hiding in this town? My eyes pleaded with Jude as I reached out, my fingers tightening around his wrist. Together, we ran toward the nearest house.

"What are we doing?" His voice was barely a whisper.

"Let's go to the church, something's drawing me there." It was as if this church was hiding in my memories, and the only way it would come to light was if I got to it. I couldn't exactly describe the feeling, but it was familiar.

Jude gulped audibly. "Go to the building surrounded by Dogs? Being killed wasn't on my to-do list today."

"Maybe this is where we were traveling to all along. Maybe we found it ourselves?" My words lingered in the air as the realization that I may be correct weaseled its way into our minds. Why would the Dogs all be here guarding a specific building? Surely they aren't God worshipping contraptions.

To say the least.

Jude nodded hesitantly, his grip tight on my hand as we dashed around the side of the house. A weathered red fence, the color bleached by sun and rain, sagged gently backward along the perimeter.

"What's the plan?" Jude paused, eyeing the sledgehammer leaning against the weathered shed, before asking his question.

"Let's make our way toward the church," I answered, looking around. "I was hoping we could run through the back of each house to get closer."

"Why can't we?" Jude swung the hammer toward the fence, blasting a hole through its exterior. The wood was so old it barely made a sound as it crumbled under the impact.

I crouched low, feeling the damp earth against my

knees as I duck-walked through the narrow hole. "I thought we'd be a bit more subtle."

"Subtle isn't part of my vocabulary."

Most humans aren't; they use their ego to blow things up and start wars. At least vampires were methodical.

I chose not to engage in his flirting at this moment because I knew he resented it when I made comments about how lowly I thought of humans. My attention was drawn to the next house's fence, which was newer than those around it. It was resin, where most of the others were made of wood. There was no way Jude's sledgehammer would bust through it without attracting attention. "Any idea how to get to the next yard?"

Jude silently approached a swaying rope ladder, his eyes focused on the treehouse nestled high among the branches. I watched as a lime-green beanbag flew out the window, landing with a soft thud in the neighbor's yard. Jude tumbled out right after it.

I gasped, my breath catching in my throat as he soared through the air, with a silent prayer on my lips, hoping he wouldn't get hurt. When did I start caring about someone else's safety over my own? Running to the fence, I put my cheek to its cold exterior. "Jude?" I whispered. "Are you alright?" Not a sound reached me, only an unsettling quiet that made me fear he lay unconscious from the fall. "Jude?"

Two heavy, black cable wires flopped over the fence, narrowly missing my face. Jude's hushed whisper carried on the breeze from the other side of the fence. "Tie these to a tree branch so you can get over here safely."

"Are you okay?" I whispered back, taking the wires in my palm.

"I-I'll be alright." His tone wasn't convincing. "I didn't expect it to hurt as much as it did."

With a grunt, I pulled the cold, damp cables across the yard and carefully climbed the ladder toward the treehouse. Inside, mounds of untouched snow sat amongst discarded toys and half-read books. I wrapped the thick steel cables tightly around the massive trunk, reaching through the treehouse's center. A metal baseball bat sat in the corner of the room, rusted and unusable. I balanced the bat precariously on the two taut cables, my hands gripping either side before I pushed off from the treehouse, hurtling toward the next yard.

I soared through the air, and it took every ounce of my strength to keep from letting out a scream. I knew I had to release my grip on the rope before I reached the end. Otherwise, I'd collide with the tree Jude secured the other end to. Once I passed the top of the fence, I released my fists, sinking into the soft, pillowy snow with a muffled thud as the bat clattered to the ground next to me.

Jude ran over to me, his face etched with worry, eyes wide with concern. "Vinny, are you okay?"

I instantly sprang to my feet to prove to him I was unharmed. "Good idea with the wires."

"I can be smart sometimes."

He winked at me, and I remembered when his flirting used to annoy me—and still sometimes does—but I've learned to find it endearing. Secretly, it made me melt. How could someone infuriate and infatuate me at the same time? What was this hold he had over me?

Behind the house, a stone pathway led to a pale-yellow storefront. Jude gave a quick wave, urging me to follow him through the small trail. "This leads to one of the shops in the village square."

We walked down the path together, our footsteps muffled by the thick undergrowth that eventually forced us into a single-file line. As we were hidden on the side of the shop, I saw what awaited us just outside the confines: an area filled with Dogs. We held our breath, knowing even the slightest sound—a cough, a creak of our boots—could betray us and give away our position. With hushed footsteps, we entered the small building to quietly devise our plan.

The back door opened into a cramped kitchen, cluttered with rusted tables and neglected cooking equipment. A stack of rusted ovens sat precariously on top of one another, surrounded by discarded ladles and knives. I closed my eyes and imagined the pristine stainless-steel kitchen this pizza shop once utilized.

Inside a small doorway, a chipped paint counter separated the entrance from the bright storefront beyond. Two large windows overlooked the village square, and a chill went down my spine as I ducked behind the counter after catching a glimpse of the menacing Dogs outside. Heart pounding, I crouched low and ran back to the kitchen with Jude.

"What do we do? How can we get into the church?" I asked. "We're so close."

A smug smirk stretched Jude's lips as he pulled a worn cardboard box from behind the pick-up counter. "I have an idea." In the center of his palm, he held a vibrant bundle of sticks—purple, blue, yellow, and red—that oddly resembled dynamite. "It's a box of fireworks, I haven't seen these in years!"

I cocked an eyebrow and looked at a calendar on the wall. Above the printed word 'JULY,' a small picture depicted a brown doe with her kin, all focused intently on the still blue lake behind them. I completely forgot that businesses closed due to the BRETH outbreak on a long-forgotten holiday—the Fourth of July. A time when Americans would proudly display their flags and gather with friends and family to celebrate their nation. I looked back at Jude and nodded. A realization came over me. "A distraction!"

We immediately got to work, the crackling of the firework wrappers adding to the crisp winter air as we angled them in the snow for a clear shot above the fences. If the fireworks functioned correctly, they would launch a mile down the road with a booming crackle and whistle, enough to pique the Dogs' interest.

I went to a stove in the kitchen and turned the knob, the metallic click echoing in the otherwise quiet room, as I waited to see if the pilot light would catch. Nothing but a tiny clicking sound reached my ears. There was no gas left. "How are we gonna light the fireworks?"

There was no response from Jude, only the quiet tinkling of glass hitting the tiled floor. I ran to the doorway, my feet skidding to a halt on the smooth floor, just before I stumbled through. Did the Dogs see Jude when he opened the door? Was I walking into a room of Dogs? My hand instinctively went to the cold steel of the gun hanging at my side, the weight familiar and slightly unnerving as I shook my head, needing to banish these thoughts. Jude needed me.

I was relieved to find the next room's windows undamaged and the pizza shop surprisingly Dog-free. Instead, Jude had his arm above his head with a dowel from the table. "Turn the light on."

Next to the doorway, a dusty light switch beckoned, and I flipped it upward with a decisive click. The broken lightbulb above Jude cast an eerie orange glow, the frayed wires humming with a low electrical buzz. With a focused gaze, Jude carefully positioned the dowel near the wire. The spark was bright and quick, setting the wood ablaze with a tiny, dancing flame. Clasping his hand around the sputtering flame, he ran outside and began to light each string attached to the fireworks.

I ran outside after him and heard a hissing sound that grew louder as more and more began their countdown until the first shot into the air. More fireworks joined the first, and the air filled with the crackle and whoosh before exploding in a flurry of green, red, and blue sparks.

Heart pounding, I ran back to the kitchen, peering through the doorway to catch a glimpse of the square. The Dogs' ears perked up with each firework bang, their heads swiveling, and their noses twitching, as they strained to locate the source of the booming sounds and vibrant colors lighting up the sky. Eyes glued to the dazzling display and ears ringing from the booming explosions, the Dogs leaped into action. Their tails began wagging, and a series of menacing barks pierced the air. It only took a few seconds before the village square was clear of the Dogs.

I could have hugged Jude. He was so smart for thinking of this distraction. He didn't tell me we couldn't do it. He found a way. He cared.

"I guess one thing will never change, even if they're mechanical." He laughed. "Dogs *hate* the sound of fireworks."

I rolled my eyes, a playful gesture that couldn't quite mask the wide, happy smile stretching across my face. Grabbing his hand, our fingers intertwined with each other. I was full. He was my person.

"Run."

Together, we burst from the pizza shop's front door and ran across the snowy town square, our boots crunching on the crisp snow. I wasn't thinking of anything while running with Jude at my side. I felt invincible, like not even a Dog could take me down.

We raced up the worn stone steps to approach the

imposing, dark wooden doors of the church. We placed both hands on the cold, damp left side and, with a synchronized heave, pushed hard. The heavy door creaked open ajar, revealing a sliver of darkness beyond.

Gasping for breath after our sprint, we slammed our bodies against the door, the wood groaning under the impact as we secured it against the approaching Dogs.

With our backs to the wooden door and the church spread before us, I breathed, "Let's find out what's going on in this town."

Chapter Twenty-One

A rainbow of light streamed through the stained glass windows, illuminating the biblical scenes depicted in vibrant colors, while the intricate stone carving of Jesus on the cross behind the pulpit felt ancient and powerful. The scent of old wood and incense lingered in the air, while empty, smooth pews gleamed faintly under the dim light, facing the altar. A faded red carpet, worn smooth from years of use, stretched the length of the aisle to a large, polished wooden podium at the head of the room.

Why were the Dogs outside this building?

Jude's fingers reached for mine, and we began walking down the aisle together. Vampires didn't believe in weddings, and I didn't know if the humans still did, but being here felt very strange. It was like we were getting married. Years ago, I'd entertained the thought of it one day, surrounded by people I love, but that seems more like a fairytale than reality at this point. I never imagined I'd find myself here, in a forgotten church, with a reminder of a world where faith had been abandoned after the apocalypse.

I shoved aside the thought of weddings and focused on the rows of aged pews, imagining past ceremonies within this hallowed space. Directly in front of the church podium, a weathered wooden door, slightly ajar, revealed a dark, narrow spiral staircase descending into the earth. My gaze flickered between Jude's anxious face and the ominous wooden door, its dark varnish seeming to absorb the light. "So…do we go in?"

"Well, we didn't almost get eaten by hundreds of Dogs to not go through a hidden door."

I rolled my eyes, but a smile tugged at my lips despite my best efforts to suppress it. I liked his sarcasm; it was a lot like mine. I hung my feet over the side and pushed myself off without another thought. My boots struck the cold metal landing at the bottom, the sound echoing upward. Before my body could react, there was a heavy thump behind me and a hand clamped down on my shoulder.

"Let me go first," Jude whispered and scurried ahead. "In case there's any danger."

I thought it best not to argue so as not to alert anyone (or anything) that may be lurking at its end. Wrapping my fingers around Jude's shirt tail, we scrambled down the darkened staircase. Holding tightly to the metal rail, we carefully descended the uneven steps, our shoes echoing softly on the metal.

Eventually, at the bottom of the staircase, we found ourselves in a green and white tiled hallway, the grime on the walls thick with the scent of mildew and age. As we neared the end, a high-pitched whirring reached my ears, punctuated by the sharp crackle of electricity, casting an eerie, flickering glow in the distance. I patted the wall as we walked, hoping to find a light switch or something to illuminate our way. My fingers brushed the cold metal of the lever, pushing it upward, and the room ignited with a harsh fluorescent light.

My vision was clouded by black spots from the sudden brightness, struggling to adjust. A sterile feel pervaded the room, and the walls, sheathed in pristine white tiles, met a floor of cheap, imitation marble vinyl. The air smelled of oil and metal as I gazed upon rows upon rows of tool benches, each laden with an assortment of parts. To my right, a colossal metal box, easily the size of three cars, hummed with a low, whirring noise vibrating through the ground. Rusty bolts and nuts were scattered across the grimy ground, and a thin trail of black oil snaked from the back of the room to a drain in the center.

"Wh-where are we?" I whispered.

"It looks like a workshop." Jude took a tentative step forward, his head slightly forward, scanning his surroundings. "But who's keeping it running?" His finger extended at the black liquid on the ground, keeping his eyes focused forward. "The oil on the floor is pretty new, and the large box to your right is the generator keeping the electricity running for the entire town."

One question was answered, but now we were here, the bigger question on my lips was who created this hidden room…and for what? I caught Jude taking his gun from the holster, holding it in front of him. "Let's go forward together. This place is giving me the creeps."

Following his nod, we traced the trail of oil leading us to the back of the workshop. As we stepped inside, the automatic lights flickered to life, illuminating the space with a soft glow. In the next room, rows of metal tables stood under a large triangular mechanism, each reflecting the cold, metallic light. A network of wires, like a spider's web, hung from each robotic arm. In the center of each, a pyramid-shaped metal claw hung silently, cold and still.

The entrance to the workshop groaned open, the sound accompanied by a chilling draft, filling us with sudden dread. "We need to hide," I whispered, my voice trembling. A wall of oil cans was stacked on top of each other on the far wall of the room. Without another thought, I grabbed Jude's hand, and we crouched behind them, hoping they'd provide enough cover not to be seen.

The slow, rhythmic thud of footsteps grew louder as they approached. Was this who lived here? Peeking through a narrow gap between the barrels, we watched the door, our breaths held tight. To me, it sounded like two pairs of footsteps were stumbling, like they were drunk. My mind was racing, thinking about what we would do next if found. A large shadow crawled up the wall and decreased as the footsteps drew near and the creature came into view.

It was a Dog. Great.

I closed my mouth, hardly daring to breathe, as I waited for the Dog to turn towards us, its ears twitching at the slightest sound. A long hiss escaped its leg with each step, and glossy black hydraulic fluid spurted from a metal joint.

It was damaged.

With a thump, the Dog jumped onto one of the cold metal tables, settling down on its side with a contented sigh. Like a tiny engine starting, a quiet whirring vibrated through the room, growing louder until it filled the space.

I cautiously poked my head outside our hiding place to see what was happening. The sudden flash of light filled the room, followed by Jude's hand on my shoulder. "Vinny, what're you doing?"

Crouching low, I slowly shifted my feet to get a better look. "I wanna see what's happening."

"You can't, it's a Dog. It'll kill you."

A sharp tug on my shirt from Jude threw me off

balance. My body landed heavily on the stack of empty barrels, sending them crashing to the floor in a clatter of metal on tile.

Shit.

My muscles tensed, every hair on my body prickling, knowing full well the Dog heard me. The noise was too loud for their ears and sensors not to catch the ruckus. It was only a matter of seconds before it would descend on me. I heard Jude make a swift movement, but no other sounds reached my ears. The Dog didn't come. What the hell was going on?

I scrambled off the ground, my hand reaching to my side and brandishing my gun in front of me. Where was this Dog? It must be toying with me. My head turned quickly to look for Jude, who was also holding his gun pointed toward the doorway to the other room. We waited for an attack for what felt like forever, but it never came.

The Dog continued to lie on the metal bed, but what was happening to it was miraculous. With a whirring sound, the claw above the table spun before piercing the Dog, each wire above it reacting with a frantic jump and jolt. With a slow, deliberate motion, the pyramid-like claw unfurled its segmented parts, then snapped shut into a deadly point. A white-hot electrical current, crackling and spitting, surged toward the Dog, creating a blinding flash of light. Its arms extended, grasping a heavy, metallic pipe from a cluttered box filled with various metal components. The device emitted three quick bursts of light as it rested the pipe on the Dog's leg.

"What's happening?" Jude asked quietly, his eyes lighting up with each flash.

"Is it being repaired?" I didn't know exactly what I was seeing, but the new pipe replaced the broken one and was being welded and attached to the Dog's leg. Moving slowly,

I saw the Dog's eyes—two empty, dark pits staring blankly ahead. "I think it's turned off…at least for now."

"Look." Jude was pointing straight ahead to a large metal door.

It was as if a sinister energy radiated from what was inside. I almost felt the danger, but at the same time, it intrigued me so much that it drew me closer. Another flash of bright light from the claw made me wince, and I quickly looked from Jude to the door. "Together?"

He nodded, wrapping his fingers comfortably around mine. "Together."

Chapter Twenty-Two

The massive metal door, cold and imposing, appeared to have once sealed a vault or perhaps a nuclear weapons stockpile. It had a sense of danger about it, like whatever was behind it needed something indestructible to keep it contained. With a deep breath, I gripped the smooth, cold handle—the chill seeping into my skin—and pulled.

Locked. Not surprised.

Next to the door, a keypad, its buttons worn from countless presses, was built into the wall. Using my sleeve, I wiped away the thick dust, revealing a dim red light emanating from the pad's surface. "Any idea what the code is?"

"Actually, I may." Jude bit his bottom lip as he looked at me. "This is what Michael and I were discussing while you talked with Nessa. He had cracked a code from the mainframe within Elysium, but we didn't know what it went to. Should I try it?"

I craned my neck and nodded. "Duh!"

Jude walked to the keypad and reached into his shirt,

pulling out a crumpled square of paper. Delicately, he unfolded the fragile paper, its edges crinkling slightly as he pressed it against the tiled wall, smoothing it out before turning to the pad. After eight precise clicks, the low red light flickered off, replaced by a reassuring blink of green.

"I...think that worked?"

No shit, Sherlock.

I pulled on the door handle, and with a loud creak, the heavy door swung outward. The room was dark, a sickly green glow emanating from an unseen source illuminating the walls. Stepping inside, we were met with the momentary darkness before the fluorescent lights sputtered to life. The dim lights flickered and sputtered, their warmth slowly returning after years of disuse, casting a weak, hesitant glow.

The room, though spacious, felt smaller than it was because of the towering bookshelves lining every wall. Books and binders were thrown around the room, each with a heavy coating of dust resting on their shoulders. Amidst piles of papers that threatened to topple at any moment, a computer sat on a desk in the middle of the room, its brass desk lamp poised over the dusty keyboard.

"Vin, look at this." Jude's voice was barely a whisper as he gently lifted an ancient-looking paper from the floor.

I allowed him to call me Vinny, not Vin. Who did he think he was?

He lifted the heavy, dust-laden tapestry, revealing a meticulously detailed pencil sketch of a Dog's exoskeleton. Directly underneath it was another scroll-like tapestry, and when I unrolled it, details of the internals of the creature met my eyes. Lines and arrows reached from the inside, connecting to spaces filled with words and frantic scribbles. "This-this is a diagram of a Dog. This is how they're made."

I couldn't believe it—one of our greatest enemies' weaknesses was scattered among a bunch of papers on the ground. The mix of disbelief and hope was almost overwhelming.

"If we already found *this*, what else could be hiding in here?"

"I think we're about to find out." I crept to the desk, the eerie green glow from the computer periodically illuminating the dusty spines of the books behind it. Surrounding the computer, stacks of papers overflowed, their edges dog-eared and ink-stained. Picking one up, I recognized a symbol I hadn't seen in years—a seal from the President of the United States. "This letter is thanking this laboratory for mass-producing the Dogs."

Jude was looking intently at a clipboard, flipping the pages back and forth. "And this is a maintenance log. Look at the dates."

With a flick of his wrist, he spun the board, revealing the final entry in the log, most of the ink faded but still legible. I squinted in the flickering light, and the most recent date was a week before my birthday. Someone was here a couple of weeks ago. The air turned heavy, as if the atmosphere was still haunted by the presence of the person who had been here prior. I scratched my back, the noise punctuating the silence between us.

Two photographs, their edges curled and cracked from age, were taped haphazardly to the computer monitor. A flip of the photo revealed three figures standing in a line, their arms entwined with a Dog nestled at their feet. Their smiles, though faded with time, still shone through the photograph, although their faces were warped by age. Crisp white lab coats were worn by all but one man, who added a touch of whimsy with a bow tie.

The other picture, taped to the bottom left of the

monitor, showed a blurry image of a boy, perhaps five years old, on a rusty swing set. Pure joy was plastered on his face as he pushed his feet outward. A young woman with pale skin and raven-black hair stood behind the boy, her arms outstretched, head thrown back in joyous laughter. Despite never having been in this room, I had a strange sense that I knew these people. Maybe I was feeling nostalgic about a simpler time before the apocalypse. It was happening more and more often as I aged.

"Who do you think they are?" Jude asked quietly.

Knowing I had to hide my thoughts, I shrugged and looked at the glowing screen of the computer, taking a second to roll my eyes at the logo that looked like fruit in the corner. "Do you even know what this is?" I laughed and looked sideways at the man next to me, bumping his shoulder with mine.

"Uh, yeah." Jude nervously returned my laugh. "I've seen a bunch of them…they've just never worked."

A mess of zeros and ones, interspersed with strange symbols and punctuation marks, filled the screen. Random letters were strung together, but one word caught my eye: Diagnostic. "Look."

Jude leaned closer to the desk, scanning all the gibberish in front of us.

A sudden flash of light came from the room we just left, making me run to the doorway. A red laser scanned the Dog, who lay calmly on the table. "I-I think this computer system is what's keeping the Dogs alive."

"Close the door," Jude breathed. "The computer is saying its diagnostic is at ninety percent, and I don't want it to decide to attack us once it's at full capacity."

I pushed the metal door closed, hearing the satisfying click of the lock. My eyes reached Jude, whose chiseled jaw was illuminated by the green words on the screen. How was it that I felt completely safe with him? What was the reason behind the pit forming in my stomach?

"I'm positive this is the mainframe for the Dogs. When they get injured, they come back here to get fixed."

"Let's just smash it, then! If the computer doesn't work, it can't help them, right?" I grabbed the gun slung around my shoulder and pointed it at the ancient technology in front of me.

"Hold on a sec, let me see something." He squinted, slowly shaking his head. Extending one finger, Jude traced the cool, smooth surface of the computer, his pupils following each line of code. His head dropped to the keyboard, the keys clicking rhythmically under his fingers. The lines in his forehead deepened, etching themselves further into his skin as he peered at me over the monitor, his eyes wide with shock. "We can shut them down."

His words didn't immediately register in my mind. Could the Dogs be deactivated with a few keystrokes? Was it this easy? Jude and I were staring at each other; the same thoughts were likely running through both our heads. I nodded to him. "Let's do it."

"We're going to shut down the Dogs." His voice lightened with excitement. "We're going to do this!"

He grabbed my hand, and a smile spread across his lips. His voice was full of promise and filled me with excitement. "I can't believe it." I squeezed his hand and bit my lip in anticipation. The greatest threat to both humans and vampires was about to be destroyed.

And we're doing it. We'd be heroes.

With a few sharp clicks of the keyboard, the screen flickered, then displayed three ominous green words: Initiate Project Shutdown? Jude pressed the arrow button, moving the green cursor over the affirmative option. We stole one last look at each other and clicked the Enter key.

With a few violent blinks, like a dying lightbulb, the screen cut to a chaotic field of static.

"You did it, Jude!"

A voice sounded from the computer. "Hello? Hello? Is this thing on?"

My heart dropped. I knew that voice. Was it the creator of the Dogs?

"Ah! It works!" The static cleared to reveal a man in a white lab coat, his magnified eyes peering out from behind enormous, round glasses. "You've opted to shut down Project G-298-001-559, also known as the Dogs. The United States government regulates this advanced monitoring technology; therefore, there is not just one key to disable Project G." A Dog came into the camera frame and nuzzled the man's arm. "Doing so will kill an entire species, my life's work. I can assure you, they do much more good than harm."

I was shaking; my brain wouldn't allow me to believe what I was seeing and hearing. More than one key? Where could it be?

"There are two labs that use robotics and programmed intelligence to repair injured Dogs. If you have the authority to do so and enter the correct alphanumeric code on the next screen, the Dogs that report to this lab will be disabled. If both laboratories are disabled, the Dogs will shut down permanently until my partner or I can repair the code."

Great, so we still have to worry about Dogs *and* find the second location in a month before we're free from these beasts?

"The Dogs were built to protect all Americans, so disabling them will leave our country vulnerable. Keep this in mind before making your decision. God bless the United

States of America." The man gave a crisp salute before the screen faded to black, leaving only a pulsing green box.

"Hurry, put in the code you used to open the door." My heart was in my throat, so the words came out as a croak.

Jude unfolded the piece of paper once again and clicked the keyboard, one at a time. The box around the numbers turned red, and two words I didn't want to see appeared below: Passcode Failed. "What could it be?"

A piece of paper whose font looked like it was constructed on a typewriter caught my eye. The paper's corners were curled from age, and its face was faded and brittle, looking like a generous amount of coffee had disfigured the text. I picked it up and held it toward the light, attempting to piece together the words.

"What's it say?" Jude asked, squinting. "Code… computer…pictures, what could all that mean? Is this some sort of puzzle?"

I looked at the photos taped to the edge of the computer screen. The four scientists in lab coats and the family swinging now looked as if secrets were hiding behind each of their eyes. "Jude… I think I know the code."

"What? How?" His eyebrows furrowed, his brain trying to piece together information.

A low growl rumbled from the doorway, making our heads snap around so fast I'm surprised we didn't get whiplash. The fully repaired Dog stood in the doorway, its glowing red eyes piercing the dim light.

My eyes darted toward the looming threat in the doorway. "Just hold the Dog off while I give it a try."

With a sharp nod, he reached for his gun and lifted it from the desk. The Dog scanned the weapon in his hands, and a growl escaped from its lips once again. It began rearing its back legs, ready to unleash a powerful jump.

My fingers, trembling with fear, fumbled on the keyboard, hitting wrong numbers. With bated breath, I silently prayed this code was correct; otherwise, Jude and I would be Dog food. I pressed the Enter key, and my stomach dropped. A red error notification popped up on the screen: INVALID PASSWORD.

Click click

My head shot up, my heart leaping into my throat before plummeting to my stomach. I knew that sound. His gun was out of bullets. My jaw hit the floor as Jude's head whipped around, his eyes wide with a terror that mirrored my own. Frantically, I scanned the desk, trying to find something that would help him while my trembling fingers clicked the last key before submitting the code once again.

INVALID PASSWORD.

The Dog barked and sprang at Jude, his voice echoing through my ears. "Vin, hurry!"

The Dog's disruption threw me off, and I realized I may have entered incorrect numbers due to my lack of focus. My eyes locked onto the heavy, brass desk lamp, its metal body heavier than it looked, hoping it would buy me time to recall the code. I had one more try; time was running out. "Use this!" I hurled the desk lamp toward Jude, and it landed with a loud thud next to him, skidding across the concrete floor.

The bulb's glass shattered, leaving a trail of shards leading to Jude. With fear etched on every crease of his pale face, he twisted and grabbed the desk lamp, positioning it horizontally into the Dog's mouth. Although its strength was mighty, he did a great job at pushing back.

Taking a deep breath, I centered myself, and my fingers flew across the keyboard, each keystroke a familiar dance. The final number appeared on the screen, and with a swift click of the Enter key, the action was complete. I glanced at Jude, who was inches from the dog's gaping maw, its teeth like daggers, poised to strike. I knew once it reached Jude, he'd be a goner.

The Dog, its body taut and quivering, stood over Jude, its red eyes blazing with a predatory hunger. The computer screen blazed a harsh, electric green, and the dog's body tensed violently before collapsing. Its glowing red eyes flickered and died, its jaw hanging slack to reveal rows of wickedly pointed teeth. With a heavy clang, the metal body plummeted from the air, crashing to the ground with a resounding collapse.

"You-you did it! Vinny, you fucking did it!" Disbelief choked Jude's words, his breath short and ragged. "But how did you know the code?"

I pursed my lips, a knot of confusion tightening in my stomach as I realized the volume of information I still needed to process. There had to be a reasonable explanation, right? "The passcode was the birthdays of the two people in this photograph." I gulped. "The little boy in the picture is me. The woman is my mother." Tears pushed themselves behind my eyes, and air caught in my throat. "That's why the Dogs never attacked me. One of their creators is my father."

Chapter Twenty-Three

We stood in silence, our gazes locked in awkward tension. The weight of the newly revealed information was overwhelming, and I could sense Jude grappling with it too. Maybe even more. Would he turn his back on me? Would this knowledge taint the feelings we share with one another?

My questions were answered when his biceps wrapped around my shoulders in an embrace. An insufferable itch, like a thousand tiny needles, made me want to tear my skin off. Wrapped in his arms, I was shielded from the thoughts I had just spoken into reality. Burying my face into his chest, I breathed in his musk, which was strangely calming.

"Vinny, look." Jude's chin moved from the top of my head toward the computer screen. "There's a folder with your name on it."

Ugh, don't even tell me there's more.

Pulling back from Jude's comforting embrace, I squinted at the ominous glowing screen. Among the countless files lining the digital interface, one stood out that was labeled: Vincent Trials. My heart instantly dropped. Trials? What could this mean? Could this be a record of all the Extractions over the years, or a guide on how to replicate my blood? I was transfixed, unable to look away, knowing I had to open it. I didn't want to, but I knew I had to.

Straightening my spine and pivoting my body toward the screen, I placed one hand on the dusty mouse connected to the computer. Navigating the cursor over the folder marked with my name, I double-clicked. A screen opened from the folder, displaying video files named with dates, their thumbnails hinted at various events. I took one glance at Jude, who looked as confused as I was. "Let's start with the first." I took one large breath and double-clicked the oldest video.

A man wearing circular glasses and a pristine white lab coat appeared in a newly opened window. I pressed play, and the man's lopsided smile sprang to life on the screen. "Is this working?" he asked, adjusting the camera and centering himself in the shot. "My name is Salvatore Asposito, and I'm here with my partner, Dante. Together, we created the Dogs for the government, and I'm here to document our new, completely self-funded project. Since unleashing BRETH on the world by accident, I believe we've found the cure."

Jude clicked the mouse, pausing the video. "Are you sure you want to watch this?"

Tearing my eyes away from the flickering screen showing my father, I met his intense, blue gaze. "I have to."

Draping one arm around my shoulders, Jude replayed the video.

A small vial of blood was pinched between my father's thumb and forefinger. "This substance offers healing benefits, but while the side effects are still unknown, it effectively eliminates all traces of BRETH in those who consume it. Dante and I are in our lab and believe we have perfectly replicated his blood for mass consumption." He waved to someone off-screen and lightened his voice. "Come over here, don't be shy."

A boy with a fair complexion and a smattering of brown freckles across his nose entered the scene. His black hair was unruly, sticking up at all angles, and his grey eyes were glazed over, like he was tired. A small smile resembling a half-moon was hanging on his lips. My mouth completely dropped. It was me.

Only it wasn't.

My body had a visceral reaction to seeing the dad I kept sacred in my mind. The man who protected and loved me. Shock spread through my bones, knowing whatever was to come would change everything. My arms fell limp, and I found myself holding a breath hitched in my throat.

My father put his arm around the boy's shoulders. "We've used Vincent's DNA to create a perfect clone. Using its blood, we've conducted extensive tests to confirm it's identical to my son's." He lifted his chin and yelled, "Bring it in!"

My dad and the clone twisted their heads to the right. I squinted in the direction of their gaze, but all I saw was a shifting mass of pixels. I noticed a previously unseen door open, and an old man was shoved inside. His knobbly arms and legs looked like they were about to fall off, while its gray skin was tightly stretched over its bones.

My father turned toward the camera. "To test the clone's blood, we've brought in a subject who's been diagnosed with BRETH. We'll inject him with fresh blood, then monitor for side effects while doing extensive testing."

He raised the clone's arm and secured a rubber band around it. Plunging a needle into its arm, I saw his eyebrows flinch at the prick of pain. Dark red blood, thick and gleaming like liquid gold, filled the vial attached to the needle.

The frail old man limped toward the table, positioning his gnarled wrist before my father. He reached his other hand to his mouth, unleashing a wet, hearty cough. With a new needle inserted, the man's gray skin shifted to pink during the injection, before turning purple minutes later. With a choked cry, he threw his arms to his neck, then spurted red liquid across the room.

My father's expression shifted from serious to horrified. "Dante! Dante! Get in here! I think he's choking!" Reaching for the camera, he caused the image to become static, but when it cleared, only my father and the clone remained. "This experiment was not a success," he said to the camera, defeated. "The test subject's blood caused the man's throat to close, and upon further research, we found an allergen infused with this clone's DNA."

Jude's hand tightened on my shoulder. We both saw my father take the boy's hand and lead him out of sight. A gunshot rang from the speakers, followed by an audible thud. Even if we hadn't imagined it, the proof was undeniable: a white forehead and a mass of dark hair lay in a pool of blood on the floor before the body was removed.

My father carefully returned to the camera, setting a gun down on the table before wiping the blood from his hands. "We'll review the data and knowledge gained during this trial, then make a new clone, and try again." He took a deep breath, then expelled a heavy sigh. "I know we can do this."

The picture froze on my father's defeated face before I moved the cursor to the X in the right corner of the video. I was at a loss for words—it almost felt like what we just witnessed was fake. As my mind caught up, the strange detachment I experienced while viewing slowly faded, replaced by a clearer sense of my surroundings.

"What the fuck was that?" Jude gestured to the computer screen. "What did we just watch? And...what are all these other videos?"

"I-I had no idea," I breathed. I just watched him kill someone, no, not just someone, me. The shock left me both numb and violently shaking. "There were...*clones* of me?"

Jude pointed to the computer screen, his finger hovering over the brightly lit pixels. "Is this your *loving* father, Vin?"

I remained quiet. I knew my dad wasn't an angel, but the things I found out about him lately continued to depreciate my unwavering admiration for him. Walking through this secret lab, I didn't want to admit he was the creator of the Dogs and likely the person who kept them active. Now I'm learning he used my DNA to create clones to harvest their blood? My blood. What other secrets was he hiding?

I clicked on the following video, and my father's face appeared once again, looking well-rested and excited. Driven by curiosity, I needed to know the content of those videos and if his efforts eventually paid off, no matter how much time it took. The Dogs were disabled, what did I care?

"Trial number two," he said to the camera. "With extensive research, I believe Dante and I found the anomaly in the last subject's blood. We have found a way to correct it and created another clone of my son."

We watched as a large woman, wheezing and coughing violently, was shoved into the room. My father proceeded to extract the blood from the clone and inject it into the woman's bulbous arm. As the last of the vial's contents were used, a look of pure ecstasy washed over her face as her persistent cough subsided.

"I-I think we did it." My dad's voice trembled, a questioning edge cutting through the tremor.

My eyes were fixed on the woman, waiting to see her face turn blue or experience another unprecedented adverse reaction. At first, she stood frozen before the camera, her breathing slow and steady. I expected her to start choking again, but what unfolded was far more horrifying. Her eyes started bulging out of her head, and her legs began to spasm. It was like her extremities were trying to remove themselves from her body. A bloodcurdling scream tore from her throat as she launched herself at my father and the clone.

Fear glowed on my father's face as the woman began clawing at them and throwing her fists in the air. Her face blazed red, and the raw power in her roar sent tremors through me. I watched in horror as the crazed woman's fist connected with my father's face, the sickening thud echoing through the speakers, then her long fingernails raked down the clone's arms, leaving crimson streaks.

"Dante! Dante!" my dad screamed in terror as the woman hurled a nearby trash can with surprising force against the wall behind him.

As the woman descended upon them, I watched my father push the clone—push *me*—into the arms of the feral human. The woman grabbed the clone's shoulders firmly before lifting it up and sinking her teeth into its neck, tearing off a piece of flesh. A gunshot cracked through the air, and the woman crumpled to the ground.

"Research will continue, and we will develop a third trial." With a shaky hand, my father furiously clicked the camera and walked off camera. "Goddammit, Dante, we can't continue draining my son every year. We need to find the code, so our replicated blood doesn't have an expiration, so we can mass produce it for our benefactors." He must have thought the camera stopped recording, but it continued to document the empty room for an additional thirty minutes.

I don't know when I covered my mouth, but once I removed my hand, it was like I was able to breathe once again. Did he have any conscience? The image of him callously tossing the clone to its doom haunted me, and a chilling thought wormed its way into my mind: would he do the same to me?

"We don't need to watch anymore," Jude whispered. "All we're going to see is more of his heartless trials. It's disgusting."

I shook my head. "I need to see more. He's trying to find a way to copy my blood to last longer, and I need to know if there was ever a success."

"I don't think that's a good idea, but if this is what you want, I'll be here with you."

I smiled at him to show my appreciation. The only other person who would've been by my side was Gabe, but his response would likely be completely different. Less supportive, more dutiful. It was strange to have this feeling of someone who genuinely cared if I was okay, rather than because he had to be.

We sat together, the hours melting away as we watched video after video of the trials my father continued to record. For every trial, he followed the same procedure: first, outlining the experiment's parameters, then explaining the enhancements to the clone's blood, and finally, presenting a human suffering from BRETH. The only difference was that a loaded gun sat on the desk, ready in case the reactions posed a danger.

Each experiment led to disastrous results: allergic reactions and becoming dangerous, like the first two were common, but the non-standard trials were visions that would haunt me forever. One man, driven mad by an unbearable itch, scratched his skin raw until he bled to death, while another savagely attacked the clone, tearing its limbs from its body in a frenzied rage before a bullet reached his head. Some of the more traumatizing cases involved a few experiments who got hold of my dad's gun and ended their lives in front of the camera, showing a mixture of fear and relief on their faces before pulling the trigger.

Then we came to the last video.

"It is with regret to announce that Dante and I have agreed to halt the trials." My father's face was drawn, and the deep shadows under his eyes hinted at many sleepless nights. "We haven't been able to find a way to replicate the exact blood we need, which has caused us to reach its expiration. There have been many safety concerns, and I'll be unavailable to conduct these trials further as I'll be focusing my efforts on creating self-sustaining living quarters for all. Dante will be taking over in a secure environment going forward."

He was tired. My father was used to seeing results. He was a scientist, accustomed to experimentation, but the bitter taste of failure was something entirely new to him. It made sense he was passing the experiment to someone else to focus his efforts on something he knew he would excel at.

"It seems that finding a cure for the sickness we accidentally unleashed upon the world is more difficult than expected, but I know Dante will rise to the occasion. He's just as passionate about perfecting this cure as I. We will continue to manage the Dogs and remain in contact throughout this process while I negotiate with world leaders to end this war. Dante and I hold a great sense of guilt for our part in initiating The Great World War and are hoping to correct our mistakes."

He looked at the camera, a glimmer of light in his eye. He looked…human, like he cared.

"Holy shit," Jude breathed. "Your dad and Dante created the sickness, built the Dogs, *and* started the war in this lab. Together, they created the end of the world."

Chapter Twenty-Four

I'd been driving the electric car we charged at the gas station back in town for hours in silence. At one point, Jude attempted to turn the radio on to try to find anything to break the silence, but the static put me on edge. I needed to be alone with my thoughts. My body was shaking, and I was seething with anger. As we drove away from the small town, disbelief washed over me at what I discovered. There were thirty-five videos. Thirty-five versions of me were killed. Salvatore Asposito was one of the inventors of the Dogs. He's been maintaining them this whole time.

I felt ashamed. Embarrassed. Confused.

The long drive was a perfect vehicle to get lost in my thoughts. I totally forgot what it was like to just…drive. I'll admit, my initial reaction to Jude's request was far from enthusiastic, but after a brief argument, I gave in. I remember having my license before the apocalypse—my friends and I used to drive without a purpose, listening to music, and going wherever the sunset took us.

It reminded me of right now. The only difference was that when I was with my friends, I didn't want to murder my father. The sunset in front of us was magnificent. Hues of orange, blue, and pink painted the sky, each cloud resembling a breathtaking patchwork of farmlands. It was almost strange seeing such a beautiful landscape amid the desolate wasteland around us. The light coming through the windshield was a gorgeous amber color, as if infused with glitter.

It was the perfect time. Golden hour.

I turned to look at Jude in the passenger seat. His skin looked pristine in this light and almost exotic. How could he be this gorgeous? He was also in his thoughts as his head was turned to look out the grimy window, never blinking.

He squirmed uncomfortably in his seat, feeling my gaze on him. A half smile played on his lips, his eyebrows furrowing in a gesture of empathy, his face etched with concern. "So, uh… d'you wanna talk about everything we learned in the lab?"

I shook my head. I didn't. Not at all. But I needed to before we got back to Silvertown.

Jude began speaking before I could answer. "I just don't know why your father would keep the Dogs in commission. I've been racking my brain to think of what he would gain by making a deadly force that threatens both humans and vampires." He shrugged and squinted his eyes. "I mean, the Dogs have killed both species, it would make sense if they only attacked humans, you know?"

"Isn't it obvious?" I asked in disbelief, my eyes trailing the splotches of itchy red skin leading to my hands gripping the steering wheel. I knew he was smarter than this. "Control. He orchestrated all of this."

"Controlling each side with fear." Jude squinted, and his pupils shot back and forth. "And keeping this war between humans and vampires alive."

I nodded as the light in the sky started to wane. Even though I trusted Jude, I still cringe thinking about the look of suspicion and pity he gave me when we realized my dad did all these terrible things. I mean, he's the reason the entire human species is living like rats. The weight of my father's actions and the realization of how blindly I'd idolized him filled my body with shame. The feeling was both physically and emotionally draining, like a weighted blanket pressing down on me. How could I be so stupid? The golden glow slowly began to fade as the conversation progressed. "The Dogs were originally used to monitor citizens within the United States for the government and are essentially still used for the same purpose today. It's disgusting."

"At least he designed them not to hurt you. Every time they got near you, their eyes would blink white and retreat to the next person." Jude sat forward in the seat. "What d'you think your dad's using the intel for?"

"Whatever it is, there are only two things he cares about: wealth and power." I shook my head, thinking about the betrayal. "Oh, there's one more thing he cares about—manipulation."

"And how did he use you? Weren't you his precious son?" Jude's voice dripped with sarcasm as he drawled out the final two words.

"I always thought so, yeah." My voice shook with each syllable. "I always knew he was using me, but now that I know what he's done and how everything was meticulously planned, the betrayal feels like a knife in my back." I couldn't bring myself to look at Jude, so I kept my eyes on the cracked and broken road. "Back in Elysium, he locked me away. I wasn't allowed to leave my room. He kept me from everyone he could. To use me. To control me. The only time I was allowed out was for the Extraction."

"What's that?"

"They drain me until I'm a raisin, then lock me back up until the next year." I heard Jude gasp next to me. "The vampires need my blood to survive, and my father found a way to replicate it, but the shelf life only lasts a year. That's why I'm so valuable. Not because I'm his son. Because the vampire race depends on me."

Jude's eyes, intense and unwavering, didn't leave my face as he shifted closer. "Vinny, you can't tell anyone this information. If Arthur knew the only thing standing between him and the downfall of the vampires was you… he'd…he'd…"

"Kill me? Yeah, like that hasn't run through my mind since I got kidnapped."

"Arthur thought you were the key to turn off the Dogs, so he must've known your father was involved with them, but he definitely doesn't know *this* bit of detail. Let's keep it that way. I can't lose you. I won't."

We crested a hill, and I breathed a sigh of relief as the box-like building called Silvertown Mall came into view. The silence in the car was thick with unspoken words, and I needed some time alone to escape the awkward tension. As much as I appreciated Jude's support and care, it's not what I wanted right now. I need to be alone and wrap my head around all of this.

As we neared the mall, I got the sense that something wasn't right. The light around Silvertown had a strange shift, as if something had happened recently and the effects were still lingering.

"Holy shit," Jude yelled, jumping toward the dash. His face was inches away from the windshield, and his finger pointed toward the eastern wing of the defunct shopping center. "Our medical sector!"

A gasp caught in my throat as I struggled to contain a

scream. I pressed my foot harder on the pedal, the engine's low growl rising to a roar. An entire wing of Silvertown was completely gone. Debris from the mall was thrown all around, and dust hung low in the air. "What the fuck happened here?"

Barely a mile away, a sudden jolt and a screech of metal on asphalt signaled the wheels giving way. With a sharp twist of the steering wheel, I fought to keep the car from skidding off the icy road, the tires screaming in protest. I knew Jude was screaming next to me, but my ears didn't hear any sound. His arm crossed my chest, and the car slowed to a halt.

A dozen men, clad in gleaming white helmets and armor, charged toward us, their guns slung across their shoulders. "They shot at us." My words came out in breaths, and my body was fully tense.

The men reached the car, and they lowered their guns, ready to attack. Jude and I slowly raised our arms above our heads, palms open, to signal we meant no harm. The cold steel barrels of several guns smashed through the car windows, and I stared into the dark visor of one of the helmets. His aggressive stance softened instantly the second he saw the man beside me.

"Jude?" one man asked. "Is that you? We need to bring you to your father immediately."

"What happened here?" Jude screamed at the guards. "Is everyone alright?"

"A bomb exploded," the man dutifully advised. "Those in the wing died, but there were far more injuries."

We were forcefully pulled out of the car and made to stand in the middle of a circle of soldiers. Each of the men in armor surrounding us held their guns across their chests, ready to pull them down if any threat revealed itself.

Jude grabbed my hand as we briskly walked away from the broken-down electric car. "We cannot split up."

I nodded, my fingers intertwining with his, a feeling of safety washing over me as I knew Jude would keep me safe. We marched for what seemed like hours, though it was probably only a few minutes. You don't know how difficult it is to keep up a quick pace without stepping on the person directly in front of you.

The army led us to an old loading dock with a ramp leading downward. With a deafening rumble and a series of metallic clanks, a large metal gate groaned upward. Walking through the basement of the old mall, the army surrounding me began to disperse, revealing one person waiting for us ahead. With a sigh of relief, the figure removed their heavy silver mask. Arthur was present, his hands lost within the long sleeves of his white robes.

"Jude! Vincent! You're alive!" Arthur's eyes shone with an inner light, a wide, joyful smile stretching across his face. "What happened to the rest of the crew?"

"The Dogs got them, but the two of us managed to escape."

Arthur scanned me. "And you, Vincent? Are you okay?"

My abrupt statement tightened the air with tension. The only person who knew why is standing next to me. Jude's arm slid behind my back, and I closed my eyes, feeling tears prick my eyelashes. "Just really tired."

"Dad, what happened here?" Jude spread his arms wide. "How can I help?"

"We believe it was an attack by the vampires, although we aren't sure how they did it yet. We have troops scanning the area, looking for who may have planted the bomb." Arthur ran his fingers over his beard. "It happened shortly after you left, so our priority was caring for those that were still alive as well as fixing what we could so the Dogs couldn't get inside."

"They won't be an issue," Jude confidently smiled. "Well, at least most of them."

Arthur's eyes lit up, a grin stretching his lips as he considered the comment. "We must go to the council and hear of your findings immediately."

He began ushering us forward, but my feet felt rooted to the spot. I couldn't go and explain what we found out. Not yet. I still hadn't come to terms with all of this information myself. Plus, I was scared if Arthur found out, he and the other humans might turn on me. They could throw me back in jail or worse—decide I was no longer worth protecting as their captor.

Jude's grip on my shoulder tightened, and he shook his head. "Can we go to our quarters for the night?"

"I really feel the council should hear—"

"No." Jude's voice turned stern. "We need rest. Let's make sure everyone in Silvertown is safe. We have time to meet with the council."

There was a moment of silence before Arthur's upper lip stiffened. "Very well."

Jude's gorgeous eyes looked into mine, and he gestured ahead. We crept past Arthur and his army, their gazes burning into our backs, and walked down the hallway toward our sleeping chambers.

"Thank you," I said quietly.

"Don't thank me." Jude shook his head before stopping in front of my room. "Want me to join you?"

"Maybe later, I need some time alone." In truth, I craved Jude. More than sleep. More than a shower. I wanted to feel him once again. But the conflicted feelings and betrayal I festered in my core took over.

"I'm gonna go help those who are displaced from the

bomb." He placed a comforting hand on my shoulder, his brow furrowed with worry. "You sure you're okay?"

A heaviness settled in my head, blurring my vision, as a lump formed in my throat. Without allowing Jude to see my emotions, I opened the metal door to my small living quarters and closed it silently behind me. My body slammed against the door, and my legs turned to jelly. No more being strong. No more worrying about what Jude may think of me.

I crawled over to the bed on the far wall and threw myself on top. Silent tears streamed down my cheeks, each one hot and heavy, as my fingers fumbled blindly across the rumpled bed sheets in search of the pillows. I planted my face between two pillows, burying myself in their soft, downy fluff. In response, I let out a guttural scream, and my body began to convulse as I was finally ready to acknowledge my feelings.

I became lost and swallowed by the night. Alone.

I carry on, I carry on.

Chapter Twenty-Five

I lay in my tear-soaked bed with my knees tucked to my chest, wondering if I had another ounce of water in my body. It'd been years since I'd cried so uncontrollably. It was one of those scream into a pillow, rip your heart out, and try to catch your breath before you pass out kind of cries. The kind when you're *really* hurt.

There was so much I wasn't able to fully express to Jude. My dad was the catalyst for the end of the world. He made several copies of me, hoping to find one whose blood would serve his purpose. Were all the failed experiments considered my brothers? Through the years, this man's power remained absolute, using his pack of Dogs to intimidate both humans and vampires, a constant threat fostering an atmosphere of fear and division. He did all of this. And he used me to do it. To him, I was nothing more than a tool for power.

While he took away my own.

My body felt like a shell of itself. Completely hollow. My entire being was pouring out from my eyes and soaking into the rough sheets beneath me. My heaving sobs subsided, leaving me breathless and weighed down by exhaustion. I didn't want to continue…both on this journey and in life. I guess that's what happens when someone you love dies in your mind.

I'd been lost and consumed in my thoughts for what seemed like hours, slowly letting my thoughts eat away at my sanity. The sudden pressure of a strong arm encircled me, their body a comforting weight against mine. The scent of dirt and campfire engulfed my nostrils. Jude. When did he get here? How didn't I hear him enter?

He nuzzled his head into my neck, lightly kissing my shoulder. "I'm not here to make a move." His voice was soft and caring. "I just don't want you to feel alone."

I let him hold me. I needed it.

From the moment I was kidnapped by the humans, I knew Jude was my safety. I may have hated him and didn't fully trust him at the time, but I knew he would protect me. And he continued to do it. This was different for me. I wasn't used to someone caring for my feelings and showing physical emotion. I knew Gabe loved me, but it was always hard for me to get him to show affection. He had the capability, but it didn't come as easily as it did for Jude.

My body relaxed, and I eased into him; it was like our souls were merging. His excitement pressed against my back, his breath warm on my neck. I knew even though he was excited, he'd never act upon his desires. For that, it made me want him more.

I flipped around and burrowed my face into his warm, pillowy chest, my arms holding him tight. Venturing a glance at him, I saw the ghost of a smile on his lips as he lifted his hand, his touch gentle as he tucked my wild hair behind my ear. Heat rushed to my cheeks, turning them pink as I rubbed his back, feeling the warmth of his skin through my palm.

I lifted my head and felt the soft, warm press of two plump lips against mine. The kiss was tender but full of passion. White hot lust radiated off each of our bodies, tugging at our clothes as if they were expected to melt off.

And I knew I needed more.

I reached my arm out and grasped his underwear, feeling his girth in my hand. I began stroking him through the soft fabric, hearing his breathing grow heavier with each flick of my wrist.

"Vinny," he breathed. "This wasn't why I came in here."

I look down. Boxers? The least sexy underwear. Maybe humans wore them because they're easy to make with limited material? A low groan escaped his lips, barely audible, and I pushed the thought out of my head to focus on the task at hand.

Literally.

"I want you to fuck me," he moaned. His breathing became labored, and his eyes rolled back in his head. "I need to know how it feels."

"Okay." I nodded and bit my lip. "But I need *you* to fuck *me*, too. I need to feel something."

In response, Jude yanked his shirt over his head, and I shoved him onto his back with a grunt. Pulling myself close to his warm body, I lightly licked his neck, and his body squirmed beneath me. His movements as he slipped out of his boxers were so deliberate, it was clear he was ready, and the sound of his cock smacking against his abdomen confirmed it.

"Suck my cock."

I bent down and took him into my mouth, savoring the taste of the member I fantasized about since that night in the barn. Feeling his legs around my shoulders, I ran my tongue along the rim of his head, savoring the moment.

"Just like that," he breathed. "But be careful—I don't want you to get me close."

His back arched, causing his hole to come dangerously close to my pelvis. Reaching my fingers to my mouth, I generated enough lubrication before placing one hand on his chest as I inserted myself. As soon as I passed through, I threw my head backward.

Damn, he felt good.

I inched myself further and further inside, careful not to go too quickly. I didn't want to hurt him; I wanted him to enjoy every second of this. His body took well to my cock because after a few moments, he was able to fit my entire manhood, and his body wrapped around me. I slowly began to rock my hips in a circular motion, and Jude grasped my hand.

"Holy," he breathed, "fuck."

I looked down at him, feeling powerful. This man was looking at me like I was his god. His eyes were full of light, and his mouth agape as he watched me thrust in and out of him. With each movement I made, Jude expelled a breath of air like he died and came back to life.

I wished I had fangs, so he would be able to feel the intense pleasure of sex with a vampire. I wanted to feel in control. With a sigh, I moved my hands from his chest and clasped them around his neck. "Do you like this?"

A surprised twitch of his face showed in his wide, startled eyes. Maybe he was scared? He didn't resist or respond, so I continued tightening my fingers around his throat. My cock swelled as it slid in and out of him, as pleasure painted his face. I didn't clasp as hard as I wanted, only enough to put a slight, controlled pressure on his neck. I should have been nervous he wasn't into it, but I was having too much fun to care.

I could kill him right here if I wanted to.

Jude's breath quickened, and desire blazed in his expression as I pressed against his thighs, putting me further inside him than I'd ever been before. His cock was wet from precum and from inside my palm, and a moan traveled from his esophagus and out his mouth. He liked this.

Pressure built inside me, and I knew if I stayed in Jude, it would be over. I needed more from him. "Let's switch, I want you to fuck me, Jude."

"Huh?"

"I said. *Fuck. Me.*" I gently withdrew my throbbing cock from his quivering ass and positioned myself on all fours, eager for his response.

"I-I'm so close, though."

"I don't care," I barked at him. "*Just fuck me.*"

As he positioned himself behind me, I heard a sound escape from his lips and felt the warmth of his head against my core. He reached for my hip bones before ushering himself inside. His girth expanded gradually with each slow stroke, reaching deeper inside me.

"Fuck me, Jude," I begged. "Harder." Feeling his movement quicken, I let out a satisfied moan. I needed this. I needed him. His perfectly timed thrusts sent waves of pleasure through me, causing me to let out unrestrained moans as he hit just the right spot.

Oh my God, his cock felt amazing. Heavenly.

Biting his bottom lip, Jude loosened his grip on me, slowing his pace. "You okay?"

I needed more. I twisted my head around and looked deep into his eyes, gritting my teeth. "Shut the fuck up and keep going."

His lips curved into a smirk as he spun me around, his manhood never leaving my center. His arms held me close, and my cock twitched every time he administered long, intentional strokes. With a forceful touch, he grabbed my inner thigh, urging me to welcome him even further.

"I want to watch you come."

His entire length was inside me, the pleasure radiating out of my every pore. My knee was near my ear, and the warmth of his breath was on my cheek. I was captivated by the way his mouth hung slightly open, and his eyes would roll intermittently as he thrust into me.

"Oh fuck," he whispered.

I whimpered, feeling my legs begin to shake as he pumped harder. I felt my orgasm building to its peak as the pressure mounted inside me. Stretching my leg over his shoulder, Jude's cock found its place perfectly, and a rush of euphoria pulsed in my core. I struggled to see clearly as a surge of pleasure consumed me as ropes burst from my cock, painting my stomach and chest.

"Oh my God, Vinny." Jude's face twisted, and his eyebrows furrowed. He pinched his eyelids closed and let out a series of moans, his face looking as if he found paradise.

Maybe he had.

His cock pulsed inside me, twitching uncontrollably. He released my leg from his grip before entirely collapsing on top of me. His blond hair tickled my chin as his head lay atop my chest, his light chest hair sticky with our aftermath. He hadn't removed himself from me, and although he wasn't as strongly erect anymore, I could still feel him.

"I-I'm sorry," Jude whispered, his breath blowing across my nipples like a gust of wind. "I should've made it last longer."

Threading my fingers through his hair, I put my other hand over his arm. "It was perfect, stop apologizing." We lay together for a few moments, our breaths completely in sync.

"I just want to be as good as-as-what's his name?"

A pain pierced my chest just before the sounds of shouting and crashing echoed from the hallway. A terrifying yell ripped through the air, followed by the sickening thud of bodies repeatedly slamming against the outside wall. A loud crash, followed by shouts and the scrambling of feet, echoed down the hallway toward my room, making me strain to hear what was going on. I heard one man say, "apprehend his hands," while another yelled, "stop fighting or we'll sedate you."

The next sound I heard caused my body to freeze. I knew Jude could feel something was wrong the moment my muscles tensed, a cold sweat prickling my skin, and a strangled gasp tore from my chest. From the hallway, a man's voice, strong and resonant, echoed, each word distinct and clear.

"Where's Vincent, you fucks? I need to see him! BRING ME TO HIM."

It was Gabe. He was here.

Chapter Twenty-Six

I stormed through Silvertown Mall, the dirty tiled floors echoing under my feet. A furious fire burned in my eyes, and my skin crawled with an army of unseen bugs. Blind rage consumed me, my head spun, the taste of bile rose in my throat, but I remained determined. I knew I heard Gabe. Where was he? Was he safe? If a single hair on his head was harmed, I swear I'd burn this whole sanctuary to the ground.

"Vinny, slow down!" Jude ran up behind me, grabbing my arm.

Feeling his touch, I slapped it away. "Lemme go!" I spun around, and my voice, amplified by the adrenaline, was far louder than I anticipated. "I don't have time for you right now. I need to find Gabe."

"I need you to stop."

Jude's grip on my shoulder was like a vise, and he shoved me against the wall. If I weren't so concerned and angry, this would've turned me on. His face was a mask of stone, immobile and emotionless, the muscles of his jaw clenched tight. This is how I knew he meant business. I tried pushing away from him, but he held firm.

"Breathe." His voice was calm, like the ocean at midnight. "I need you to take a breath."

He was right. I needed to calm down. There were too many emotions flying around today, and I need to re-focus. This is why I grew feelings for Jude. He was kind and considerate. He cared about me. I took a few deep breaths, feeling the muscles in my shoulders loosen.

"Thank you," he cooed. "I called for an immediate meeting with my father. I did it for you." His crystal-clear eyes were full of adornment. "Let's go to the theatre, he should be waiting for us there."

Of course he did this for me. Do I deserve someone so nice?

I wrapped my arms around his neck and gave him a hug. "Thank you," I breathed into his ear. The strength of his arms squeezed me, and his lips brushed my neck. I laced my fingers through his, the warmth of his hand a comfort as we walked to the room where Arthur awaited.

Ascending the stairs, a wave of people flowed past us, up and down, more than we ever saw before. Even stranger, they were dressed in civilian clothes; this wing was strictly for military personnel.

"They're displaced," Jude advised, seeing me lock onto every human that passed. "Since they're our healers, all medical equipment has been moved to the safety of our old town underground until we can rebuild or at least find them somewhere to live."

We left the military wing of Silvertown and went down the hallway to the old cinema. Entering the gates, we passed the old popcorn machine and ticket booth, then proceeded down the dimly lit hallway on the faded carpet.

Passing numerous doors with imposing numbers, we arrived at number thirteen, which hung slightly ajar.

Standing inside, Arthur stood with his back to us, his fingers clasped together, resting just above his buttocks with his shoulders pushed back. A wide smile stretched across his bearded face as he saw us, his arms extending in greeting. "Jude, Vincent! Thank you for calling this meeting with me."

"Where's Gabe?" I pushed Arthur's arms out of the way, looking around the room for the vampire man. I didn't want to waste time on pleasantries; I needed to know he was okay.

Arthur's white eyebrows lifted. "Gabe? Is that the name of the vampire man who blew up our medical wing that we found half frozen outside?"

My heart jolted, then skipped a beat, as if it stopped entirely for a second. Gabe couldn't have detonated the bomb, could he? My brain said no, but my heart had other assumptions. Could he have been convinced to do it in order to save me? "Where is he?"

Arthur held up one knobbly finger. "First things first. I need to know what you found when you followed the homing device we extracted from the Dog's head."

Jude cleared his throat before summarizing the events in the town and laboratory. He told Arthur that half the Dogs were temporarily disabled, and to reset them all, they needed to find the secondary deactivation site. Thankfully, he left out any mention of the unsettling clones of me—a detail I was grateful for.

Arthur shook his head with a snarl pulling at his upper lip. "I knew Salvatore had something to do with those damn Dogs. There's no way he couldn't have."

"Not just the Dogs." My voice was shaking. "He brought about this whole apocalypse."

"And how do you feel about that?" His voice rose in pitch, the inflection hinting at a genuine interest in my response.

I lifted my head and locked eyes with the leader of the humans. "It's completely irredeemable. When I first got here, I thought humans were the enemy, but now I know you're just like me—forced to be locked away by my father, hoping for one day to be free." Arthur lingered on me for a few moments. I wasn't sure if it was disbelief or if he was scanning me for verification. All night, I'd been thinking about what I was going to do next. The thought of returning to Elysium and pretending everything was fine was unbearable, but I also couldn't stay in Silvertown living in shambles for the rest of my life. There was one thing I knew: I needed to end my father's reign. "You have my complete cooperation to bring him down."

"How will you do that? Do you want to see his end at your own hand?"

I shook my head. "I'd like to be clear: taking him down will not involve his death. I-I can't let him die. We need to take away his power, that's a fate worse than death in his eyes, and I know exactly how to do it."

"I trust you." Arthur clasped his fingers together. "I'll leave you to handle your father, but in exchange, I need to get into his vault. We suspect the code for creating vampires is inside, along with blueprints for the Dogs. I want both of those secrets."

"Deal." I nodded. I knew if any of the humans got hold of my father, the likelihood of his survival would decrease. So I needed to do it myself.

"My goal is to bring vampires and humans together and rebuild a new world. I'm excited to start this new chapter with you and our mutual respect for one another."

Arthur put a reassuring arm across my shoulder. "Did you find a file showing where the second location is?"

Jude shrugged and shook his head. "There was no indication where, just a video stating there was another that is managed by his partner, Dante."

"Ah, yes." Arthur snapped his fingers and gestured to me. "When we first met, you asked if I knew anything about this Dante character. I discovered through my father's old journals that sixty-five years ago, he was banished from Elysium and found his way underground, where we were living at the time. He assisted us in siphoning electricity from the vampires, which gained him trust from our leaders."

I was hanging on every word Arthur was telling me. What happened to Dante? If he were still alive, he'd likely be just as dangerous as my dad.

"He helped create the Silvertown you see today, he aided us in harvesting crops, developing medicine, and assited in stealing technology from the vampires for our own use. As time went on, his own hubris was his downfall. He thought he could overthrow our democracy and, like Elysium, was dismissed from Silvertown as well. Any mention of him was removed from texts due to his mutinous attempt."

"Did your father write where he went after his banishment?" The story didn't surprise me. Dante also turned his back on my dad, which led to their falling out.

Arthur shook his head. "There has been no word from him since, and considering his age, it's safe to assume he passed away many years ago. Nevertheless, his laboratory must still be operational, and we need to find a way to disable the Dogs to take down your father."

I knew what I had to do and exhaled a long breath of air. "I can find out, just tell me where Gabe is."

A flash crossed Arthur's pupils, and he paused. He opened his mouth to answer several times, but then paused, a thoughtful frown etching itself onto his face as he reconsidered his response. Moments passed before his deep voice echoed off the walls. "Guards, please enter."

The two guards, stiff in their identical uniforms, pivoted inward. Almost in perfect unison, they walked toward Arthur and crossed their chests dutifully with guns before stopping, their backs taut.

"I need you to bring Vincent to our most recent prisoner, who is being housed in a cell downstairs."

Jude clasped my hand in his. "I'm going with him."

Arthur placed his arm between us, severing the space we shared. "You are not. We have much more to discuss."

"But Dad…"

"I will not hear anymore." Arthur's voice went stern. "If Vincent can find out where this laboratory is through the vampire man, let him do it alone." With a flourish of his hand, he dismissed the guards, still locked on Jude.

As I stepped out the door, I turned my head back to see Jude staring at me. His face was etched with worry, as if he wanted to rush to my side and hold me forever. To put him at ease, I offered a reassuring smile. I can do this.

The two soldiers led me down a seemingly endless series of dimly lit hallways and echoing staircases, each step taking us deeper into the bowels of the mall. The familiar string lights hanging from the cracked walls cast a warm glow, reminding me of my first visit. Following the downward curve of the steps, we were deposited at the bottom, where a massive metal door stood, barring the way into the jail.

One of the guards opened the door and spoke to me in a gruff voice. "Your friend is in cell six."

I nodded and hesitantly breached the threshold, feeling

the weight of countless prisoners watching my every move. The lighting cast an eerie orange glow along the walls, and my shadow jumped at me with every step. Passing the pale, zombie-like humans in each cell made me wonder what they did to be thrown in here. The echoing silence and the musty smell of mildew made me think of a haunted house, and I half-expected someone to jump out and scare me.

"Gabe?" I whispered into the vast area, hearing only sniffles and coughs in the dank space. I stopped walking and quieted my breathing, straining my ears for any sound.

A rustling sounded in a cell toward the far end of the jail. A surprised voice penetrated the silence. "Vin? Is that you?"

My heart leaped into my throat, and I practically ran toward the cell from which I'd heard his voice. The metal bars blurred past as I glimpsed a large, hunched shadow on a cot in the dimly lit prison cell. The number six glared at me from a heavy padlock that detained him. "Gabe?"

The shadow straightened, its head turning slowly as it brushed the long, dark hair from its face. The shadow's intense gaze pierced my soul, and it darted towards the metal bars. "Vinny! It is you! You're safe!"

Hearing his voice, my body felt lighter, though the persistent itch remained. It was a sound I didn't think I'd ever hear again. I inhaled deeply, drinking in the familiar sound of his voice before I dropped to my knees, my arm sliding through the rusty bars. "Are you alright? Please tell me you're okay. Did they hurt you?"

The weight of his thick body pressed against the cell as he wrapped his calloused palms around my slender fingers. "I'm fine now that you're here. Have they hurt *you* at all?"

The unexpected question made me stop short, a knot of surprise tightening in my chest. The humans haven't hurt me. Everything we've been told about them was wrong. I shook my head, relief washing over me. "They said they found you almost frozen to death."

"I've been traveling for days in the snow, hoping to find you."

"You found me." A smile crossed my face before a thought struck me. Gabe was part of my father's entourage. A loud, hearty cough emanated from a nearby cell, and the prickling sensation of bile rose in my throat. I took a breath, not prepared for his answer to my next question. "Did you detonate the bomb?"

Confusion etched itself onto his face as his thick eyebrows furrowed. "Bomb? What are you talking about?"

"Gabe, I need you to be honest with me. It's the only way I can save you."

He shook his head and brushed the hair out of his eyes. "I'm being truthful, I swear."

I searched his face, hoping to catch a flicker of deception in his pupils. But I found only an honest gaze staring back. "Did my dad send you here?"

His lips turned into a straight line, and his jaw clenched. "After you were kidnapped, your father turned cold. I begged him to let me organize a search party, but he refused. We got into a heated argument before he threatened me and my job."

This news didn't shock me. My dad was spiteful, and in the face of any opposition, he needed to prove who was in charge. Nevertheless, a gasp escaped my throat, and I clutched my palm over my open mouth. Besides me, Gabe's job was the only other thing he loved. It was part of him, a defining aspect of his identity. How dare my father threaten to take that away from him?

"After he did that, I packed a bag and left Elysium to come find you." He tightened his grip on my hand. "If he wasn't going to help, I'd do it myself...or at least die trying. Without you, my world ended, and I've always said—"

"You want me to be near so if there's ever another apocalypse, your life can end where it began." My heart elated, feeling like a balloon inside my chest as he nodded. "I need to ask you one more question."

"Anything."

I swallowed the lump that formed in my throat. "I found out a lot about my dad while I have been here. Do you know what he did?"

"Are you talking about the Dogs?" His mouth frowned. "Only his inner circle knows he controls them, and we've been sworn to secrecy. I've seen him feed many friends of mine to the Dogs for so much as using his name and the Dogs in the same sentence." His eyes were wet and pleading. "I couldn't tell you without fear I'd be next."

He knew this entire time. As hard as it was to grasp, I did understand why he couldn't tell me. "So you don't know what he did to this world? To me?"

His face reddened, and his voice grew angry. "What did he do to you?"

I held my wrist out to feed him while recounting the events that had unfolded since my arrival at Silvertown Mall and the horrors I witnessed inside the laboratory. Well, maybe not everything. I, of course, left out the portions about Jude and I. Which I still didn't really understand yet.

I described how my father profited from the end of the world, and his face went slack with shock, his mouth hanging open. Then, when I recounted the video on the computer and the failed clones, he gasped. To me, his reactions validated he knew nothing. And I believed him.

"That motherfucker." Gabe's voice was an angry whisper. "I can't believe I did that man's dirty work. He was like a father to me."

"He *is* my father—how do you think *I* feel?" My voice quivered, but I remained firm. "I'm done with him. I'm going to bring him down for everything he did."

"How? Are you-are you going to *kill* him?"

A cold stare adorned my face. Did I want to kill him? If the roles were reversed, I'm sure he'd have no hesitation ending my life. "I'm not like him. To bring him down and make things right with the humans, I won't let him harvest my blood. I'm refusing to take part in the Extraction and without my blood, his empire will fall."

Gabe's warm brown eyes met mine, and he nodded. "I'll be by your side through it all."

I reached through the metallic bars and ran my fingers through his thick, wavy hair. Wrapping my fingers around his head, I brought him closer to the bars until our lips touched. His soft rose petal lips brushed against mine, and his strong hand gently cupped the side of my head. Gabe didn't kiss me often, but when he did, it was raw passion. This is what I missed. I know if he were out of this cell, he'd rip my clothes off.

Through our strained breaths, I pulled away. "I've missed you."

"You don't even know how much I missed you, Vin."

We pressed our foreheads together, my voice trembling with a mix of fear and excitement. "I-I need to hurt him like he hurt me. D-do you know w-where Dante's lab is? Or have any idea? W-we need to disable the Dogs to get to him."

Gabe grunted and shrugged. "I have an idea. Years ago, I accompanied your dad to a hidden location in the mountains that was surrounded by Dogs. He didn't allow me to go inside, but if I had to guess, it's there."

I nodded, knowing he was telling me the truth.

"I love you, Vinny. I'd do anything for you." He smiled and let out a slight chuckle. "I guess that's how I'm in this jail cell."

I wasn't sure if it was the exhaustion weighing on me, the turmoil in my heart, or the unexpected comfort I felt with Gabe, but we both laughed. I didn't have it in me to say it back because my new relationship with Jude made my feelings all the more complicated.

It was reassuring to know that even though our environment was grim, we still had each other.

Chapter Twenty-Seven

"We *have* to stop meeting here!" Jude, Arthur, and I returned to the room, only to find it filled with the hushed whispers and serious faces of the council members. I'd hoped my sarcastic quip would lighten the serious mood in the council chamber, but the council members remained as stony-faced as gargoyles.

"Where did the vampire advise the second laboratory is?" The red-haired woman looked at me expectantly, like I owed her a response.

"He didn't." Arthur's head turned to the council, then to me. "Vincent, care to explain?"

I nodded. "*Gabe* remembers going there once, a long time ago, but cannot pinpoint where it is by memory."

"Then what good is he?" With a sigh, the short council member threw his arms up, his sleeves falling slightly. "He bombed our medical wing. Kill him!"

"He didn't bomb anything!" I screamed. "You don't know what you're talking about."

"Let's not do anything rash. How about we bring him in to get more information?" Arthur raised his stubbled white beard to the door. "Men, please bring us the prisoner."

My mind was put at ease, knowing Arthur was on our side and would make sure nothing happened to Gabe, despite what the council wanted. He wanted the Dogs deactivated as much as anyone else, so why not work together? I held my breath, every nerve ending tingling as the distinct sound of approaching soldiers' boots neared the room. Jude tenderly grabbed my hand, but I snuck a look at my boyfriend before shaking it away.

Gabe entered with both men on each side of him. His hands were secured behind his back with a thick, knotted rope, and a heavy, suffocating mask was strapped to his face. The cold steel of a gun barrel pressed against his back, urging him forward, while the hum of tasers poised nearby threatened any sudden movement.

"Gabe!" I ran to him, the buzzing of the bat-like tasers filling my ears as the guards waved them menacingly close to my face.

A jolt ran through the air as Gabe shifted uncomfortably upon seeing me, the distinctive buzzing and crackling of tasers filling the silence. The bat in the guard's hand came to life, and a blue light flashed through the room as it touched Gabe's skin. His screams, sharp and piercing, echoed through the empty room and the long hallways as he fell to his knees.

I spun around, fury blazing in my eyes, and glared at the council. "Release him right now."

"He's a criminal, a danger to all of us."

"He is *not*!" My voice cracked as I yelled at them. "Am I? Is that what you think of me?" I scanned the council's stoic, unmoving faces before finally settling on Arthur's. I breathed out a large puff of air. "Please."

"Do you take responsibility for him?" A flash of light,

like a sudden spark, glinted in Arthur's eyes. "If he chooses violence, we'll shoot him dead."

I searched Gabe's face and found my answer, nodding slowly. The guards backed away, both with their guns locked onto the back of Gabe's wavy black hair. I carefully removed the mask from his mouth and the tight cuffs from his wrists. "Are you okay? Did they hurt you?"

He was breathing heavily and whispered each word. "I'll kill all of them. I'll-I'll rip them to shreds and-and drain their blood until they're nothing but an Exile."

I gently cupped his face, tracing the line of his jaw with my thumbs. "You *need* to stay calm. I need them to trust you." A silent understanding passed between us as Gabe's gaze held mine, a connection deeper than words. He gave in and entrusted his life to me. I grabbed his hand, and together we rose to our feet, a united front against the council. It felt good not to be so alone, to have people I could truly depend on. "You have our full cooperation."

The red-haired woman's chin jutted out in a clear show of disdain. "Prove it. Where's the second lab?"

Gabe looked at me, lingering for a moment before he turned back to the hushed council. "In a small valley within the mountains. I don't know exactly where, but I remember the general location and various markers to find it."

The council members threw their heads back, laughing. "So you *don't* know where it is? Fabulous!"

"Hold on." Arthur raised his hand. "I'm confident that if Gabe were in the mountains, he'd be able to find the location. Am I right?"

I turned to look at the man beside me, a sneer twisting his lip. His eyes flickered from one person to another before resting on Arthur. "Absolutely."

"So it's decided." Arthur clapped his hands together.

His chin pointed at Jude. "My qualified son will organize a group to head into the mountains with Gabe as our navigation."

"B-but Dad," Jude stammered, his voice shaking nervously. "I cannot trust that-that vampire. Will he have a mask and handcuffs on for the whole trip?"

I gasped and spun my head. Is Jude really saying this in front of me? The way he spat the word 'vampire' left a sour taste in my mouth. My lip curled, a grimace tightening my jaw as my fingers clenched into a fist.

"Not at all." Arthur extended an arm toward me, his palm facing upward. "Our friend Vincent here will join you on this mission. He has taken full responsibility for all of his friends' actions."

"B-but…"

"And you trust *him*, correct?"

Jude's head jerked toward me, his eyes both scared and confused. "Of course I do."

"Then it's settled." Arthur's jaw tightened, a snarl on his lips as he addressed Jude. "Gather a group, pack supplies, and ensure the snowmobiles are charged." He snapped his fingers, and the two guards who were pointing their guns at the back of Gabe's head ascended onto him. "Restrain the vampire and get him back into his cell."

My knuckles turned white as I squeezed Gabe's hand, terrified of letting go. "If I take responsibility for him and you're confident enough to have him join us on the mission, he shouldn't spend the night apprehended in jail."

Arthur narrowed his eyes, a calculating glint in them, as he considered my request. "As you wish, but if any harm comes to my people, it'll be both of your heads."

I looked at Gabe, who gave a silent nod in understanding. "You have nothing to worry about."

"As you wish." Arthur slightly bowed. "Our meeting is adjourned."

Jude turned to leave, his gaze lingering on me, a silent, burning intensity in his eyes that made my skin tingle. A negative vibe permeated my soul as daggers were being thrown my way by the man I loved.

Well, one of them, anyway.

"You saved me." Gabe's voice was appreciative, and his body enveloped me in a meaningful hug as Jude left the room.

"Someone had to." I laughed and hugged him back. "Let me show you around."

Leaving the movie theatre, no words escaped our mouths as we were surrounded by the growing number of guards, their presence a heavy weight. There was one in front of every door with guns crossing their bodies, their eyes watching us from beneath their metal horse masks. Exiting the tense area, the palpable tension in the air dissipated, and Gabe and I both breathed a sigh of relief.

"Was that weird or is it just me?"

"It was weird." He nodded, lowering his voice. "Are you really trusting these *humans*?"

Passing by bustling shops, the vibrant energy of the mall enveloped us as we turned right toward the center. "I don't know who to trust anymore," I admitted. "But I know my dad is the enemy. The humans have only been kind and supported me while I've been here."

"You know you can trust me, right?"

I glanced over my shoulder, noticing a lone guard trailing us. I didn't care; it made sense if Jude couldn't be with me, someone else would protect Silvertown's residents. "You're one of the only people I can trust, Gabe." I needed to figure out what my relationship with Jude meant now that my boyfriend had shown up.

We entered the bustling center of the mall, where a sea of people bustled before us. As twilight deepened, people gathered around the carts, their hands reaching for the steaming dinner packages.

"Should we grab something to eat?" Gabe asked, looking at the lines of dirty humans. "All I've had is slop while in my cell."

A sharp, acidic taste developed at the back of my throat. My hand flew to my mouth as a spasm of nausea hit me, but vanished as quickly as it appeared. "The food out here is probably comparable to what you ate in jail."

"Are you okay?"

My stomach was gurgling, and I had no idea what was happening to me. Itching the back of my arm, I nodded. "Just been feeling sick lately, I'm sure it'll pass."

His face scrunched as he looked around the area. "These people are disgusting." Gabe craned his neck, looking in all directions. "Is this how they *live*?"

"It was a shock to me, too."

To our left, a loud gasp was followed by a wet splat. Turning my head, I saw a girl with a halo of wild, dark curls surrounding her oversized glasses. At her feet lay a tray of food, scattered across the ground. In shock and surprise, she gasped, her hands flying up to cover her mouth.

A large smile graced my face, and a laugh caught in my throat. I waved my hand, beckoning her to come over. "Hi, Vanessa!"

With a shy smile and a small, trembling wave, she timidly sauntered toward us. "H-hi, Vinny." She scanned Gabe from head to toe, and she bit her bottom lip. "Is this who I think it is?"

"Nessa, meet Gabe. My boyfriend from Elysium." I

held my arms out like I was presenting at an award show. "You know, the one I told you about?"

An excited squeal escaped from Nessa's mouth. "A tall, dark, and handsome man with perfectly coiffed hair and a gorgeous five o'clock shadow? I instantly knew it was him as soon as I saw you two together!" She danced around in front of us. "You're right, he's even *hotter* than how you described him!"

"Uh…I'm right here?" Although he was accustomed to adoration in Elysium, Gabe secretly relished the attention. The murmur of compliments was a soothing balm to his ego.

I giggled. "How's everything been here?"

Gabe held her gaze, and she was captivated by him. I'm sure it felt as if she was looking at a mythical being, and if she blinked, he would vanish. With a heart-struck smile plastered on her face, she made sure her eyes never left him. "Here? Good, fine. Everything's fine."

I crossed my arms and snapped my fingers in front of her face. "Everything's fine? What about the bomb?"

She shook her head as if she had come out of a trance. "Right, the bomb, yes." She scrunched her frizzy hair. "Not many people died, luckily. Some of those that did had families, and now we're unsure what to do with the orphaned children."

"Do you know who did it? Are there any rumors?" Gabe asked.

Nessa's large eyes panned over to me. "Even his voice is dreamy, like warm molasses."

Whatever that means.

"We don't know who detonated the bomb, probably the vampires, if I had to guess."

"Gabe," I turned to him, "if it wasn't you, is there a chance it was someone who worked for my father?"

"I was traveling here for days and didn't see anyone out there." He shrugged and shook his head. "But I suppose it is possible, your dad is a powerful man. He's done many things I thought weren't possible."

Nessa grabbed my hand. "Come, please have dinner with me tonight, both of you."

I shook my head. "It's really okay, we should rest."

Her fingers traced the contours of Gabe's muscular arm. "Just a bite?"

Gabe nodded to me, his fangs fully extending. "Just a bite."

Chapter Twenty-Eight

An icy wind whipped against my body, but I held my arms firmly around Jude's waist. The snowmobile rattled and bucked its way through the snowy landscape, the occasional jarring bumps a welcome distraction for my itchy, restless body. We'd been driving for what felt like an eternity, and my body felt numb from the freezing cold.

As we navigated the vast, windswept tundra, the biting wind stinging our faces, my mind replayed the events leading up to our departure. I'd been sleeping soundly, the thin pillows cradling my head, feeling soft and luxurious against my cheek. The scratchy blanket wrapping around my body felt like a heavy comforter, and the hard mattress I lay upon could've been made of spikes, but I was so tired that I didn't mind. Throughout the night, dreams came to me easily, and my subconscious drifted from one restful dream to another.

A loud *bang* interrupted my slumber, and hearing the noise caused my body to jump. My eyes snapped open in terror, expecting a snarling pack of Dogs to be in my room, ready to pounce. Instead, I saw Jude standing in front of the metal door to my room, holding two large fur-lined jackets with a scowl adorning his face.

Gabe ran in from the adjoining room with an angry look on his face. "Are you okay?"

I found myself unable to look away from his sculpted body, admiring the way his hair perfectly complemented his toned abs and chest. Sitting up in bed, I tore my gaze from the breathtaking figure standing before me, turning to the surprised blond man now at the foot of my bed. I'm sure he expected Gabe and me to be in the same bed, but seeing him realize how wrong he was filled me with quiet satisfaction.

And I reveled in that.

The helmet I wore made the gusts of wind with pancake-sized snowflakes almost disappear. Gabe's tall frame was rigid as he sat on the snowmobile, his powerful arms gripping the handlebars, the roar of the engine vibrating through the snow. I bit my lip to stifle my laughter as a large man slid wildly back and forth in the car due to Gabe's reckless driving. Behind us, another snowmobile trailed, carrying two more, and together, the three machines formed Jude's lab-finding team.

Gabe pointed to our left, his finger sharp and precise, and the vehicles smoothly veered in the correct direction. How long were we going to be out here? Did Gabe know where he was going? I looked toward the sky, and the muted sun, a hazy orange orb, dropped lower. Night would be coming soon, and we needed to find a hidden spot to set up camp, especially if we were getting closer to the lair.

Ahead of us, large snow-topped mountains loomed, their peaks piercing the gray sky, as our snowmobiles entered the pristine, untouched terrain. A path opened at the bottom of the hill, and Gabe's vehicle came to a gentle halt, signaling us to follow. With a collective groan, we pushed ourselves up from the uncomfortable seats, kicking out our legs to ease the stiffness. I wasn't even sure if my legs would work; I couldn't feel them. I was shocked when my body lifted from the hard seat, but I soon fell sideways, feeling a void in mobility stemming from my buttocks. As my body crashed to the ground, my face slammed into the snow, the sharp icy crystals digging into my skin with the force of a thousand tiny glass shards.

Of course I'd make an ass of myself.

Jude and Gabe ran to me, one on each side, and hoisted me up with a surprising ease. Their words melded in my mind, their inaudible concern muffled in my ears. Extending my arms, I pushed both of them away. "Both of you! Get the hell off me!"

Gabe hooked a finger under the chin strap of his helmet and swiftly pulled it off. The helmet hit the ground with a dull thud, sending a small cloud of fluffy snow into the air. His brows were narrow, and his pupils completely took over his eyes. "Why are you touching my man?" With one palm, he pushed Jude's shoulder. "He said to get the fuck off of him."

"I was just helping him," Jude snarled. "Back off, bro."

Gabe's jaw clenched, his teeth grinding together, a muscle twitching in his cheek. "Back off? You're telling me to back off? Who the fuck are you, *bro*?" He pushed Jude once again, who stumbled backward.

"What's your issue?"

"What's *my* issue?" Gabe spat back. "What's *your* issue?" With that, he lunged at Jude, the force of the impact sending a spray of powdery snow above as they tumbled together.

I watched in horror as both of their bodies entwined. Fists blew through the air as they tumbled through the snow. The other two guards sprinted toward them, weapons drawn. I ran in front of them. "Stop! You can't hurt either of them." I turned my head to the two men punching each other on the ground. "Can you two STOP?"

Gabe's knuckles connected with Jude's face, a sickening crunch accompanying the whoosh of air leaving Jude's lungs. The next thing I heard was Jude mutter something under his breath, followed closely by a grunt from Gabe. If I allowed this to continue, they'd kill each other.

Maybe it's for the best.

"Both of you. STOP!" I screamed so loud, it's a wonder how all the snow didn't avalanche from the mountains. Blood stained the pure white snow in beautiful splatters that could rival any painting. I thought about intervening, but the sheer intensity of their anger made me back down; their rage was too powerful.

Out of nowhere, the twin blasts of gunfire echoed. A sharp crack echoed as the blow landed squarely on Jude and Gabe's necks, sending them to the ground. Fresh red liquid splattered on top of the old, bloodstained snow. The two men froze in their spots, and two more gunshots sounded through the air, hitting them squarely in the chest. Both of them fell to the ground, and their fighting ended.

My eyes widened as I saw both of them lying on the ground with red gunshot wounds, covered their chests. "Gabe! Jude!" My initial reaction was to rush to them to make sure they were okay, but I needed to know where the shots had come from. Otherwise, I'd be next. The two soldiers behind me raised their guns and scanned the landscape, their faces grim as they tried to pinpoint the source of the gunfire.

Despite my heart rhythmically thumping against my chest, it felt like it was slowly breaking as I scanned the craggy mountains. I just got Gabe back. I wanted to explore my relationship with Jude further. And now both of them were gone. I was all alone in the world. Once again. A hollowness cascaded over my body—whoever did this was going to pay.

"Holy fuck! What was that?"

Jude. That was Jude's voice. But he was shot once in the neck and again in the chest. There's no way he'd still be alive. I scanned the mountains, thinking I saw movement, but it was just the tendrils of snow floating in the wind.

"That got da both o' yer to stop, di'nt it?"

A shadowy figure slid down the steep, snow-covered slope, his feet kicking up a small cloud of powdery snow. I raised my arm at the two people behind me and quietly whispered, "Don't shoot." I wanted to see who this was. With a groan, Jude and Gabe pushed themselves up from the snow, the cold seeping into their numb arms. How were they alive?

The man walked closer, and I squinted, trying to make out his features in the dim light. The stout man wore faded blue overalls, their denim worn soft from years of labor, and his sturdy build filled them out. A scraggly white beard, coarse and thick, cascaded from his chin, reaching his torso. His bushy white eyebrows, thick as caterpillars, were perched so high on his forehead they almost appeared to be part of the brown hat atop his head. In his hands, he held a strange-looking gun.

"I don' mean no trouble." The man's accent was unidentifiable and seemed to be a mesh of many. His gravelly voice occasionally lightened with surprising inflections on key words. "If yeh want ter still be alive after tonight, yeh might want ter come with me."

"Come with you?" I yelled, crossing my arms. "We don't even know you."

"What is this?" Gabe wiped the red liquid on his neck.

"Paint." The man held his weapon in the air. "I use my pain'ball gun ta blind those goddamn Dogs."

"How do we know we can trust you?" Jude stood and brushed the snow from his pants.

The man shrugged. "I guess yeh don't. But yeh can either trust me or trust da Dogs. I'll let yeh in on a secret: yeh have a better chance o' survival wit me." He turned and threw the paintball gun over his shoulder. "Don't see many folks up here, so I figured I'd help ya out."

It was getting dark, and we all knew the Dogs would spot us as soon as the first touch of night came. Right now, the light and the snow shielded us from being seen. We needed to find shelter. Fast.

"Hide yer vehicles, but bring da batteries. Yeh can charge 'em at my house." With that, the man began walking up the trail into the mountains, leaving us behind.

"What do we do?" I whispered. "Do we follow him?"

"Get the bags and restock your weapons," Jude ordered, pointing to the two military personnel. "Move the snowmobiles out of sight and put the white cover over them to blend in with the snow. The Dogs won't pick up on three inactive vehicles."

The three of them nodded, and each went to a snowmobile and turned the keys. As the vehicles roared to life, the guards tossed the heavy bags into the snow before speeding off, leaving a trail behind them. The light around us turned hazy yellow as the sun dipped below the horizon, and the air grew noticeably cooler.

"So are we going with him?" I was too tired to get ambushed by Dogs.

"We have no choice." Jude strapped one of the bags to his back and threw another forcefully at Gabe. "Keep your distance. We aren't finished."

"We certainly aren't," Gabe muttered under his breath as he threw the bag across his back.

We trudged up the hill in silence, following the man's snowy footsteps. The boot steps veered off course, to the left, where the terrain became rocky, and travel became unsteady. We followed them until we came to a narrow passage between two rocky masses, only wide enough for single-file passage. The wind whipped through the pass, but very little snow reached its innards.

"The wind blew his footsteps away. Let's keep going to the other side," Gabe suggested. "They should reappear once we're back in the snow."

Up ahead, the man's round head peeked out from the rock wall itself. "Ah! There yeh are! Come on in."

A dark cave came into view, its mouth a gaping maw in the cliff face, and the old man stood in its entrance, holding back a heavy, black velvet curtain. "Welcome to mah home, folks!"

Chapter Twenty-Nine

I wasn't prepared for what I saw inside the cave. Hesitantly, I stepped inside, every nerve ending screaming that this crazy man was luring us to our death, but the sight before me stole my breath. The roof of the cave was strung with bright orange light bulbs, their coiling filaments casting a hazy yellow light. A large, flat-screen television, displaying a vibrant image, hung on the wall above a plush couch and loveseat. The living room's perimeter was lined with bookshelves, leading to a full kitchen with stainless steel appliances, ample cupboards, and a large prep island.

"Wh-what is this place?"

The six of us were in shock, our minds unable to grasp how this crazy old man had such an excellent living space. While the world was struggling, he was living a luxe life, it almost didn't seem fair. To everyone except Gabe and I, this was unheard of.

"Welcome to mah home!" The man smiled. "I'll start fixin' ya some food. Yeh must be starvin'. He looked at us huddled together, our mouths agape. "Come on in, yeh don't need ta be scared. Make yerself at home."

"Th-thank you," I whispered. "Why are you being so nice to us? We're strangers."

He shrugged. "Don' see many people up here. Figured I'd help yeh out, yeh'd either freeze ta death or da Dogs woulda ripped yeh apart. My life's almost at its end, so if bein' a good person is goin' to be the death o' me, it's a good way ta go out." The man walked to a beautiful bar separating the living room from the kitchen. Each of the bottles sparkled, their faded labels disguising the liquid inside. He carefully arranged seven short glasses on the polished bartop before pouring a precise ounce of amber liquor into each. "Name's Pete, I've been livin' here for the past fifty years. Come, have a drink an' warm up."

We followed him to the bar, and I took a seat on one of the stools. The last time I was at a bar was The Carlton, right before I got kidnapped. It seemed like so long ago. A different life.

But was it a better life?

The six of us introduced ourselves to Pete, then, with a quick cheers, we downed the brown liquid. The alcohol burned my throat with a searing caramel flavor. Every drop of liquor reached my stomach, but Pete wasn't wrong—I was warm.

The old man wiped a dribble of alcohol from his mustache. "What brings yeh up here?"

"Our mission is confidential." Jude's authoritative voice boomed as he puffed out his chest, his presence filling the room.

I rolled my eyes, and Gabe shook his head. "We're looking for a large building hidden in the snow within these mountains. Do you know where that may be?"

Jude's head snapped at Gabe. "Don't release confidential information! We don't know if we can trust him!"

"*He* trusted *us*." I pursed my lips. Why was he being so difficult?

"Fuck off, dude," Gabe huffed.

"Yeh mean the laboratory in the valley?" Pete walked to the refrigerator. "The one that fixes the Dogs?"

Once again, our mouths dropped. Would this place cease to surprise us?

A deep guffaw rumbled from Pete's chest. "Why're yeh so surprised? Livin' here for so long, o' course I know about that place. I steal da food that's sent ta it. Ain't no one livin' up there, so why not?" He opened the refrigerator and rummaged around in the back. "Speakin' of… care for filet mignon tonight?"

Another surprise: filet mignon!

"You know where it is?" Jude's eyes lit up. "So you can bring us there?"

Pete nodded. "Aye, but we have ta wait 'till mornin' when da Dogs leave ta hunt. Yeh could find it by climbin' the mountain, but there's a shortcut down the hallway over yonder." He nodded to the far end of the room. "This place used ta be a storage room, so they built a tunnel that leads right outta the lab."

"If this used to be a storage room, how did it turn into…this?" Gabe asked.

"I ain't no angel." A sly smirk crossed Pete's face. "Them vampires left one person in charge up there, an' when they stopped comin' ta visit, I took their food an' equipment for myself."

One of the military guards named Nine spoke up, his demeanor completely unreadable. "So there's someone still in the laboratory we need to be concerned about?"

"He ain't there anymore. It's empty." Pete solemnly shook his head.

Jude, Gabe, and I all exchanged uneasy glances. We were all thinking the same thing: Dante. But where did he go?

"I go there once a month to fill out the order form, them vamps must think he's still up here an' alive." He raised an eyebrow. "Yeh didn't answer my question: will everyone eat filet?"

I laughed and nodded.

"Good, I've been savin' these fer a special occasion." He grabbed a rectangular black remote control and pressed the bright red button in the upper right corner. The television on the wall flickered to life with a soft hum and a static hiss. "Why don't y'all get cozy an' relax. Watch a movie while I cook dinner." He turned to me and winked. "I'm limited on entertainment. See anything you like?"

On the TV were four rows of digital movies, which must have been downloaded over sixty-five years ago. I mean, they had to be; the internet hadn't worked since the societal collapse. We'd tried to get it back online, but nothing worked. At least, that was what my father told us, but he'd clearly figured out some way to have the computers communicate with the Dogs.

"Oh my God," I breathed. "I haven't seen Mamma Mia in years!"

If they didn't know I was gay, I fear my comment made it obvious.

"Me neither," Gabe laughed. "Remember when we were in high school, and you forced me to watch it with you?"

I rolled my eyes. "Yes, you said it was the worst experience of your life because I quoted the movie the whole time."

"And you did interpretive dances to all the songs!"

Tears welled in our eyes as we laughed together at the shared memory. I noticed Jude scowling at us from the corner of my eye, but I didn't care. This was a happy memory. A memory before all of this. Back when my mom was alive, and the world was so carefree. At least to me.

How I yearned for those days back.

"I think we found a winner!" Pete clicked the remote, and the screen shimmered to life, displaying the glistening blue waves of Santorini. "Takes a few minutes ta load, but it'll get there."

One of the plush couches sank under the weight of the three military guards whose names were all distinguished by numbers—Fifteen, Nine, and Four—their heads tilted back.

"You knew my brother, didn't you?" Four's kind eyes looked toward me, legs spread wide on the couch. "Three?"

My mouth dropped as I looked at the man before me. He was a very tall, muscular man with a bald head and a black bushy mustache sitting on top of his lip. I stared, dumbfounded, at the uncanny resemblance—the same eyes, the same smile—it was as if I were looking at his brother. The last few seconds of Three flashed through my memory as I remembered how he valiantly saved me from a Dog right before his death. My lips formed a straight line, and I looked toward the ground, nodding. "I did, he was a good man."

Four wiped the top of his head, which was beading with sweat. "He *was* a good man, the best brother."

A pang stabbed through my heart, and I had to look

away before the pain deepened. The television screen held Jude captive, its mesmerizing glow reflected in his wide, wonder-filled eyes. I suppose it never dawned on me that humans had never watched a movie before. In Elysium, each of our living quarters contained a device that housed every movie made before the collapse. Now that I think about it, there aren't TVs in Silvertown at all, so this must be an otherworldly device to them.

I picked up the three snowmobile batteries. "Where can I charge these?"

"Wherever yeh can find a plug," Pete waved his hand. "When yer done, come help me prep dinner for all o' yeh."

I knelt on the ground and attached the three rechargeable batteries to the wall. Each device emitted a small, warm light, indicating the start of the charging cycle. I stopped to glance at the television before heading into the kitchen to join the old man. This was a movie my mother and I watched together. It was our comfort movie. I smiled as the main character, Sophie, and her best friends ran around Greece, reading her mother's diary. Gabe looked at me while sitting at the dining room table, far away from Jude, and smiled as I mouthed the words to the song they were singing. "Dot, dot, dot."

I met Pete in the kitchen, where he maintained a perfect mise en place setup in front of him, complete with knives, produce, and cutting boards. "Where do you want me to start?"

"I'll help too!" Jude stood abruptly from the couch, interrupting Donna's mid-song lament about her financial struggles.

"Me too!" The chair Gabe was sitting in screeched backward.

The two men nudged each other out of the way, trying

to be nonchalant, but it was incredibly obvious. I didn't know how much more of them trying to top the other I could take.

Pete whipped around, sporting a white apron and putting a fist on his hip. "Calm down, yeh two. Me an da young man here got this. Yeh just relax, an dinner will be ready soon." His wrinkled eyes grew hard, and without another word, both men retreated from the kitchen, finding seats in the living room.

"You must be magic," I joked. "Those two usually never listen to anyone's orders."

Pete laughed. "They'd be losing da battle with me, son. I haven' cooked fer more than one in a minute."

"Really? When was the last time you had visitors?" I grabbed the bag of green beans, tearing open the paper-thin wrapping. "These are the skinny ones! My mom and I used to cook together. Would you mind if I make the vegetable dish?"

He nodded at me with a warming smile. "My wife, Patty, and I found this place an made what yeh see here. We loved camping in these mountains before the Da Great Worl' War."

I began to slice the ends off each of the beans, the knife gliding smoothly through the firm skin. "If you don't mind me asking, where's she now?"

He tossed a pile of potatoes into the bubbling, steaming pot, his expression turning somber. "Yeh'd think with everything that happened—pandemic, war, the Dogs, that one o' those got her. But it was her own clumsiness. She tripped while we were out walking one day, an' she fell off the side of a cliff." He shook his head. "Patty was a clumsy gal, but I knew that. I shoulda been holding her hand."

With a fine grater, I moved the lemon back and forth, its pungent scent tickling my nostrils as the zest collected in the bowl. The acidity of the juice stung the microscopic cut I didn't know I was there. A sharp, burning sensation spread through my fingertip, and a quiet yelp escaped my lips.

"Thought ya'll would be immune ta pain or somethin'." Pete strained the steaming potatoes and began mashing them, adding sharp cheddar and rich cream. "Yer one of those vampires, aren' yeh?"

"Me and Gabe." I nodded before instantly regretting my decision to tell him. "But-but you don't have to be scared or worry about us."

"I wasn't scared of yeh." He laughed. "I knew yeh weren't a threat when I saw those two bozos fightin' in the snow. What were the fightin' about anyway?"

My cheeks blushed as I grabbed a bowl full of water, adding a few ice cubes before I boiled the beans. My mother always blanched her green beans, plunging them into ice water afterward to give them an extra bright color and a delightful, almost snappy, crunch. Each time, she would offer me one to sample, a treat I never refused. "Me," I answered. "Their egos, I suppose, too."

"Ah, ego. Always da downfall of men." Pete took out a frying pan and added some olive oil, waiting for it to heat up before adding the steaks. "Yeh must be pretty special ta them if they were fightin' over yeh."

As the beans chilled in the ice bath, I went to the stove, where Pete was already working. The clatter of pans and sizzle of oil filled the kitchen with noise and a delicious scent. In a frying pan, I added some oil and minced garlic. As the fragrant smell of the herb wafted into the air, I added the beans. "They seem to think so."

"Don' be so modest, yer in demand!" The last piece of steak landed in the pan with a loud sizzle, the rich smell of browning meat filling the air and silencing the music from the TV. "My Patty was a big believer in doin' what makes yeh happy, so follow yer joy. It may be one o' them or neither. Do what's right fer you."

I laid the steaming, tender beans into a ceramic bowl and added a sprinkle of lemon zest. "Can I borrow the potato peeler?" I took it from him and shaved off some strips of a block of parmesan, then tossed the two new ingredients, incorporating them into the beans. I reached my hand into bowl and brought a single bean to my lips. The familiar crunch and flavors on my tongue unveiled a long-forgotten memory.

"I think with everythin' that's gone on over the past fifty or so years, everyone forgot how ta live their lives. What it means ta be happy. We gotta get dat back, even when da world seems grim." Pete piled the cooked filet mignon on a platter and handed me a large black bottle. "Yeh might like this with yer meal."

I opened the cork and put my nose to the entrance. I expected the familiar cranberry and spice notes of wine, but a strange metallic sweetness filled my nostrils instead. "Is this blood?"

Gabe's ears perked. "Blood? I'm almost out of my reserves."

"Aye, they included it with the shipment. Take all yeh want!"

I threw the bottle to Gabe. "I've never heard stories or rumors that Dante was a vampire. Why would the lab be sent blood?"

He shrugged. "Either he's a vampire...or someone else is."

I looked at the movie and smiled. "This is a good place

to stop, after dinner, Gabe and I will show you the dance we used to do during the Super Trooper song."

"No, we won't!" Gabe's cheeks were red, but a hidden smirk was tugging at his lips.

"Everyone, come an' get a plate. Dinner is served!"

Chapter Thirty

After a night of laughter, movies, and one too many cocktails, I felt Gabe stir next to me. Lazily, I opened my eyes to the stone ceiling of the cave, scratching at the irritating prickles on my skin. My boyfriend was staring at me intently, while soft snores rumbled gently from Jude on my other side. It was odd waking up in a dark cave. Even in Silvertown, the fluorescent lights turned on at a particular time, so although there were no windows, we knew it was morning. However, this cave was perpetually black.

"Morning," I whispered.

"Good morning, handsome." A subtle lilt colored Gabe's quiet, almost hushed tone.

I cringed at his greeting, hoping Jude didn't hear, and extended my arms and legs, stretching my body. Jude's body stirred with a groan, his breath heavy with sleep. His pained face and the lingering scent of liquor told me the alcohol had taken its toll. I wriggled free from between the two men, their bodies warm against mine, and stood. Fifteen, Nine, and Four were sleeping on the couches, but as soon as they heard me, all six of their eyes opened with a jolt. "Just me." I smiled at them.

I went to the kitchen, the linoleum cool beneath my feet, and opened the refrigerator, grabbing a chilled bottle of blood and an ice-cold water. With a crack, the blood vial's cap came off as I knelt on the ground and offered it to Gabe. He grasped the bottle's neck, his large hands tightening around the cool glass. I've never been in this situation before, being wanted by two men. The worst part is I don't know what to do…or if I even want either. I couldn't imagine choosing one over the other. The turmoil in my heart forced me to divide my time carefully, ensuring each received some portion of my attention.

I turned toward Jude and opened the bottle of water. The warmth of his skin registered as I cupped his face, lightly rubbing his cheek with my thumb. His eyes fluttered open, heavy-lidded and bloodshot, then closed like a heavy theatre curtain once a show was over. A pained smile stretched his lips as I tilted the bottle, the liquid dribbling down his chin.

"My head is pounding," Jude muttered, running his fingers through his perfect blond hair. "Thank you." He lifted the bottle to his pink lips and took a long swig. The gulping of water down his parched throat filled the room, pulsing each second as if he had never tasted water before.

The bulbs within the cave flickered to life, their harsh glare made Jude wince and shield his eyes. The sudden brightness was overwhelming after the cave's darkness. Pete hobbled into the room, his white hair sticking up in tufts.

"Ah, good." Pete rubbed his beard. "We're all still alive this mornin', yeh never know with vamps in yer house, but I s'pose yer not like the others." Pete winked at me and led us into the kitchen.

Within moments, the rich, nutty aroma of freshly ground coffee beans filled the room, accompanied by the cheerful whistle of a percolator, signaling a fresh brew was beginning. My heart leaped because in Elysium, I drank coffee every day. I lifted my head to the ceiling and breathed in the delicious fragrance wafting around me. I swore I couldn't live without coffee, but the coffee-less hallways of Silvertown proved me wrong.

They may have had coffee, but I'm sure it'd be similar to swill.

"Do you need help with breakfast?" I leaned on the counter, looking at the short man. A wave of nostalgia washed over me as I gravitated toward him, the feeling strangely familiar, like being with my long-forgotten grandparents. It made me yearn for their connection once again.

"Quick breakfast," Jude moaned, cupping his eyes in his hands.

"I agree with him." Gabe nodded. "We need to get to the laboratory, and once we shut it down, we can go back to Silvertown. I expect we can do this all by the end of the day."

The coffee maker began to bubble, indicating the brew was nearly complete. With a gentle clink, Pete poured the dark, rich liquid from the glass pot into two mugs, offering one to me with a smile. "I'll take yeh through da tunnels. It'll lead yeh right to the lab yer lookin' fer."

"Let's go now." From a chipped fruit bowl on the cluttered dining room table, Gabe grabbed a speckled banana and threw it to Jude. "It amazes me that there's fresh fruit here."

Pete shrugged. "All genetically modified, I'm sure."

Jude scrunched his face, turning the yellow fruit like it was a grenade. "What the hell is this?"

I lowered the steaming mug from my lips, the warmth lingering, and fell silent for a moment. It never occurred to me Jude had never seen a banana before, but it made sense because it wasn't a fruit native to our geography. The gap between vampires and humans continued to astound me.

With a second banana in hand, Gabe peeled back the slightly bruised yellow skin and sank his teeth into the soft, yielding flesh. Everyone's eyes were on Jude, who hesitantly followed suit. My breath was bated, waiting to see the reaction on his face. Would he love it or hate it? Surprisingly, his face went from confusion to disgust, then to surprise.

He raised his head to look at all of us. "This is kinda good, I wish we had more of these back home."

I shrugged. "Maybe one day, when this is all over, you will."

"Maybe." He continued to chomp on the banana, wiped his mouth, and nodded to the three military guards. "Why don't the three of you install the charged batteries back in the snowmobiles, then we'll go through the tunnels all together?"

Fifteen, Nine, and Four nodded and wrapped their masks around their heads. Before they disappeared behind the curtain, they put their fur-lined hoods up, each with a metallic battery beneath their arm.

"Hey, Four." I raised my chin before he disappeared out the door. "Be careful, alright?"

He nodded and gave me a thumbs-up signal, putting me as at ease as I could be. Witnessing his brother's final breaths filled me with a sense of responsibility for his safety.

"While they're doin' that, I'll get everythin' ready for yeh." Pete nodded to me. "Mind helpin'?"

"Not at all."

Pete guided me to the back of the cave, where a massive metal door loomed, its cold surface reflecting the dim light. It was so tall and rusted, it almost looked like part of the cave itself. With one hand, he wrapped his thick, calloused fingers around the cold metal lever, pulling with all his might. The lever shook, but never once budged.

Letting go of the lever, Pete wiped his hands on his overalls.

"One sec," I said, seeing his struggle. Running back to the main room, Gabe was leaning against the kitchen counter while Jude lay groaning on the ground, nursing his hangover. "Can one of you help us?"

"Ughhhh, do you mind going, Gabe?" Jude moaned. "I'll wait for my guys to come back."

"Humans are so weak." Gabe laughed as he sauntered over to me. Under his breath, he scoffed. "Can't handle a little hangover."

Whether Jude heard him or not was unclear, but the lack of response told me all I needed to know about his state of mind. Gabe followed me to the large door, wrapped his palm around the rusty lever, and pulled. His biceps swelled, straining against his skin as the rusted lever screeched, its metal protesting with each upward inch.

"Not as easy as it used ta be." Pete brushed by us and disappeared inside the door.

A large, metallic clang echoed, the vibrations resonating through the air. I cautiously opened the door a crack and saw Pete, struggling with a huge, old lever. The vibration grew louder, and an orange light came to life, causing the bulbs in Pete's home to flicker. Lightbulbs were haphazardly strung on the walls, illuminating the way through the tunnels like stars in the night.

"Be careful where yeh walk." Pete pointed to the wall where a bunch of dusty wooden boxes sat. "Those are all filled with explosives. They mus' be unstable and crystallized by now, so any handlin' or sudden movements could set 'em off."

Two rusty metal beams, spanned by decaying wooden planks, formed a precarious bridge across the tunnel's midpoint. The air smelled of rust and felt heavy in my lungs. "Did this used to be a mining tunnel?"

"Yeh got it!" Pete nodded. "These used ta be tracks miners would transport goods and any precious stones they found." He hobbled ahead and waved to us. "Follow me, I wanna show yeh somethin'."

The tunnel sloped downward, the air growing cooler and damper as we continued. Traveling through the mine, discarded pickaxes and other equipment were strewn across the ground, likely never to be used again. The stone tunnels twisted and turned, their damp surfaces slick and cold under her fingertips, making travel treacherous. It was as if the cave itself had grown smaller, like it were a living being that expanded and contracted over the years.

"Look at the ceiling." Pete pointed his stubby finger upward as we neared a fork in the road. A massive pipe, as thick as a person, snaked across the tunnel ceiling, twisting and turning down the right side of the path. "This is how I get food. There're these tunnels all over the country now. The vamps created them—"

"To exchange goods with other Elysiums," Gabe finished. "Each building has a central location in the basement where the pods carry food and other goods to each vampire compound to distribute to their residents." He stopped and awkwardly shifted on his feet. "They're how your dad gets blood all over the country."

"Pretty cool, huh?" Pete sipped his coffee. "Easiest way ta get ta the lab is ta follow the pipe."

"What about the other path?" I curiously asked, looking down the darkened cave.

"Leads deeper into the tunnel, but if yer smart, yeh could take a few rights an' be re-routed back ta da lab."

I nodded in understanding and followed Pete as he turned to retrace our steps back to his home.

"Just lettin' yeh know—be careful when yeh climb the ladder an' get inta the lab. It's a large facility dat fixes those nasty Dogs, so they're everywhere."

"How do you usually get by them to get your food?" Gabe asked in curiosity.

"I don'," he admitted. "I cut a hole in da pipe and made a barrier, so the pod stops right at da bottom o' the ladder. Too dangerous ta go up there. I just keep signin' the paperwork fer refills."

"Pretty smart," Gabe admitted, with a laugh.

Closer to the door, my vision slowly adapted to the dim light, the oppressive darkness starting to recede. Truthfully, I wasn't sure if my eyes were adjusting to the dim light or if the bulbs were warming to a brighter glow. Nearing the massive metal door, a shiver wracked my body. The sight of the dynamite—red sticks seemingly sprouting growths, crudely packed in worn wooden boxes within the dark, echoing mine, was unnerving.

Jude moved from his makeshift bed, albeit not far. Instead of lying on the ground, contemplating his life choices, he was now sitting upright on the couch. As soon as we emerged from the door, his head swiveled. "Where've you guys been?" He threw his arm up and slapped his knee. "It should not be taking the three of them this long to install the batteries. I'm gonna see what's going on." Throwing on his jacket, he disappeared beyond the curtained door.

"What's his problem?" Pete's lip was upturned in disgust.

Jude's body was thrown back into the cave, landing roughly on the ground. Nine burst through the door, colliding with him, and Four followed close behind, both leaving a trail of blood.

"D-Dogs k-killed F-F-Fifteen."

The words that left Four's mouth hung in the air, and everyone's bodies stiffened. The environment grew tense, and the next few moments felt like they happened in slow motion. With a sudden leap, a Dog bounded from behind the curtain, its paws landing squarely on Nine's shoulders. It opened its mouth, revealing rows of razor-sharp teeth glinting in the dim light before clamping down onto the man's head with a crunch. With a twist, the Dog ripped Nine's head from its body, a spray of blood and gore coating the surrounding area like rain.

I stared, completely stunned, as Jude stumbled toward me, his clothes soaked and dark with blood. Nine's limp body landed heavily on top of him, a thud echoing in the room as the Dog's eyes scanned the room. Five more beasts walked in, sniffing the mangled head on the floor.

I don't know exactly when it happened, but Gabe grabbed my hand with his gun pointed at the Dogs and pulled me toward the metal door leading to the dark mining tunnels. With a grin, Pete grabbed his weapon and unleashed a volley of paintballs at the bloodthirsty Dogs intruding within his home.

A daze enveloped me as I ran, slightly behind Gabe, the world blurring around me. "G-gabe, we need to get Jude. We can't leave him behind." My words came out in a choke as my body was pulled down the mine.

"My only concern is for you," Gabe growled back.

Following the tunnel's dimly lit path, we took a right at the fork, where the air grew noticeably colder. The barks and cries seemed to drown out the further we ran. I looked toward the ceiling and saw the large pipe, knowing we were heading in the right direction. Only a few moments passed before we neared the tunnel's end, where a rusty metal ladder was bolted against the cave's cold stone.

"You go first." Gabe moved out of the way, putting one hand on the ladder and shaking it. "Actually, I'll go first in case this breaks."

I nodded, my body shaking. The rhythmic clang of Gabe's boots on the metal ladder echoed through the cave as he climbed. He swiftly moved upward, and I placed my foot on the first rung of the ladder, reaching for the next with a slightly trembling hand.

"Vinny, where are you?"

It was Jude. My heart jumped. It was like whatever daze I was in was lifted. I couldn't leave him behind. Gabe looked down at me, and I lifted my chin to him. "I gotta get Jude. We can't leave him."

"Vinny, no—"

The echo of Gabe's voice faded as I began sprinting down the tunnel. I tried to keep my breathing and footsteps quiet, running on my tiptoes. As the fork came into view, I saw the silhouette of a round man. Coming down the tunnel, a pack of Dogs emerged, their red eyes gleaming menacingly in the dim light.

"Pete!" I yelled. "Run!"

He turned to face me. "Turn 'round, Vincent. Go up the ladder, it's not safe for yeh here."

I saw a flicker of light dance near his overalls, and his eyes shifted downward. At his feet was a box of dynamite, and in his hands, he held a stick, the fuse sparking dangerously. My mouth dropped. "Pete, what-what are you doing?"

"There's no way we're all makin' it out o' this an' those bastards will notify their pack of anyone who escapes." He held up the sparked dynamite. "I'm makin' sure ya'll get outta here."

"No, you can't, there must be another way!"

"It's time for me to be with Patty. She's been waitin' fer me fer far too long." Pete touched my face, water glistening in his eyes. "Run back ta da ladder, so you don' get caught in da crossfire."

"I-is Jude okay?" I started backing away slowly, knowing my pleas were useless.

Pete nodded and cocked his head down the other tunnel at the fork. "Don' forget what I told ya—listen to yer heart and live yer life because yeh only got one to live."

I watched in horror as the six Dogs ascended upon Pete, their claws scraping against the ground as they launched themselves at him. With a rush of wind, they landed on the round man and the box of dynamite. My last memory of Pete was his hand in the air, reaching for his wife, even though his body had been pummeled to the ground.

The sudden loud bang echoed through the empty space, replaced only by an unsettling, heavy silence. A high-pitched sound ran through my ears. The impact hit me with the force of a runaway train, throwing me forward and ripping my legs out from under me. A white-hot pain shot through me as I slammed against a wall of the stony tunnel.

"Vinny! Where are you?"

It was Gabe. His voice was scared and hoarse. I never heard him like this. It scared me because I knew something was wrong. I tried yelling back to him, but I couldn't speak.

A wave of paralysis washed over me, and though I tried to move, I was trapped within my own body. I felt useless, like my brain and body weren't connected.

Fear ran through my mind. Was I dying?

A high-pitched squeal vibrated in my ears, drowning out Gabe's terrified screams as darkness consumed me.

I CARRY ON, I CARRY ON.

Chapter Thirty-One

The weight of my eyelids was nearly unbearable, and my body felt as heavy and unresponsive as if it were made of stone. Every nerve throbbed, as if I'd been flattened by a bus and my body was still vibrating from the impact. I pushed against the invisible force pinning me, but my body refused to move. What happened to me? Someone grabbed my arm, and I mustered all the strength I had to croak, "Jude? Gabe?" The person's fingers quickly left my arm, and footsteps pitter-pattered away.

I strained my ears, listening intently for any sound that might give any indication of my location. A low, rhythmic beeping pulsed to my left as I struggled to open my heavy eyelids. My vision was blurred, a milky film obscuring the world like a dirty pane of glass pressed against my forehead, each object hazy and indistinct. A thick woolen blanket covered my feet, barely visible as my brain pieced together surroundings. I was in a bed.

Where the hell am I?

A woman with thick, slightly smudged glasses walked toward me, her footsteps barely audible. Vanessa noticed me stirring, and her jaw dropped in surprise. "Vinny, are you awake?"

My throat tightened, a suffocating pressure building, and I strained to force it out. "Y-yes." It was all I could muster while my body and mind were in a battle for control. Hopefully, Nessa could help me. Wherever I was.

"Hold on." In a flash, she was gone, then reappeared with an older man whose presence conveyed quiet authority. His lips were so cracked, it looked like he constantly sucked on a lemon. Nessa directed him, "He's awake, see? Can you take him off the medication?"

The man pursed his lips and walked to my left, fiddling with a plastic bag of liquid hanging from a rusty hook. "This will be good for him. He may have a slight allergy toward the medication because his body has broken out in a mild rash."

I tried to tell the doctor that the rash was from my constant itching, but my jaw wouldn't move. My tongue felt thick and heavy, refusing to cooperate as I struggled to form words. I strained to recall the events that led me here, but my memory was a foggy maze with no clear path to the truth.

"Vincent, I'm so happy you're awake." Nessa excitedly clapped her hands. "You're underground, in the infirmary at Silvertown."

"Is he awake?" A voice boomed from behind Nessa, the sound echoing in the room as a large, round man strode in.

She nodded and moved out of the way to give room to whoever was entering.

"Well, you're probably wondering how you got here, right?" Four's large body settled heavily onto the wooden stool next to me, the wood groaning under his considerable weight, a low creak echoing the strain. "After the explosion,

Jude and your vampire friend ran to your aid. You were buried under the collapsed tunnel, and they thought you were dead, like Pete."

I felt like I had no control of my body, but a lone tear slid down my cheek. Pete was dead. And he did it to protect us. He was finally with his wife.

"When Jude and Gabriel found you, you were barely breathing. They begged me to abandon the mission and bring you here to get help. I agreed and strapped you onto my snowmobile. I tried to get here as fast as I could, and it's good I did because we were able to save you."

"The infirmary made sure you were able to live and hooked you up to machines while your body healed." Nessa pointed to the beeping screen next to me. "You've been asleep for two days."

TWO DAYS? How have I been asleep this long? "Wh-where's J-Jude and Ga-be?" The medicine was wearing off, and I was regaining my ability to speak.

With a frustrated groan, Four shook his head. "They stayed behind, hellbent on completing the mission."

I wish I could've screamed. Jude and Gabe stayed behind in order to disable the computer? Without me, they'd likely kill each other. My stomach plummeted with the chilling thought that one, or perhaps neither, might not make it back. Why are men so stupid, and why are their egos their biggest downfall?

Well, second biggest.

"Where are they?" When we were at Pete's house, they said we could disarm the computer and return to Silvertown by nightfall. It's been two days, meaning the mission was harder than expected or... Well, I didn't want to think about it.

Nessa shrugged. "We haven't heard from them."

"Until now."

The three of us whipped our heads toward the door to see two men walk through the door. Gabe's wavy hair was pulled back tightly, revealing fresh scratches on his face, while Jude's shredded clothing was stained crimson with blood. Regardless of how disheveled they looked, their presence brought a wave of relief. I was relieved to see them alive and in one piece.

"G-Gabe! Jude!" I tried to stand, but my body felt heavy as lead, refusing to obey. With a frustrated grunt, I tried to rip the cords from my arm, but the incredibly sticky medical tape wouldn't budge.

Vanessa tackled me, her body heavy on mine as she pinned me to the bed. "Vinny, you have to wait until you're strong enough."

My eyes burned with tears. I didn't think I'd see them again. Since waking, I've been thrust into a rollercoaster of emotions.

Gabe nudged past Jude and hastily beelined to me. He nuzzled his face into the corner of my neck and wrapped his strong arms around me, holding me close. "I'm so happy to see you're okay," he whispered in my ear.

"We were so scared," Jude said, standing behind Gabe, looking relieved. "Thank God Four got you here safe."

My pupils darted nervously back and forth between the two men. The last thing I wanted was for them to get into a fight in the middle of the infirmary. I was holding my breath, waiting for Gabe to see Jude holding my hand. I looked fearfully at Nessa, whose smile was ear-to-ear, most likely in hidden jealousy. "What happened out there?"

Gabe held my hand in his with concern-ridden eyebrows, while Jude put a comforting hand on the man's shoulder.

"We'll let you three catch up." With a casual lean

against the doorframe, Four raised an eyebrow at Nessa. "Would you, uh, like to grab some dinner?"

Heat rose in Nessa's cheeks, staining them a bright red as she fought back a smile that threatened to break free.

Jude raised his eyebrows. "Hey, Vanessa, before you go—"

I watched as Nessa turned, her bright eyes shining with a mixture of hope and excitement.

"Thanks for taking care of Vinny. Can you let my dad know we're back?"

With a push of her glasses and a quick nod, Nessa was guided from the infirmary by Four.

"When the tunnel collapsed, we were beside ourselves," Jude started. "We helped Four load you onto the snowmobile and prayed for you to get here safely. Once you both disappeared from our view, we went back to the mining tunnels, finding our way to the ladder."

"It brought us to the basement of the lab, but let me tell you, Vin, it was gorgeous." With a flourish, Gabe fanned his hands in the air, each movement a sweeping gesture. "Everything was so sterile and white. It was like a beautiful modern hospital, well, modern from fifty years ago." He chuckled, knowing I'd understand what he meant. "The whole basement was these large pod-like things, filled with liquid. Some were broken, and some had sludge in them. It looked like they hadn't been used in years."

A long, slow breath escaped Jude's lips. "They were the same ones we saw in the church. You know, the ones from the video?"

I nodded, knowing exactly what he meant. As the church only harbored a couple of pods, it couldn't accommodate their growing needs, so they relocated their facility to a secluded mountain lab with ample space for multiple, large-scale experiments. More failed versions of me. A nervous twitch pulsed in my eye as I thought about it.

"When we went upstairs from the basement, we found this massive room with beds and Dogs that needed help, but it felt different from the church." Jude held one finger up. "Half of the facility was used to fix Dogs, while the other half was robots *making* them."

Making new Dogs? For some reason, I hadn't considered there were any new Dogs, just maintaining and fixing the old.

"They were all lined up, like an army." Gabe's hands were rigid, showing parallel lines. "Their eyes were dark, but it was eerie to think they could come to life at any moment."

"To be honest, I was shitting my pants." Jude laughed. "We snuck around the laboratory, making sure we weren't seen by any of them. We found a staircase leading to the upper level, where the computer was. Thankfully, the code was the same as before, so we instantly got access."

"The room was completely made out of glass; it kind of reminded me of the cockpit of an airplane." Gabe smoothly curved his hands. "There were blinking buttons, panels, and levers— so many things we didn't know what to do, but as soon as we accessed the computer…all hell broke loose."

I felt both of them tense, their posture becoming awkward yet rigid. It was like they were reliving the moment.

Jude squeezed Gabe's shoulder and patted him on the back. "I wouldn't be here if it weren't for this guy. I owe my life to him." Gabe's eyes flickered, and a smile touched his lips as Jude awkwardly hugged him. "The computer glowed alive, and all the Dogs in the lab came to life, with their sights set on us. Without a moment to think, Gabe told me to figure out how to disable them and left the room, firing his gun."

"You idiot!" I screamed, throwing my arms in the air. "How could you be so stupid? What if…what if…"

"It didn't," he reassured. "The gunshots made all the Dogs follow me, giving Jude time to get into the database. Believe me when I say there were hundreds of them." He shook his head and covered his mouth with his hand. "I dunno how I even survived. Everywhere I looked, a Dog was chasing me. Their red eyes are seared into my brain. I don't remember much, except for climbing a rope, and they were jumping into the air, trying to reach me. When I looked down, it was a sea of metal." He shuddered. "I honestly didn't think I'd make it out. But then the barking and growling from the Dogs ended. Their red eyes dimmed, and they fell to the ground."

"Sorry, bro." Jude laughed. "Before the computer gave me the option to disable the Dogs, it made me watch a video explaining why it's a bad idea, like the one below the church." He turned to me. "Although this time it wasn't your dad, just a blank screen with a recording of someone's voice."

"Dante?" I already knew it; his nod was only a confirmation. "Was he in the lab?"

Jude shook his head. "No sign of him, and we didn't even find bones or a skeleton, like we were expecting."

"So he's still out there." Even if we brought my father down, Dante could still be hiding or could've even been turned into a vampire. He could be biding his time, quietly amassing an army far surpassing the might of the Dogs. He could sweep in to seize control once my father is gone. For all we know, he could be long dead, but we have to take it into consideration.

"My boy!" A voice came from the doorway. Arthur ran

in, engulfing Jude in a tight hug. "As soon as Four told me you were here, I ran through town and didn't stop until I reached the infirmary…" He placed a hand over his heart, a silent gesture of respect, and nodded to Gabe. "You have my thanks for bringing my son back to me safely."

Gabe's body tensed, his muscles locking in surprise. "N-no problem." His initial visit had been a nightmare, so his astonishment at the kindness he now received was understandable.

"Dad, the Dogs are disabled. We did it!"

Arthur's mouth fell open in disbelief, his eyes shining with an almost feverish excitement. "We need to move swiftly. I'll start the preparation tonight, and we will discuss our strategy tomorrow. Get rest because we're on the precipice of the war we've been building." With a gleeful look on his face, he added, "The humans will rise once again!"

Jude nodded dutifully, then cocked his head at one of the nurses. "Can you ask for two beds to be rolled in here? I don't think Gabe and I want to leave Vincent again."

And you know what? They didn't.

Chapter Thirty-Two

"Storming Elysium wouldn't be an ideal strategy." Gabe crossed his arms, his stance defiant as he stood before the murmuring council. "There's not only a vampire army, but there's also a secret military always at the ready, but they won't deploy it unless there's a threat of a large-scale war. On top of that, the gates and walls are infused with more electricity than a strike of lightning, which would likely kill any human on the spot."

"Why are we taking advice from a vampire?" One of the council leaders sneered, a cruel twist of the lip that spoke volumes. "How do we know he isn't leading our troops into a trap?"

With a sharp glint, Arthur's eyes turned to me before he began to speak to the council. "You may have forgotten, but this *young man* helped to disable one of the biggest hindrances to our army—the Dogs. He's proven to be trustworthy, so we have no reason not to trust him."

"I trust him," Jude stepped forward.

"And I take full responsibility for him." The three of us

stood together as a unified front, like an impenetrable force. Finally, we were all on the same page.

"Oh, great," the short council member huffed. "We have Arthur's posse giving their input, that's rich."

"Have I steered you wrong before?" Arthur's face was stern, his jaw tight. It was clear the council wasn't taking him seriously as their whispers and dismissive glances betrayed their lack of respect.

"What do you propose, considering we are the last known human compound in the world?" The council began to chatter. "We'll need more than our military to start and end this war."

"Time is of the essence." Gabe hooked his thumb under his chin, his forehead etched in thought. "Allow Vincent and I to return to Elysium, under the guise that I saved him. Together, we'll disable all power and open the gates for your army."

"We can have the first wave of military travel under white camouflage, making it difficult to see us against the snow. Then, when the gates open, the battle will begin, and we can signal to bring the second wave as backup to help." Jude turned his head away from the council, turning to me and Gabe. "But I'm coming with the two of you."

"We must trust them," Arthur pleaded to the council. "At least have faith in my son. This is what we've been waiting for."

"If this fails, Arthur, you'll have the end of the human race on your shoulders."

"That won't happen, trust me."

Heads bobbed in agreement as one council member softly confirmed the decision. "You may proceed. Prepare our army and develop a contingency plan. If the gates open, we must give it our all. We may not get another chance with the Dogs being disabled."

"You won't regret it." Arthur backed out of the room with us in tow. "You three, follow me right away."

We walked through the cool, carpeted hallways of the movie theatre toward the exit. I secretly hoped that if everything went according to plan, I'd never have to lay eyes again on those ghastly numbered doors or that dreadful carpet.

"Jude, how will you get inside Elysium?"

"We have a plan," Jude answered his father.

"Do we?" I asked with an eyebrow raised. "When the humans first stormed Elysium and kidnapped me, they didn't have many guns…what's your plan this time?"

Jude laughed. "You mean the pitchforks and axes? We wanted to give the illusion of an attack without sacrificing our plans and weapons. We were hoping to get an idea of what this secret army was, but only the normal military was deployed." Turning his head, he looked into the wrinkled face of his dad. "Get us new guns and ammo, ones we can easily hide and meet me outside."

Arthur stopped abruptly, locking onto Jude. It was as if he were peering into the depths of his mind, searching for a solution, the faintest frown etching itself onto his brow. He nodded and walked toward the military sector of Silvertown as we headed for the exit. Jude nodded curtly to the guards, whose machine guns were against their bodies, and they allowed us to pass.

"Vinny!" a voice shouted, followed by a traipse of dainty footsteps behind me.

Nessa was running toward us, her hair bouncing behind her, with Four trailing not far behind. A mischievous look crossed my face. "How was *your* night?"

Reaching me, her cheeks burned with a deep red, and her eyes were wide with exertion. "Oh, I have *a lot* to talk to you about."

"Hopefully, you have a *large piece* of information to share."

Our giggles, high-pitched and unrestrained like schoolgirls sharing a secret, grated on the two men waiting impatiently by the door. Reaching into her jacket pocket, Nessa pulled out a smooth, cool silver circle from her jacket pocket and balanced it on her index finger. "I know you have a long way, so I thought you might want this."

She handed it to me, the rainbow streaks from the CD catching the light. I opened my arms and embraced her. "Thank you for being a friend."

"Good luck," she whispered and waved as Jude and Gabe opened the door.

Blinded by the intense glare of sunlight on the snow, I stood for a moment, letting my eyes adapt to the brightness before exiting the mall. Everything seemed quiet and still without the potential of getting your body chomped off by a Dog. A brilliant, cloudless blue sky stretched above us, and the bright sun illuminated the world. The boys walked a few feet in front of me, their footprints in simultaneous procession. Knowing their history, I was still surprised at how their unlikely friendship blossomed. They were both so strong-willed.

I guess that was what happened when you nearly died, and someone saved you, right?

I followed their footsteps to a small white car that sat low to the ground, and Jude unraveled a map on its hood. He traced the script on the parchment with his fingertips, then lifted his gaze, sunlight making him squint as he peered into the distance. Biting his bottom lip, he pointed to the east. "We need to go toward the vampire compound."

I craned my neck, straining to see the map, before finally settling on the spot Jude's fingertip precisely marked.

It showed a city circled in black marker, and I caught my breath. I had an idea of Elysium's size, but seeing it laid out on the map showed its incredible width. The building we lived in spanned an entire city, minus the small area where the Exiles resided.

I heard the distinct crunch of snow and turned to see Arthur trudging through the drifts, his arms laden with three small pistols and cardboard boxes packed with ammo. Arriving at Jude's side, he halted, extending a smooth, cherry-red stick about the length of chopsticks. "When the power is shut off and the gates open, shoot this into the sky to alert us." He thrust the rod into Jude's hands and embraced him with a hug. "Good luck."

"I won't fail." Jude's hand rested gently on Arthur's shoulder as they shared a silent, understanding moment before turning to me and Gabe. "*We* won't fail."

"Get going, and I'll start rallying the troops."

"We'll see you soon." I waved and climbed into the backseat of the car. Each of the cracked black leather seats was reclined so far back, it felt as if we were lying down. The ceiling was so low, I couldn't sit upright. "What's this? A toy car?"

Jude snorted as Gabe struggled to get his large body inside. "It'll hide us from prying eyes." He pressed the ignition, the dash lights flaring to life, and the engine's purr vibrated through the car's frame. The car began to move through the empty parking lot until we were on the open road.

"Where are we going? What's the plan?" I asked, crouching forward between the two men. "Or are we going to pull up outside Elysium and ask politely to be let inside *with a human?*"

"Yeah, that's exactly what we're going to do." Gabe rolled his eyes, a smirk dancing on his lips.

"I actually got the idea from Pete," Jude answered, never looking away from the road. "We're going to sneak into the vampire compound through the transport pods."

"But aren't those just for food and goods?"

Gabe nodded. "It's a risk because the speed is so fast, our bodies may not withstand the stop, but it's truly the only way I can think of getting the *three* of us inside."

I raised my eyebrows. "There's not another way besides potentially crushing ourselves?"

"Yeah," Jude sarcastically answered. "I like your idea of knocking on the door. Let's try that and hope I'm not instantly shot dead."

He wasn't wrong. Any human—actually anyone—who gets close to Elysium is likely to be a target since the Dogs have been disabled. I'm sure my father has been notified of the shutdown and, by now, is assembling a team to reactivate both locations.

I took the disc Nessa gifted to me and slid it into the port within the car's dashboard. The car groaned, and a whizzing sound quietly hummed through the silent car. Within a few moments, a sultry woman's voice sang through the speakers with an upbeat back track.

The song ended, and an infectious wave of laughter erupted from Gabe, shaking his shoulders. "This is the worst song I've ever heard."

"We don't have music like this in Silvertown, but the people who bang on plastic buckets sound better than this."

We laughed together, the joyful sound echoing with the music's rhythm, until the song repeated. Interestingly enough, neither of them turned the song off. I suppose we figured even bad music was better than silence during our drive, a welcome distraction from the fear of a Dog ambush. Approximately ten songs filled the car as we drove along, the catchy tune a soundtrack to Jude's fingers drumming on the steering wheel.

There was a vast expanse of water in front of us with no bridge in sight. I'd never seen a body of water this close before. A fierce wind roared as we drew closer, the car fighting against the gusts, pushing and pulling at it. As the road plunged into the dark tunnel, the headlights flickered on, cutting a swathe of light through the blackness.

Jude slammed on the brakes, the tires squealing, and the car lurched to a halt. "This was an underground tunnel used for vehicles that led to the city, but it has since caved in. When you get out, don't be surprised if there's water underfoot."

I stowed the gun in the band of my pants and stuffed the cardboard ammunition in my pockets. We exited the car, and a disgusting stench reached my nostrils. The air was damp, with a musty smell clinging to the moisture that soaked my ankles. The lights from the car revealed that the tunnel extended deeper into the earth—we were at a dead end.

Jude popped the trunk and took a shovel out from the back. He moved to the tunnel's edge and began attacking a jutting pipe with a flurry of blows.

Initially, I thought the oddly shaped piping might be part of a generator, maybe to redirect water in the event of flooding or to safely house electrical wiring, but I was clearly mistaken. Jude used a drill to bore a hole in the pipe while Gabe crouched down, carefully peeling back the sharp metal edges to create a wide enough opening for us to squeeze through.

"We'll go first," Gabe explained. "I'll let the guards in the receiving area know it's us." He turned to Jude. "Don't go directly after us; give me five minutes before you enter. I'll be waiting for you."

Jude nodded, and a high-pitched whistling echoed through the busted tunnel. Balancing precariously on the aged pipe, he thrust the shovel downward. "The vacuum suction being disrupted should slow the pod, and putting the shovel in its center should be enough to stop it. Once we have the pod halted, both of you can get inside."

"You're saying 'should' a lot, does that mean it may *not* work?" I looked into the busted pipe, knowing if I made one wrong move, I'd instantly be dead after the vacuum-sealed tunnel took me.

Before he could answer me, the whistling grew louder. "Here comes the first."

The shovel's handle shook back and forth, reverberating as a car-sized metal pod struggled to get by the carefully placed obstruction. Gabe ripped open the door to the pod's innards and plunged headfirst inside. Within an instant, he threw a flurry of cans of beans, fresh produce, and packaged goods through the air, each with its own distinct collision against the wall behind us.

"You two need to go. The second pod will be coming soon, and we don't want them to collide."

Gabe nodded and ushered me inside. "Lie down."

Carefully, I lowered myself into the cramped pod, noticing that the majority of the remaining goods had been pushed to the front. I inched backward, my body pressing against the boxes, causing them to shift and creak below me. In the darkness, Gabe lowered himself inside, and the clicking of the lock pierced the silence.

"If anything happens, I'll be crushed, but you'll be safe," Gabe whispered. "If that happens, wait for Jude and make sure he gets out of here safely."

"It won't happen." My anxiety was skyrocketing. How are we playing with our lives so easily? There has to be a better way. But here we are. Inside a pod going hundreds of miles per hour in a vacuum-sealed pipe, heading straight to Elysium.

Gabe knocked twice on the metallic pod, the dull thud echoing in the confined space, and we were instantly propelled deeper into the dark, twisting tunnel. We went from zero to a hundred miles an hour in seconds.

"You okay?" Gabe's voice was shaky. I'd never heard him scared before.

"I'm fine." A wave of dizziness washed over me as the relentless speed and the horrifying possibility of being crushed threatened to make me vomit.

Until we came to an abrupt halt.

The suction disappeared, and gravity soon became nonexistent. Were we being lifted? The door to the pod hissed open, a blast of harsh, white light revealing two indistinct black shapes hovering above.

"Don't shoot!" Gabe yelled, his hands above his head. "My name is Gabriel Rodriguez, Captain of the Guard. I have Mr. Asposito's son with me. I saved him."

He hesitantly stepped from the pod, his calloused hand outstretched, a silent invitation to join him. As I stepped out, I saw two vampire guards with both their guns out—one on me and the other on Gabe. As soon as I tucked my disheveled black hair behind my ear, I knew they recognized me. Their eyes grew wide, and they lowered their weapons, sniffing the air around me, smelling my blood.

"Please," Gabe begged. "Alert Mr. Asposito and let him know his son has returned." The guards stopped in front of us, dumbfounded. "Go. NOW!"

Chapter Thirty-Three

As I opened the door to my penthouse, a wave of relief washed over me. It was a familiar feeling, like a warm embrace after coming home from a long day at work. This was my sanctuary, the place I spent the most time. It may have once felt like a prison, but it was also the place that gave me the most comfort and familiarity. Despite the relief in my body, I knew our work was just beginning.

The scent of me and my home reached my nose. It's strange—when you're living somewhere, you can't smell it, but as soon as you leave for a period of time and return, you know what your home smells like. Entering my penthouse, a wave of stale air hit me, and an overwhelming sense of loneliness floated around the room. Was this lingering from the years I never left or from my absence?

The sunlight, filtered through the dark blue-tinted windows, cast an ethereal glow across the cool, polished marble floor. Everything was just as I left it, not one thing out of place. Cleaner, even. I walked into my dimly lit bedroom and threw myself onto the plush bed. Unlike the stiff, uncomfortable mattress I'd grown accustomed to, this one cradled me like a cloud, sinking gently into the plush foam. I wanted to fall asleep right in this moment; it was like I was missing something and needed to catch up.

A light knock came from my door. I lazily rolled off my bed to find Gabe and Jude standing outside my door. Jude donned a crisp vampire guard suit, shielding his face from any cameras. Gabe quickly shoved Jude inside, the door slamming shut with a loud bang to prevent any bystanders from seeing them.

"Vinny..." Jude's voice was soft. "Holy fuck, this place is ridiculous! It's huge! I've never seen anything like it." He stepped inside my penthouse, a look of wonder and amazement on his face. "Whoa...and you *live* here?"

"You mean my luxurious prison? Yeah." A burst of laughter escaped me at the sight of his shocked face. "Don't forget I was locked inside for years, so to me, it's just home." I looked at his clothes. "By the way, where'd you get that?"

"We, uh, borrowed them from a military locker," Gabe answered. "He couldn't be walking around looking like a human." Delving further into the penthouse, he scanned the room. "Weird to be here, isn't it? It's like everything happened, but at the same time, nothing has changed."

He was right. It *was* weird.

A second, more forceful knock rattled the door, and my face went white. I quickly ushered Jude into the dimly lit coat closet and pressed a finger to my lips to signal silence. Walking to the door, I opened it to find a man in a tuxedo, his face impassive, standing behind. "Mr. Vincent, you're back."

I nodded. "And you are?"

"Eddie!" Stepping out of the room, Gabe shook the

man's hand. The grip was firm, and his eyes were intense. "What's up, my man? Did ya think you'd see me again?"

"Gabe!" The man's face lit up. "You were the one who brought Vincent home? You both need to come with me. Mr. Asposito is asking to see you."

With a click of the lock, I secured the door, ensuring Jude's safety, before meeting the two pale men at the elevator. With a low creak, the doors opened. We stepped into the hushed interior, while the button for my father's office pulsed with a faint, ominous light.

"How's everything been while I've been away, Ed?"

"Crazy," he breathed. "There's a lot going on right now. D'you think if Mr. Asposito offered you your job back, you'd take it?"

Gabe looked at me, a silent understanding hanging heavy in the air. I bit my lip to keep from smiling, knowing it would never happen.

"Yeah, definitely."

Ding

The doors creaked open, and Eddie beckoned us into the dimly lit hallway leading to my father's office. The large painting of the ship loomed over me, its rich colors and textures mesmerizing, as if it were about to swallow me whole.

"Vincent!" The door to the office swung open, the sound echoing in the silent hallway, and my father strode out, his arms open wide in greeting. "My boy, I was so scared for your well-being. I'm *so* relieved to see you safe."

Over my shoulder, I looked at Gabe as he stared at my limp, dangling arms. His eyes almost told me to try to pretend, no matter how much anger I felt toward this man. I had to play along. Like I always did. Unwillingly, I lifted my arms and returned his embrace, the warmth of his body doing little to quell the burning anger igniting in my stomach.

With a slow turn of his bespeckled head, my father opened his arms wide, a warm welcome. "Gabe, you did it! I knew you would—come here."

I watched Gabe hesitate, a flicker of uncertainty in his face, before slowly ambling into my father's embrace. The display of affection was brief, and when they parted, we were ushered into his office. The large mahogany desk, polished to a high sheen, sat in the middle of the room, its imposing presence radiating corporate coldness. What secrets did this desk hide?

Today, my father wore a grey plaid suit, the white shirt underneath contrasting sharply with the dark fabric. A white bow tie adorned his neck, while a crisp and neatly pressed pocket square peeked from his breast pocket. His salt-and-pepper hair was slicked back, and his round glasses were the statement—a beautiful shade of purple made his pale skin pop. The stubble on his usually clean-shaven face felt rough, and his eyes, shadowed and dull, spoke of countless hours without sleep.

Was it because he was worried about me? Or scared his Dogs were disabled?

"First things first," he held one finger in the air. "Gabe, you wonderful boy, I'd love for you to re-join my team. When Vincent was taken, and you left to find him, I didn't expect you to come back. Apologies for doubting you, but I hope I can make up for my emotions getting the better of me before you left."

"I'd be honored." Gabe reached his hand over his heart and slightly bowed. "I needed to find him."

"It was inadvertently a test to prove your loyalty to me and your devotion to my son." My father clapped his hands with one loud smack. "I have the perfect idea, let's plan a wedding!"

"Dad, stop!" I yelled, horrified. "We just got back, stop talking crazy."

"What?" He looked hurt. "I'm excited to have you back, and my heart is bursting seeing the two of you. There's nothing I'd love more than to see you happy and protected with Gabe."

I shook my head, waving my arms in front of my face. "We can talk about this later. Do you need anything else from us? We're tired from the journey and need to sleep."

"I'm sure you are. We can plan this later." My father turned to Gabe, clapping him one more time on the back. "I'm happy to have you back on my team."

With a gentle squeeze, Gabe clasped my hand in his, his touch both reassuring and tender. "Wanna head back to your room?"

I nodded, and as we started toward the exit, my father's voice cut through the air. "Gabe?"

We paused.

"You're dismissed," he started. "But I'd like to have some time to talk to my son."

Gabe and I caught eyes, silently asking if being alone with him was a good idea. I nodded, knowing I'd be fine. I'm stronger than I was before I was kidnapped. Plus, I have a gun in my waistband, armed and ready for use if anything gets out of hand.

"I'll be waiting in your apartment."

I nodded, a silent agreement passing between us, knowing he'd look after Jude. The door clicked shut, and I turned to my father, the sound echoing in the quiet room. Disgust filled my body as the man in front of me smiled. I now know everything about this man is a lie. He's been feeding me lies my entire life, but I knew holding my cards close was my best bet.

"Vincent, my son, I'm so thankful you've returned unharmed." His voice was genuine, unlike the formal tone he used with other leaders. It sounded like he was genuinely happy. "This snag has delayed the Extraction. We're behind schedule."

Ah, there's the reason why he's happy.

"We must perform the Extraction as soon as possible."

A large yawn escaped my lips, stretching my jaw and releasing a tired sigh. "I'm exhausted, I don't think I can handle it right now. Do you think we can postpone for a few days until I get my strength back?" I saw my father's eyes squint. "I know it's my duty to the Elysium."

He was quiet for a moment, contemplating my request. "You've been through a lot. Take some time to rest. I'm going to schedule some time for us to connect. I want to hear *all* about what you went through and where the humans took you. I'll make sure they pay, you can bet on that."

I'm sure you can, Dad. I'm sure.

I need to choose my words carefully. My first instinct was to tell him it wasn't necessary, but I don't want him to know I was working with the humans. I needed to continue to let him believe I find them despicable. "I'd like some time for the two of us, Dad. Like in the old days."

"How I wish we could go back." My father came over and gave me one more hug. "I'm just happy you're home."

"I'm happy too." Returning his embrace, I breathed in his scent of tobacco and blood. I no longer knew who this man was. He was a stranger.

"Do you need me to have security bring you back to your room?"

I shook my head, both of us knowing there's only one

floor I can access. "I know where it is." Before leaving his office, I offered him a reassuring smile. Pressing the elevator button, I stepped inside and rode down to my floor. Stepping out, I turned to my penthouse door and went inside. I couldn't wait to debrief with Gabe and Jude.

Walking in, everything was quiet. The sound of a heavy breath, thick and labored, reached my ears from the living room, urging me to investigate. Jude's blond hair came into view, sitting on my couch with his head rolled backward. I hesitantly walked closer. "Where's Gabe?" I stopped in my tracks, and my questions were answered. Jude sat on my couch with his pants pooled at his ankles, and Gabe's face was in his lap.

Startled by my sudden question, both jumped and their faces flushed. I didn't know what to do, so my instinct was to run away. Sprinting to my bedroom, I closed the door and locked it.

"Vinny, it's not what it looks like!"

"Come out!"

They were banging on the door, and I slid down it with my knees clutched to my chest. Their words were muted in my mind. What did I just see? When did this begin? Where does this leave me? They stole my heart and time. If they were to choose each other, what would become of the mission? These two men, whom I once saw as heroes, now seemed like thieves who stole my heart and deceived me. Which were they—heroes or thieves? Lines blurred until I couldn't seem to tell them apart anymore.

I knew staying holed up in my room wasn't a reality. I needed to face them. I needed to find out how this happened and what it meant for us going forward. I always felt completely secure with these two men, but now, a deep unease settled in my heart.

Hesitantly, I opened the door. Both of them were standing there, looking concerned.

Gabe started, "Vinny, I—"

I stopped him abruptly, his words hanging unfinished in the air, before capturing his lips in a fervent kiss. His strong hands wrapped around my waist, and he kissed me back, the taste of Jude on his lips. He cared.

I then pulled away and turned toward the human standing next to us.

"I-I'm sorry—"

Ignoring his unfinished sentence, I reached out, my touch gentle yet insistent, drawing his head closer until our faces were inches apart. His tongue was warm and wet, exploring my mouth as I kissed him deeply and fully. The intoxicating feeling of kissing them both, one after the other, while the other watched, was intoxicating. Pulling back, both men were looking at me with lust in their eyes. Like they were hungry and I was their breakfast, lunch, and dinner.

I leaned over, pressing a kiss to Gabe's lips one last time, feeling Jude's warm breath ghost across my own. A third pair of lips entered the intimate moment. The three of us were kissing. Maybe we could make this work?

We stumbled toward my bed, our lips locked in an impassioned kiss, ripping at our clothes until they lay in a tangled heap on the floor. Together, Jude and I collapsed onto the cool, silken sheets, our kisses deepening as Gabe trailed kisses down my skin. I swear, when he got close to my neck, my body sent out a signal to bite. I craved it.

Gabe forcefully grabbed my chin, wrenching it away from Jude's lips. Leaning in closer, a subtle smile tugged at his lips as he gently sucked on my bottom lip. Jude's hand grasped my cock and began working me harder.

As Gabe pulled away from me, his tongue left a trail of warmth from my nipples to my pelvis. He sensually explored my shaft with his tongue, teasingly circling the tip of my dick before sucking on it like a lollipop. His wavy hair bobbed rhythmically, getting deeper and deeper into his throat with each gulp.

It wasn't the greatest head—not like Jude's—but he was trying.

Jude's fingers grazed my skin as he pulled me close, his lips crashing against mine in a passionate kiss, our tongues tangling together. Gabe stopped sucking me and leaned over to Jude, taking his manhood in his mouth. Our kiss paused as he let out a low moan, his eyes fluttering shut and rolling back in his head.

As much as I was enjoying myself, it was amazing to me Gabe was taking his time to please both of us. Usually, it was quick foreplay, he'd suck my blood, then pound me until completion before his erection went away. Tonight was different. He knew Jude and I were the only two who could get hard without blood, so he was taking his time before feasting.

Jude pressed on the back of Gabe's head, urging him lower. A low gagging sound echoed from his throat before Jude finally allowed him to rise. "Fuck." Gabe came back up and longingly kissed Jude, his flaccid member hanging below Jude's belly button. "Can I?"

A mischievous glint sparked in Gabe's eyes as his eyebrows shot up and a smirk stretched across his face. With his stomach to the bed, he raised his hind in the air, like one of the Dogs. Kneeling behind him, Jude exposed Gabe's buttocks and buried his face. A whine escaped from his mouth as Jude lapped at his sensitive hole.

What was happening? Gabe doesn't allow this. Every

time I've tried so much to enter a finger, he quickly ushers me away. Who was this man?

"Vin, come here." Gabe gasped. "Put your cock in my mouth."

Seriously, who *was* this man?

Following his instructions, I pressed myself against the headboard, my legs tightening around Gabe's head as his hand caressed my member and his wet mouth enveloped the tip.

His moans grew in intensity, his warm breath caressing my cock as he powerfully grinded backward onto Jude's tongue. His puppy dog eyes looked up at me in pure ecstasy. "I want you to fuck me, Vin." With a few swirls of the expert tongue, he gasped. "Please."

Gabe never asked this before, but I was more than happy to oblige. Was it Jude? What magnetic hold of passion did he have over us? I firmly grasped Gabe's hips and swiftly moved him until his knees were right at the edge of the bed, positioning myself behind him. I placed my fingers in the two dimples above his butt, feeling the slight arch in his strong back.

Spitting into my hand, I made sure my dick was well-lubricated for him, although I knew Jude had already prepared him with his tongue. I brought my throbbing cock to his entrance, feeling a sudden rush of sensation as I inhaled sharply. "Damn, you're tight." As I eased my way into the confined area, I noticed Jude thrusting into Gabe's mouth, his abs flexing with every thrust.

"Give it to me," Gabe grunted as I inched deeper into him. "All of you."

He was pushing his ass out, asking to take more. I began with gentle thrusts, gradually guiding him into me. Who knew my strong boyfriend, who only topped, would be the one begging for me to fuck him?

"Give him what he wants." Jude bit his bottom lip. "But don't come."

I quickened the pace of my hips, moving smoothly in and out of him. With each reentry, I increased the pressure, and his pleasurable moans assured me I found the perfect spot.

"That's it. Harder," Gabe breathed. "Like I do to you."

I took my hand off his hips and gave his ass a forceful smack, making sure it would leave a lasting impression. With each thrust, my cock hit his prostate forcefully, causing him to moan in pleasure to a point where he momentarily stopped sucking Jude's cock to focus.

Sensing I was nearing the end, I slowed down, relishing the sensation of his tight walls gripping my cock. I wanted Jude to know how it felt to be with a vampire. "Suck him."

"I-I am," Gabe stammered.

"Not his cock," I spat. A bead of liquid leaked from Jude's cock, and I turned my attention to him. "Don't come."

"Do you trust me?" Gabe whispered to him.

In response, Jude slid underneath Gabe, angling his head to the side. "Oh my—" Jude breathed. "God." Rivulets of blood rushed down his chest, covering his pale skin and pink nipples with the crimson liquid. Jude's face looked like he was orgasming as Gabe sucked on him. There is no more pleasure than a vampire feasting on you.

I continued my slow but intentional thrusts into Gabe, trying to control my urge to climax. From between his legs, I saw Gabe's cock slowly begin to inflate until it was standing at full attention, the head fully exposed from his foreskin. "I want you to fuck him," I instructed.

Jude flipped on his stomach, and I paused, giving them a moment to settle. Gabe took one hand and expertly guided his cock to its destination. I knew he entered when

Jude's head rolled backward, and a grunt released itself from his throat.

"You better be able to take all of me," Gabe ordered before planting his entire cock into Jude, who let out a surprised yelp.

Gabe completely took over, as he does when his cock gets full of blood, and Jude let him. As I remained inside him, he started moving his hips slowly at first, then picked up speed. With his movements, my dick was also being worked inside him. The three of us were fully connected.

"Good boy," Gabe growled into Jude's ear, thrusting a bit harder.

His every stroke tightened the hold inside me, pushing me closer to the edge of losing control. I feared much more of this would cause me to bust. I wiped the sweat from my forehead and gently extracted myself from him, settling down beside Jude, who looked lost in bliss.

"Holy shit," Gabe breathed.

"Give me all your come," Jude cooed as he arched his back.

"I'm gonna—I'm gonna—" With one final pound, he unloaded into Jude, his face contorting in the sexiest way possible.

"Wow," Jude breathed. "That was amazing." He reached back, his fingers tangling in Gabe's soft, dark hair, before gently kissing him on the lips. "But it's my turn now."

His eyes narrowed, a predatory glint in them, and he grabbed me, pulling me closer. With a firm grasp on my legs, Jude lifted them onto his broad shoulders, letting his erection tease my hole. His chin, neck, and chest were covered in blood, and it made him look sexy and dangerous at the same time.

He inserted himself, and my body wrapped around

him, like he belonged there and I was reclaiming what was mine. The curve in his cock seemed to ease its way in, rubbing gently against my prostate. With his full girth inside me, he pressed his body against mine, moving in a slow and steady rhythm.

He felt *so* damn good.

My cock rubbed against Jude's muscular body, the precum making our stomachs sticky. "Jude," I breathed. "I'm not going to last long. You both have me right on the edge."

"Me too," he admitted and began increasing the rate of his strokes. The smooth, slick friction of his cock sent jolts of pleasure pulsing through my body.

I became lightheaded, and my body trembled uncontrollably. Was I going to pass out? I was seeing stars as my balls grew tighter and tighter with each stroke of his shaft.

"I'm gonna come," Jude moaned.

"Give it to me," I pleaded as I pushed back, tightening my hold around him. "Give it all to me. I need it."

With a single forceful thrust, Jude unleashed a primal moan, his pelvis convulsing and pulsing deep within me. I knew I couldn't hold on any longer and felt my body tighten as I shot ropes of come over the two of us, like a cream filling in the middle of a snack. Following the orgasm, my body was quaking, and my heart was skipping a few beats.

"Holy shit," Jude breathed, a smile escaping his lips.

"I know." A wave of tingling sensations washed over me as love ignited in my veins like a thousand tiny jolts of electricity, and I prayed it'd never fade. Maybe this could work out between us. My heart burned with desire and contempt. "Where's Gabe?"

From the bathroom, a rich, resonating laugh erupted,

and a damp, gray towel arced through the air. "Thought you two may want this for afterward." He threw himself down on the bed next to me. "Damn, that was fun, wasn't it?"

It was… It really was.

Chapter Thirty-Four

Deep into the night, just before the sun rose to grace the land with its radiance, I stirred from an overwhelming itchiness spreading over my body. I was utterly worn out from the previous few hours and sleepily rolled over, scratching my back against the sheets. I tousled Gabe's wavy hair, flopping across his brow, and lightly kissed his cheek. He flinched at my touch, a subtle movement that made me smile. He looked so damn cute sleeping. I rolled over to look at Jude's cherubic face. His full, soft lips curved into a perfect heart shape, and I pressed my lips to the corner of his mouth.

I'll never need more than this.

Jude stirred. "What're you doin'? Everything okay?"

I smiled and nodded. "Don't worry, I'm just going to the kitchen to grab a glass of blood. I'll be right back."

He rolled over, falling back into his soundless sleep. I scooched to the bed's edge so I didn't disturb either of them. Looking back at the sleeping men, I was whole. These were my guys. The two that have stolen my heart.

The two I completely trusted. While I didn't know what the future held for us, I knew I'd never be without them.

My legs trembled as I pulled one of Gabe's shirts over my head and crept towards the kitchen. Bracing myself against the polished wood of the small bar, I removed the crystal stopper from the decanter and tipped the vessel, filling a heavy rocks glass with the ruby liquid. My dry mouth craved a sip as I dropped one cube of ice inside, hearing it clink softly against the glass.

A hand clamped over my mouth and nose, shoving a perfumed cloth into my face, its cloying sweetness filling my nostrils. The scent was somewhat intoxicating and slightly nostalgic, though I couldn't place where I knew it from. My mind became hazy, and with one last shuddering gasp, my body went limp. Before my vision blurred, a silent scream tore through my throat, a desperate attempt to rouse Gabe and Jude from their sleep, but no sound escaped my lips.

Where was I being taken? How will Gabe and Jude know where I am?

I didn't know how long I'd been out, but when I opened my eyes, a bright light seared my retinas. Was it the sun? The air in the room smelled sterile, like a mixture of bleach and burning hair. My vision was blurred, but the shining light didn't disappear. I was strapped to a cold table with leather belts wrapping around my legs and chest. My arms were stretched out wide, like a T, the rough white gown scratched against my skin.

As my eyes focused, I knew exactly where I was—the lab used for the Extraction. The place I'd come to know once per year for the past sixty-five years as a symbol of my dad's control over me. The place, many times, I thought would kill me.

Two tables flanked me, each laden with racks of vials and a single, menacingly long needle. Fear and anger delved into my core, creating a potent mix of emotions. My father knew I wouldn't be willing to take part in the Extraction, so he took matters into his own hands. He forced me to be his puppet once again.

Two doctors, clad in crisp white jackets and surgical masks, entered the sterile lab. I knew them well; they were always the two who conducted the Extraction. They used to chat with me and make me feel comfortable before they started this procedure, which essentially left me on the verge of death. Now, I only felt a seething hatred toward them, knowing their complicity in my father's cruel plans.

"Good morning, Vincent," one of the doctors started. His voice reminded me of an actor saying lines. Totally scripted and rehearsed. "This is your yearly routine Extraction, we've done this many times, so there's no need to be alarmed."

"Just relax." The other doctor, a woman, sat next to me. With one eye closed, she inspected her needle, which was the length of my forearm.

I tried to scream once again, but nothing came out. I summoned every ounce of strength I could muster and began to writhe on the table, jerking my body erratically so they couldn't get a clean poke from their needle.

"Vincent, I need you to calm down," the male doctor cooed. "Or else we'll have to sedate you."

"And we know how much you hate that."

Each convulsion sent jolts of pain through my body as the straps bit into my flesh, holding me fast to the table. I didn't know exactly what I was doing, but I refused to go down without a fight. I hated my father. I hated how he continued to use me for his own benefit and power. This entire interaction made my decision to take him down all the more easy. I was no longer the good boy standing idly by. I was determined to fight back, no matter the cost.

"Get the sedative!"

The woman next to me abruptly stood from her chair, its legs scraping against the floor, and began rummaging through a nearby closet. She filled a small needle with a clear liquid, holding the syringe between her fingers, like a cigarette, with one bead of substance glistening on its tip. Taking a seat beside me, her eyes crinkled in each corner. "Calm down, or you'll force me to use this."

In response to her, I thrusted my body in the air. I knew as soon as the needle reached my skin, I'd already be asleep. I'd be useless. I needed to do anything in my power to get out of here. Tears pricked my eyes as I watched the doctor rest the needle on top of my skin, ready to push it in.

I tried one last glance at her, pleading not to sedate me, but to pity me instead. Her eyes darted from the syringe, then glazed over, losing all focus. Like whatever she was thinking about, she completely forgot. The doctor slumped in her chair next to me, her shoulders heavy, while the man standing over me crashed backward, hitting the floor hard.

What the hell just happened?

Gabe and Jude stood in the doorway, their guns pointed inwards, the heavy weight of their presence filling the space as I looked toward the door. The table holding the needle next to me filled with blood as her injury grew. I let out a low groan from deep within my throat, hoping to alert the two men's attention.

They hesitantly stepped into the sterile, brightly lit operating room, their arms outstretched, weapons ready to shoot at anyone else who may emerge. Once they deemed the room safe, they ran over, their faces etched with relief, and swiftly removed the gag from my mouth. The straps around my legs and chest finally loosened, and a wave of relief washed over me as the pressure disappeared. I sat up, rubbing the red wounds around my wrists. "I've never been happier to see both of you."

"Aw, come on!" Jude pursed his lips and smiled. "You can't *only* be happy to see us when we're saving you."

"I don't *need* saving."

"Why can't you ever admit you need help?" Jude's lip curled into a half-smile. He whirled around, keeping his gun pointed toward the door. "Anyways, we need to move, it won't be long before these dead bodies are found."

Gabe threw me a pair of spare black medical pants and the T-shirt I was wearing when the doctors abducted me. "Get dressed, we have to go. Once they're found dead, they'll be looking for you. We need to disable the gate right now."

Damn. I knew this time would come, I just didn't expect it to be so soon. I thought we'd maybe have another day to plan. No time like the present, I suppose. Stuffing myself into the unflattering pants and throwing the oversized band shirt over my head, I ran my fingers through my hair. "Let's start this war."

Gabe handed me a pistol and a box of ammo, and I put them in my pocket. "We have silencers if they're needed."

I nodded, now understanding why I didn't hear the bang from their guns as they shot both doctors in the head. "What's the plan?"

"Now that I'm reinstated as a guard, I'll head to the electrical control room and turn off all power." Gabe turned to Jude and me. "And the two of you are going to open the gate to the city. Vin, I think you know where the controls are."

I furrowed my brows. Do I know how to open the

gates? I delved into my mind, thinking back to the limited places I went outside my penthouse, but my mind only showed me the same image. The heavy, black metal door at the hallway's end struck me with a sudden realization. "The Carlton."

"Bingo!" Gabe nods. "The code to the room is zero, two, one, four. I created it."

I put my hand to my heart. It was our anniversary. Back when Gabe and I started dating when we were humans, he bought me Valentine's Day candy and asked if I'd be his boyfriend. Though I roll my eyes every year at our anniversary's predictable date, his thoughtful passcode was undeniably cute. It showed I actually meant something to him.

"But what about you?" Jude asked, exasperated. "I'll make sure Vinny doesn't get hurt, but how will we know you're okay?"

"Once the war breaks out, meet me at the fountain in The Wastes, it's in the middle for both of us. We'll help the humans fight off the vampire army." Gabe's strong hands found my waist, pulling me close as his lips met mine. "You can do this, I know you can."

"I have to," I breathed. "To atone for my father's sins."

"What about the secret vampire army? Shouldn't we figure out a way to stop them?"

"I know nothing about them, so we'll have to hope we have enough manpower to defeat them all." Gabe turned to Jude, putting one hand on his shoulder and looking at him dead in the eye. "I'm trusting you to protect him."

"If you can't be there, I'm his next best protector."

With a gentle pull, Gabe brought Jude near, their lips meeting in a sweet kiss. I watched as Jude lifted his arms, grabbing at Gabe's jaw to pull him deeper. The kiss lingered far longer than mine, and I crossed my arms.

"Alright, you two, let's go. We can discuss how this will work *after* we're done saving the world."

With a shared smirk and a lingering look that spoke volumes, they turned, and we parted ways with our guns loaded and our hearts burning with desire.

Chapter Thirty-Five

"And *I* thought the Silvertown was grim," Jude commented as we made our way outside Elysium.

The Wastes remained unchanged, the same desolate expanse I remembered, though crimson stains marred the stone walkways—remnants of the humans' last visit. Exiles, with their feeble and skinny bodies, lay piled all around. Some lay sprawled in the streets, while others slumped haphazardly against buildings or on benches. A thick blanket of snow covered the area, settling over the Exiles like a layer of fine white dust.

"What are these...things? I don't know how else to describe them, but they feel sad— hopeless."

I nodded, running my hand across my welted skin from the constant itching coursing through me. "Exiled vampires are banished to The Wastes for one reason or another by the vampiric authority." He looked at me. "The people my father and Gabe work for, well, used to work for."

"What makes them look like that?"

"That's what happens when you don't drink blood.

Your body still lives, but slowly withers away. When they get too old, they're usually thrown to the Dogs." I looked around, seeing mounds upon mounds of Exiles around. "Although it appears there are more of them than usual because the Dogs have been disabled."

We passed the large fountain in the middle of the courtyard, and I knew we were getting close. It was weird to be out here in the daylight. When I snuck away on my birthday, this place seemed so mysterious and dark, yet in the light it was dangerous and run-down. I can see why I was always told not to come here, aside from the thieves and Exiles who were looking to drain me.

I noticed the alleyway and waved to Jude. "This way."

"You sure?" He stopped, looking at the crumbling buildings. "This seems sketchy."

"Trust me." Together, we crept down the shadowy alleyway, the rough brick of the hotel scratching against my hand as the familiar building loomed. The sign, though unlit in the daytime sun, still clearly displayed its faded yet powerful letters, confirming our arrival: The Carlton.

I led Jude through the front door and into the once grand lobby, its faded grandeur now hinting at past glories. We went through the door next to the large desk where the wizened man sat, checking people in. Glancing right, I saw the men's locker room and remembered when the lights started blinking when the Unicorns first attacked.

At the end of the hallways was the bamboo-clad tiki bar, where freshly washed plastic coconut cups were heaped on top of each other. A stack of rattan chairs sat beside the drained hot tub, its smooth surface cold and slick to the touch.

"Sauna? Play Room? What is this place?" Jude's head was on a swivel from seeing a contraption like a hot tub for the first time.

"It used to be a hotel, but it was repurposed when the vampires took over."

"Repurposed into what?" He opened the sauna door, showing a quiet room with rows of worn, wooden benches.

"Uh…" My cheeks reddened. "It's a place people go… to have fun."

He poked his head into the Play Room, and his mouth dropped. "What the hell are those swings used for?"

"Don't touch anything." I couldn't help but laugh at his naivety. There was no way I could tell him what each of these rooms was used for—or that I was yearning to come here just to let loose before we met. This adventure scratched that itch for me, but I never want to go back to being controlled like I was.

I walked halfway up the staircase to the second level and leaned over the railing. "C'mon, Jude, we have to hurry."

He put a finger to his lips. "Shh! We don't know if anyone is here."

"Why would anyone be here? It's only open at night once a month."

With a careless shrug, he trailed behind me up the steps. Our feet clinking on the cool, smooth tiles echoed as the familiar faded red arrow on the sign beckoned us forward. "Executive Lounge, that's exactly where we need to be."

With his gun held high, Jude followed me down the hallway. We passed endless rooms, each identical to the last, and I wondered if I'd recognize the lounge. I remember it being a big black door, but it didn't have a sign or anything on it. I just got a weird feeling when I passed it.

A strange, unsettling feeling of intrigue settled deep within my bones, intensifying with each step we took.

Straight ahead was the Diamond Bar, where I met that sleazeball Trent, who tried forcing himself on me. My heart fluttered as I remembered Gabe showing up and putting a knife to the man's neck.

So romantic.

An inexplicable urge made me look down the hallway, where a heavy black metal door stood out, its keypad emitting a faint, warm glow against the cold steel. "This is it." I hurriedly typed the code Gabe gave me and heard a click as the door unlocked. A disconcerting flicker of the hallway lights was accompanied by a distorted, unsettling sound—a misplaced resonance—that seemed to distort the space. With electricity, there's a constant humming in the air, but when that power is removed, it's replaced with a strange silence.

"Gabe must have disabled the power."

We entered the room behind the door to find a fairly large lounge, complete with a bar along one wall, velvet chairs, and couches all situated around a stage lined with a circle of light bulbs that had a shining pole in its center, affixed to the ceiling. Surprisingly, the room felt luxurious, despite the events that took place here. A strange smell lingered from the lounge, one I shudder to describe.

The electric hum, a low thrumming sound, started up again, and the circular ceiling and floor lights flickered to life. My lip turned upward as I passed a velvet couch, seeing stains on the armrest. Disgusting.

"Wh-what happened? Did Gabe fail?"

"I don't think so," I answered hesitantly. "Only certain lights came on. I think this hotel may have a generator that would provide power for necessities in the event of an outage."

There was a sudden flash of red and green lights from a small, oddly placed door at the back of the room that startled us, and then we immediately ran towards it. A standard hotel-style card reader secured the door, its metallic surface slightly worn from frequent use. A faint green glow pulsed gently, beckoning me to turn the cool metal handle.

"Another shock that this door is open," I breathed.

"It has to be because the power went out," Jude whispered, keeping his gun pointed downward, ready for anything.

The next room had textured black walls which seemed to absorb the light, drawing the eye to the plush red headboard of the large bed, which dominated the space. The bed was so big, at least five people could fit in it. I rolled my eyes—of course, the vampiric council and military, who are majority men, would create a secret room to bring their flavor of the night. Men will be men.

On the far side of the wall, a door with a glowing red keypad hummed faintly. "Well, I think we found where the power is going."

My hands grew slick with sweat as I gripped the cold, metallic handle of my gun, my heart pounding in my chest, knowing what lay beyond the door. I lifted my finger, pressing the code Gabe shared onto the keypad, and a satisfying click echoed as the red light blinked green. I looked at Jude, his expression serious, as he nodded and, with a powerful kick, sent the door swinging inward.

Jude and I stepped inside, guns raised, and three surprised faces stared back at us. The three men fumbled for their weapons at their hips, but our draw was faster. Jude's silent shot sailed through the air, and the man closest to me stumbled backward, a look of shock on his face. The recoil jolted my arm as I pulled the trigger, but my shot went wide, the bullet striking the man farthest away.

"Fuck!" the man yelled and clasped his leg.

I looked at the vampire I'd missed, his sharp fangs catching the dim light, their points gleaming menacingly. A cruel smile stretched across his face as his finger tightened on the trigger of his gun. It was like everything happened in slow motion. A deafening gunshot ripped through the air, and I shoved Jude to the ground, our bodies hitting the floor just as the bullet ricocheted off the wall.

Jude's hand moved like a blur as he brought up his weapon. The gunshot was sharp and immediate, correcting my earlier miss. The man fell to the ground in a solid heap while the last remained seated. The room felt cramped, a suffocating density of objects making it hard to tell if it was actually small or just overflowing with machines. Floor-to-ceiling monitors displayed various zones of The Wastes, their flickering screens showing specific points along the perimeter of the wall outside the city.

Jude sprinted toward the final man and swiftly wrapped his arm around the vampire's neck, pressing the cold steel of his gun to his temple. I scanned the several monitors displaying live feeds of the outside world, focusing on those pointed toward the city's exterior wall. No sign of The Unicorns, they must be hiding well.

"How do we open the gate?" With a decisive shove, Jude pressed the barrel of his gun to the man's temple.

"You'll never take down the vampires, you filthy human!" The man's voice was laced with disgust as he turned to me. "And you should be ashamed of yourself, you asshole!"

"Don't talk to him like that!" Jude screamed. "Help us, or you'll feel a bullet in your head."

The man held his hands up. "Okay, okay, fine. What do you want?"

"Unlock the gate."

"I can't do that without Mr. Asposito's direction."

Jude punched the man hard in the face and then returned his gun against his head. "Does it look like we care about Mr. Asposito's direction? Just fucking do it!"

"Whatever you say." A rhythmic clicking filled the air as the man typed furiously, his eyes flitting between the glowing screens and the keyboard, a blur of motion.

I stared at the wall of screens, each displaying various areas within The Wastes and the slow, agonizing movements of the Exiles. My head bounced between the multitude of monitors, each displaying a different camera angle—I had no idea the surveillance was so extensive. I was drawn to a bright red button, encased in a plastic box on the dashboard that seemed to mock me.

Of course it was a red button. My father is always *so* dramatic.

"All set!" The man smiled and reclined in the chair. "I've notified the vampire army that there's been a breach in the security room, you both can go fuck yours—"

Before the man could utter another word, Jude's swift movement ended his life, the bullet piercing his temple. He hunched over, the warm blood trickling down his face and splattering onto the cold, hard floor below. I opened the plastic box and pressed the red button, my gaze glued to the flickering screen. A loud sound, reminiscent of a fire alarm, blared through the air, and white lights began blinking atop the gates to enter the city.

"We did it!" Jude smiled as he watched the screen with me. "We really did it!" He hugged me in his excitement.

"C'mon, let's get outside and let Arthur know this war can start."

Jude clasped my hand, and we ran through the echoing hallways of the hotel. The air felt lighter, and each step propelled us forward with surprising ease. We did it—the regime of vampires will soon be over. We pushed the doorway leading to the hotel lobby open and ran into The Wastes outside. Scaling the alleyway, we came to the main road.

I watched as Jude reached into his shirt, revealing the stick Arthur handed him. He ripped it open with his teeth, and three red balls shot into the air, leaving a bright red streak in their wake before exploding with a pop. A searing red light filled the sky as the explosion boomed, and a ferocious battle cry echoed around us.

Then the gate opened.

Chapter Thirty-Six

With the gate slightly ajar, humans slowly started trickling into The Wastes in droves. Each person wore pristine white armor, their faces hidden behind their signature metallic horse masks. Jude and I, fueled by determination, sprinted towards the gate, passing several Exiles that'd been attempting to lift themselves from the ground. Many were walking away as briskly as they could; perhaps they knew a war was imminent.

"Vincent! Jude! You did it!"

Our hearts leapt as we heard a familiar voice. The man lifted his mask, and Arthur's face stared back at us. Relief washed over me as we ran to him, the sounds of the approaching human army a thunderous roar in The Wastes.

"Here, take these." Arthur threw a couple of horse masks at us. "I figure you'd wear these to hide your identity from the vampires and also to let our team know you're one of us."

A terrifying, high-pitched screech pierced the silence as a colossal black beam shot upwards, expanding to form a net-like structure across the sky. Reaching the high poles on the city's wall, the thick covering cast a heavy veil over the city, muffling the sun's warmth and creating a shadowy atmosphere.

"Impressive tint your father has here." Arthur smiled. "This must only be used if there's an attack during the day, so the army can fight and deter us from getting inside."

"Pretty smart," Jude acknowledged.

"Our first wave is fully prepared to combat the vampire army," Arthur confidently said. "Hopefully, our second wave will be enough for the secret army. Did you find out any more about them?"

Jude shook his head. "It's a mystery."

"I do have a secret third army to help us if we need it as well." A triumphant smile stretched Arthur's lips, a sure victory already tasted on his tongue as he watched the humans. "We'll take your father's power today, Vincent." He clapped me on my shoulder. "And create a new world where humans and vampires live in harmony."

Instead of reveling in the show above, my eyes remained fixated on the grim figures of the Exiles. "Something isn't right." Those with enough strength walked toward Elysium, while others, weakened and desperate, clawed at the ground in a slow approach. I looked at Arthur, putting on my mask. "Rally the troops, Jude, and I will check this out."

With a curt nod, Arthur rejoined the human army, the air thick with anticipation. I cocked my head to Jude, indicating for him to follow me. With the weight of our weapons heavy in our hands, we stealthily followed the Exiles. Each one looked sicker and paler than the last, almost like zombies. They all crept toward the same direction, their movement ominous and silent, as if fleeing some unseen terror. Could it be the humans?

We followed them through the park to the courtyard where the empty fountain sat in its center, my eyes searching for Gabe. The Exiles were flocking around the fountain, some were even inside the empty basin. Familiar alarms sounded around me—the same ones I heard the night I was kidnapped. The vampires knew they were under attack, and the troops would soon be deployed.

"What're they doing?" Jude whispered. "It's like they're trying to hide."

"Put on your mask. The vampire army will soon be coming out of Elysium."

We secured the masks over our faces, peering through the small eyeholes, watching what happened next in stunned silence. A metallic crunching echoed from beneath the courtyard, like some trapped creature clawing at the pipes. The sound soon stopped, and the metal fountain began to shake. I braced myself for an explosion, but instead, water started spraying from its openings.

"What…is that?" Jude breathed.

I squinted at the fountain. It wasn't water; it almost looked like rust, and my eyes grew wide once I realized what was spurting out of the top. "It's blood."

The metallic scent overwhelmed the Exiles as they surged towards the fountain, a chaotic mass of flailing limbs and desperate cries. Some toppled into the basin with a splash, while others carefully climbed the treacherous ladder of Exiles to drink from the fountain directly. With each drop of blood re-entering their body, the Exiles were becoming stronger. Their arms and legs, once thin and weak, began to fill out with muscle, and their pale skin started regaining a healthy color.

"J-Jude, we gotta get out of here and warn your dad." With the majority of the vampire army gathering, it was nearly impossible not to stammer. "*This* is the secret army."

The Exiles' hearing must have improved, for a group perked up their ears in my direction, their eyes fixed on both of us. A piercing scream ripped through the quiet as Jude and I scrambled back towards the human army. I glanced back and saw the Exiles, their teeth bared in snarls, scrambling towards us on all fours like crazed animals. Like Dogs.

Rounding the corner, the imposing gates came into view, and with a sense of urgency, we waved our arms, trying to get Arthur's attention. The intense thumping from the handful of Exiles behind us indicated others were on their way. The human army ahead of us began sprinting toward us, weapons outstretched, a terrifying wave of shouting and clashing steel. A war cry came from ahead, while a shriek of bloodlust came from behind, heightening our sense of impending danger.

Two sharp gunshots cracked through the air, followed by a heavy thud that vibrated through the ground behind us. I looked over my shoulder and saw the two newly grown vampires who were chasing us were shot dead. Humans, guns blazing, rushed past, spraying bullets at the vampires in the courtyard.

"Now's the time," Arthur boomed over the rushing humans. "Protect our families! Protect the human race!"

Doubled over with my chest heaving, gasping for air, Jude put a reassuring hand on my back. "C'mon, let's see if we can find Gabe. He should be around here."

My gun's metal handle was in my hand as I regained my composure. Unicorns were still rushing by me, their white coats a dazzling sight, and I realized there were many more people in the first wave than I expected. From underneath my mask, I nodded to Jude. "Let's go."

We turned around and joined the throng of humans running toward the courtyard. Now that the Exiles had time to drink deeply from the gushing fountain, many were at their full potential. Their pale bodies were crisscrossed with long, blue veins like a roadmap, and their fingers ended in unnaturally long claws.

A bloody scene unfolded in front of us. Unicorns shot at the vampires with their guns and also used various other methods to distract them, like smoke bombs and paralysis gas. As much as the vampires may have had the upper hand with brute strength, there was much more white than red.

Dodging the pale skin of vampires and the desperate faces of humans, Jude and I ran through the thick, surging crowd until a massive explosion engulfed us in a wave of heat and debris. A thick, white smoke surrounded us, obscuring everyone within its swirling embrace. My lungs burned as I coughed, waving my arms wildly, searching for Jude amidst the confusing chaos. "Where are you?" The smoke was so thick, I might be standing directly next to a vampire, and I'd have no idea.

A hand wrapped around mine. "Don't worry, I'm right here."

A touch to the side of my mask brought a screen to life before my eyes, its glow warm against my skin. Faint outlines of the people around me materialized before my eyes, their features blurred except for the sharp horns on their unicorn masks. We crept forward until a powerful force slammed me to the ground. A vampire was on top of me, its fangs glistening even through the thick fog.

Two deafening gunshots rang out, and the vampire crumpled next to me. Through the deafening scream, I saw Jude beside me, a thin, acrid plume of smoke curling from his smoking weapon. "Th-thanks," I whispered. "Let's go!"

We found the courtyard's perimeter, its rough stone walls beneath our hands as we carefully moved along, escaping the choking smoke. Splashing water and murmuring voices from the Exiles drinking at the fountain reached my ears. Gabe stood in the middle of them, his gun pointed and firing.

This may be the wrong time to say this, but he looked *so* hot.

Gabe was surrounded on all sides by vampires, their eyes glowing menacingly in the dim light. It seemed no matter which way he turned, there was another one there. When one vampire fell, two more took its place. Although many bodies were lying at his feet.

I pointed my gun and began running toward him, firing. Gunshots came from my weapon and from Jude, who was directly next to me. Our bullets sailed through the air, reaching both their targets, leaving Gabe to continue his fight.

"About time you guys got here!" he yelled to us with a smirk.

A small, soft blue ball appeared in Jude's hand as he reached into his pocket and threw it high. It clinked against the uneven stone walkway and exploded, creating another shield of smoke. Through the fog, we neared Gabe, and I grabbed his hand. With a powerful pull, I yanked him from the circle of deadly vampires.

"Where to?" I whispered.

"The vault." He coughed. "That's where your dad is."

Chapter Thirty-Seven

Jude and I followed Gabe back into Elysium, heading upward to the level where the vault was located: thirteen. Each step we took was heavy with anticipation, our breaths labored. Going from the chaos outside, it seemed odd to hear silence. It made me feel on edge and kept my senses heightened, as if expecting an ambush at any moment.

"There's a direct elevator to the vault from your father's quarters," Gabe explained through heavy breaths. "Just in case there's an attack, so he'll likely already be inside." He increased his speed, taking two steps at a time. "Hurry, I don't want any of the vampires to find us."

"Isn't the army outside?" Jude asked as he trailed directly behind Gabe, our heavy feet echoing in the stairwell.

He shook his head. "That's the Exiled, they're the first wave of protection for Elysium. The second wave is hundreds of military-trained vampires. Their training quarters and weapon safehold are on the same level as the vault, so we have to be careful not to run into any of them."

"Let's take these off." I lifted the mask from my face and tucked it under my armpit, as Jude did with his own. A sickening dread filled me, the pit in my stomach deepening with each step, a feeling I couldn't shake. What will I do once I get there? I knew I had to take down my father, but I wanted him to admit to everything he did. I needed validation in knowing I was saving the vampires and humans by removing this man from power.

As we reached the bottom of the stairs, we saw an elevator door and two smaller doors on either side of it. A large black metal door to the right seemed to pulse with the echoes of a thousand battle cries, while the golden door across from it remained still and quiet. "Let me guess which one is the vault." I rolled my eyes. "Could my father be any more obvious?"

"Men's ego will always be their downfall," Jude breathed.

Gabe swiped his security card at the glowing electronic screen, hearing a satisfying click as the door unlocked. He gripped the handle with one strong hand, pulling the door open with a loud creak.

"I thought you cut the power?"

Gabe lowered his head, his perfectly arched eyebrow conveying skepticism. "Do you think your father wouldn't have a generator inside the vault?"

I rolled my eyes again. "Of course he would."

Inside, a towering wall of wooden crates, overflowing with canned goods, created a narrow aisle leading to a sturdy metal door. The door featured a combination lock dead center, with a large Dog wheel directly underneath. The hatchway resembled the kind of vault door used by banks—imposing, steel, and clearly designed for maximum security. How subtle.

"I don't know the combination, do you?" I asked Gabe. "I suppose we could try all the numbers I can think of—birthdays, anniversaries, important moments."

"I don't think we'll need it," Jude answered, opening the thick door. "It's already open."

"I'll go first," I whispered, circling Jude and stepping foot inside. "Don't lock us in." The door was so thick, and the locks were so definitive that I was scared if it closed fully, we'd be stuck inside forever. Trapped.

As soon as we delved deeper, the overhead lights slowly flickered on, casting a warm glow on our surroundings. Jude's mouth fell open, his shock apparent as he took in the opulent room. The room was a bizarre mix of luxury and tackiness—plush seating sank under the weight of its own opulence, while gold leaf clashed with the cold, hard surfaces of numerous, oddly placed animal statues. To someone who didn't know, this room would've looked very rich and over-the-top, which I'm sure it was.

I hated my father's taste. And this was *all* him.

Continuing deeper into the bunker, the musty smell intensified as we entered a room filled with exercise equipment, followed by a surprisingly large kitchen and living area. These rooms looked similar to the first we were in—old and garish. It was clear this vault had been designed over sixty-five years ago and hadn't been updated since. Then again, why update something you hope never to use?

From the kitchen, a man straightened from his crouched position, his face pale, letting out a slight yelp when he saw us. Once his mind registered it was me, he clutched his chest. "Vincent, you startled me. Did my guards find you?"

"What?" I was confused; it was like he was expecting me.

His eyebrows pinched together. "I told my staff to find you and bring you here for safety." He shifted toward Gabe. "Ah, there's my boy. I knew I could count on you for bringing Vincent to me." His eyes flashed to Jude with distaste. "Who's your friend?"

"Dad, wh-what is this place?" I ignored his question, trying to subtly shift the focus from the human in the room.

"It's my bunker," he answered, extending his arms like he was welcoming me home. "I made it in case we were ever attacked, another nuclear war broke out, or a new sickness affecting vampires came to fruition."

"For us?"

He laughed. "Of course, who else would I want to be with at the end of the world?"

Me, for my blood. He was playing a game.

"There are rumors outside Elysium that this vault holds the key to killing all the vampires." Gabe stepped in and scanned the room, clearly searching for answers.

My father laughed again. "Nope, just a bunker. I don't believe there's a way to kill the vampire race. We are here to stay. That is, as long as we have enough blood to sustain our bodies, which we always will thanks to my son."

Gabe, Jude, and I subtly exchanged shared looks. "I've heard that too. Why would everyone think that if it's not true, Dad?"

"Hmm, maybe for the secret room I created?" He crept toward a secluded door on the far side of the living room. "I needed this place to be a true safe haven, so I developed this room and stocked it to last a few years, just in case."

I walked toward my father, the smile on his face crinkling the corners of his eyes, as he held the door open for me. Jude and Gabe remained, their hands hovering over their holstered weapons, ready for action. The air crackled with tension. As I leaned into the room, the sudden burst of light from the motion sensors startled me, revealing a surprisingly tidy space. A long hallway stretched before me, filled with shelves upon shelves of large crystal decanters that were filled to the brim with blood.

"What is this?" I breathed as a sudden wave of prickliness scratched at my skin.

"Isn't it obvious? Blood!" he screamed in delight. "Years ago, when I started experimenting, I found a way to create a longer-lasting strain of blood and stocked this bunker with it. See the big red button at the far end of the wall?"

I nodded. Knowing my father, a big red button didn't mean anything good. He's such a cliche.

"It's the last resort. If pressed, that button will detonate bombs all over the city. But not us." He smiled. "We have this new blood that stays fresher longer, although it has a shorter rate of effectiveness. We've actually had it for quite a while, but have never distributed it to other Elysiums." He shrugged once he noticed the disgust on my face. "What? Supply and demand increases the price of goods."

"Speaking of that…there's been something I've wanted to talk with you about." I knew my voice was shaking, but I tried my hardest to remain calm and steady. "I heard some things about you while I was kidnapped."

"My dear boy, you cannot believe a word the humans say. They're all liars." He poured himself a drink and took a swig. "Look at their politics before the collapse. They cannot be trusted."

No more beating around the bush—I have to finally be direct and honest. "Dad, did you help create the Dogs and keep them in production this whole time?"

I've never seen my dad's face lose sense of control. It was like hearing my direct question made him glitch. Everyone he knows speaks to him like he's the most important person in the world. And I suppose to them, he is. But not me, not anymore.

"It's widely known Dante created the Dogs."

"That wasn't the question," Gabe spat. "Answer him."

His eyes, cold and sharp as ice, threw daggers at the man before him. "Remember who you're speaking to, Gabriel." He squinted, peering at each of us intently before pushing his glasses up his nose and planting one hand firmly on his hip. "Dante and I created the Dogs as well as the automation for their repair in the event of damage. That was the directive of the United States government at the time."

"And what of after?"

"Dante and I had a falling out. I wanted to use the Dogs for the vampire's advantage, and he wanted to disable them completely."

"And what did you do to him?" He must know I now have knowledge of all the despicable things he's done. "Did you kill him? Turn him into a vampire?"

He shrugged. "I haven't heard from him in years. I assume he was at the laboratory in the mountains. We continue to send him supplies and food because our order forms keep being completed."

Why was he continuing to lie to me? "Do you take responsibility, even partially, for the apocalypse we're in?"

He paused, a finger tapping thoughtfully against his chin, before answering. "Partially, I suppose, but it was all to preserve the people I loved."

"Let's be real—it was for power and wealth." This was the first time Jude spoke, and though his voice trembled slightly, he wasn't wrong. His face blazed with fury and anger. "Stop lying to your son. He knows the truth."

A sly smirk stretched across my father's face, his eyes twinkling mischievously. "Well, yes, I made a lot of money and became the most powerful individual in the world. With all my wealth, I created Elysiums across the globe, safe vampire compounds away from humans. My initial thought was to live separately but harmoniously."

"Until you used the Dogs to kill the humans," Gabe said under his breath.

"Look at what I created!" The sound of buzzing filled the room as Salvatore clicked a button, turning on the old television screen hanging on the wall. Four quadrants displayed horrific visions of The Wastes—a bloodbath of chaos and destruction happening outside, each quadrant a different angle of the carnage. "I created the strongest army in the world, and we're winning! I cannot be stopped. It's my responsibility to ensure the vampire race continues."

I gazed at the television and saw Exiles launching themselves at the humans, taking them down one by one. A horrifying expanse of white snow was stained crimson where the soldiers lay, their bodies scattered across the field. The only color was their white coats, now red.

"Speaking of responsibility." My dad swept across the room. "I understand the Extraction was unsuccessful today. We found our poor doctors completely dead. I didn't raise you to be a killer, Vincent."

"I-I'm not giving my blood to anyone anymore. Without me, you'll turn into an Exile, and this war will be over. We can finally start to rebuild what you've broken."

"Oh, you'll give it to me, whether you give it willingly

or I force you to." With a roar, my father launched himself across the room, knocking me onto the floor. I screamed, my legs thrashing wildly as his fangs tore into my neck, and a chilling cold ran under my skin as he began to drain me.

Chapter Thirty-Eight

Sounds of my father feasting on me blared through my eardrums. A snarl and moan rumbled from deep in his throat as he drank deeply from the artery in my neck. My body and mind were completely in shock and paralyzed. It all happened so fast. I couldn't even hear Jude and Gabe screaming until they removed my dad from on top of me.

Gabe's powerful hands gripped my dad's shoulders, sending him sprawling backward against the wall with a heavy thud. With a swift, decisive movement, Jude unsheathed his gun and pressed it to my father's temple. "I'm only keeping you alive because Vinny would never forgive me if I made a move. Don't try anything, or I'll be forced to put a bullet through your head."

His eyes wide with worry, Gabe fell to his knees, his warm hand cradling my neck. "Vin! Are you okay?"

I swallowed the saliva pooling in my throat. "I-I'm fine."

His fangs pierced his skin, a bead of blood welling up

before he offered his wrist to my mouth. "Drink me to help you regain your strength."

I wrapped my lips around his wrist and drew in a deep breath. Blood cascaded into my mouth like water from a lake once the dam had been removed. His blood was sweet, and I couldn't get enough. Is this how I tasted to him? No wonder he loved sex so much. As my body grew stronger, I gradually released his wrist from my mouth. I wiped my lips with the back of my hand. "Thanks."

A bloodcurdling scream, sharp and piercing, echoed from the wall. My father started making gurgling noises, his face turning pale, and his body heaved as if he were about to vomit. His face drained of color, and his cheeks swelled as his skin took on a sickly gray hue. He doubled over, clutching his stomach in agony, and collapsed onto the floor in a fetal position.

"What's happening? What's wrong with him?" Jude asked, locked onto the man with his gun extended.

Is it bad of me to say I didn't care what happened to him? On one hand, I wished Jude would pull the trigger, but my conscience wouldn't allow it. I didn't know why he was sick, but I also didn't care. He deserved it.

A hearty laugh boomed from the doorway. "Evil is a disease that infects the body and mind."

Every eye in the vault snapped to the door, a tense silence between us as we waited to see who entered. With a slow, deliberate movement, a man in a white robe reached up, his fingers finding the surface of his unicorn mask before he let it fall to the ground. From the shadows emerged Arthur, a triumphant smirk playing on his gray beard as he brandished a gleaming pistol.

"D-dad, what're you doing here?"

He held his chin high, eyes locked onto my father, a

steely gaze that dared him to challenge him. "I'm here to end this war."

My dad was still on the ground in pain, but managed to croak, "End the war? The vampires will never lose. We're-we're winning."

"Oh, are you?" A chuckle came from Arthur's mouth. "I had a trick up my sleeve, too. Why don't you see for yourself, Sal?"

We stared at the screen, the four quadrants of the war outside painted in stark, flashing colors, the air heavy with the unspoken screams of those fighting. The vampires were growing tired. The battle looked about even, with both sides slowing down. From the gate, a larger wave of humans appeared, brandishing pitchforks, axes, and other barbaric weapons.

A horrifying eruption of red liquid sprayed across the floor as my father let out a massive belch. "The vampires will be victorious. If the Exiles fail, my military will step in."

"So you say." Arthur shook his head in disbelief before turning to me. "Vincent, what's wrong with your father? It seems he has fallen ill after trying to drink your blood."

Why did Arthur's tone change? The once fatherly man now radiated dark energy. Something different, something sinister. "Yeah, it-it has never happened before."

"Never happened before, isn't that strange?" With a frown, Arthur tapped a finger to his chin, feigning deep concentration. "What might be different from the last time he drank from you?"

I had no idea what he was getting at. There was nothing different about me.

"Your blood is no longer drinkable, thanks to my son."

Gasps of horror filled the room, a chilling counterpoint to my father's labored moans and the sounds of his vomit.

Gabe's eyes were wide, his chin almost hitting the floor. With his mouth clamped shut, Jude expelled ragged breaths through his nose, his eyes glistening with moisture. The revelation hung in the air, heavy and shocking.

How could this be true? Did Jude somehow deceive me? The thought was like a dagger to my heart, shattering the trust I had in him and leaving my thoughts in a whirlwind of confusion and betrayal.

"You liar!" My father's accusation pierced the air. "That dirty human is gaslighting you!"

Arthur cocked his head at me. "Am I lying, Vincent? Have you been feeling…ill? Maybe even itchy?"

All eyes were on me, boring into me like daggers. How did he know I've been nauseous and my constant itchiness? What was Arthur trying to get at? "Yes, but that doesn't mean my blood is bad."

"And that's where you're wrong." Arthur held one finger in the air like he remembered something. "You're special, Vincent, you're the blueprint. I had a thought after hacking into the files Sal created on extending blood lifespan—maybe, just maybe, I could delve into the data to see if there was a way to render your blood unusable. And after years of experiments, *I did*. You needed fertile semen injected into your bloodstream, it seemed so obvious once I realized. Something alive would cancel out the death—the fertile human DNA caused a cellular-level rejection and had manifested as a full body rash." His eyes glinted in the light. "But there was no way of confirming the validity of my experiment, which is why we staged an attack to kidnap you…and I made sure my son was there every step of the way."

"Wait a sec…" Jude lowered his gun from my father's head. "Did you-did you *use* me?"

Arthur's pupils drifted upward, and he moved each of

his hands up and down, like he was trying to balance something. "I wouldn't say I used you exactly…more like I initiated your meeting and forced the two of you together with the hope you may get close…too close. And I was right." He held up a finger. "That was part one of my plan. The second was to continue to fuel Vincent's hatred for his father after the first laboratory fell, and that's when I set off the bomb at Silvertown."

"You're disgusting!" I yelled over my father's screams of pain. "You killed all those innocent humans, leaving children without parents!"

"But I wasn't wrong. You wanted nothing more than to help me." Arthur smiled, his larger-than-normal incisors peeking out of his lips. "After intercourse with my son, your blood was infiltrated and unusable by the vampires going forward." His chin gave a slight nod toward my father, who was fixed on him. "Vincent is no longer able to be used to continue the vampire race." He sidled closer to Jude with a smug smile painted across his lips. "But I believe I can."

"What do you mean?" I screamed. "How's that possible?"

"Throughout the years, I've been microdosing on vampire blood, leaving just enough human in me. Equal parts human and vampire." He couldn't hide his triumphant smile. "After a few experiments, I believe my blood can create the next generation."

A gasp caught in my throat. His experiments were the sick people in Silvertown jail. He was experimenting on his own citizens, whom he vowed to protect.

"Dad, I-I can't believe this." Disbelief etched Jude's face as he shook his head, his whole body trembling in anger.

It was unreal. This man, who was so nice, so caring,

was a monster. He was the puppet master, pulling the strings behind everything that transpired between Jude and me. I was sick, and I felt dirty. We played right into his hands. He was the king, and we were his pawns. Despite my best efforts to break free from my father's grasp and forge my own path, I had fallen into the hands of someone else's control.

"Now we can create our own world. One without Salvatore Asposito. We can rebuild the world with super-humans. Doesn't that sound exciting?"

"Hold on," my father groaned. "I know you, aren't you —ahh!" With a pained expression, he grabbed his aching stomach and puffed his cheeks. Whatever was happening to him wasn't good.

Arthur walked closer to the trembling Jude. "Move out of the way, let me take a look at this man before I put him out of his misery."

Jude remained steadfast, a silent sentinel between my father and his father, his presence unyielding.

"I said move, or *he'll* get the bullet." Arthur's arm stretched out, the gun steady in his hand, aimed squarely at me.

Gabe stood, shielding me from Arthur. "You won't hurt him."

"Gabe, move," I yelled. "Don't be stupid. Don't die for me."

"I'd always die for you," he answered. "You're my beginning and end."

"See, Jude?" Arthur spat. "If you don't move away, he'll get the first bullet, and Vincent will get the second. Is that what you want?" He glared at Jude and narrowed his eyes, like a master schooling his disobedient dog.

"Just listen to him!" I yelled. I couldn't bear the responsibility if anything happened to Gabe, knowing his stubborn streak and the immense love he held for me.

Jude reluctantly ran to us, collapsing into our embrace. "We have to get out of here. I need to know you're both safe."

Arthur bent down and spoke quietly to my father, whose gasps for breath echoed in the stillness. I watched as my dad's pupils dilated, his jaw dropping slightly in shock. I strained my ears, desperate to catch the murmur of their conversation.

My father vomited a small pool of blood and muttered, "But how did you do all of this?"

Arthur turned to us and solemnly said, "I'm sorry for doing this, Vincent." There was a metallic click of the trigger as he pointed the gun at my father, and the subsequent gunshot shattered the silence.

It was like everything turned black and white. My father's body went limp, his blood pooling around him. The look on my dad's face—etched with terror—is all I remember. The gunshot itself was completely silent to me. His eyes, wide with shock, slowly drooped, mirroring the crushing weight of defeat and loss. He was always one of those people you never thought would die, who would live forever. Yet when he did pass on, it almost seemed surreal that someone so important was nothing more than a normal being.

Arthur muttered a silent prayer under his breath.

"Come on, Vin, let's go!" Jude tugged insistently on my arm, but I remained rooted to the spot.

"You'll be safer here. At least until the war is over." Arthur pointed to the screens. "Ah, it looks like my third wave finally joined."

The screens showed humans and vampires locked in a desperate battle. The ground was covered in blood, yet both humans and vampires continued to battle on. Broken bodies lay scattered across the muddied ground, their chests crushed under the relentless march of soldiers on both sides. I was fixated on the imposing gates, where a wave of animals in perfect formation stormed the gates. I squinted. "What are those?"

"My babies," Arthur whispered, his voice full of love and relief. "I've been waiting for this day to come. I created my own Dogs to help us win the war."

A squadron of metal animals marched onto the screen. Their red eyes, burning with intensity, were laser-focused on the vampires, who screamed as they desperately tried to escape. The Dogs exploded into a frenzy of barking and snapping teeth, launching themselves at anyone who dared to approach.

"How did you—why did you?" Jude stuttered next to me.

It all clicked in my mind, like a puzzle coming together. The vampire blood kept him alive longer than the average human. Arthur knew the passcodes for both laboratories. He even knew the dates to shut off the Dogs in the mountains. The Polaroid pictures on the computer. He had the knowledge to create new Dogs. He called my father Sal.

A wave of realization washed over me, and the words seemed to choke out of my mouth. "You're Dante."

Arthur turned to me, a surprised look on his face as he shrugged. "Sal had the ego, I had the brains."

A gunshot rang out through the bunker, and Arthur—Dante—fell to the ground with a smoldering bullet through his forehead. Tears streamed down Jude's face as he collapsed onto the ground, his gun clattering to the ground with a metallic clang.

"I had to do it." He sobbed. "I had to. He created

more of them. He was going to be another version of your dad—worse probably."

I knelt, cupping his face in my hands, feeling the warm tears stream over my fingers. "Jude, I love you." I looked at the black-haired man behind me. "I love both of you."

Gabe kissed him on the cheek, licking the salty tears from his lips. "You did what you had to do for the greatest good."

The greatest good. What *was* the greatest good in this moment? I stood, a knot of dread tightening in my stomach, and walked over to the screens to watch the Dogs rip the vampires apart. I couldn't let this continue. The Dogs should never be allowed to walk this Earth again.

Gabe held Jude's head against his chest, his hand gently rubbing Jude's shoulder, and I smiled, feeling the warmth of my love for both men. "I have to do what's right for everyone—for us."

They didn't try to sway me, so I ran before they could. I opened the door to the secret room lined with blood, opened the glass box, and punched the red button protruding from the wall. Red lights started blinking around me, and just as I ran back to the two men, all of the doors within the bunker closed shut.

"Vinny, what did you do?" Gabe yelled.

I did it for the greater good. I did it for us. I did it for our future.

We watched the screens as several large explosions erupted in a blinding flash, the sound delayed slightly before the connection was lost. Killing every vampire, every human, and every Dog battling within the war outside.

My gilded cage was destroyed. Elysium was no more.

Epilogue

"You okay?" Jude asked, his wild, wavy blond hair bouncing in the sunlight, a halo of gold around his head.

He snapped me out of a daze, a daydream I found myself in—maybe more like a nightmare. A strained smile stretched my face as I nodded, the muscles stiff and uncomfortable. "I-I'm fine, are you heading out?" He slung a worn leather bag over his shoulder and impatiently rifled through papers haphazardly thrown inside.

With a thoughtful nod, Jude pushed his circular wire-framed glasses back up the bridge of his nose. "We found more humans who were living in abandoned subway tunnels underneath a city for all these years. We're planning an expedition to meet them."

More humans. More people. More growth.

It's been seven years since I pushed the button. Seven years since I made the decision to sacrifice everyone within the city gates. The innocent lives lost still tormented me, and the light from the explosion continues to curse my dreams. Leaving the safety of the vault with Gabe and

Jude still haunted me. Dead bodies covered the ground, both human and vampire alike. The mechanical Dogs exploded into a million different pieces. The world seemed so still and silent amid the grotesque aftermath.

But I needed to do it. To move on.

Golden sunbeams streamed through the kitchen window as I made chocolate chip cookies for our daughter. The air was thick with the sugary scent of baking as I wiped flour and stray bits of dough from the countertops. We lived in a modest house, nothing compared to my old penthouse, but it was ours. That's all I could ask for.

"Say hello to Four and Nessa for me." I smiled, remembering their wedding. It was the first time since Elysium fell that we felt that we were allowed to relax. The last seven years have been a struggle, but we all banded together to build a better world. I like to think we're on our way.

Jude crept to the slightly open window and carefully peered outside. "How's he doing today?"

A lump formed in my throat. Seven years have passed, and without my blood to sustain them, all the vampires have long since perished. Well, all but one. Call me selfish, but I took every last drop of blood hidden in my father's vault for Gabe, and the final bottle dried up over a month ago. It has been hard on all of us to see his slow decline, but I think Jude was taking it the hardest. He never had someone he loved die right in front of him. He knew I was struggling, and though he tried to stay strong for me, the cracks in his own facade were more visible than mine.

I joined him at the window, the scent of freshly cut grass wafting in as we looked out at the vibrant green backyard. A warm, golden light danced around our little utopia as the summer day slowly faded away, accompanied by the soft sounds of crickets chirping in the distance. A garden of multicolored flowers ravaged the yard, crawling up the sides of the expansive fence surrounding our property. Dancing around the area and reaching her arms in the air to catch butterflies flitting overhead was a little girl with brown hair and light green eyes. Beneath a canopy of leaves filtering the sunlight into dappled patterns, a pale man sat on a wooden bench. His skin was the color of ash, his body frail and shrunken, as if all life was leached from him.

"He-he's doing okay." I managed to choke out. "I'll be here with him."

"You're getting older, too." Jude's arm braced my back as he moved his head to kiss my neck. "You need to take some time for yourself, Vin. You can't be chained to this house."

A prison of my own making.

His comment was common, and it always struck a chord with me. Once my blood lost its healing properties that made the vampires, I started aging at a normal rate again. I knew he was looking out for me, since we're the same age, but it's easy for me to slip into old ways. I shook my head. "This is different. I need to be here for him. We've been through hard times together, but I want to love him and love him right, especially before he goes."

"And I'll be there for you."

A snort of laughter escaped my nose. "Let's be real, *I'll* be there for *you*."

He smiled, a melancholy look crossing his blue eyes. "Let's try to be there for each other, however that may look to each of us." He looked out the window one last time and let out a defeated breath. "Stay close to him, alright?"

"Always."

Jude brushed his lips lightly against my cheek before sprinting out the front door. Luckily, he didn't have to go far because our house was built near the old Elysium. After clearing the rubble from the exploded buildings and wall, the remaining residents of Silvertown decided to use the resources the vampires created. They built a small village for all, complete with electricity and fresh water. Partial remains of an exploded Elysium sit where it once stood, a poignant memory of what once was.

The wounds may never mend, but they're a reminder of how far I've come.

With two freshly baked, warm chocolate chip cookies in hand, I joined my family outside. The wind had a warmness threaded into its being, and the sun's warmth hugged me as I walked down the walkway to the garden. Who would have thought, after all this time, this was where my life would lead?

"Daddy! Daddy!" With a squeal of delight, the five-year-old jumped up and down once she saw me. "I'm trying to catch butterflies!"

"I see that." I smiled. Somehow, this kid always seemed to brighten my mood. The joy she brings is a reminder of the beauty that still exists in the world.

Years ago, Jude, Gabe, and I traveled to an abandoned Elysium on the East Coast, where we found a baby girl at the building's entrance, wrapped in blankets. We camped there for at least a week, waiting for the baby's parents, but they never came. Collectively, we decided to bring the baby back to Silvertown and raise her as our own.

I knelt, the warm, slightly sweet scent of the cookie filling my nostrils, and held it in my hand. "I brought you a treat."

She squealed in delight and snatched the baked good, leaving melted chocolate sticking to her fingertips.

I turned to the man sitting on the bench, and my heart lurched at the sight of his hollow eyes and gaunt face. He was a shell of what he used to be—now skinny and sickly with wrinkles covering his face and body. Thin wisps of hair, remnants of a once glorious head coif, blew gently in the light breeze across his bald head. I held out the second cookie, and Gabe hesitantly lifted his arm, gingerly grabbing it from my hand and taking a bite.

"Delicious," he murmured as he munched, getting crumbs all over his lap.

I know he was lying because he hasn't been able to taste any food in weeks, but I appreciated his sentiment nonetheless. Settling beside him, his hand clasped mine as we watched our daughter run around the garden with her imagination running wild.

"Don't run too fast, Bella," Gabe lovingly warned.

Bella was her name. We agreed upon it in honor of Gabe's mother. I'm happy he had the chance to be a father, even if only for a short while, and to feel the joy of that unique bond. He nurtured her growth, played with her daily, and built a strong bond with her until he was no longer able. I gazed into Gabe's honey brown eyes and smiled. There he was, my Gabe. He might look different, but he was still in there.

"Every day is getting harder," he breathed, tightening his grip on me. "Don't go too far, you know I need you near. My world is ending, and I want my last moments to be with you—where my life began again."

He always said this, ever since his parents died. But what he doesn't understand is that it's not just his world ending, mine will too. Thinking about living without Gabe, my best friend, my protector, was more than I could bear. My heart ached thinking about it. How was I going to be able to comfort Jude and our daughter when I was so much more hurt and devastated? A rapid heartbeat pounded in my chest, accompanied by a tightening pressure building in my head. Every time I thought about the aftermath of my world ending, my mind started to race, and my body began to lose control.

Watching his slow decline, I've taken the time to reminisce about the moments that made me fall in love with this man. Like when we first met at a school dance, and it felt like we were the only people in the room. How every Valentine's Day, without fail, he would offer a gift to show his affection. When he loved, it was with all his heart. And for a long time, I took him for granted.

All I could do right now was be in the moment with him. While I still had him.

Gabe wrapped his arm around my shoulders, pulling me close. I rested my head on the nape of his neck, breathing in his scent, trying to make sure I never forget it. If the world were to end right now, I'd die with a smile in my heart.

"I want to hold you and enjoy this moment together, just for a while."

And we did.

WE CARRY ON, WE CARRY ON.

Acknolwedgements

First and foremost, I want to thank you, the reader, for giving this book a chance. This story and the characters stayed with me far longer than I anticipated, I hope they stay with you, too! If you enjoyed Swallowed By Night, please consider leaving a review on Amazon or Goodreads.

To my beta readers - Seb, Joy, Veronika, Aaron, and Clare, thank you for all your insight and assistance with this book. It went through many iterations and you saw the good, the bad, and the ugly. Thanks for sticking with me!

Ramona and Charlie – Thank you for polishing this story to be the best it can be. Good editors are the true heroes of any story.

Maria – This cover... I mean look at it! You took my scatter-brained notes and created an absolutely gorgeous cover that perfectly translates to the core of the story. So many thanks to you!

Rae – Thank you for tying everything together and putting up with my frequent change requests.

To Beka, Hannah, and Kait – Thank you for cheering me on when I needed it most.

Acknolwedgements

Britt – Your support and attention to detail were so helpful while writing my sophomore novel. Unfortunately (For me? For you?), you *know* my crutch words and my writing improvement areas. Thank you for your encouragement and always pushing me to be better.

To Emily Rose (not the exorcism of) – Thank you for introducing me to the world of Vanessa Carlton, whose music was a huge inspiration for this book.

Michael, my ride or die, my home. Words cannot express how much I appreciate your unwavering support, humor, and love.

Lastly, to Harper and Sophie—my writing buddies—for always sticking by my side and reminding me that love is being in uncomfortable sleeping positions, loud pug snores, and without a doubt, completely unconditional.

About the Author

Jeremey Harrison lives in Rhode Island with his husband and two pugs. You can connect with him on all social media platforms under @jeremeyhwrites, or subscribe to his newsletter at: www.jeremeyharrison.com

www.ingramcontent.com/pod-product-compliance
Lightning Source LLC
LaVergne TN
LVHW091704070526
838199LV00050B/2269